I0592413

Robert Nisbet Bain

**Hans Christian Andersen**

A biography

Robert Nisbet Bain

**Hans Christian Andersen**
*A biography*

ISBN/EAN: 9783337028725

Printed in Europe, USA, Canada, Australia, Japan

Cover: Foto ©Raphael Reischuk / pixelio.de

More available books at **www.hansebooks.com**

# HANS CHRISTIAN ANDERSEN

## A BIOGRAPHY

BY

## R. NISBET BAIN

*Un esprit de femme dans un caractère d'enfant.*—AMIEL

LONDON
## LAWRENCE AND BULLEN
16, HENRIETTA STREET, COVENT GARDEN
NEW YORK
DODD, MEAD AND COMPANY
1895

# INTRODUCTION

A LIFE of Hans Christian Andersen will, I venture to think, not be unwelcome in England. He is the one foreign author whom we can never regard as an alien; whom, from long familiarity and association, we have come to look upon as one of ourselves. His stories have been the delight of our children for three generations, and their popularity among us increases rather than diminishes as time goes on; scarcely a year passes without bringing with it a new edition or translation of the incomparable "Fairy Tales."

But even if Andersen had not written a single line of a single fairy tale he would still remain a tempting subject for a biographer. In practical life he was essentially a shrewd, observant man of the world, who saw more than most people, because he took the trouble to keep his eyes open. Half his life was spent in travelling up and down Europe; he was more or less intimately acquainted with most of the leading men of letters of his day; he had at his finger ends the literatures of half a dozen languages, and he was as much at home in the prince's palace as in the peasant's hut. Such a man can tell us a good deal, and is well worth listening to.

The materials available for a life of Andersen are copious, not to say complete, as no appreciable addition thereto is to be anticipated. I will now set out the principal documents, which are, briefly, as follows:—(1) *Breve fra H. C. Andersen*, udgivne of C. A. S. Bille of N. Bögh, 2 vols., Copenhagen, 1878. This collection contains 479 original letters of Andersen's, extending over a period of more than forty years, and filling nearly 1500 pages. (2) *Breve til H. C. Andersen* (same editors), Copenhagen, 1877, containing 329 letters to Andersen from literary colleagues or contemporaries and private friends in Denmark and out of it. (3) *H. C. Andersen og det Collinske Hus* ("H. C. Andersen and the Collin Family"), Copenhagen, 1882. The first 518 pages of this notable book consists of some scores of Andersen's most characteristic letters, addressed to his intimate friends the Collins, interspersed with numerous original documents relating, principally, to his literary

career, with very valuable explanatory and illus-
trative notes. It goes back as far as his student
days, but breaks off somewhat abruptly at the year
1855. It is on these three documents that the
ensuing narrative is mainly based.—Next (4) comes
Andersen's own autobiography, entitled, *Mit Livs
Eventyr* ("The Story of My Life"), first published in
1855, a bulky volume containing, with its supple-
ment, nearly 700 pages. This autobiography, which
has never been translated into English, is an ampli-
fication of the earlier *Das Märchen meines Lebens*,
Englished anonymously in 1852, and is a document which should only be used with the utmost
caution. Herr Edward Collin, Andersen's oldest
and most intimate friend, has, severely but not
unjustly, called it "that production of daily shifting
moods," and certainly a more misleading book can
scarcely be imagined. It is mainly responsible for
what I have elsewhere called "The Ugly Duckling
Theory of Andersen's Life," I mean that widely
received but perfectly gratuitous idea of him as the
constantly misunderstood and mercilessly persecuted
victim of captious and malicious critics. As a matter
of fact, whenever his critics are concerned, it is impossible for Andersen to be I will not say fair and

just, but even reasonable and coherent. At least
one-third of *Mit Livs Eventyr* is taken up with
Andersen's literary squabbles, nearly another third
of it relates to matters of considerable interest to
Danes, but to Danes only, while in the remainder
the facts are often too obviously grouped with an
eye to dramatic effect. Nevertheless, though of
somewhat doubtful value as a historical document,
*Mit Livs Eventyr* is, psychologically, of immense
importance, as showing, better perhaps than anything
else, the peculiar bent and bias of the author's mind.
It naturally abounds, too, with entertaining anecdotes not to be met with elsewhere, and consequently furnishes a goodly supply of those piquant
seasoning ingredients which no biography can dis-
pense with. Finally, it gives us the only detailed
account we possess of Andersen's infancy and youth,
in some respects the most interesting period of his
life. Very important also to Andersen's biographer
are his four great travel books or itineraries—
(5) the *Skyggebilleder* ("Silhouettes"), 1831, (6)
*En Digter's Bazar* ("A Poet's Bazaar"), 1842, (7)
*I Sverrig* ("In Sweden"), 1852, and (8) *I Spanien*
("In Spain"), 1863, poetic but perfectly veracious
expansions of the diaries which he so conscientiously

kept during his principal continental tours. Many
biographical data, too, are scattered up and down
Andersen's novels, notably in (9) *O. T.*, (10)
*Kun en Spillemand* (" Only a Fiddler "), and (11)
*At være eller ikke være* (" To Be, or not to Be "),
which a diligent student of his correspondence can
detect at once, though, of course, extreme care is
necessary in disengaging them from their environ-
ment of fiction. Finally, I am indebted for many
interesting particulars to various Danish monographs
and essays. Thus in (12) J. M. Thiele's *Af mit
Liv's Aarböger* (" From my Life's Diaries "), I find a
vivid description of Andersen in his gawky hobble-
dehoy days by one who knew him personally; (13)
Örsted's *Breve*, Samml. ii. (" Letters," 2nd collection), and (14) Sibbern's *Breve*, edited by Mynster,
supply a few literary details; (15) Brandes' *Kritiker
og Portreter* (" Critiques and Portraits "), contains the
best critical estimate of Andersen's Tales existing or
conceivable; and it would have been quite impossible
to have told the story of Andersen's last days without the valuable assistance of (16) Dr. Wilhelm
Block's *Om H. C. Andersen* (" About H. C.
Andersen ") in *Nær og Fjern*, and (17) Herr
Nicholas Bögh's *H. C. Andersen's sidste Dager*

("H. C. Andersen's Last Days") in the *Illustreret Tidende.* I have also gleaned a few odd facts from (18) Mrs. Howitt's Autobiography, and from (19) X. Marmier's *Histoire de la Littérature en Danemarc.*

R. NISBET BAIN.

BRITISH MUSEUM,
*July* 1894

# CONTENTS

## APPENDICES

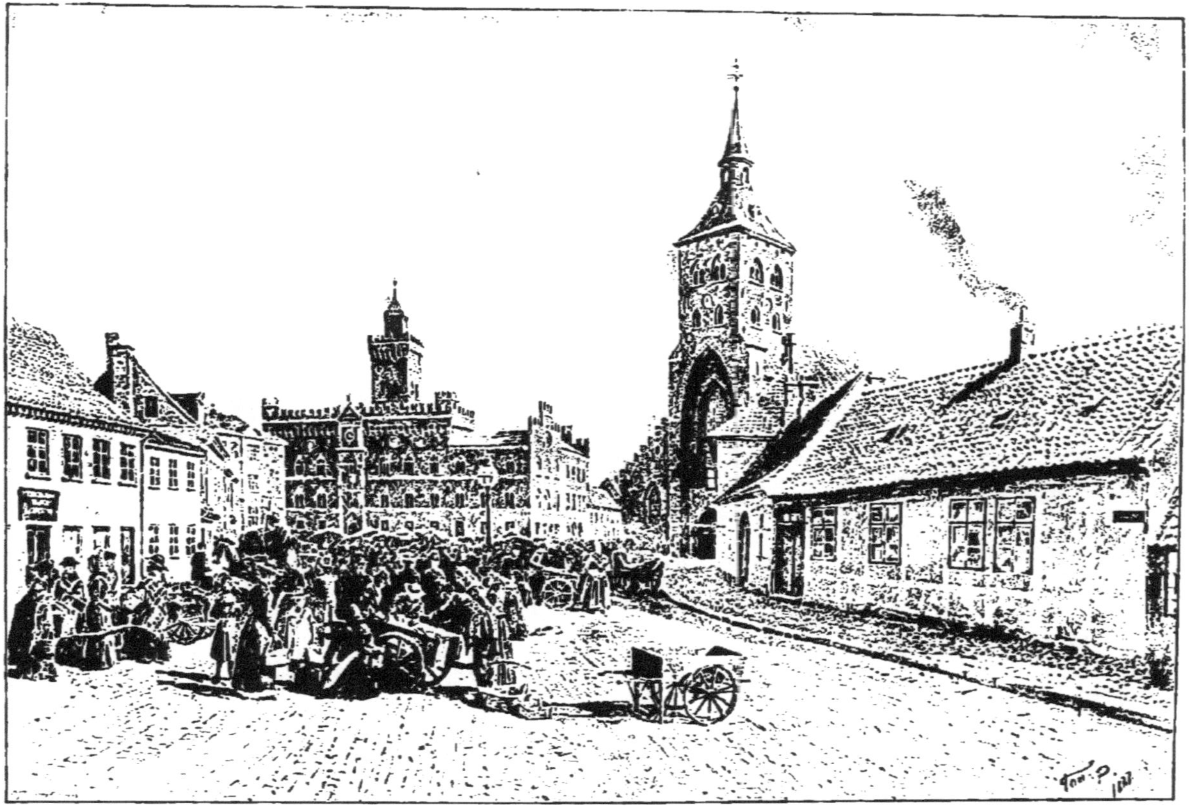

Market Place of Odense with St. Knud's Church

# HANS CHRISTIAN ANDERSEN

## CHAPTER I

### ODENSE

THERE is no more venerable place in Scandinavia than
the little city of Odense. Its antiquity is so remote
that Odin himself is popularly believed to have been
its first burgomaster, though it was the murder there,
in 1086, of King Canute at the altar of St. Alban's
church, whither he had fled from his pagan pursuers,
that first gave the place a name in history. Round
the shrine of the royal martyr a great mediæval city

A

rapidly arose, and tradition tells us that at a time
when Copenhagen itself was nought but a second-
rate fishing-village, the wealthy citizens of Odense
were wont to entertain princes with more than
princely pomp, and burn cinnamon instead of wood
upon their ample hearths to show their contempt for
wealth.   In Odense hoary traditions meet us at
every step.   At one point in the river, not far from
the shore, is the so-called bell-hole, a fathomless
depth.   Tradition says that long, long ago, when St.
Alban's church stood where St. Knud's church
stands now, a bell flew from the tower into this hole,
and now, whenever a rich burgher of Odense is about
to die, the bell tolls beforehand beneath the water.
The very sanctuary of St. Knud's vast church has
been invaded by legends old.   Let one example
suffice.   Visitors are shown, on a column near the
altar, the effigy of a lady with folded arms and
painted face.   This lady is said to have danced
twelve squires to death in one night, but the thir-
teenth, when it came to his turn, suspecting that
something was wrong, watched his opportunity and,
in the middle of the dance, deftly unloosed his
partner's girdle, whereupon she instantly fell down
upon the floor—a corpse.   A city of so many hoary
memories, the hearth and home of Danish legend,
was a befitting birthplace for him who was to open
the eyes of all good and true children to the glorious

mysteries of fairyland, of which, till he came, they had only caught fitful glimpses. Here on April 2, 1805, was born Hans Christian Andersen.

The early surroundings of the future Fairy King were lowly in the extreme. He first saw the light in a little room which served the whole family as workshop, kitchen and parlour; and half of this room was taken up by the big bed on which he now lay wailing. This bed, by the way, was something of a curiosity; Andersen's father had fashioned it out of the trestles on which the coffin of a great nobleman had once reposed. The walls of the room were covered with pictures, and in the spring time whole heaps of fresh birch branches stood behind the polished stove, and bunches of sweet herbs hung down from the crevices of the rafters. On the solitary chest of drawers stood shining cups, glasses and knick-knacks; pots of mint were on the window-sill, and right above the little workshop, which had been rigged up close to the window, was a shelf full of books and ballads. The door itself, the panels of which were painted with rude landscapes, was as good as a picture-gallery to the child's observant eyes. When he grew a little older, it was his delight to adorn his home with flowers from the fields and lanes; but he seems to have loved it best in the evening, when he was put out of harm's way into his parent's big bed till it was time for his own little sofa bedstead to be got ready for him—the room was too tiny to hold both beds at once. There he would lie staring at the light of the candle through the calico curtains which were drawn closely all around him, listening to every sound in the room where his parents were working, and yet as much wrapped up in his own thoughts and fancies as though there was nothing else in existence. "How nice and quiet he is, the blessed child!" he would hear his mother say at such times. A ladder led from the kitchen end of the room into a loft, and in the roof-gutter up there, between the Andersen's cottage and their neighbour's, stood a box of earth full of chives and parsley—that was their whole garden, and it still blooms in the story of *The Snow Queen.*

Of Andersen's mother, whose maiden name was Anna Maria,* we know but little, and that little is not very much to her credit. The idyllic picture given of her in the autobiography of her son, shows her not as she was but as his filial piety imagined her to be. It was only natural and right that he should be very fond of a mother who, at any rate, was never actively unkind to him; always a good son, he is absolutely reticent about the miseries of her later years. It is easy enough, however, to gather from various other sources† that she was a

---

* Collin, p. 510 ; compare Bille og Bogh: *Breve til Andersen*, pp. 6-14.                              † Bille og Bogh ; Collin.

poor thing at best, one of those good-natured, silly, thriftless, happy-go-lucky creatures who are quite content to live from hand to mouth, and never look to the morrow so long as they have got a decent roof over their heads, and can sit down once a week to a square meal. As a mother she was mischievously careless of her only child in his infancy, and at a later day was not ashamed to draw upon his slender purse when he himself was living upon the charity of others, nay, frequently reproaching him when his poverty could not respond liberally enough to her exacting demands. Extreme misery, however, and growing habits of intemperance had by this time quite demoralised the poor creature, and until her son was able to get her into a comfortable private alms-house, she had been driven to earn a precarious livelihood by washing bottles for an apothecary.

Andersen's father was also a somewhat unsatisfactory, though a much more remarkable, character. He came of a well-to-do yeoman stock, which had been ruined by a series of misfortunes and then migrated to Odense. There his father became deranged, and the best thing his penniless mother could do for him was to apprentice him to a cobbler, despite his intense longing to be sent to the Latin school. Some friends had talked of clubbing together to enable him to go the way he would; but nothing

ever came of it, so the elder * Andersen settled down
to cobbling with great bitterness of heart. Books now
became his only solace, he was never seen to smile
except when he was reading. His favourite authors
seem to have been Holberg,† La Fontaine and *The
Arabian Nights*, but Holberg he particularly admired
and knew nearly all his plays by heart. It was from
his father, whose character was evidently closely akin
to his own, that little Hans Christian first learned to
love literature. The young cobbler would read aloud
to his family of an evening. His wife used to listen
to him with puzzled admiration (she could never
quite make him out), but not a single word was lost
upon the lad, and as he grew older he and his father
became close companions. The elder Andersen devoted all his spare time to his son, made him toys
and pictures, and in the summer time took him for
long walks in the woods, where he himself would sit
buried in thought for hours at a time while the
little fellow capered about, plucked strawberries, or
made garlands of wild flowers. The elder Andersen,
by the way, mixed very little with his fellows, who
no doubt regarded him as an oddity. He preferred brooding over his books at home, and sometimes startled his little circle by expressing the
result of his excogitations aloud, for in his small

* Old he cannot be called, for he died at 35.
† The Danish Molière, one of the world's greatest comic dramatists.

way he was something of an original thinker. On one occasion he suddenly closed his Bible with the exclamation : "Christ was a man like us, although an extraordinary man." His wife was so horrified by these words that she burst into tears, while little Hans Christian, full of terror, prayed God to forgive his father such a frightful blasphemy. On another occasion he heard his father say that the only devil in existence was the devil that every one has in his own heart, and again Hans grew very anxious indeed about his father's soul, especially when, shortly afterwards, that sinner woke up one morning with three deep scratches in his arm, caused no doubt by a nail in the bed. The neighbouring gossips were of the opinion that they were the marks of Satan himself, who had been there in the night to convince the sceptic of his existence.

But even if the devil did not come to the cobbler, it is pretty plain that the cobbling business itself was about this time going to the devil. What with brooding over his books, and building castles in the air, the elder Andersen seems to have forgotten that this dull earth also has its claims upon us which we neglect at our peril. At any rate the following anecdote seems to prove not only that customers at Odense had begun to fall off, but also that the cobbler's hand was losing something of its former cunning.

It was the dearest wish of Andersen's father to move into the country, and it happened at this very time that a shoemaker was wanted at one of the Funen country houses. He was to settle down in the village close by, and there have a free house, a little garden, and pasturage for a cow, and with this and regular work from the squire, he would be able to make a livelihood. A piece of silk stuff was sent from the squire's, out of which Andersen's father was to make a specimen pair of dancing shoes, finding the leather himself. For the next two days the family could talk and think of nothing else, and little Hans prayed God from the bottom of his heart to fulfil his own and his parents' wishes. At last the shoes were finished. They were gazed upon with awe and admiration. The whole future of the family depended upon them, and off the cobbler went with them in his apron, leaving his wife and child behind in joyful expectation. He returned pale and angry. The squire's lady, he said, had not even tried on the shoes, but looked askance at them the moment she saw them, said that the silk was spoiled, and that the bungler could not be engaged, whereupon, full of rage, the poor cobbler had whipped out his knife, and cut the offending slippers to bits. Thus all their hopes of living comfortably in the country came to an end; all three fell a-weeping, and Hans thought to himself that God might surely have heard him.

Had his prayer been answered in the way he wanted, he might have lived and died a yokel.

The best head in the family appears to have been Andersen's grandmother, the prototype of all the ideal old grandmothers whom we meet with in the fairy tales. She is described by Andersen as a cheerful, quiet, and very amiable old woman, with gentle blues eyes, and a fragile figure. She used to come nearly every day to his parents' house, chiefly, he gives us to understand, to see *him*, and he certainly seems to have been her darling. She was fond of talking of her mother's mother who had been a gentlewoman at Cassel, and there married a " play-actor " as she expressed it. The old woman had a little garden to look after, close to the lunatic hospital where her husband was, from which she used to bring to the Andersens' cottage, every Saturday, bunches of flowers, which it was the child's delight to put into glasses of water on the chest of drawers. Twice a year she used to burn all the refuse of this garden in a large fire-place at the hospital, and it was a prime treat for her little grandson to be with her on such occasions, when he would roll about on the big soft heaps of cabbage leaves and pea-stalks, and get better food to eat than he generally got at home. He also used to follow the idiots about the hospital grounds, and listen with mingled curiosity and terror to their

talking and singing. Occasionally he would even·
venture into the house where the dangerous lunatics
were kept, and once his curiosity led him into quite
a terrible adventure. He had strayed into a corridor
between the cells, and knelt down to peep through
the crevice of a door; inside he saw a naked woman
on a heap of straw, her hair was hanging down over
her shoulders,. and she was singing with a pretty
voice. Suddenly she sprang up and rushed shrieking towards the door outside of which he lay. The
keeper had.gone away; he was quite alone, and she
banged so violently against the door that the little
lid just above him, covering the aperture through
which they used to thrust her meat, sprang open
and she looked through it right down upon him,
and stretched out one of her· arms towards him.
He shrieked with terror, and squeezed himself
still closer to the floor, but for all that could
feel the tips of her fingers touch his clothes, and
was half dead with fright before he could get
away.

Another place he was fond of frequenting was the
spinning-room at the poor house, where he became a
great favourite. Here he used to astonish the old
women by parading all the odd scraps of information
he had picked up from his father, and would chalk
up on the door a lot of rubbish which was supposed
to represent the heart, lungs, liver, and the internal

organs of the human body generally. The old dames used to listen admiringly, and declare that he was much too clever a child to live long, which flattered him mightily. Sometimes they rewarded his chattering by telling him fairy tales. Here doubtless it was that he first made the acquaintance of *The Tinder Box*, *The Travelling Companion*, *Soup on a Sausage Peg*, and their fellows.

Of his weak-witted grandfather little Hans stood in great dread. He had only spoken to the child once, and on that occasion he addressed him in the third person plural, a mode of speech the urchin was not used to.\* The old man, however, had a talent. He could carve out of wood odd-looking figures, men with beasts' heads, beasts with wings, and very curious birds; these he would pack into a basket, and take into the country, where the farmers' wives used to entertain him, and even give him hams and vegetables in exchange for the toys which he used to bestow upon them and their children.

With lads of his own age little Hans never mixed at all. Even at school, of which more anon, he took no part in their games, but remained sitting inside the school-room. At home he had plenty of toys which his father had made for him, such as

\* The familiar second person singular was what Andersen and his parents would naturally employ.

pictures which changed their shapes when they were pulled with a string, a mill which made the miller dance about when it was set in motion, a peep-show and comical rag dolls. But his greatest pleasure was to make dolls' clothes, or to sit in the yard close beside their solitary gooseberry-bush with his mother's apron extended between it and the wall with the help of a broomstick. This was his tent in sunshine and shower, there he would sit and watch the gooseberry leaves day by day, from the time that they were small green buds, till they broke loose in autumn as large yellow leaves.

One of his earliest recollections is the comet of 1811. His mother had told him that it would smash the world to bits, or that something equally dreadful would happen. He listened intently, and accepted the prophecy as gospel truth. Out in the square in front of St. Knud's churchyard he stood with his mother and some neighbouring gossips ; looked at the terrific ball of fire with its large shining tail, and listened to their talk about evil omens and the Day of Doom. Then his father joined the group. The learned cobbler was not of the same opinion as the others, and gave a proper explanation of the phenomenon, but Mrs. Andersen and the neighbours only sighed, and shook their heads. This was another proof of his heterodoxy, and again the child was terribly grieved and frightened that his father did not believe as they did.

Of anything like proper schooling the lad, thanks to the foolish indulgence of his parents, got little enough. He was sent first of all to a dame's school, but it was expressly stipulated beforehand by his mother that the birch-rod, which was kept in reserve for the other scholars, should never be exercised on him. One day the school-mistress forgot this injunction, and gave him a tap with the birch. Little Hans instantly arose, put his books and slate under his arm, marched off home without saying a word, told his mother what had happened, and asked her to send him to another school, which she accordingly did.

This other school was a boy's school kept by a Herr Carstens, but there was one little girl there, too, quite a wee thing, with whom Andersen chummed up immediately. It was this little girl's ambition to become a dairymaid at a large country house when (as she told Andersen in confidence) she had learnt enough arithmetic for the purpose. " You shall be a dairymaid at my castle when I am a gentleman," he replied jokingly, and one day he showed her something which he had drawn upon his slate which he called his castle. Then, in his fanciful way, he invented a little tale about himself, assuring her that he was of noble birth, only the fairies had changed him in his cradle. He wanted to astonish her as he had astonished the old women at the hospital, but, to his dismay, the prosaic little Philistine looked at him very oddly, and said to one of the boys close by : "He is mad like his grandfather !" An icy shiver of horror ran through him, and he never talked to her about such things again. For the rest Andersen, by his own confession, idled or rather dreamed away most of his time at Herr Carstens' school, to the frequent disgust of that pedagogue, whom he tried, not always successfully, to propitiate with bouquets of wild flowers.

Andersen's father died in 1816 when the lad was only eleven years old.* The poor cobbler seems never to have got over the misadventure of the dancing shoes, and enlisted shortly afterwards, partly out of admiration for Napoleon, who was one of his many heroes, and partly in the hope of returning from the wars a lieutenant. He had got no further than Holstein, however, when peace was concluded, and he returned home to die, the unwonted fatigues and privations of campaigning having very soon ruined his feeble health. His widow speedily consoled herself by marrying another young cobbler, Jür-gensen by name,† "with lively brown eyes, and a good even temper,"‡ and Hans Christian was left

---

* Collin, p. iii.                            † *Ibid.*

‡ *Mit Livs Eventyr* (" Story of My Life"), henceforth contracted : *M. L. E.*

more than ever to his own devices. At first, indeed, there was some talk of sending him to a cloth factory close by, and he actually did work there for a short time ; but the rough horse-play of his fellow journeymen scared him home again, and his mother was easily persuaded to promise that he should never go there again. So he remained at home playing with his peep-shows and theatres, making dolls' clothes, and eagerly devouring all the books he could lay his hands upon. About this time a clergyman's widow, Madame Bunkeflod, and her sister, who lived in the neighbourhood, took an interest in the lad, and were very kind to him. It was the first civilised house he had ever found a home in, and he was often there the best part of the day. It was here that he read Shakespeare's works for the first time, and he tells us that, despite the wretchedness of the translation, they made a great impression upon him, "the bloody incidents," and the ghost and witch episodes, being particularly to his taste. He was already well acquainted with the works of the great Danish dramatist Holberg, and we know that from a very early age he had felt a mysterious attraction towards the stage, which in the event was to be most mischievous to him. His friend Collin has preserved for us the *titles* of no less than five and twenty plays jotted down by him about this time on the last page of his father's military account book, which he intended to write when he was older, and very curious some of them are.* Andersen himself informs us that he used to play Shakesperian dramas in his dolls' theatre, killing off as many of his characters as he could. His first piece, as he calls it, was a savagely sanguinary version of Pyramus and Thisbe, which ended in a perfect holocaust of all the *dramatis personæ*, including a hermit and his son, who were introduced, seemingly, for the express purpose of making love to Thisbe. But his ambition took a still higher flight; he wanted to write a play in which kings and princesses appeared, but the difficulty was to find language grand enough for such exalted personages. He had observed indeed in Shakespeare's plays that monarchs talked very much like other men, but this did not appear to him to be quite natural, so he consulted his mother, and several other wise women about it. They, however, could not give him very much information on the subject. It was a long time, they said, since a king had been to Odense, but they thought such a potentate would be pretty sure to talk some foreign language. So little Hans Christian got a sort of lexicon containing lists of French, German, and English words with the Danish equivalents opposite, and with its assistance put into the mouths of his royal personages such

* Collin, p. iii. The spelling is, of course, very eccentric, we find, *e.g.*, " Celia and Physke."

polyglot sentences as the following: " *Guten morgen, mon père! har de godt sleeping?* " which perfectly satisfied his idea of the fitness of things.

Young Andersen—*little* Andersen he could no longer be called, for he was now shooting up apace into a lanky gawky lad of an almost comical ugliness —young Andersen continued to dream away his time for the next few years, dressing dolls in clothes of his own sewing; practising singing in the lanes and meadows in the firm belief that his voice would make his fortune; cramming his overwrought brain with a jumble of plays, poems and romances, and living in a fantastic morbid world of his own, which had nothing whatever in common with the world of actual solid fact around him. By the time he was fourteen the queer creature (for queer indeed every one thought him) had become the wonder or the laughing-stock of the neighbourhood. From lads of his own age and class he shrank instinctively, but he always had a wistful longing for the society of his betters socially, which reminds one of the ugly duckling's dim feeling of kinship with the lordly swans. The *gamins* of Odense, therefore, naturally regarded him as " stuck up," and fair sport, and chivied him unmercifully whenever they met him with derisive yells of " there goes the play-scribbler ! " while poor Andersen would fly panic-stricken homewards, hide himself in a corner, and there " weep and pray to God." Heaven

B

only knows what he must have suffered. The local gentry, on the other hand, took a half-amused, half-compassionate interest in the poor cobbler's son, who could recite whole plays from memory, and tried to write poetry before he had learnt the rudiments of grammar; but all their well-intentioned efforts on his behalf came to nothing, for the lad, vaguely conscious of his own genius, though its true nature and scope was quite hidden from him, had extraordinarily ambitious ideas, which must have seemed supremely absurd to his well-wishers in those days. Colonel Höegh-Guldberg, whose whole family circle took the liveliest interest in young Andersen, tried to get him into the local Latin school through the influence of Prince Christian, afterwards Christian VIII., who was then residing at Odense Castle. The Prince, however, good-naturedly pooh-poohed any such idea; but promised to look after the lad if he would adopt some honest trade, a turner's, for instance. Andersen wouldn't hear of it, and left the castle in high dudgeon. Then he was sent to the Ragged School, to learn Scripture-history, writing, and arithmetic, for though he could read Holberg and Shakespeare, he candidly confesses that he could scarcely spell a single word correctly. But his dreamy, abstracted ways, a dislike of application, due more perhaps to pride than sloth (he tells us himself that he never looked at his lessons except when on his way to and

from school), naturally irritated his master, and the upshot of it all was that he left the Ragged School pretty
nearly as ignorant as when he entered it. Shortly after
this happened the first great event of his life, his
confirmation, which took place at St. Knud's church,
the first Sunday after Easter, 1819.* The family
did what it could in honour of the occasion. A
tailoress was called in to metamorphose Andersen
senior's old overcoat into a confirmation jacket for
young Hans, and for the first time in his life he wore a
pair of boots. His joy over these new boots was extraordinary. His only fear was that everybody might not
see that they *were* new, so he drew them right over his
trousers, and walked in that guise up the aisle. The
boots creaked loudly, and he inwardly rejoiced, because
the whole congregation could now hear that they
were new, though at the same time he had terrible
qualms of conscience at the thought of forgetting his
Maker at such a moment for the sake of a pair of
boots. It was this incident which suggested to him
many years afterwards the story of the Red Shoes.

Andersen's own family was now getting anxious
about him, and beginning to think it high time that
he put his hand to "something sensible." His

* Collin, *H. C Andersen og det Collinski Hus.* p. iii. There is an
interesting entry in the church register on this occasion : "He [Ander-
sen] has good parts, and a good knowledge of religion ; if his application cannot be praised, his general conduct nevertheless cannot be
blamed."

mother, under whose eye he was always making dolls' clothes, thought him cut out for a tailor, and certainly his skill with his needle was something extraordinary, and is even put down by his friend Collin as one of his standing accomplishments. Collin also tells us * that Andersen, to the end of his life, never travelled anywhere without thimbles, needles and thread, and that he always sewed on his own trouser buttons, and darned his own stockings. On the other hand, his grandmother, who had seen better days, and held more liberal views, would have preferred to see him in a counting-house. As, however, no agreement could be come to, nothing was done, and the youth led the same sort of desultory life as before. For this unsatisfactory state of things, which proved so mischievous to Andersen in later years, his mother is to be chiefly blamed. As already stated, she was by no means a model mother, but her chief sin against him was her neglect. She never seems to have made any serious effort to wean him from his lazy dreamy ways ; nay, instead of scolding him for scamping his lessons while at the Ragged School, she would let him " buzz away," as she called it, over his romances and comedies, and then boast that although her Hans Christian never looked into a school-book, he always managed to come up to the scratch in class.

* Collin, p. 510, and *ib.* p. 486. Compare Bille og Bogh : *Breve til Andersen*, 6-14.

But now the lad determined to take his fate into his own hands—he resolved to go to Copenhagen to seek his fortune. The idea appears to have first occurred to him the year before his confirmation, when a troupe of actors from the Royal Danish Theatre visited Odense, and gave a whole series of operas and tragedies which the good folks of Odense did not soon forget. Young Andersen made friends with the bill-poster, and was allowed not only to see all the performances from behind the scenes, but also, to his intense delight, to appear on the boards as a page or shepherd; nay, on one occasion, he took a minor part in the opera of "Cinderella." His childish enthusiasm amused and interested the players. They were kind to him, and he looked up to them "as if they were gods." Of course he at once jumped to the conclusion that he was a born actor himself, and that the Royal Theatre at Copenhagen was the only proper goal for his Olympian strivings. He naïvely tells us that he also heard the actors talking of a thing called a "Ballet," which, according to them, was far superior to even a play or an opera, and they added that a certain *danseuse*, a Mme. Schall, was the presiding genius of this mysterious art. This was quite enough for Hans Christian. His imagination instantly pictured Madame Schall as the fairy queen whose generous protection was to help him on to fame and fortune, and full of this idea he called upon the printer

Iversen, one of the leading citizens of his little native town, who had frequently entertained the actors during their stay at Odense, and therefore, so Andersen argued, must needs know all about the great *danseuse*, and asked him for a letter of introduction to her. The old man, who now saw him for the first time, listened in the most friendly manner to his request, but dissuaded him most earnestly from venturing upon any such journey, and told him he ought to learn a trade. "But surely that would be a great sin!" exclaimed Andersen. Iversen was so struck by the emphasis with which the lad uttered these words, that he actually did give him a letter of introduction to the great *danseuse*, though he himself had not the honour of that lady's acquaintance, and Andersen gleefully departed, imagining that the door of fortune now lay open before him.

He had now to settle with his mother, but he did not meet with much difficulty in that quarter. She asked him, indeed, what he meant to do at Copenhagen when he got there, and he replied that he was going to be famous like so many other remarkable men he had read about who had been born in poverty. "You go through a frightful lot of hardship first," he explained, "and then you become famous." His mother was duly impressed, but, in order to make assurance doubly sure, she consulted a "wise-woman" from the hospital, who, after a careful inspection of sundry coffee grouts, predicted that Hans Christian would become a great man, and that Odense would, one day, be illuminated in his honour. Andersen's mother was now quite satisfied. After shedding a few joyful tears, she packed up his little bundle for him, and arranged with the postillion of the stage coach that he should be taken at a cheap rate as an extra passenger all the way to Copenhagen, so with fifteen rix dollars* in his pocket, and endless hopes in his heart, Hans Christian departed on as mad an errand, judged from a common-sense stand-point, as ever suggested itself to a human brain. When he came to the Little Belt at Nyborg, and the ship bore him away from his native isle, he felt for the first time how utterly alone and forsaken he was, but the novelty of the scenes around him sustained his flagging spirits, and, besides, was he not hasten-ing at last to the goal of his desires ?

* About £1 17s.

# CHAPTER II

## THE UGLY DUCKLING AT COPENHAGEN

Arrival at Copenhagen—The ticket tout—The *danseuse* takes him for an escaped lunatic—Snubbed by the Director of the Royal Theatre—"Paul and Virginia"—Utter destitution—Befriended by Siboni and Weyse—Loses his voice—Makes the acquaintance of the poet Guldberg, who helps to educate and support him—Rapacity of his landlady—Becomes a dancing pupil of the Royal Theatre—First appearance on the boards—Brutality of an actor —"My first tragedy"—Terrible privations—An instance of Andersen's superstition—Admitted into the Chorus School of the Royal Theatre—The bully Brand—Takes to play-writing—Comical interview with Admiral Wulff—Personal description of Andersen at this period—A guest at the "*Bakkehus*"—The beautiful blue coat and the playbills—Fresh attempts at play-writing—Jonas Collin recommends him to the King—Sent to school to Slagelse.

ON Monday morning, Sept. 6, 1819, Andersen entered Copenhagen, and the first thing he did when he got there was to go to the theatre. He walked round it several times, gazed up at the walls, and regarded the whole building as a home that was not yet opened to him.* A ticket tout close by, observing him, came up and offered him a ticket, and Andersen, innocently supposing in his ignorance that the man meant to make him a present of it

\* *M. L. E.*

accepted it, and thanked the fellow so effusively that he fancied this country lout was trying to make a fool of him, and flew into a violent rage, where- upon poor Andersen took to his heels in terror. The next day, arrayed in his confirmation clothes, not forgetting the boots, which he took care to ostentatiously display, and with a hat which slipped down over his ears, he set off for the house of the great *danseuse*, Madame Schall, to present her with his letter of recommendation. The Ballet Queen naturally looked at and listened to him with the utmost astonishment. She knew absolutely nothing either of old Iversen who had written the letter to her, or of the odd creature who had brought it, and Andersen's whole appearance and behaviour was singular, to say the least of it. He expressed the ardent desire he had to get upon the boards, and in answer to her question in what play he thought he would like to act, he replied, " Cinderella," which was one of the pieces he had seen at Odense. Then, to give her a specimen of his skill, he forthwith took off his boots, and, improvising a drum out of his big hat, proceeded to dance and sing in character. His strange elephantine gambols filled the lady with considerable alarm, and she speedily showed her strange visitor the door. Many years afterwards she told Andersen that she had taken him for an escaped lunatic.

Andersen next went to the director of the
National Theatre, Chamberlain Holstein, and
audaciously asked for an engagement. Holstein
looked at him and said he was *too thin* for the
theatre. " Oh ! " cried Andersen, " when once I get
a permanent engagement with a salary of 100 rix
dollars (£11 13s. 4d.) I shall get fat enough." The
director then allowed him to give a specimen * of
what he could do, after which he dismissed him
with the solemn snub that only educated persons
were engaged for the stage.†

Andersen was so cast down by this rebuff that he
thought the best thing he could do was to die on the
spot ; but after a good cry, and a fervent prayer to
his Heavenly Father, he comforted himself by buying
a gallery ticket for the opera " Paul and Virginia."
The parting of the lovers affected him to such a
degree, that he burst into a violent fit of weeping.
A couple of tradesmen's wives who sat beside him
did their best to console him, and were good enough
to explain that it was only a play, and therefore
meant nothing at all. One of them also gave him a
large piece of bread and butter, and some potted
meat. Andersen, out of the fulness of his heart,
immediately confided to them that he was crying,

* In their official report to the King on the subject, the directors of
the theatre say that the applicant had neither the proper talents nor
the proper figure for the stage (Collin, viii., ix.).    † *M. L. E.*

not on account of Paul and Virginia, but because he regarded the theatre as his Virginia, and if he were separated from her he would be as unhappy as Paul had been. The worthy tradesmen's wives were puzzled, as well they might be, and then he went on to tell them why he had come up to Copenhagen, and how lonely he was, and they gave him more bread and butter, and fruit and cakes.*

The next morning, after paying his account at the little inn where he had put up for the night, he found that all his worldly possessions consisted of a single rix dollar (2s. 4d.). He must now either return home by the first coasting ship that would take him for nothing, or settle down at Copenhagen to learn a trade. He chose the latter as the less humiliating alternative, for the thought of returning home to Odense to be laughed at, and made a fool of, was intolerable to his pride. Accordingly he apprenticed himself to a joiner the same day, but the brutal horseplay of his fellow 'prentices so shocked his girlish delicacy, that he quitted the place a few hours after he had entered it. As now he was pacing up and down the streets, bitterly conscious of his utter friendlessness and abandonment, he suddenly remembered that he had read in the Odense papers of an Italian named Siboni, who had been appointed director of the Royal Musical

* M. L. E

Conservatoire at Copenhagen. What if this kind-hearted man would take him as a singing pupil? So to Siboni's he went. The musician happened to be having a dinner party just then, and the famous poet Baggesen, the composer Prof. Weyse, and many other celebrities were among the guests. When the maidservant opened the door, Andersen was so over-come by the feeling of his own misery, that he told her not only the errand on which he had come, but also the whole of his past life. She listened with the deepest sympathy, and going away, brought back with her the whole of the company, who re-garded the odd intruder with considerable curiosity. Siboni then took him into the room where the piano stood, and made him go through his scales, listening attentively all the time. After that Andersen recited some scenes from Holberg, and a few poems, till the feeling of his miserable situation so overcame him, that he burst into real tears, the whole company loudly applauding. A collection of seventy rix dollars* was made for him on the spot, and he was told to go next day for singing lessons to Prof. Weyse. In the joy of his heart, Andersen immedi-ately wrote a triumphant letter to his mother, in which he said that fortune † was already within his grasp.

For the next nine months Andersen was supported

---

\* £8 3s. 4d.        † Collin, viii.

by the generosity of Siboni, Weyse and a few other
"noble-minded men," as he himself gratefully calls
them.   He drew ten rix dollars (£1 3s. 4d.) a month
from Weyse, who acted as his cashier, while Siboni
opened his house to him, and gave him food and
singing lessons gratis.   From early morning till late
at night Andersen stayed in the worthy Italian's
house, while at night he found a lodging where best
he could.   As the ten rix dollars he received every
month from Weyse was all he had, he could not
afford to stay at a tavern.   He therefore had to look
about for cheap lodgings, and, in his innocence and
ignorance of the town, pitched upon the *Ulkegade*,
which then had the worst reputation of any street in
Copenhagen, and here he fell into the hands of an old
harridan who, as we shall see presently, fleeced him
unconscionably.   And now a fresh misfortune overtook
him.   He suddenly lost his voice, and Siboni counselled
him to return to Odense, and learn some useful handi-
craft, as there was now no prospect whatever of his
becoming a singer.   But rather than return home to
be the laughing-stock of his native place (especially
after his jubilant letter) the poor lad was prepared to
suffer every hardship, and while he stood there reflect-
ing what he should do next, and to whom he should
turn now, he recollected for the first time that the poet
Frederik Höegh-Guldberg, a brother of the Colonel
who had been so kind to him at Odense, was living in

Copenhagen. Andersen soon found out his address,
wrote to him for an appointment, and finally went and
found him "among his books and pipes." The poet
received him kindly. He promised to teach him Danish
properly (he had been struck by the villainous spelling
of Andersen's letter) and on examining the lad in
German, the rudiments of which he had picked up at
Siboni's, found that his German was, if possible, even
worse than his Danish, so he undertook to teach him
German also. But Guldberg's generosity did not stop
there. Convinced that the lad had "natural gifts which
deserved to be cultivated," and that his "character
was uncorrupted"* he raised a subscription on his
behalf, to which he contributed the proceeds of one of
his recently published works, and dispensed sixteen rix
dollars (£1 17s. 4d.), a month to Andersen, besides
giving him regular instruction and entertainment at
his house. Andersen might have made shift with
this for a time, but for the rapacity of his landlady.
When this harpy heard about the money her lodger
got from Guldberg and Weyse she said she couldn't
afford to keep him any longer under twenty rix dollars
(£2 6s. 8d.) a month. As all Andersen's resources, put
together, brought him in no more than sixteen rix
dollars, out of which he had to clothe and feed himself,
he was at his wit's end what to do. During the short
time he had been there, the helpless confiding creature

* Collin, vii., viii.

had got to love the woman like a mother, and felt quite
at home in the wretched hole.   Besides, where else
was he to go, and who would take him in ?   But the
landlady was inexorable.   He must pay her the twenty
dollars or pack his traps, and off she went giving him
a couple of hours to decide—yes or no.   The tears
ran down his cheeks, and such a child was he that
seeing a portrait of her dead husband hanging over
the sofa, he went up to it, and smeared its eyes with
his tears, in the belief that the dead man could feel
how distressed he was, and then, perhaps, might
work upon his wife's heart, and prevail on her to
keep him for sixteen rix dollars.   The woman must
have seen that there was no more money to be
squeezed out of him, for on her return she said
that he might stay for the sixteen a month.   "I
was so happy" says Andersen, "and thanked God
and the dead man."   Next day he brought her all
the money, unspeakably happy at having a home
over his head,* though he now had not a farthing
left wherewith to buy himself even the necessaries
of life.

In the course of 1820, apparently through the
kindness of Herr Dahlen, who had a dancing-school
in connection with the Royal Theatre, Andersen was
admitted as a dancing-pupil.   By his own showing,
however, he made but little progress in the art,

* It was a wretched unfurnished attic at the top of the house.

though he toiled away at it heroically; but he seems
to have regarded it as a mere makeshift until he
could obtain a place as singer and actor at the
theatre,* for all along the theatre was the goal of his
ambition.  As a theatrical dancing-pupil, moreover,
he had now free access behind the scenes, and he
tells us that he felt as happy as if he already had
had his foot on the boards and was a regular member
of the company.  Nay, one evening, to his inexpressible delight, he actually *did* appear upon the stage.
On this particular evening the operetta "The Two
Little Savoyards" was being played.  The actress, Ida
Wulff, afterwards the Countess Holstein, but now a
singing-pupil like Andersen, whom she had first met
at Siboni's, and always treated well, chanced to
meet him behind the scenes just before the operetta
began, and good-naturedly told him that in the
market-scene which was about to begin, every one,
even the machinists, could come on just to fill the
stage, only he must take care to dab a little rouge
on his cheeks first of all.  He did so at once, and
came in with the others, overjoyed.  He saw the
footlights, the prompter, and beyond them the whole
of the dark space full of spectators.  He wore his confirmation coat which still held together, but looked
wretched enough for all the care and skill with
which he had patched it up, while his hat was too

* See his petition to the King, Aug. 6, 1820, in Collin, viii.

big for him, and fell down almost over his eyes.
Conscious of these defects, he did his best to conceal
them by all sorts of awkward antics.  He durst not
hold himself upright for fear of betraying the scanti-
ness of his waistcoat, and he had worn the heels of
his boots so crooked that no ingenuity in the world
could hide the fact.  Then, too, he was preternatu-
rally long and lean, and knew from bitter experience
how ridiculous he could be made to look.  But at
that moment he thought of nothing else but the
supreme joy of coming before the footlights for the
first time.  His heart beat violently as he stepped
forward, and then one of the leading singers, to
raise a laugh, seized him by the hand, and, with a
mock bow, congratulated him on his *début*.  "Allow
me to present you to the Danish Public" said he,
and dragged the wretched scarecrow towards the
footlights, to have a good laugh at his expense.  Poor
Andersen's triumph was turned to shame.  His eyes
filled with tears, and wrenching himself loose, he
rushed off the stage.  Nevertheless he seems to
have found some compensation shortly afterwards by
appearing in a hideous mask as a troll in the ballet
"Armida," on which occasion his name actually
figured in the play-bill.  It was the first time in his
life that he had ever seen himself in print; he
fancied himself crowned with a nimbus of immortality; gazed rapturously at the letters on the poster

c

all day long, and took it to bed with him in the evening.  " That was something like happiness ! " he cried.

While he was still in the dancing school he wrote
his first complete dramatic work, a tragedy in five
acts, called *Skogskapellet* (" The Forest-Chapel "),
a jumble of absurdities and horrors, the last scene
of which Collin is cruel enough to quote from the
MS. in his possession.*   Even Andersen, enamoured
as he always was of his own works, had not the
courage to show "my first tragedy," as he called it,
to anybody but an enthusiastic old lady friend, who
brought tears of joy to his eyes by prophesying that
he would certainly be a poet one day, though not till
long after her death.   His condition at this time was
wretched in the extreme.  The money that Weyse and
Guldberg had collected for him was exhausted, and
he had too much delicacy to apply to them for more.
" I couldn't bear to tell people of my dire distress,"
he says pathetically.  He had removed to still
humbler quarters, kept by a sailor's widow, where
he had nothing but a cup of coffee every morning,
making the woman believe that he dined at midday
with families of his acquaintance, when, as a matter
of fact, the only meal he had was a roll furtively
devoured on a bench in the park.  His boots were
in pieces, his feet were wet through for weeks
together, and he had no warm clothing to wear in

* Collin, p. xii.

winter.* Yet for all this he was quite happy. He tells us that when he lay down to sleep of a night in his little attic after saying his prayers, he was sustained by a wonderful trust in God, and an invincible belief that things would and must come right in the end.

That there was a strong ingredient of superstition mixed up with his piety, however, the following anecdote of what he did on New Year's Day, 1821, sufficiently shows. He had the firm belief that as it fares with one on New Year's Day, so will it fare for the rest of the year. It was the wish of his heart to act in a play during the coming year, and full of this thought he went to the Royal Theatre while it was closed, crept with fear and trembling past the purblind old caretaker, who was sitting in the corridor leading to the stage, made his way thither through the side-wings, and fell upon his knees before the empty orchestra, but not a single dramatic quotation could he recollect. As, according to his theory, however, he was bound to recite *something* aloud there and then, if he were to have any chance of acting in the course of the year, he said the Lord's Prayer, which was the only thing that occurred to him at the moment, in an audible voice, and went away with the firm conviction that he would infallibly make his *début* during 1821.

* *M. L. E.*

Nor was he altogether disappointed. In May his voice improved so much that Herr Krossing, the singing-master of the Royal Theatre, resolved to give him a trial, and admitted him into the chorus-school. Andersen was enthusiastic. He saw before him a fresh possibility of getting on in the way he liked best, and had the satisfaction of taking a part, if a very subordinate part, as a soldier, a sailor, and such like, in opera choruses. But he was not content with this. His burning desire to play more important parts led him to pester the directors of the theatre continually, and he anticipated the objection that play-acting might interfere with his studies, by observing that leave to play one or two small *rôles* would only inflame his zeal for literature, adding that "two such pretty sisters as Minerva and Thalia might well be suffered to walk hand in hand."* In fact the theatre had now become all the world to him. In it he lived, or rather dreamed, away his time, frequently absenting himself "with or without an excuse"† from his Latin lessons (Guldberg had found him a tutor to whom he was supposed to go regularly) in order to go to the pit, where he was allowed free admittance whenever there was a vacant seat. Guldberg, who got to know of it, was naturally very angry, and for the

---

* Collin, xiii. The directors replied that they could hold out no hope of any such thing.        . † *M. L. E.*

first time in his life Andersen received a severe and solemn rebuke which nearly crushed him to the earth.*  " I don't think," he says, " that a criminal on hearing sentence of death pronounced upon him, could be more appalled than I was by Guldberg's words : " the upshot of it was that his Latin lessons were stopped. And he had other troubles about which he, in his autobiography, says not a word. The shameful way in which he was treated by some of his fellow-pupils in the singing-class again reminds one of the undeserved sufferings of the poor " ugly duckling " in the poultry yard. There was one bully in particular, called Brandt, who seems to have taken a coward's delight in annoying and harrassing the poor unoffending creature. He used to throw snuff in Andersen's eyes and mouth, tweak his nose, and threaten to " crush " him if he dared to complain about it. The poor lad seems to have endured these insults for weeks, but at last his patience was exhausted, and, turning upon his persecutor, he exclaimed : " I have never known such an impolite *Monsieur* as you." The bully, no doubt irritated by even this feeble show of resistance from one whom he must have looked upon as dirt beneath his feet, instantly retorted by giving Andersen a couple of ringing boxes on the ear, at the same time loading him with curses. Andersen,

† *M. L. E.*, p. 48.

though very unwillingly, reported Brandt to the directors, and it is satisfactory to learn that the blackguard was obliged to publicly apologise to Andersen before the whole singing school.* This was in November 1821, and in the following June Andersen was dismissed from the singing-school altogether, with the intimation that he was only wasting his time there, and that it would be as well if his friends took him in hand, and gave him the instruction necessary for every-one who wanted to make his way in the world, and without which mere natural talent was of no use at all.

Andersen felt as if he were cast adrift, rudderless, in the midst of a vast sea. But his self-confidence was unshakable, and he speedily came to the conclusion that he *must* write a piece for the theatre, and that it *must* be accepted. This was the only remaining hope for him ; so he set to work and wrote a tragedy entitled *Alfsol*, suggested by a tale of Suhm's.† He was positively transported with joy by the first acts, and immediately introduced himself with them to Shakespeare's translator, Admiral Wulff, in whose house and family circle he afterwards found a real home. Wulff humorously relates how they first became acquainted. Andersen suddenly put his head inside the door and exclaimed : "You have

---

* Collin, xiii., xiv., where Andersen's complaint to the directors of the theatre is given *in extenso.* ·     † *M. L. E.*, pp. 53, 54.

translated Shakespeare, and very fond of him I am ;
but I have written an *original* tragedy, so pray listen
to it ! " Wulff invited his strange unbidden guest
to sit down, and have a little breakfast first, but
Andersen was too full of his play to think of anything
else, and after reciting it from beginning to end,
stopped for breath and cried: " Well, now, what do
you think of it ?  Have I got it in me ? "  Wulff
evaded the question by asking him to come and see
him again soon.  " Yes," replied Andersen, " Yes, I
will come when I have written another tragedy ! "
" Then it will be some time, I suppose, before I
have the pleasure of seeing you again ! " said the
Admiral.  " Oh, no ! " cried Andersen, " I'll have
another ready for you in a fortnight."*

Andersen's *amour propre* makes him insinuate
that Wulff's description of him is a little exaggerated.
There is every reason, however, to suppose that it is
literally true, for we have the independent evidence
of a shrewd observer to the same effect.  It was
about this time (most probably in the course of 1821)
that Andersen made the acquaintance of the poet
Just Matthias Thiele, already famous for his masterly
collection of " Danish Folk-tales,"† who was to be

* Edward Collin points out (xi.) that Andersen appropriated Suhm's
language holus bolus.  " At this rate," he adds, " Andersen might very
well promise Wulff to have another tragedy ready in a fortnight."

'† *Danske Folkesagn*, first published 1818-1823.  Hansen, *Illustreret
Dansk Litteraturhistorie*, ii. 3 and 4.

one of the best friends he ever had, " one of the few,"
says Andersen, " who told me the truth while others
made merry at my expense." Andersen himself indeed does not tell us how the acquaintance began, but
Thiele, fortunately, has been more communicative,
and his account of their singular first interview
is valuable, as giving us the only full and authen-
tic portrait of Hans Christian, at this time, that we
possess.

Thiele was sitting one afternoon at his writing-
table, with his back towards the door, when some
one knocked. " Come in ! " he cried, without raising
his head, but when he did look up he was astonished
to see a lanky hobble-de-hoy, of the oddest appearance
imaginable, standing at the door, and making him a
deep theatrical bow, right down to the ground. This
strange apparition had already thrown off his hat by
the door, and when he had raised his long figure,
which was encased in a shabby grey frock, the
sleeves of which fell short far above the skinny
wrists, Thiele encountered a pair of small Chinese-
like eyes which seemed to require a surgical operation to enable them to see clear of an abnormally
prominent, obstructive nose. The strange intruder
wore round his neck a striped cotton kerchief tied so
tightly that his long neck looked for all the world as
if it were striving to wriggle out of its wrappings—
in short, a startling apparition which became still

more startling when, after taking a couple of strides
forward, and making the astonished author another
low bow, the strange visitant began his pathetic
oration thus : " May I have the honour to express
my sentiments with regard to the stage in a poem
of my own composition ?" Thiele's amazement
prevented him from moving a muscle, and taking
silence for consent, the lanky visitor plunged incontinently into the middle of a long declamation which
he followed up by another low bow and an announce-
ment that he was now about to recite a scene from
another drama, into which he rushed forthwith,
taking all the different parts himself. Thiele sat
dumb, waiting for an opportunity of putting a
question and receiving an answer ; but in vain, for
the performer dragged him along from one scene in
this tragedy to another scene in that comedy, and
when at last he had run through an epilogue (also of
his own composition), he concluded with a series of
theatrical bows, snatched up his cap, rattled down
the steps, and was gone. Thiele related his strange
encounter at a dinner party that same evening, when
he learnt that the odd apparition was a talented
youth whom Weyse and some others had taken in
hand, and that his name was Hans Christian
Andersen.*

It was to this passion for declaiming in season and

* J. M. Thiele : *Af mit Livs Aarböger*, pp. 204-6.

out of season, that Andersen owed his nickname of
"Der kleiner Declamator," first given to him by
the celebrated actress Madame Andersen. It was,
in fact, the name he generally went by, and Collin
tells us that even the maid-servants used to announce
him as "the Klamator "* which was as near as they
could get to it.

It is not surprising that this strange original
creature soon became the talk of the town. He was
regarded as a sort of curiosity whom every one was
free to make fun of, while he, poor fellow, saw in
every smile a smile of approval. In this way,
however, his circle of acquaintances rapidly enlarged,
and he soon numbered amongst them some of the
highest in the land. He even found his way at last
to the *Bakkehus*,† that classical cottage, "the Temple
of the Muses," where the veteran poet and critic,
Knud Lyne Rahbek, with his gifted wife, the incomparable and irresistible " Kamma," assembled around
them everything of literary distinction and splendour
which the Danish capital had to show for two
generations. "In this home of hospitality," says
one‡ who knew it well, "people were weighed by a
standard quite different to that of the world outside.
It was like Heaven, where rank and riches count for

* Collin, p. 3, *note*.

† Lit., Hill-house. It was situated in the village of Valby, near
Copenhagen.

‡ Madame Gyllembourg in *Extremerne*.

nothing. The poor man whom the world looked down upon, if only he possessed some artistic merit, some accomplishment, was sure of being received there with a warm shake of the hand and a friendly look. If Socrates had lived in those days, he would have visited that house, and brought Plato and Alcibiades along with him."

Andersen also was warmly welcomed beneath the "shade of those linden trees where the birds of song could sing, and the friends of song could listen," * and here he seems to have met most of those who were to befriend him in after-life, such as the aristocratic Colbjörnsens, Thiele, Madame Andersen, and many others. Like every one else he was enchanted by Madame Rahbek, and wrote a comedy for the express purpose of reading it to her. "Why!" exclaimed the lady, after listening attentively to the opening scenes, "there are whole passages in it that you have copied from Oehlenschläger and Ingemann!" "Yes!" cried Andersen innocently, "but they are so charming, you know"— and he went on reading. On another occasion he went there in a beautiful blue coat, nearly new, which had been given him by Edward Colbjörnsen. Its only fault was a looseness about the breast, and to remedy this, Andersen, before buttoning it up to the neck, had stuffed the vacant space full of old

* Heiberg, "*Bakkehuset.*"

play bills, which made him look as if he had a hump
on the breast, and, in this guise, he presented himself before Madame Rahbek and her friend, Madame
Colbjörnsen. They immediately asked him what
was the matter with his breast, and why he didn't
wear his coat open during such hot weather (it was
in the middle of the dog days), but Andersen took
good care not to unbutton it for fear of all the playbills tumbling out.

All this time he was still engaged in authorship,
which, as I have said, he had now begun to consider his last chance. Throughout the summer
of 1822, indeed, his condition was truly pitiable,
it was as much as he could do to keep body and
soul together. There were many who would
gladly have helped him if they had only guessed
how dire his need was, but noble pride or a false
shame tied his tongue, and besides, he was upheld
all along by a strange confidence in his own
powers. If he could not be a great actor, at least
he was determined to he a great playwright, and
shortly before his dismissal from the theatre he
had composed an original tragedy called : *Röverne
i Vissenberg* ("The Robbers at Vissenberg"), paid
some one who spelt better than he did to fair copy
it for him, and sent it to the Royal Theatre anonymously. For the next six weeks he was perfectly
happy, never doubting for an instant that his

play would be accepted, and then it was returned
to him with a curt note from the directors of the
Royal Theatre to the effect that the piece in question
showed such an utter want of elementary education
in every page that it was absurd to expect any
audience to tolerate it.* Nevertheless, nothing
daunted, Andersen now sent to the theatre a fresh
tragedy, *Alfsol* the same piece that he had before
recited to Admiral Wulff. He had previously
shown it to the kind-hearted provost Gutfeldt, one
of the leading broad-church preachers of his day,
and Gutfeldt thought so well of it that he recommended it to the notice of Ruhbek who was one of
the four directors of the Royal Theatre. For the
next few weeks Andersen lived between hope and
fear. If this piece were also rejected, he really did
not know what he should do. While waiting for a
reply he attempted to publish this same play,
together with an original story called *Gjenfærdet ved
Palnatoke's Grav* ("The Spectre at Palnatoke's
Grave"), in one volume by subscription. The book
was actually printed in 1822, but not a copy was
sold, and it was ultimately disposed of as waste
paper.† The manuscript sent to the theatre was
more successful, though not in the way that

---

* Compare *M. L. E.*, p. 53, and Collin, p. xv., where the letter of
the directors is given in full.

† Collin, p. xi.

Andersen himself anticipated. Rahbek, to whom
the play had been especially recommended, took the
trouble to read it, and reported to his co-directors
at the next meeting of the board, that, although
*Alfsol* was quite unsuitable for the stage, nevertheless its young author "ought to be recommended
[to the king] for such assistance as might enable
him to develop and cultivate his unmistakable
talents."* Andersen was then sent for, and the
directors undertook to interest the king in his
behalf if he would promise to devote all his time
and attention to the studies so necessary for him,
an offer which he naturally accepted with joy.
Another of the directors, the noble-minded and
large-hearted Jonas Collin, who had already made
inquiries about the lad, and satisfied himself that
his was a most deserving case, now took the matter
in hand with his usual prompt and energetic benevo-
lence, and represented all the facts to Frederick VI.†
in a private audience. It was ultimately arranged
that Andersen should be sent at once to the Latin
school at Slagelse for three years at the public
expense, by which time it was hoped he would be
able to pass the university examinations for his
degrees. Collin, moreover, undertook to act as a sort

* Collin, p. xvii.

† This worthy prince was, I may remark in passing, the prototype
of the patriarchal type of kings we meet with in Andersen's fairy tales.

of guardian to the youth, and provide him with a home at his own house. Andersen called upon Collin to thank him just before his departure for Slagelse, not without fear and trembling, for, at their first interview, the well-known Privy Councillor had struck him as a somewhat awful personage. Now, however, he found the great man kind and encouraging. " Be sure you always write to me without reserve," said Collin, " whenever you want anything, and let me know exactly how you are getting on." " From that moment," says Andersen, " I grew fast to his heart. No father could have been more to me than he was . . . . . No one has sympathised more with me in all my sorrows; he felt for me just as if I were one of his own children. His charity was given without a word, without a look, that could make it hard for me to bear, which is more than I can say of every one to whom I had to convey my thanks at this change in my fortunes." *
It is pleasant to add that Andersen's gratitude to his " fatherly benefactor," as he called Jonas Collin ever afterwards, was deep and lasting; indeed, his affectionate devotion to all those who had, at any time, shown him the least kindness, was one of the many amiable traits of his character.

On a fine autumn day shortly afterwards, Hans Christian set off by the stage-coach from Copenhagen

* *M. L. E.*

to Slagelse to begin his schooling. Thus, what, looking back upon it long afterwards, he has called "the days of my degradation," were over once and for all. Henceforth his troubles and grievances were for the most part to be either sentimental or imaginary.

JONAS COLLIN

D

# CHAPTER III

## THE "TYRANT" MEISLING

Slagelse—Simon Meisling—His character—Misrepresented by Andersen—Andersen's own character at this time—Suffers from the
abrupt transition from his old to his new mode of life—His dislike
of and difficulties with grammar—Hatred of the "dear old classics"
—Tragico-comical account of an examination—"Herr von Cicero"
—A specimen of Andersen's sensitiveness and Meisling's chaff—
Meisling at home—Extract from Andersen's school-diary—Dull-
ness of Andersen's school-days at Slagelse—The theatre there—
Intercourse with the Ingemanns—Meisling transferred to Elsinore
—Andersen goes with him—Rupture between them—Its possible
causes—Imprudence of Andersen—Increased severity of Meisling
—Jonas Collin intervenes—Rudeness of Meisling—Andersen with-
drawn from Elsinore.

Slagelse is a small town of some 6000 inhabitants,
in the north-west corner of Zealand between Sorö
and Korsör, and about 12½ miles from Copenhagen.
It was chiefly remarkable at that time for its Latin
school,* and the rector of this school, Prof. Simon
Meisling, was certainly the most important personage in the little place. This worthy man was a
sound and graceful scholar, an able and conscientious
teacher, and, above all, a strict disciplinarian who
flattered himself on his success with boys in general;

* It has since then been transferred elsewhere.

his name, however, would have been long ago forgotten but for the unenviable notoriety he has
obtained as young Andersen's tyrant and persecutor,
on the sole authority, it must be added, of Andersen
himself. In *Mit Livs Eventyr*, that "production of
daily shifting moods,"* as Edward Collin severely
but not unjustly called it, Andersen describes
Meisling as taking a peculiar delight in turning all
his pupils into ridicule; † as being quite unfit, for all
his learning, to bring up young men; ‡ as habitually
treating him in particular like an idiot; § as brow-
beating and bullying him, not for the sake of discipline or correction, but from sheer ill-humour, and of
making his school-life, generally, a sort of "spiritual
torture-chamber," ‖ a worse than Do-the-Boys Hall.¶
Now there is no reason to suppose Andersen guilty
of wilfully misrepresenting facts. He was quite
incapable of an untruth, and clearly believed every
word he wrote, at least *while* he was writing it. On
the other hand, in his own letters, written at the
very time that he was at Slagelse, he actually acquits
Meisling of any intentional unkindness, and takes all
the blame upon himself. The truth seems to be that
Andersen's super-sensitiveness and morbid imagination made mountains out of molehills, and read the
most sinister meanings into the most innocent

---

* Collin, p. 455.      † *M. L. E.*, p. 61.      ‡ *Ibid*, p. 65.
§ *Ibid*, p. 74.      ‖ *Ibid*, p. 79.      ¶ *Ibid*, p. 76.

accidents. To explain what I mean I will try
to give some idea of his character at this time, so
far at least as it can be gleaned from his daily
correspondence, and the memoranda of intimate
friends.

Andersen came into the world with an extraordinary, extravagant, imagination, out of all propor-
tion to his other faculties. If ever there was any one
who needed the constant control of a kindly but
watchful eye, of a firm but loving hand, it was he ;
but this, at any rate at the most critical period of his
life, was just what he never had. On the contrary,
he was, as we have already seen, left entirely to his
own devices ; his vivid, volatile imagination, nursed
in dreamy idleness, and nourished by the indiscrimi-
nate perusal of endless romances and plays, gradually
gained the upper hand, and the result was a one-
sided mental development, a want of intellectual
balance, from which he was to suffer for the rest of
his life. His other great natural gifts, such, for
instance, as his retentive memory, quick apprehension,
remarkable powers of observation, and that keen
and rapid sense of the ludicrous which was one day
to make him a prince of humorists, lay dormant
for want of exercise. He lived in a world of his own
creation, a world of day-dreams, or, as he himself
expresses it when looking back upon these early
days : "I could not picture life to myself as anything

really solid, but only as a phantasm."* Still more
mischievous was the reaction of this abnormal state
of mind on his moral development. Andersen was
naturally the most impressionable of beings. In him
the mind of a great poet was united to the heart of
an innocent child, and the nerves of a sensitive woman.
His susceptibility to outward impressions was extraordinary. A smile, a friendly word, could always fill
his soul with gladness, while a single cold look would
make him utterly wretched. He knew this very
well, and never made the slightest effort to conceal
it. "I am a strange being," he once wrote.† "If the
wind blow a wee bit sharply, the water always comes
into my eyes, though I know very well that life
cannot be a perpetual May Day." Such a morbidly
sensitive creature, even if brought up amidst the
most congenial surroundings, and carefully prepared
for the contact of a rough and ready world by the
healthy give-and-take discipline of ordinary family
life, was bound to suffer, and suffer severely, in the
battle of life. But poor Andersen entered upon his
life's struggle heavily handicapped. He had never
known what it was to have a proper home. His
mother was a foolish negligent gossip, with a taste
for excitement which she ultimately concentrated
on the bottle; fit playmates of his own age he

---

* Letter to Madame Andersen, June 1824, Collin, p. 12.
† Letter to Madame Jörgensen, Oct. 1826, Collin, p. 57.

had none, and he shrank instinctively from the rough companionship of the village lads. Thus he was thrown back more and more upon himself, and such self-concentration naturally fostered still further his exalted ideas of himself. For it is worth remarking that he was conscious, only too conscious, of his own genius, although he was so little aware of its true field of activity, that he may be said to have strayed into it by accident. His belief in his own powers, moreover, was encouraged by the kindly but mistaken praises of his early benefactors and protectors at Odense, and it was then, doubtless, that the seed was sown of that naïve, almost comical, vanity, that childish delight in flattery, that fretful impatience of anything like disparagement, which was to plague him, and his friends too, in later years,— and yet with all his ridiculous and irritating follies and foibles, Andersen was always the most lovable of creatures. It was impossible to mistake or resist his truthfulness, his loyalty, his gratitude, his readiness to forgive, his reluctance to offend, his transparent conscientiousness, and, finally, his touching, childlike faith in God's providence, which he himself looked upon as his solace in all the troubles and his safeguard amidst all the temptations of life.

Such, then, was the new pupil who joined Dr. Meisling's Academy in the autumn of 1823. No doubt Meisling had been properly primed as to the antecedents and the idiosyncrasies of the long, lean youth who was now placed amongst the small boys in the very lowest class because he was found to know absolutely nothing; no doubt, too, Meisling tried to do his duty by Andersen, as he himself understood it, but the attempt proved a failure, for the simple reason that Meisling was Meisling, and Andersen, Andersen. Like all professional disciplinarians, the Rector of Slagelse was something of a martinet, and he seems, from the first, to have taken up a harsh attitude towards his new scholar varied by occasional interludes of bluff pleasantry. Now this, of course, was the proper way to deal with ninety-nine boys out of a hundred, but Andersen, unfortunately, was the hundredth, the exception, and instead of being braced by this drastic regimen, he nearly broke down under it altogether. Besides, the transition from perfect freedom to the trammels of scholastic discipline was a little too abrupt, and this is what he, at first, seems to have felt most of all. "The factory-like regularity of school-life," he writes to a friend, "was bound to make a strange impression upon one whose flaming fancy had hitherto only been wont to roam from flower to flower."* And in another place† he adds : "I was really like a wild bird put into a cage. I had the

* Letter to Madame Andersen, June 1824, Collin, p. 13.
† *M. L. E.*, pp. 60, 61.

best will in the world to learn, but kept fumbling
about in the endeavour every moment. I behaved like
one who is thrown into the water without being able
to swim. It was a matter of life and death for me
to make progress, but there came one billow after
another, one called Mathematics, another called
Grammar, a third Geography, &c. &c., till I was fairly
overwhelmed, and began to fear I should never swim
through them all." This nervous fear of failure, the
fear of being found unworthy of the confidence and
kindness of his benefactors, haunted him daily, and
caused him the most intense misery. There were
times when he even fancied himself a blockhead, and
felt quite persuaded that his friends in Copenhagen
were simply throwing away their money upon him.
Collin, however, encouraged him from to time with
brief but cheery little notes, assuring him of his un-
abated confidence, declaring himself quite satisfied
with his progress, and bidding him take things
quietly and sensibly. And indeed there was no
ground at all for these wild alarms. Meisling's private
reports to Collin showed he had no mean opinion of
his new pupil's talents, and Andersen's zeal and diligence were, from first to last, exemplary. In those
studies he liked, or had a natural aptitude for, he
made rapid progress. His theology, Bible-history,
and Danish composition are always described in his
conduct-book as "remarkably good." Indeed the

superior quality of his Danish composition was so generally recognised, that boys from all the classes, even from the highest, used regularly to come to him for help; "only don't let it be too good, or it will be found out," they used to say.* In history, geography, mathematics, he was generally "pretty good," but his great stumbling blocks were languages, especially Latin and Greek,† just the very things in which the pitiless Meisling excelled, and was anxious that his pupils should pursue. Andersen hated all grammar, "that hideous, grinning, linguistic skeleton," as he has called it,‡ with an almost personal hatred. "All grammar is hard to me," he writes, "and when I get anxious about it, the blood flies to my head at once. and I give stupid answers."§ "I cannot get on with these languages at all," he writes to Jonas Collin on another occasion.‖ But it was "the dear old classics," as he ironically calls them,¶ which brought the water into his eyes most frequently. His descriptions of what he suffered on this score read comically enough, but the paper on which he wrote then must certainly have been moistened with his tears. Take, for instance, this tragi-comical account of an examination

* *M. L. E.*, p. 66.

† Of the two he fancied, at first, he preferred Latin (Collin, p. 4) ; but a closer acquaintance with it convinced him that it was a "hostile demon." Collin, p. 39.

‡ Bille og Bogh : *Breve fra A.*, i. p. 17.     § Collin, p. 11.

‖ *Ibid*, p. 29.     ¶ Bille og Bogh : *Breve fra A.*, i. p. 19.

contained in a letter to Collin,* at a comparatively
late period of his tuition : "The examination began a
fortnight ago, and we had all the Latin we had learnt
for the last two years. It was not Ovid I was afraid
of but Courtius (*sic*). I had gone over them both in
the summer, but hadn't time to get them *both* up, so
I took Ovid, and left my fate to God. How my
heart did beat when I had to stand up ! I prayed
God that I might merely hold my own as heretofore,
but the Fates willed that I should be examined in
Courtius (*sic*). Then my courage broke down. I
stammered and stuttered, and so I only got 'mid-
dling' (in my conduct book). I was quite desperate.
I no longer saw any career before me. . . . . I
already fancied I had lost everything, and I really
thought it was quite a sin of our Lord to allow me to
be unfortunate with my Latin." On another occasion
he made a fervent vow to God that if only He would
let him get into the fourth class, he would go up to
the altar the very next Sunday, a vow he was able to
accomplish ; † and on the eve of an examination he
frequently used to open his Bible at random, and
read his fate on the morrow from the first text that
caught his eye. Yet by dint of dreary plodding he
managed to get a fair knowledge even of the classics,
though he was never very enthusiastic about them.
Virgil he liked pretty well at last, but Horace never

* Collin, p. 38. † *M. L. E.*, p. 72.

appealed to him at all, and at the very end of his schooling he confided to his friend Ingemann that he would much prefer practising the moral precepts of "Herr von Cicero" throughout life, than construing them in class.*

Nevertheless we have Meisling's own testimony that Andersen, thanks to his own conscientious application, gradually "apprehended and appropriated with more or less of success the various branches of study† presented to him," so that fourteen months after his arrival he had reached the highest class but one.‡ Up to this point, and for some time afterwards, the rector and he seem to have got on pretty well together. At the same time Andersen always quaked before him in the school-room, and was scared almost out of his life by the caustic banter and rough chaff in which the pedagogue frequently indulged. Though he dared not say a word to the rector by way of remonstrance, he frequently pleaded with him by letter, excusing his own stupidity, and endeavouring to propitiate the stern mentor in a way both comical and pathetic.§

Stern as he was in school, however, out of it Meisling could be agreeable enough. At home he was generally full of fun, would tell waggish stories,

* Bille og Bogh : *Breve fra A.*, i. p. 14.
† *M. L. E.*, pp. 74, 75.
‡ Bille og Bogh : *Breve fra A.*, i. p. 4.
§ See Appendix No. 1.

crack jokes, and play at tin soldiers in the evenings
with his children and his pet pupils. Andersen
seems to have been one of the favourites, at any rate
he was invited to the house oftener than any one
else, though his delight at the distinction thus
conferred upon him was tempered by doubts as to
how long it was likely to last. The following
extracts from his private diary show how nervously
eager he was to conciliate, and how desperately
afraid he was of offending his master. " The rector
bade me good-night ; oh, if he only knew how his
friendliness encourages me he would always be like
this in future. . . . . Read diligently, rector kind
and courteous. Oh God ! let me retain his friendship ; he is stern, but his heart is in the right
place. . . . . R[ector] particularly good-humoured ;
had a walk with me . . . . lent me all the papers.
Have enjoyed myself splendidly this evening.
Oh ! he bubbles over with wit ! We play blind-
hookey together. Oh God ! good God ! if only I
may preserve his favour. . . . . The rector's frock-
coat was covered with fluff; he called to the
servant-girl for a brush, she did not come at once,
so I rushed out and brushed him ; he was so
kind, and I felt quite at my ease again. In school
we read about the French Revolution. Poor Louis !
how unstable thou wert, violent and weak. I believe
thy character is mine. . . . . Read Byron's biography.

He was just like me, even down to his little tattling ;
my soul is ambitious like his, it can only feel happy
when admired by all. . . . . The rector gave me
some fruit this evening, but I dread to-morrow's
Greek. . . . . God ! how my heart is like to burst !
Now I am going in, and when I come out again then.
. . . . Got *bad* for Greek also. . . . . What *will*
become of me ? . . . . My strong imagination will
bring me to the mad-house, my violent emotion will
make me a suicide ; both combined might have made
a great writer of me.   My God, forgive me !   I am
ungrateful.   By my hope of eternal peace I promise
Thee never more to doubt the guidance of Thy
fatherly hand, if only, this time, I may get into the
fourth class." *   It is satisfactory to learn that the
examination, so far as Andersen was concerned, went
off "splendidly" after all ; he had the wish of his
heart, and *did* get into the fourth class.†

Andersen was three years and eight months‡ at
Slagelse, and a very dull and uninteresting place he
found it.   The one bright spot in the sombreness
of these Slagelsian school-days, was the privilege
enjoyed by the pupils of the Academy of frequenting
the rehearsals of the local theatre, a privilege he
never failed to take advantage of.   This theatre had

---

* Collin, pp. 84–93.   The entries cover a period of many months.
† *Ibid*, p. 38.   Letter to Jonas Collin, Oct. 2 1825.
‡ Oct. 1822.

formerly been a stable, was situated in a backyard,
and the lowing of the kine in the neighbouring fields
could be plainly heard during the pauses in the
rehearsals. It is this theatre which is so vividly
described in the fourth evening of the immortal
*Picture Book without Pictures.** Another dis-
traction was Andersen's intercourse with the novelist
Ingemann, one of Walter Scott's imitators, who lived
at Sorö close by, and was rector of the academy there.
Ingemann had been very kind to Andersen at
Copenhagen, and frequently invited him, during the
summer, to stay with him and his wife, for a day or
two, at their pretty little cottage amidst the woods
and lakes of one of the most picturesque parts of
Zealand. The garden where " the flowers of the field
and the forest had leave to grow as they liked," must
have been a veritable sanctuary to Andersen in his
Slagelsian days. Whether Ingemann was as wise a
friend as he was a kind one, is another question. He
was certainly a very indulgent critic of his young
friend's early works, and Andersen, in his correspondence with him† at this period, speaks of his own
studies with an impatience, and of his poetic effusions (for he had begun scribbling again‡) with an

* Better known in England, perhaps, as "What the Moon
Saw."
† Bille og Bogh : *Breve fra A.*, i. pp. 8-20.
‡ At first Andersen had made the abstention from poetising quite a
case of conscience.

enthusiasm, which Collin would certainly not have commended.

In May 1826 Meisling was transferred from the academy of Slagelse to the still more important academy of Elsinore, and Andersen, who was now in the first class, went with him. Under the new arrangement Andersen was to board at the rector's house at a fixed rate, and receive private instruction from him after school hours, to prepare him for taking his degrees at the University of Copenhagen. Collin seems to have left the matter entirely to Andersen's choice, and Andersen came to the conclusion that he had better go with Meisling, as he could scarcely expect a new rector to take as much interest in him as the old one.* So to Elsinore he went, and was quite charmed with the picturesque old place so delightfully situated on the Sound. His first letter to Collin, after his arrival, is full of enthusiasm, and contains his earliest description of scenery, which his friends thought good enough to be printed in one of the leading newspapers. A happy time therefore seemed to be in store for Andersen at Elsinore. Meisling, too, was unusually pleasant, and we hear of his taking little tours into the country with his pupil every Sunday, and showing him the prettiest parts of the country. But this ideal state of things was not to last. Andersen had

* Collin, pp. 47, 48.

not been six months at Elsinore, when the relations between master and pupil began to be strained, and by the end of October there was a downright rupture. The causes of this final catastrophe, for so it proved, though still somewhat mysterious, are not difficult to divine. Andersen was now of age, and, with increasing years and knowledge, his old self-confidence had revived, and he began to believe himself a greater genius than ever. He no longer regarded himself as bound to abstain from "pouring out his feelings on paper." On the contrary, he had already written several little poems, one of which, *The Dying Child*, was much admired for its tender feeling, and had the distinction of being translated into German. Moreover, during his vacation visit to Copenhagen he had moved in the best society, and society had looked at and even listened to him. Great ladies had praised his poems; Lord Chamberlains had stopped to congratulate him on the progress he was making; nay, the immortal poet, Oehlenschläger himself, had actually crossed a crowded drawing-room to shake hands with him, despite the humiliating fact that he was the only person present who was not dressed in conventional black.* And after all these triumphs to return to Meisling, and find him—old Meisling still!

* Collin, pp. 97–101. Andersen's own account of his summer vacation at Copenhagen.

E

No wonder that Andersen began to think himself
very hardly used, though there are indications that
he was not quite so diligent now as he had been
before, and gave to his friends the Muses some of
the time that ought to have been given to his
enemies the Classics.    Nor was this all.    There is
good reason to believe that Meisling now began to
positively dislike his eccentric pupil, and, it must
also be admitted, not without some cause.    Andersen
had been imprudently communicative to his friends
at Copenhagen, especially to his lady friends.*    He
had complained of Meisling's conduct to more than
one sympathetic soul, and had even shown them
some of his master's sarcastic epistles which had
been meant for no eye but his own.    Meisling
apparently heard of this, and was very angry.    He
naturally resented any interference from outsiders,
and seeing, as he thought, in Andersen a disposition
to kick over the traces, he tightened the reins ;
became more and more severe as the time for his
pupil's final examination approached, snubbed him
in season and out of season, and punished every
excursion into verse without mercy.    Andersen
quailed beneath this treatment.    He durst not
openly rebel against it, but he chafed and fretted in
secret, and finding that letters of remonstrance to

* One lady told him to assert himself, and not allow his master to
trample upon him.

the rector had now no effect at all, appealed piteously
to Collin. His letters show how much he suffered,
and that it is no exaggeration when he calls his
school days at Elsinore "the darkest and bitterest
period of his whole life." At last he really began
to think that he was good for nothing at all, and it
was while in this state of mind that he wrote a des-
pairing letter to Jonas Collin, in which he declares
it to be quite impossible for him to endure Meisling's
brutality any longer. That he himself may have
been stupid and flighty, he candidly admits, yet he
implores his benefactor not to throw him over,
although he has made him such a poor return for all
his kindness, but to give him another chance in
some office far away across the seas. "At any rate I
am honest," he says, "and that, surely, is something!"
Collin sent by return of post a sensible, soothing
little note, bidding him cheer up, as things would
certainly turn out all right, and assuring him that
the rector meant to be benevolent, though he might
have a queer way of showing it. Then he courteously wrote to Meisling, asking him point-blank
whether he was satisfied with his pupil or not.
To this letter Meisling sent a somewhat sour
reply. He began by saying that Andersen would
do very well as long as "thoughtlessness and lazi-
ness did not throw hindrances in the way," but
added that as "backbiters in society had been

attacking him [Meisling]," he was quite willing to leave the honour of preparing Andersen for his final examination "to worthier hands." This letter decided Collin to take Andersen away from Elsinore, though it was still some months before a move could be made. Finally in April 1827, Andersen settled down in Copenhagen, in a little attic at 131 Viin-gaardstraede, the same little room with "the slant-ing wall under the roof" which is described in the romance *Only a Fiddler*,\* and in the *Picture Book without Pictures*, where the moon used "to pay her nightly visits." His lodgings had been paid for a month in advance, and he had an allowance of five rix dollars (11s. 8d.) a month for breakfasts and suppers. It had also been arranged that he was to dine in turn at the houses of various friends, such as the Collins, the Wulffs, the Örsteds, the Guldbergs, and some others, and a private coach, Ludvig Christian Möller, then a candidate for holy orders, was found for him at fifteen rix dollars (£1 15s.) a month.† Happier days had began to dawn upon him at last.

\* *M. L. E.*' p. 80.                    † Collin, p. 81.

# CHAPTER IV

Andersen at the Collins' house—"The family candle-snuffer"—Passes
his examinations—Appearance of his first work, *Fodreise til
Ostpynten af Amager*—Description of it—Favourably received—
*Dödningen*—Trip to Jutland—Andersen's first love—Its general
mysteriousness—His mildly Heinesque erotic poems—Appearance
of the *Gjenganger-Breve*—Its savage assault on the writers of the
day—Falls foul of Andersen—Crushing effect of "The Spectre's"
criticism on Andersen—His first continental tour—Describes it
in *Skyggebilder af en Reise til Harzen*—Its defects and great
merits—Extracts—Andersen's itinerary—Tieck and Chamisso—
Andersen's dramas—The dramatic censor Christian Molbech and
his bitter sarcasms—Mortification of Andersen—His condition of
mind alarms his friends—Obtains a travelling stipend.

DURING the next two years we catch but an occasional glimpse of Andersen. His studies now took
up most of his time. Twice a day he walked backwards and forwards from his lodgings to the house of
his tutor at Christianshavn, a suburb of Copenhagen,
and his evenings he spent with the families that
befriended him, though he always looked upon the
patriarchal dwelling of the Collins as his real home.
It is from this time that Edward Collin's acquaintance with Andersen begins, and he has given us some
very interesting details about him. Andersen was

almost a daily visitor at the Collins' house at this
time, and as the younger Collin undertook the
duty of being a sort of extra coach to him in Latin
composition, always his weak point, the intimacy

THE COLLINS' HOUSE

between them became pretty close.    It is as the
family candle-snuffer, however, that Edward Collin
has the most vivid recollection of his friend at
this period.    Tallow candles were then in general
use, and of course required constant snuffing.    Andersen's abnormal elongation of limb enabled him,

without leaving his place, to trim all the candles on
the table, with a sure and steady hand, at almost
incredible distances, and so it became a recognised
thing that only he was to perform this useful office.
He was also a very amusing talker. In that sort of
conversation where irony had free play and Andersen's peculiar humour found a chance of asserting
itself, he could be irresistibly comical. " I never
knew any one," says Collin, "who could so seize upon,
and make so much of, a simple, and in itself insig-
nificant, trait of character." Almost every evening
he brought home a funny story about something or
other that had happened to him in the course of
the day. His best tales, however, were about Meisling and his household, "but these," we are told,
"do not bear repetition, only he could tell them
properly." *

Andersen's only serious trouble, at this time, was
with his inveterate enemy Latin Grammar, which
seemed for long to be an insurmountable barrier to
his progress. Frequently he despaired of ever passing his examinations at all. He bids one of his most
sprightly and sympathetic young lady friends, Miss
Henrietta Wulff, not to judge him too severely if he
fails in his examinations after all, as it costs a mind
so volatile as his, an immense amount of trouble
to gnaw its way through dry grammar. If the

* Collin, pp. 81, 82, and 458–60.

worst come to the worst, the world is large enough, and he can find a grave anywhere.* On another occasion he gloomily predicts that he will, in all probability, die of starvation like Camoens. Nevertheless, things did not turn out so badly as he had anticipated. In October, 1828, Andersen passed his first academical examination *in quo haud illaudabilem in artibus liberalibus profectum probavit.* The reading for the second and final examination began at once, his tutor, this time, being the theologian, afterwards Bishop, Bindesböll, and he passed it with distinction in the autumn of 1829, obtaining the highest certificate, *laudabilis.* Moreover, the same year which saw his scholastic apprenticeship come to an end, saw his career as an author begin. In the course of 1829 appeared his first considerable work : *Fodreise fra Holmens Kanal til Östpynten af Amager* ("Journey on Foot from Holm Canal to the East Point of Amager "),† which Edward Collin brought out for him by subscription, as no publisher would look at it.

The *Fodreise* is a confused and confusing jumble of the most extravagant images and fancies, after the manner of Hoffmann in his maddest moods, the

* Bille og Bogh : *Breve fra Andersen*, i. pp. 26-8.

† The Isle of Amager, Copenhagen's kitchen-garden, and connected with it by a bridge, is about two miles long and one mile broad. It is a flat, monotonous stretch of land planted with carrots, turnips, and cabbages.

Hoffmann of *Kater Murr* and *Elixire des Teufels*, whom Andersen at this period idolised. Scarcely one page in ten of it is original, and some of the best ideas of Chamisso, Tieck, and Jean Paul are half appropriated, half parodied, with the most perfect frankness. What of originality there is consists in a running fire of persiflage chiefly directed against the stupidity of professors, the wickedness of critics, and the author's own absurdities. The effect produced upon the reader now-a-days by this literary phantasmagoria is very much the same as that of a nightmare. Even Andersen himself, always so ready to regard his own new-born spiritual children as veritable nonpareils, seems to have been rather doubtful about the reception of this work while he was writing it. Looking back upon it years afterwards, he could complacently call it a "poetical improvisation," and a "fantastic arabesque;" but at the time he was actually writing it he made one of the chief characters express the belief that if the *Fodreise* went round the town at all, it would most probably do so wrapped round soap and sugar. Yet even amidst this heap of fantastic, exotic rubbish, a few native grains of pure poetic gold, a few traces of the Andersen of the fairy tales, whom we all know and love, are to be found. Here, for instance, we find the first faint suggestion of two of his best known

tales, *Oli Lockeye* and *The Story of the Year*,\* and
the description of the Temple of Fame contains
many happy passages, though, perversely enough,
E. T. A. Hoffmann is placed on an equal pedestal
there with Calderon, Aristophanes, and—*mirabile
dictu*—Shakespeare himself. Here, as I have said, we
have a stray hint, a faint foretaste of the famous
fairy tales, but in the following year, at the end of a
small volume of poems,† we actually find the first
complete *Eventyr*. It is entitled " Dödningen,"‡
and is, in point of fact, the rough draft of what
Andersen afterwards developed into the now
universally known and admired *Travelling Companion*.

The *Fodreise*, strange to say, was, on the whole,
favourably received by the Danish public, ran
through two or three editions, and was published
ten years later in a collection of Danish classics.
P. E. Müller, in the *Dansk Litteraturtidende*
(*Danish Literary News*), praised the " light-hearted

---

\* See Appendix II.　　　　† " Digte," 1830.

‡ " The Deadman." Unfortunately I have not been able to get hold
of this little volume, of which only a very limited number of copies was
printed, and Andersen rightly excluded the immature *Dödning* from
his collected works. However, the celebrated Danish critic, Dr.
Brandes, has been more fortunate, and in his masterly analysis of
Andersen's genius in *Kritiker og Portraeter*, has compared the two
versions together. It is not often that one has the privilege of following
out the genesis of a favourite story, and the subject is so interesting to
all lovers of Andersen, that I have translated Brandes' remarks for the
benefit of English readers. They will be found in Appendix III.

humour" and the unmistakable talent of its author,
"which deserves to be encouraged"; while even
the great Heiberg, who in those days gave the
tone to Danish criticism through the columns of his
celebrated review, *Flyvende Posten* (*The Flying
Post*) was friendly and encouraging, though he
compared "the young poet" to a collector who
goes in more for quantity than quality, and accepted
the book mainly as a transitional essay containing
within it the promise of something better to come.
Many of Andersen's private friends were delighted
with it. Guldberg grows quite enthusiastic, though
he evidently approved of it more on moral than
on æsthetic grounds, and congratulates the young
writer on having found his legs at last and made
his *début* "like a man." The most intelligent
and far-seeing of all his critics, however, was
a lady, Mrs. Ingemann, who alone at this time
appears to have foreseen wherein Andersen's real
strength lay. Writing to him *apropos* of *Dödningen*,
she says: "The little elves of our childhood seem to
me to be, on the whole, your good geniuses; and
when they live in the fancy and the heart, then, I
think, there is no fear of the stream of the understanding losing itself among glittering pebbles. I
am sure the little elves will show you the right way
through the bright blue sky." *

* Bille og Bogh : *Breve til A.*, p. 368.

In the summer of 1830, Andersen took a trip to
Jutland, and enjoyed himself immensely. The fame
of the *Fodreise* and his poems had preceded him,
and he was fêted and petted wherever he went,
though he comically complains that in one place
they took care to put in the papers next day how
kind they had been to him. On his return journey,
however, an event occurred which, as he tragically
expresses it, " burst the bubble of my life's joy "—he
fell in love for the first time with a young lady
whom he met at a country mansion somewhere in
Funen. Who the girl was we are not told. We
only know that she was well-to-do, had beautiful
brown eyes, and an "innocent, childlike disposition,"
and was already engaged to another young man,
whom she married in the course of the same autumn.
Andersen, I fancy, could not have been very deeply
smitten at the time. He only saw the lady for three
days in the country, met her casually once or twice
in society at the capital a few months later, and
does not seem to have ever exchanged more than a
few words with her. Nay, in his autobiography,
when he could look back upon the whole circumstances of the case from the philosophical standpoint
of middle-age, he distinctly says that it was all
self-deception on his part, and that the lady could
have had no idea of his state of mind. If he had
only held his tongue and gone about his business, he

would, no doubt, have speedily forgotten all about "the brown eyes all aflame [sic] with genius and childlike peace ; " but in an evil hour he took it into his head to confide his budding sorrow to the tender care of a lady friend, Madame Laessoe. This lady at once took the matter *au grand sérieux*, instantly jumped to the conclusion that the love was mutual, and implored Andersen, in almost as many words, not to corrupt another's bride, or "take possession of a heart which is already, perhaps, torn asunder by remorse and self-contempt." A long correspondence ensued, but as we have only the lady's portion of it (there had been an understanding between them that all the letters on the subject should be destroyed, an understanding which Andersen does not seem to have strictly kept), we know no more than half of the story. But it is pretty plain that Andersen, in his inordinate self-conceit, was secretly flattered at being taken for an irresistible lady-killer whom the fondest husband had perhaps some cause to fear. Complaining to Edward Collin at the time of the latest development of this love romance, he says that he desisted from the pursuit because the lady was rich and he was poor, and people might therefore have regarded his suit as a mere commercial speculation. All his best friends—the Ingemanns, the Guldbergs, the Collins—were gradually admitted into the secret.

The gentle Ingemanns tried to console him with moral lectures and Scriptural exhortations. Edward Collin, much to Andersen's indignation, took no notice whatever of his love-sick letters. Bluff old Guldberg told him to be a man, and not to give way to despair. But not content with worrying his friends with his sentimental griefs, Andersen took the public into his confidence likewise, for most of the poems that he published at this period —such, for instance, as the *Phantasier og Skizzer* ("Fantasia and Sketches") 1831—are wailing erotics with a faint Heinesque after-taste (he had escaped from the yoke of Hoffmann, only to fall beneath the harrow of Heine), full of *Welt-schmerz* and desolation. His friends protested, some of them very warmly, against this morbid sentimentality. Even the indulgent Guldberg was vexed, and tried to bully him out of his sickly whimpering, which he put down to wounded vanity. "Don't imitate Heine," he concludes. "Leave your love out of your poems. Don't flutter about as if one of your wings was broken when you can use them both so gloriously."* Fortunately, this imaginary woe was now to be expelled, or rather supplanted, by a more poignant and tangible grief: the stinging lash of hostile criticism, wielded by the hand of a master of satire, was to make Andersen forget,

* Bille og Bogh : *Breve til A.*, i. p. 687.

for awhile, the puny surface-scratches of saucy Cupid.

Towards the end of 1830 a book appeared in Copenhagen which put the whole city in a ferment, and was rightly regarded as an event in the history of the national literature ; this work was the anony- mous *Gjenganger-Breve, eller poetiske Epistler fra Paradise* (" Ghost-letters ; or, Poetical Epistles from Paradise),"* which purported to be a contribution from the lately-deceased poet, Jens Baggesen, to the literary feud which had been raging in Denmark ever since the beginning of the century between the Romanticists and the Classicists. I ought here per- haps to premise that Baggesen during his life-time (he died at Hamburg in 1826) had been the most determined opponent of Romanticism, which had been introduced into Denmark by the poet Oehlenschläger, whose brilliant example was speedily followed by the majority of his countrymen. For a genera- tion Romanticism ruled supreme in Scandinavia. Baggesen, however, who belonged to quite another order of intellect, and whose clear, if somewhat narrow, judgment and keen sense of humour detected, from the first, the faults of the new school, notably its contempt for style, of which he himself was a past master, at once declared war against Oehlenschläger

---

* The title-page bore the Horatian motto : " Data Romanis venia est indigna poetis." Its author was the rising young poet Henrick Hertz, who shortly afterwards declared himself.

and his followers, ridiculed them in a splendid series of poetic satires, beginning with the incomparable *Gjengangeren* ("The Ghost"), which for spark-

OEHLENSCHLÄGER.

ling wit, Attic grace, and sarcastic incisiveness are amongst the very finest things in northern literature. But the fashion of the day was against him, he fought almost alone, and finally gave up the unequal struggle, which had become more and more virulent and personal as it proceeded. After his death, the Romanticists, who now appropriated all, or nearly all, of the rising talent of the day, had everything their own way, and Andersen as a disciple of their German brethren, Hoffmann and Tieck, and the author of the *Fodreise*, took his place among them also. The astonishment of the Danish public was therefore profound indeed when they heard once more what seemed to be the voice of Baggesen himself reasserting the claims of reason and common-sense from his abode in Paradise. To many it seemed incredible that any living being could imitate so faultlessly the Baggesenian rhythm and style, and speak so exactly the Baggesenian language. Many even went further and maintained that the ghost of Baggesen evidently possessed a clearer perception and a calmer judgment than Baggesen himself had been blessed with during his sublunary existence. This terrible satire burst like a bomb upon the camp of the Romanticists, scattering broadcast a fiery rain of ridicule which slew or maimed many a rising reputation. The more prominent poets of the day, Oehlenschläger, Heiberg, Hauch, naturally suffered most ; but none of the smaller fry, "those literary vagabonds that swarm among you as thick as sand," were forgotten, and Andersen and his followers,*

* The *Fodreise* seems to have found imitators.

"that nasty, ugly gipsy-band of versifiers which goes bellowing through the bogs behind their rhyming bell-wether," came in for more than their fair share of abuse. They were told to go to school again, to learn what a true study of the poetic art means even for those who fancy themselves to be geniuses, and they were compared to swine grubbing up the roots of the laurels of Parnassus. Andersen himself was hit off in the following lines, the sting of which lay in the spiteful allusion to his detested Slagelsian days which he couldn't bear to think of.*

> Drunk with the thin, small-beer of Fancy,
> And mounted on Slagelsian Nancy,
> The Muses' ancient nightmare hack,†
> With drooping flanks and broken back,
> The holy Andersen ‡ comes riding,
> Whom the unlettered mob takes pride in.
> They hold him—their applauses show it—
> For quite a prophet of a poet !
> If, while he plodded through the schools,
> In company with fellow fools
> (Himself a laggard 'mongst the louts),
> He'd given grammar half the flouts

---

* I feel I owe an apology to my readers for this defective rendering of these notable lines, but *ultra posse nemo obligatur.*

† An allusion to an old Slagelsian legend. In King Valdemar's days there was a priest there, Anders by name, who got a promise from the king that he should have as much ground as he could cover riding on a nine nights' old foal while the king was bathing. The holy man rode so well, that if the king had not been warned to leave his bath in time, the lands of Slagelse would be even larger than they are already.

‡ Hellig Andersen, a play upon words having reference to Hellig Anders, the worthy parson above alluded to.

That now, to her extreme dishonour,
He daily dares to shower upon her,
He would have got—my word upon it—
A breeching and the dunce's bonnet.

Any young author with a reputation to lose, might well have been pardoned for wincing beneath such a diatribe as this ; upon the sensitive, vain-glorious Andersen its effect was simply crushing.* His friends, especially his fellow-sufferers, did all they could to console him by depreciating " The Spectre " as a mere parasite of Baggesen's, who might amuse the idle public for an hour or so, but whose days were already numbered. But all would not do. Andersen remained inconsolable, and his extreme depression and morbid sensitiveness at last caused his friends some anxiety. He complained in a letter to Edward Collin that he would never be able to recover his former spirits, and that he was filled with an infinite weariness of life which made him indifferent to everything. " Oh, my dear Edward," he concludes, " I wish for death from the bottom of my heart. What great or good thing is there left for me to do in this world ? " †

This letter was written from Berlin through which he was returning home from a tour in the Hartz,

* Bille og Bogh : *Breve til A.*, pp. 268, 269, and 687, 688.

† Collin, p. 155. In this letter it is that he first breaks the news of his so-called love affair to Collin, more than nine months after the event. That "Gjengangeren," however, not the lady, was the real cause of his melancholy there can be but little doubt.

which he had been persuaded to take by Jonas Collin, who thought that a complete change would do him good and give him fresh ideas. He had saved a little money by thrift and industry, and in the spring of 1831 he set out, quite recovering his spirits by the time he had reached Hamburg. "My good humour," he says,* "came back again to me like a bird of passage; but sorrow is the swarm of sparrows which remains behind, and builds in the bird of passage's nest." His road lay through Hamburg and Lübeck, across Luneburg Heath to Brunswick, from whence he saw mountains (the Hartz) for the first time in his life. In Dresden, whither he went on his way to the Bohemian frontier, he learned to know Tieck, to whom he had a letter of introduction from Ingemann, and at Berlin he made the acquaintance of Chamisso. He diligently recorded his impressions as he went along, and published them on his return to Copenhagen under the title of *Skyggebilder af en Reise til Harzen och det sachsiske Schweiz* ("Silhouettes of a Journey to the Hartz and to Saxon Switzerland").

Between the *Fodreise* and the *Skyggebilder* there is all the difference that separates an immature juvenile essay from a genuine masterpiece. I do not mean to say that the *Skyggebilder* have the finished grace of Andersen's later books of travel, such, for

* *M. L. E.*, p. 69.

instance, as *I. Spanien* ("In Spain"), or *En Digter's Bazaar* ("A Poet's Bazaar"). The young author still writes with a somewhat hesitating hand, he evidently still only half believes in his own powers; there is also a tendency to moralise in season and out of season, and the narrative is frequently swamped by floods of indifferent verse. But with all its faults (and very trifling faults they are) the *Skyggebilder* make a delightful book which must certainly be regarded as a notable addition to the Danish literature. Take as a specimen the following description* of his journey in the diligence across Luneburg Heath:

The monotonous grinding of the wheels of the diligence in the sand, the soughing of the wind among the branches of the trees, and the postillion's bursts of melody blended together into a sleep-compelling lullaby. One after the other, all the passengers nodded their heads; even the bouquets, which were stuck into the receptacle at the top of the diligence, mimicked the same movement every time the diligence gave a lurch. I, too, closed my eyes. Presently I opened them again, feeling half-dazed. I had been dreaming, I suppose, but, anyhow, my eyes were especially attracted towards one of the large carnations in the bouquet I had got. . . . All the flowers were exhaling

---

* I translate from the first Danish edition. I may add, however, that there is an excellent English translation of the *Skyggebilder* by C. Beckwith (Bentley, 1848), entitled "Rambles in the Romantic Regions of the Hartz Mountains." The first German version, 1836 "Umrisse einer Reise von Copenhagen nach dem Harze"), is also very good.

a strong fragrance, but methought this flower overpowered the rest in odour and colour, and the curious thing about it was that right in the very centre of the flower sat an airy little being no bigger than one of its petals, and as transparent as glass.  It was the genius of the flower, and in every flower dwells one such little sprite which lives and dies with it.  Its wings were of the same hue as the carnation's, but of so delicate a shade that it seemed to be only the pink shadow which fell from the flower in the moonlight.  Golden locks, finer than pollen, floated over the little creature's shoulders, and rose and fell on the breeze.

Now when I had looked a little more curiously at the other flowers, I perceived that this sprite was not the only one.  In every flower just such another little being was rocking to and fro, whose wings and gossamer garments were like gleaming reflections from the flower in which it lived.  Every one of them was rocking to and fro on the light leaves in the fragrance and the moonlight, and laughing and singing, but the sound was like the wind passing softly over an Eolian harp.

Presently hundreds and hundreds of other little elves of all sorts of shapes, and in all sorts of garments, came into the diligence through the open window ; they came from the dark pines and the heath-blossoms.  What a chattering, and a singing, and a dancing, there was, to be sure !  They very soon sprang right across my nose, and did not hesitate to have a round dance in the middle of my forehead.  These elves of the pines looked like little savages, and were armed with lances and darts, and yet they were as lightsome as the delicate vapours which exhale in the morning sun from the dew-besprinkled rose.

And now they split up into groups, and played whole comedies, which my fellow-passengers fancied they were dreaming, each had his own particular piece all to himself.

To the merry, lively student from Hamburg, the scene was Berlin.  A whole group of elves disguised themselves as German

students, and some of them were veritable Philistines with long
pipes in their mouths, and sticks like clubs by their sides. They
stood in long rows. It was a college. One of the pine-tree elves
(he was the living image of Hegel) mounted into the lecturing
pulpit, and talked in such a learned and involved style, that I
absolutely could not follow him. . . .

For the young girl from Brunswick, however, they played a
solemn scene out of her own life's history. The tears trickled
down her cheeks, and the little elves smiled, and mirrored themselves in each tear, so that each tear-drop that fell in the dream
had an innocent smile inside it.

But the old apothecary was the worst off, for he had trodden
one of the flowers to pieces as it fell to the bottom of the diligence,
thereby killing the little elf that lived in it. So the other little
elves sat upon his legs, till it seemed to him, in his dream, as if
he had none at all, but was hopping on bare stumps through the
streets of Brunswick, where all his neighbours and friends were
standing and looking at him. But then the little elves were sorry
for him, and gave him back his legs, and a pair of wings into the
bargain, so that he could fly right up high over the copper lion
of Henry the Lion in the market-place and the high church to wer
of St. Blasius, and this delighted the heart of the apothecary,
immensely, and he laughed aloud in his dream. . . .

The elves appeared to take no notice of me till long after
the others. "That lean and lanky man, over there, is a poet!"
cried one of them suddenly, "aren't you going to show him
anything?"

"He can see *us*, and that ought to be enough for him surely,"
they replied.

"But shall we not let him see what we see? and then he will
be able to tell it to other men when he awakes."

They held a pretty long debate as to whether I was worthy
of being admitted into their community, but, as they had no

better author actually on the spot, I got a card of admission after all. The little elves kissed me on the eyes and ears, and it was just as if I had become another and a better man.

I looked out over the vast Luneburg Heath which is generally considered so ugly. Good gracious ! what nonsense people *do* talk. But then, of course, they only talk as they see and hear. Every grain of sand was a glittering piece of rock ; the long blades of grass which hung full of dust out upon the high road, were the prettiest macadamised roads for the little elves to walk upon ; from every leaf of every tree there peeped forth such a tiny smiling face. The fir-trees looked like completed Towers of Babel, and were swarming with elves from the lowest broad branches to the lofty tops, the air was full of the most wonderful shapes, and all of them were as bright and rapid as light itself. Four or five of the geniuses of the flowers were mounted astride a white butterfly which they had routed out of its slumbers, while the others were building castles out of the strong perfumes of the flowers and the delicate moonbeams. The whole of the vast heath was an enchanted world full of marvels. . . . . Legend says that only the loyal love of a child of man and Christian baptism, can give the mermaid an immortal soul ; the elves of the flowers do not require even so much as that. A single repentant or compassionate tear from a human heart is the baptism which can give them immortality, and whenever a pious sigh of devotion escapes from our hearts to God, they also rise with it. That is how they gain admittance into beautiful heaven, and grow up into angels beneath the stimulating sunlight of eternity.

The dew began to fall. I saw the nimble, lightsome geniuses romping about on the big dew-drops. Many poets say that the elves bathe in the dew. But how can the gossamer sprite, that dances on the down of the thistle without disturbing it, force its way through such a hard mass of water as a dew-drop ? No, they were standing on the top of the round dew-drop, and, when it rolled away from under their feet, and their light garments fluttered in the breeze, they looked like the daintiest miniature counterfeits of Fortune on her rolling sphere.

Andersen went down the mines at Goslar, not without fear and trembling, and in the church there he was shown the stone effigy of Matilda, the daughter of the Emperor Henry III., whose wondrous beauty had been blasted by the revengeful claw of the devil whom she had worsted in a contest of wits. The old pew-opener was not quite certain whether the monument represented the lady in the days of her loveliness, or as she appeared after the mauling of Satan, but Andersen, after a cursory inspection, was inclined to favour the latter view. He took sketches in his pocket-book from the summit of the Regenstein, near Blankenburg, whence the fields below looked like "kitchen-garden beds, and the peasant behind his plough like a snail's house creeping along the ground." At Lohmen in Saxon Switzerland, he had a pretty little bare-footed boy for his guide, who reminds him of "that wretched little rascal Cupid who runs about with the dart."

After touching at the boundary Bohemian village Herren-Bretchen, he returned to Dresden, where he took leave of Tieck, who kissed him affectionately on the forehead, and promised him future fame. Andersen was so overcome, that he burst into tears and sobbed like a child. After Dresden, Berlin struck him as second-rate and pretentious. "It looked as if it must always be Sunday afternoon there." The one oasis in this desert was the house of Chamisso, whom he describes as a tall, lean figure, with long grey locks hanging down over his shoulders, and with an open good-natured countenance—the very image of Peter Schlemihl. He wore a brown dressing gown, and a flock of rosy-cheeked children was playing about him. The country between Berlin and Spandau, as he beheld it on his homeward journey, reminded him of a chart, it was so flat, and at last the beauties of Nature shrunk up into the blades of grass which popped up here and there on the way. But Andersen was now in a very sulky humour. His holiday was nearly over, he was packed up in a dusty diligence, with half a dozen disagreeable fellow-passengers, for the best part of a sweltering-hot week, and there was absolutely nothing to look at. And then, too, every mile brought him nearer to his critics, and the thought of them awoke bitter reflections. "Copenhagen's towers," it is thus he concludes his itinerary, "Copenhagen's towers rose up before us. They seemed to me so *pointed*, so satirical, just as if they were symbols of the pens which will perhaps scratch my 'Silhouettes' to pieces."

There can be no doubt that Andersen was in his proper element while travelling. He loved to be on the move, and "was as much a bird of passage as his

prime favourite the stork."* His correspondence
shows how his spirits rose by leaps and bounds when
he was fairly off. His heart expands as well as his
mind ; he forgets all the troubles he has left behind
him, and surrenders himself unreservedly to the joy
of the moment with a delighted, childlike anticipation
of the surprises and adventures that are sure to be
waiting for him at every turn of the road. This
gaiety, enthusiasm, and lightheartedness, are reflected
in all his books of travel, and make them, quite apart
from their delicate fancy and delicious humour, as
refreshing and exhilarating things as are to be found
in literature. Oddly enough, however, Andersen
seems to have underrated his itineraries, possibly
because they flowed so spontaneously from his pen,
and cost him little or no trouble. His literary
ambition aimed at something quite different. It
was the dream of his life to become a great dramatist,
and the passion for the theatre was the will-o'-the-
wisp that seduced him again and again from the
right path, and led him into sloughs of despond
where he was fair game for the critics. It would
have been a good thing for him if his first dramatic
venture, a farce entitled *Kjaerlighed paa Nicolai
Taarn* ("Love on St. Nicholas' Tower"), had been
damned as it deserved to be, for he had little or no
talent in that direction, but, as ill-luck would have

* Brandes' *Kritiker og Portraiter.*

it, it was warmly applauded by his fellow-students, and had a run of actually three nights.* This petty triumph sufficed to convince Andersen that his true vocation was the drama, and between 1831 and 1833 he wrote, and sent to the Royal Theatre, four operettas : *Bruden fra Lammermoor*,† *Skibet*, ‡ *Festen paa Kenilworth*, § and *Den anden April*, ‖ and two vaudevilles ; ¶ *Spanierne i Odense*,** and *Fem og tyve Aar derefter*.†† Of these six pieces the young author had the highest opinion, but the dramatic censor of the Royal Theatre before whom they had to pass muster, thought otherwise. This censor was the historian and literary critic, Christian Molbech, a successful worker in various departments of literature, and especially remarkable for his severe taste and diligently cultivated style. He was the last man in the world to show mercy to anything like false quantities or bad grammar; but he was not vindictively predisposed against Andersen, as the latter in his autobiography would lead us to imagine. Molbech had praised the humour, feeling, and poetic insight displayed in the *Skyggebilder*, but com-

* Collin, pp. 132, 133.        † " The Bride of Lammermoor "
‡ " The Ship."        § " The Festival at Kenilworth."
‖ " The Second of April."
¶ The vaudeville had been introduced into Denmark by J. L. Heiberg, whose brilliant originality in this new *genre* caused a great sensation. Andersen was the first and worst of Heiberg's imitators.
** " The Spaniards in Odense."
†† " Five and Twenty Years Afterwards."

plained that the young author's fancy frequently ran away with him, and caustically inquired when he was going to begin to learn how to write his mother-tongue properly. With these dramatic essays Molbech was even less satisfied. The operettas, indeed, managed to run the gauntlet of his sarcasms, though not unscathed. Every single scene, situation, and character of the "Bride of Lammermoor," he said, was borrowed from Walter Scott, but there was poetry in its songs, and the chief incidents had been skilfully grouped together into a dramatic whole, so he allowed it to pass. "Kenilworth" he also passed for the sake of its music, although the crude and careless way in which it had been botched and patched together, made him doubt whether the author really had sufficient talent to turn a novel into a play. But it was when he came to the vaudevilles, which he treated as mere impertinences, that, as he candidly confesses, his wrath fairly over-came him. No terms of reprobation are too severe for them. They are unpoetical, tasteless, careless schoolboy scribble; they are the products of wretched, immature, villainously-trimmed, bungling goose quills; he would as soon think of allowing them to be acted as of going to see them if they were acted; if an anonymous bungler had sent in such rubbish, it would only have been in the nature of things, but that an author of Andersen's position and pretensions should insult the National Theatre by offering it such trivialities was simply outrageous. Finally he declares he will waste no more of his time, in future, in criticising Mr. Andersen's vaudevilles, and once more advises that gentleman to go to school, and learn good honest Danish.

Andersen, to the very end of his life, could never quite forgive Molbech this scathing criticism. He had such an absolute belief in the excellence of his own works (especially of his dramatic works) that he could only put down hostile criticism to malice, or stupidity, or both. A foreigner is naturally some-what diffident as to judging between Andersen and his critics on questions of Danish style and Danish syntax; but when we see Andersen's own friends, men like Ingemann, Guldberg, Örsted, and the Collins', for instance, who always had his best interests at heart, and loved him like a son or a brother—when we see such men as these "taking the part of his most severe critics," as he pathetically complains, and expostulating with him again and again about his slipshod style and contempt of grammar, we cannot but feel that Molbech's indignation was not altogether unjustifiable. Edward Collin tells us * that in the earlier days of his authorship Andersen's knowledge of his mother-tongue was very defective, and that he recognised the fact himself. For years

* Collin, pp. 452-6.

he used to make a point of bringing his manuscripts, and even his proof sheets, to Collin for revision, and at first accepted Collin's suggestions and corrections with a good grace ; but when he began to be better known he became less compliant, and regarded most of his friend's corrections as pedantic and hypercritical. Many a bitter sigh used to escape him as they went over the MSS. together and the inexorable Collin insisted upon this or that being struck out. As he became more famous, he became altogether impatient of criticism.

There can be no doubt, too, that Andersen was writing far too much at this time, though it should be pleaded in his excuse (he was too proud to say anything about it himself, even to his most intimate friends) that he was forced to do so to gain a living. Besides the *Skyggebilder*, and the operettas and vaudevilles already mentioned, he wrote, between 1831 and 1833, three small volumes of poems—viz., *Phantasier og Skizzer* (" Fantasia and Sketches "), *Vignetter til Danske Digtere* (" Vignettes to Danish Poets "), and *Aarets tolv Maaneder* (" The Twelve Months of the Year "). While praising the tenderness and delicate fancy which many of these poems undoubtedly possess, his friend Ingemann warned him that he was exhausting himself prematurely by making too much haste to be famous. In Edward Collin he found a sterner mentor who took him severely to task for his self-conceit, and assured him that he ran a fair chance of disgusting all his friends.

Andersen must have winced beneath these rebukes, but, generally speaking, he seems to have taken them in the spirit in which they were given. Sometimes, indeed, he begs Collin not to moralise too much, but he declares in the same breath that his " dear good Edward" is the only friend in whom he implicitly trusts. His defence of himself against the charges of egoism and *cacoethes scribendi* is delightfully naïve. He comically pleads that his follies and absurdities are not more numerous and rampant now than they used to be, but only more notorious. He is a public character and therefore his peculiarities are public property. Besides, even if he weaned himself of all his present faults, a censorious world would pretty soon saddle him with others. As to his alleged bad habit of always bringing forward his own poems, that, he said, was due not to vanity, but to sheer good-nature on his part. It was natural for a young man to try to be agreeable, and as he had not been blessed with good looks, he had to find out some other way of pleasing, and fall back upon his accomplishments.* From true friends who meant him well, and to whom he had reason to be grateful, Andersen could always take a great

* Collin, pp. 148, 149.

deal. Much harder to bear were the snubs and flouts of casual acquaintances. There can be little doubt that he was subject at this time to a good deal of annoyance from officious busybodies—"my educators" as he ironically calls them—who dipped into his books for the express purpose of detecting blunders. Thus, for instance, at a large party at which Andersen was actually present, a country clergyman took up a volume of his *Digte*, and proceeded to criticise them aloud, line by line, for the benefit of the company, picking holes in them freely as he went along. At last he put the book down with an air of triumph. There was an awkward pause, and then a little girl of six, who had been listening all the time with deep attention, took up the eviscerated volume, and, pointing to the word "and," exclaimed innocently, "Look! there's a little word you have forgotten!" The parson, who felt the justice of the rebuke, unintentional though it was, turned very red, but had the grace to stoop down and kiss the child.* On another occasion Andersen was accosted by an acquaintance who said to him : "So you write the word *Hunden* with a small initial letter, eh!"† and producing a copy of the *Skyggebilder*, showed him the offending sub-

* *M. L. E.*, p. 96.
† In Danish, as in German, all substantives are written with capital letters.

G

stantive which, owing to a printer's blunder, had indeed been mulcted of its capital, a mistake which had escaped the author while correcting the proofs. Andersen was rather vexed at being suspected of ignorance in such a trivial matter, but, being in a merry mood, he took the stricture good humouredly and replied: "Well, you see it was only a *little* hound, so I gave him a little h!"*

But Andersen was not always in the mood to rebuke impertinence with a repartee. There was a deep-lying morbid strain of melancholy in his anxious sensitive nature which asserted itself periodically and completely unmanned him. One of these recurrent attacks of melancholia came over him towards the end of 1832, and the beginning of 1833. He got into a low state. He brooded over his wrongs, real and imaginary. He could not shake off the haunting recollections of Hertz's sarcasms and Molbech's criticisms, and at last even the rebukes and remonstrances of his candid friend, Edward Collin, were more than he could bear. Andersen clung to Collin as the ivy clings to the oak ; had a profound admiration for his firmness and decision, qualities in which he himself was very deficient, and always looked up to him as the elder in understanding, although he was the younger in years. But there were times when Andersen was sorely troubled

* *M. L. E.*, p. 96.

and depressed by Collin's well meant, but, as it seems
to me, ill-timed zeal for his improvement, and his
sensitiveness was often wounded by the other's "hard
angularity." *   About this time Andersen wrote to
Louisa Collin that he was sick both in mind and body;
that he could no longer find any happiness in life; that
his youthful ambitions had turned out to be nothing
but empty dreams; that he was withering away in
sickness and solitude, and that the only thing in the
world which could make a man of him again was a
foreign tour.   " I must go away," he exclaims, " far,
far away ! " †

Andersen was quite right in indicating a foreign
tour as the proper remedy for his morbid state of
mind.   Travelling, as I have said before, was an
*elixir vitæ* to him, which never failed to restore to
him his mental equilibrium and elasticity.   His
friends knew this as well as he did, and both the
Collins, who had the ear of the King, used all their
influence in his behalf.   At first it was very doubtful
whether a travelling stipend could be found for
him.   The resources of the *Fond ad usus publicos*,
out of which such stipends were paid, were limited,
and an allowance had already been granted out of it
to Henrik Hertz, the author of the *Gjenganger-*

* On another occasion he says that Edward Collin reminds him of
those fruits that are spoiled by too much sugar.
† Collin, pp. 170, 171.

*Breve*, who had, in many respects, a better claim
upon it than Andersen. For a few weeks Andersen
lived in a fever of anxiety and doubt. "If I get it,"
he wrote to Edward Collin,* "'tis not merely a
whole year of my life I shall avoid losing, but I shall
save my whole spiritual existence." † Finally, however, the influence of the Collins prevailed, and
Andersen obtained from the King a travelling-
stipend of 600‡ rix dollars (£70) a year for two
years.

It was *apropos* of this stipend that Andersen had
his first audience of Frederick VI., which led to a
rather comical scene. While the Collins were still
exerting themselves on his behalf, Andersen was
advised by a friend, who knew the ways of the court
to wait upon his Majesty personally, tell him who
he was, why he wanted a travelling-stipend, and
present him at the same time with one of his works.
Andersen thought it rather odd that he should make
his Sovereign a present, and immediately afterwards
ask him for something in return ; but his friend told
him it was the usual thing, and so to the Palace
he went with his poem, *Aarets tolv Maaneder*,§ in
his hand. His heart throbbed with anxiety when
the King, suddenly entering the room, came straight

* E. Collin was the secretary to the fund.    † Collin, pp. 179, 180.
‡ Increased to 800 the following year.
§ "The Twelve Months of the Year."

up to him, and asked him abruptly what sort of a book it was that he had brought him. "A *cycle* of poems, your Majesty," replied Andersen. "A cycle, a cycle! what do you mean?" "I mean a few verses about Denmark," replied poor Andersen, covered with confusion. The King smiled. "Well, well, very nice, very nice, no doubt! Thank ye, thank ye!" and he made the author a parting bow. But Andersen who had not yet explained the errand on which he had come, pulled himself together and hastily told the King all about his studies, and how he had managed to get on in the world. "Very praiseworthy," said the King. "Make the application for the travelling stipend in the usual way." "I have got it with me," exclaimed Andersen, "and here it is." Then, in his naïve way, he protested how much it went against him to bring one of his books as a present at the very time that he had to ask for a favour; and the tears came into his eyes. But the good old King only laughed aloud, nodded kindly, and took the application, whereupon Andersen bowed, and hastily withdrew. A few days afterwards he set off for Paris, *viâ* Hamburg and Lübeck.

# CHAPTER V

Andersen in Paris—" Freedom's funguses "—Napoleon's statue—The grey trousers—Cherubini—Victor Hugo—Heine—The cruel practical joke—Le Locle—*Agnete and the Merman*—Three weeks among the mountains—First impressions of Italy—Lake Maggiore —Milan—Pisa—Florence—Job among the potsherds—Arrival at Rome—Meets "The Spectre" there—Thorvaldsen—Death of Andersen's mother—Failure of *Agnete*—Opinion of critics and friends—Anguish of Andersen—Naples—Hears Malebranche— On Vesuvius with Hertz—Capri—Economics—Meagre fare— Andersen's genius for thrift—Enthusiasm for Italy—Venice— Vienna—Prague—Reminiscences of his friends—Kindly reception on his return—His extreme poverty at this time—" *The Improvisatore* "—Its plot and character—Enormous success.

ANDERSEN reached Paris in the beginning of May 1833, and in a couple of days felt quite at home there. His lady friends, the self-constituted guardians of his virtue, had warned him beforehand against the seductions of that gay and gallant city, and he himself was considerably scandalised by much that met his observant eye there. The whole tone of society struck him as "extraordinarily frivolous," everything showed itself "without clothes," the women talked, quite innocently, about things which his more sober-minded countrymen would have blushed to mention, and the Rabelaisan pleasantry of a piece which he was taken to see at the Palais Royal, made him feel a "little queer." "I am not a bit straight-laced," he writes to the younger Collin, . . . . "but it seems to me that even in things sensual there ought to be a little decorum." * Nevertheless he gradually got accustomed to "freedom's funguses," as he calls these levities, and the more he saw of the French, the more he liked them. He employed his time, too, excellently well, saw everything and everybody, and was lucky enough to be present at a great historical event : the unveiling of the statue of Napoleon by Louis Philippe in the Place Vendôme. From his father Andersen had inherited an intense admiration for the great Napoleon, and it was with a solemn, almost religious, awe that he beheld the sleeping-room of his ideal hero at the Petit Trianon.. At the unveiling of the statue he got a good place on a barrel, where he sat in the blazing sun from eleven o'clock in the morning till five in the afternoon, and saw pass close by him Louis Philippe surrounded by his sons and his generals, and followed by 100,000 national guards. The jovial smile and *bonhommie* of the King of the French quite won his heart. He was also one of the guests invited to the splendid ball at the Hôtel de Ville the same evening, and

* Bille og Bogh, *Breve fra Andersen*, i. p. 120.

" the lanky poet," as he delights to call himself,
drove thither at eight o'clock, in silk stockings,
white gloves, and a Parisian frisure. He had
indulged in the extravagance of a fashionable pair of
light grey summer trousers, which must have been a
perfect triumph of the tailoring art, as it made even
his ungainly nether limbs presentable. "It is quite
a delight to look at one's self in them," he wrote to
Collin. "If only these trousers could be seen at
home! Unfortunately they are not long enough
to reach all the way to Denmark."* Although his
knowledge of French was so slight that he had to
employ the services of a *parleur* at two francs an hour
whenever he went out by himself, he nevertheless
ventured to call upon several notabilities. Cherubini
he found sitting at his piano, with a cat upon his
shoulder. The old musician welcomed him kindly,
and accepted some Danish music from him, though he
seems to have been surprised to hear that there were
any original composers in Denmark at all. He also
visited Victor Hugo, whose *Notre Dame* was the
first French book he had ever tried to read right
through. The great poet seems, however, to have
been somewhat suspicious of the intentions of his
strange and uninvited visitor, and when Andersen
asked him for his autograph, he took care to write
it high up in the top corner of a sheet of paper, so

* Collin, p. 189.

that it could not be utilised as a signature, a precaution which made a bad impression upon Andersen.
Heine, whom he had been especially cautioned
against by his lady friends, he did *not* intend to
visit at all; but Fate brought him into contact with
"that man of sin," in spite of himself. Andersen
had been introduced into the *Europe Littéraire*, a
sort of literary club for distinguished foreigners, by
Paul Duport, and, on his first visit there, was
accosted by a little man of Jewish appearance, who
said to him : "I hear you are Danish, I am German ;
Germans and Danes are brethren, therefore I offer
you my hand!" Andersen asked him his name, and
the stranger replied that he was Heinrich Heine.
Heine was inclined to be friendly, and obligingly
praised Andersen's fellow-countryman Oehlenschläger
as the greatest of European poets. He also called
upon the young man, and they had several walks
and talks together on the boulevards, but Andersen,
who could not get over his prejudices, continued to
avoid his new friend as much as he could.*

Andersen's sole grievance during the earlier part
of his visit at Paris was the utter absence of news
from home; he had written no less than twenty-one
letters to his friends, and received not a word in
reply. No doubt they wisely thought that he ought

* Compare Collin, p. 188 ; Bille og Bogh, *Breve fra Andersen*, i.
p. 125, and *M. L. E.* p. 126.

not to be overburdened with correspondence during
a pleasure trip ; but he took it otherwise, and his
heart was already beginning to sink within him,
when, on returning to his lodgings one afternoon, he
found at last a large envelope from Copenhagen
awaiting him.   It was unfranked, and the postage
on it was pretty dear ; but then, "it was so nice and
big" that he forgot all else in his joy at the sight of
it, and, hastily tearing off the cover, discovered—not
the long letter he expected to find, but half a number
of the *Kjöbenhavnspost*, containing an exceedingly
spiteful and scurrilous lampoon against himself,
entitled, "Farewell to Andersen !"   This was his
first greeting from home.   Happily his dejection
only lasted for an instant.   The utter paltriness of
the deed speedily filled him with mere contempt
for his anonymous persecutor, and the generous
sympathy and indignation of the Collins comforted
him and helped him to forget the mean affront.

But there was another reason why Andersen,
unusually so sensitive to the faintest disparagement,
could afford to take this cruel practical joke so
easily.   Just at this time he was engaged upon a
work which, in his opinion, would shut the mouths
of all his detractors for ever, and establish his reputation, once for all, as a great and original poet.
The idea of this masterpiece had haunted him "on
the lively boulevards" and "amidst the silent

treasures of the Louvre,"* and took visible shape during what he calls a "five days' ecstasy" at the little village of Le Locle in the Jura mountains, whither he had gone after a four months' stay at Paris, partly to economise,† and partly to acquire in that remote solitude a colloquial knowledge of French. The great work, of which he thought so much and which he sent into the world with a preface ridiculous enough to have damned a far stronger book,‡ was the dramatic poem "*Agnete og den Havmand*" ("Agnete and the Merman").

"Agnete and the Merman" is a free dramatisation of the old Danish ballad of Agnete, the girl who throws herself into the sea to become the merman's bride, but, growing weary of her splendid solitude, returns to earth after what seems but seven years (though as men count time it is really more than fifty), only to find all her kith and kin dead and gone, save her former lover, now a tottering old man, who avoids her as some unholy thing, so that

---

* Preface to "*Agnete og den Havmand*," first Danish edition.

† It must not be supposed that Andersen was extravagant at Paris. The thirty francs a month for lodging, which he paid at the Hotel Vivienne, does not seem excessive, but then his means were very limited.

‡ For instance, he tenderly alludes to it therein as the child which had grown beneath his bosom before he himself was aware of it, as " my Agnete, born among the black deathly-still pine forests," and he bids his countrymen " deal gently " with his " darling child."—Preface to *Agnete*.

poor Agnete, broken-hearted, dies on the sea-shore.
'Tis a pretty myth, but much too slight and unsub-
stantial to be spun into a drama of some 130 pages.
As one of his lady friends truly said it was a butterfly to be looked at but not handled.  In Andersen's
drama, moreover, the original story is obscured and
thrown into the background by the intrusive personality of Andersen himself, who is unmistakably
present in the character of the mawkishly melancholy
Hemming, the rejected lover.  All the other
characters are so shadowy as to be little more than
abstractions.  The best parts of the piece are the
numerous choruses of elves, nightingales, swans, sea-
mews, sea-waves, beach-trees, flowers, and hunting-
horns, which moralise on the doings and sufferings
of the chief personages, somewhat after the manner
of the old Greek choruses.  Indeed, many of the
lyrics interspersed are exceedingly pretty, notably
the little birds' plaintive lay beginning:

" Merman's wife, so young and fair,"

and the effective imitation of an old *Kœmpevise*
with its haunting refrain,

" Oh God ! how my poor heart must suffer ! "

But the piece, as a whole, is too flimsy to excite
any real interest or pleasure, and abounds with the
most absurd anachronisms.

Andersen, however, was enthusiastic about "the

only golden fruit that my poetic tree has borne this summer," and already triumphed, in anticipation, over the discomfiture of his critics. Of these Molbech was still the most vigorous and the most virulent. In a review of the first edition of Andersen's collected poems, which appeared during his absence from Copenhagen, he remarked that Nature had not indeed been churlish to the young author, but, unfortunately, he had wasted his talents upon trifles, and not allowed them time to come to maturity. "He has mistaken," concluded this Aristarchus, "he has mistaken an easily awakened, gentle and light-hearted sensibility for the fire of inspiration, and an incoherent fancifulness for the plastic power of genius." *Agnete* was to be a victorious appeal against this verdict. At the same time Andersen himself seems to have been a little anxious as to the *style* and syntax of his new poem, and humorously requests Edward Collin to practise the good child (Agnete) in grammar a bit, and make allowances for his " Northern Aphrodite," as she had been born amongst the mountains [*sic.*]

Animated by the delightful thought of his coming triumph, Andersen could now pursue his journey southwards with a light heart. He was all the better, too, for his three weeks' stay amidst the soothing solitude of Le Locle, "right among the mountains, and very near the clouds," which lay

close around his window in the early morning, as if
with a greeting from the North. Here he had rambled
about, to his heart's content, amongst the dark pine
forests, pleasantly impressed by the unbroken stillness
around him, till the tinkling bells on the necks of
the home-returning kine reminded him that it was
his own dinner-time also. The people of the house,
who were of Danish extraction, treated him like a
dear kinsman, and his creature comforts were particularly well looked after by his landlord's kind old
maiden aunts, who saw that he had a good fire in his
room morning and evening, and regaled him every
day with honey and coffee. Andersen, in return,
translated, for their edification and amusement, long
extracts from his poems into French, which was the
only language the good folks understood, and romped
with the children who, to his great amusement,
bawled at him, as if he were deaf, when he did not
understand their patois.*

Andersen quitted this pleasant retreat, the best
description of which will be found in his novel,
"O.T.," early in September, and, passing through the
Rhône Valley, entered Italy by way of the Simplon,
"where the finger of the giant Napoleon has scratched
zigzags through the earth's spinal column." He
was much impressed by his first view of the Alps,

* *M. L. E.*, pp. 135-7 ; Collin, pp. 194, 195 ; Bille og Bogh : *Breve
fra Andersen*, i. pp. 134-8.

and calls them the Earth's huge folded wings.
"What if she lifted them, I thought, and spread
abroad her mighty pinions with their variegated
tapestry of black forest, wild waterfall, and swimming
cloud!" Lake Maggiore, on the other hand, disappointed him. He thought it pretty, but no more
than pretty. There were even finer lakes at home.
Geneva was far more beautiful. Milan Cathedral,
"that sculptured marble mountain," delighted him,
but the city itself bored him in three days; it was so
silent, the people seemed to be always going to
church, and his Protestant nose was offended by the
smell of incense in every street. By the time he had
reached Pisa he had come to the conclusion that
Italy was the Garden of Eden, and words fail him
when he attempts to describe the treasures of
Florence. "As well ask a man his sensations
when he arises at the last day, and sees God and
his angels above him, and worlds and worlds
around him." He also visited the quarries of
Carrara which seemed to him an enchanted
mountain, in which the gods and goddesses of
antiquity sat bound up in blocks of stone, only
awaiting a mighty magician like Thorvaldsen or
Canova to loose the spell and give them back to the
world. But his enthusiasm did not blind him to the
vileness of the inns, and the general unpleasantness
of travelling in Italy in those days, and he had

several comically unpleasant experiences. At one country hostelry there was a perfect plague of vermin, and when he awoke in the morning, he counted no less than fifty-seven flea-bites on one hand. When he was about to depart from Florence, a wretched being, who looked like Job when he was scraping himself with the potsherds, presented himself at the carriage-door. Taking him to be a beggar, Andersen and his two travelling companions shook their heads, but the man only went round to the other side, and was again waved off. But then the coachman came and explained that the intruder was not a vagrant, but a Roman noble who had booked the fourth seat in the carriage. He was accordingly admitted, but both his clothes and his person were so filthy that at the very first resting place the three other occupants of the carriage bluntly told the coachman that they wouldn't go a step further with him if the fourth gentleman remained inside, and after a good deal of chattering and gesticulation, the Roman noble was prevailed upon to crawl up on to the box-seat alongside the coachman, where the drenching rain gave him what was perhaps the only good washing he had ever had in his life.

Andersen arrived at Rome on October 18, 1834, and one of the very first persons he came across there was the poet Hertz who, it will be remembered, had so mercilessly satirised him in "The Spectre Letters,"

and, like himself, had obtained a travelling stipend.
Jonas Collin, who had a very high opinion of Hertz,
had privately advised Andersen to make friends with
.such a useful man if he could.   After a good deal of
hesitation, Andersen honestly tried to follow this
excellent advice, and Hertz met him half way by
making the first advances.   Very soon they became
constant companions.   "There are even moments,"
wrote Andersen to Jonas Collin, "when I could
seize his hand, and say, 'Why should we not be
friends?'   But I forbear, as it might perhaps strike
him as too comical." *

Andersen lodged at Rome in the Via Sistine, where
lived Thorvaldsen, then the pride and glory of the
Scandinavian and German artist colonies at Rome.
The tenderness and *bonhommie* of the great sculptor
completely won the susceptible heart of Andersen at
their very first interview.   They soon became very
intimate, and Andersen was never tired of confiding
his troubles to his inexhaustibly patient and sympathetic friend.

For poor Andersen's troubles had now begun
again in real earnest.   First of all came the tidings
of his mother's death, which reached him through
Jonas Collin soon after his arrival at Rome.   In one
way, indeed, this bereavement was a positive relief
to him.   The miserable condition of his poor, sick,

* Collin, p. 212.

H

and helpless old mother had long been a great grief
to him ; while he stinted himself in order to send to
her every penny he could spare, he never spoke a
word about it to any one but Jonas Collin.  He had,
he says, even prayed God to take her to Himself ;
and his first thought, on hearing that she had gone,
was : " Oh God, I thank Thee ! "   Nevertheless, the
news, though not altogether unexpected, moved him
deeply ; and, as he pathetically expresses it, he felt
that now " there was not a single being in the whole
world who was *bound by nature* to love him."*

A much more poignant anguish, however, was the
tidings that " Agnete," his beloved " Agnete," had at
last come out, and proved—a total failure.   No
doubt, it had not quite a fair chance, for, as ill-luck
would have it, it was completely eclipsed by Paludan
Müller's *Amor og Psyche* ("Cupid and Psyche"),
one of the most brilliant and, with respect to style,
one of the most perfect masterpieces of the Danish
language, which appeared simultaneously, and
received a perfect ovation from the public and the
critics alike.   But even if " Agnete " had had no
rivals to fear, she could scarcely have hoped to
find many admirers.   The most sympathetic and
indulgent of Andersen's personal friends† were

---

* Compare Collin, p. 211, and Bille og Bogh : *Breve fra Andersen*,
p. 173.

† With the exception of Ingemann, who, however, as the event will

disappointed with it. Even Madame Laessoe, who
on the appearance of the *Fodreise* had promised him
honour and glory both in this world and the next,
even Hetty Wulff, who had always championed his
cause against his critics, found it difficult to say a
single word of praise for " Agnete." Nay, Jonas
Collin shook his head over it, and anticipated the
worst from the critics. Nor was he mistaken. Heiberg
called it an utterly weak and vapid piece of work,
tricked out here and there with false and empty
lyrics, and testifying to the author's usual want of
inventive power. Another critic insinuated that
many of the best parts of it were plagiarisms from
Oehlenschläger's *Aladdin.* But the opinion that
Andersen seems to have looked for most impatiently
was that of Edward Collin, who had acted as a sort
of foster-father to the unlucky book, and got it
published by subscription when not a publisher
would look at it, actually addressing and sending off
all the copies to the booksellers and the subscribers
with his own hand. Collin was more polite than
Heiberg. The plan of the poem seemed to him a
happy one, and he expressed his admiration of the
many beautiful and highly poetic ideas in it ; but he
put his finger on the cardinal defect of this as of all
Andersen's early works, when he said that it lacked

show, was perhaps the worst possible judge of his friend's literary
merits.

"objectivity," that faculty, possessed by all the greater writers, of standing aloof from the scenes and characters they describe. All Andersen's friends, moreover, recognised him at once in the unmanly, flabby, whining lover Hemming; and some of them told him so pretty plainly.*

Andersen received Collin's letter at Milan, while on his way to Rome. It was naturally a blow to him, but at first he seems to have borne it like a man. He agreed that Collin's strictures as to his lack of objectivity were just, and promised to be more careful in this respect in future. He was also brought to admit that "Agnete" had blemishes, but insisted, nevertheless, that her charms had been overlooked; and, borrowing a simile from his surroundings, declared that if she were not actually of Carrara marble, she was still very far from being mere common greystone. Finally, he thanked his friend for his salutary criticism. "I know," he adds, "that if you give me wormwood occasionally, it is only to strengthen my weak stomach." So far this was all very well, but unfortunately Andersen had the bad habit of brooding over his wrongs, till he had persuaded himself that he was the most ill-used man alive, and that his so-called friends were leagued together in an unnatural conspiracy to

* Ludwig Müller for instance. See Bille og Bogh: *Breve til Andersen*, i. p. 529.

crush him. At such moments he really cared not
what he said, and was frequently within an ace of
shipwrecking the happiness of his life altogether.
As we have seen, he had accepted Edward Collin's
criticism with a fairly good grace at the time it was
given ; but a few months of bitter meditation convinced him that it was intolerable to be treated like
a schoolboy by one so much his junior, and it was
while smarting beneath this thought that he wrote
his " dear Edward " a letter, which Edward's father,
to whom he enclosed it, put at once behind the fire
instead of delivering it, thus rendering to Andersen
perhaps the greatest service of his life. For Molbech, whose consistently hostile criticism had also
duly been reported to him, Andersen had a perfect
loathing. " He has prostituted his pen," he cries,
excitedly ; " God have mercy upon him when his
hour comes ! " The tone of his correspondence at
this time indeed is suicidal. Edward Collin's
rebukes and remonstrances make him " forget his
God," and put thoughts into his head " which no
Christian ought to have." He has drained to the
dregs, he says, the poisoned chalice offered to him
by false friends. His honour is gone. His hopes
are so many burst bubbles. He is perfectly callous
to everything. He has nothing more to live for. An
out-of-the-way corner in some distant churchyard is
the only place still open for him. His resentment

at the way in which his countrymen have treated
him is reflected in a withering contempt for his country, which he disparages in every possible way with
almost feminine spite.    In Italy, he exclaims, there
is an eternal summer; the laurels are always green,
the orange trees are all glow and fragrance, while at
home hang heavy mists, and the air is dark with
driving snow.    He laments that he, who has all the
warmth of the South in his veins, must needs die in
the North.    He protests that his life's happiness
had hung on a single thread, and that that thread
has been cut through by the hand of his friend.*    It
is the one wish of his life never to produce another
work.    He has buried in Italy the poet whom they †
have murdered.    God gave him a poet's patent of
nobility, which they have torn in pieces.    As for his
dear native land, 'tis a poor, God-forsaken place at
best.    Italy has received a full cornucopia of fruits
and flowers, whilst Denmark has to be content with
a bit of grass and a sloe or two here and there.
Here it is Paradise.    Oranges, resedas, and carnations grow everywhere like weeds; the sea is heaven,
the clouds are fantasias of colour, the air a drink for
the gods, the earth teems with grapes; while Denmark is mother Nature's neglected step-child.

Nevertheless, he managed to get a little fun out
of the carnival revels; and the day afterwards set

---

* *I.e.*, Edward Collin.          † His critics.

out for Naples in the company of Hertz, with whom
he was now quite reconciled, even to recognising his
true merits as a poet, which "human weakness," as
he puts it, had hitherto prevented him from doing.
For some weeks to come "Holy Andersen and the
Spectre" shared the same bedroom. At Naples
Andersen heard Malibran in "Norma." "It was,"
he says, "a human heart dissolved in tears. I
wept. The people applauded. Yet there was one
there who hissed! Yes, actually *hissed*. How *can*
people be so wicked?" The libretto of "Norma,"
however, did not please him, and he declared himself
ready to write a new one for the Danish National
Theatre, if only they would treat him like a gentleman. With Hertz he ascended Vesuvius, which
gave them such a warm reception (it was in
eruption just then) that "the Spectre" would
have gone back, but "the lanky poet," who,
despite his constitutional timidity, became ven-
turesomeness itself when novel experiences or
exciting sensations were to be had,* insisted upon
scrambling up to the highest cone, through ashes up
to his knees, and in the midst of black smoke, which
hid the moon at intervals and spread the darkness

* Thus, while he was travelling through the Campagna, he fervently
prayed that he might be attacked by bandits, though he was trembling
all the time, and at Rome the delight of a descent into the catacombs
was enhanced by the reflection that Molbech had been afraid to venture down them.

of night all around them.   In order to see the newly
vomited stream of molten lava, they had to cross
layers of half-dried lava crust, through the crevices
of which they could look down into the red fire
beneath ; while a few yards further on a fiery-red
cascade roared down the mountain side, and the
sulphur fumes almost stifled them.   " I felt that my
life was in God's hands," says Andersen, " and I
reeled with rapture." *   The soles of his boots, however, were the only things that suffered.   A more
pleasant experience was the visit to the Blue Grotto
of Capri, which he was one of the first to describe.†
He had already made pilgrimages to Pæstum, Pom-
peii, and Amalfi ; and it was with a sad heart that
he abandoned the idea of seeing Sicily.   But despite
the strictest economy, his funds were now running
low, and he was anxious to eke them out as
long as he could.   He had already begun to stint
himself of many of those little delicacies that he was
always so fond of.   Cream he no longer dared to
think about, and towards the close of his travels he
seems to have fared meagrely enough.   " No doubt
it is right that a poet should not overeat himself,"
he wrote, " but he oughtn't to starve ; " and he
threatened to frighten his acquaintances by coming
home a skeleton.   And here I may mention, by the

* Bille og Bogh, *Breve fra Andersen*, i. p. 201.
† In *Improvisatoren*.

way, that despite his simplicity and childishness, there was a shrewd practical strain in Andersen's character. He had a perfect genius for regulating his finances,* and making a little money go a long way, though he was never stingy or even near. On the eve of a tour he would always map out the whole itinerary beforehand, settling how long he would stay and how much he would spend at every place in the line of route. His disbursements were estimated in advance down to the very smallest item, and he was rarely so much as a penny out in his calculations. His present tour is a good instance of his really wonderful thriftiness. With very little more than £100† he travelled for sixteen months through France, Italy, the Tyrol, and Germany, including flying visits to Venice and Prague, saving enough besides to buy a few antiques and other curiosities for himself and his friends. ' Surely economy could do no more.

If Andersen was enthusiastic about Italy before he had even entered Rome, he was in raptures over her by the time he had seen Naples. " When I die," he wrote to a friend, " my ghost shall haunt Naples ; the nights there are so beautiful." Every-

* See Collin, p. 512, who reckons this as one of Andersen's most useful talents.

† He received in April 1833, a stipend of 600 rix dollars (about £75) for two years, which was increased in 1834 to 800 rix dollars (£100). He was away from April 1833 to Aug. 1834.

thing in and about the capital of the Two Sicilies
enchanted him.    The islands there looked like
swimming clouds, the children like Raphaelic angels,
and every other woman was an ideal Madonna.    All
the more downcast was he on his return to Rome,
where he arrived in time to participate in the
Easter festivities and be rude to the Pope.*    After
a few days' stay there, he took leave (not without
tears) of Thorvaldsen and his other friends, and set
off homewards across the mountains to Bologna
first, and then on to Venice *viâ* Ferrara.    As he
left Italy behind him (and for him Italy only began
beyond the Appenines), he grumbles and growls
more and more bitterly at the hard fate which
compels him to return to the inhospitable north,
where only gibes and taunts and Judas kisses
await him.    He could almost be happier as a poor
monk beneath the orange trees of Naples than
as an author in the best street of Copenhagen.
He regards everything on his way back with a
jaundiced eye.    Venice, where a scorpion stung him
in bed on the very night of his arrival, he calls an
Austro-Italian amphibian, a dead swan floating on
muddy water; and the gondolas gliding about the

* He absolutely refused to kneel when the Pope passed, although
his friend Hertz set him the example.  Andersen, indeed, at this time
was a rabid Protestant.  He looked with alarm at every monk, and
with suspicion at every nun, and ungratefully put down the urbanity of
the Jesuits (for whom he had an especial horror) to servility.

stagnant canals, like so many hearses, made him feel
quite ill. The splendid square of St. Mark and the
Rialto, " where Shylock struck his bargain," alone
interested him ; and after three days he quitted the
"corpse-like city " without regret. In the Tyrol he
travelled with a young Scotchman called Jamieson,
who was seized with home-sickness at the sight of
the mountains that reminded him of his native
Highlands. Andersen felt quite angry with himself
at being unable to share the feeling. The light
green poplars and beeches of South Germany irritated him, and Saxon Switzerland now seemed quite
trumpery. He moaned continually over the loss of
the palms and the cactuses of the south, the vivifying air full of the refreshing fragrance of oranges and
citrons, and the gigantic cypruses and velvet-leaved
olive trees. And to think that he was going to
exchange them for the thick clinging mists and the
snow-water that is always getting into one's boots !
At Vienna a stall at the theatre was placed at his
disposal during his stay there, a courtesy which
instantly suggests the reflection that his " dear
native land " had never yet offered him a similar
privilege, though there he had the right to expect
it. Bohemia, where all the roads were fragrant with
lindens, and .real gipsys with coal-black hair like
horses' manes and yellow Egyptian faces, met one at
every step, Bohemia was the only country that

restored to him his good humour for a brief moment.
With Prague he was delighted, and there, in
ascending the tower of the Hradshin Palace, his
usual good luck brought him face to face with the
exiled Charles X. . and the Duke and Duchess of
Angoulôme, who were sojourning just then in the
Bohemian capital. He learned enough of the Czech
language, which he compares to an intensified cawing
of rooks, to bawl " I love thee, lovely maiden," after
every pretty girl that he passed in his carriage ; and
he had his fortune told him in unintelligible
jargon by a pretty Preciosa with eyes like black
velvet, and the demeanour of an abducted countess.
Berlin he found more intolerable than ever, though
his vanity was flattered by the attention paid to
him by the Berlinese poets.

All this time he had been worrying himself with
groundless fears of the reception that awaited
him at home in Denmark, where " every one is so
cold and prudent." Many of his friends were
naturally annoyed at his ceaseless jeremiades, his
ungrateful attacks upon his country at the very
moment when he was enjoying the bounty of his
King, and his hysterical whimpering. But they seem
to have treated him as a sort of sick child who is
scarcely responsible for his morbid fancies, and
should be coaxed into a better humour. Madame
Laessoe, whom he regarded as a second mother, and

who ever since his unhappy love affair had quite
made up her mind that the best thing he could do
was to marry and settle down, now again returned
to the charge, and bade him choose for himself some
pretty girl or other, become a husband, a father, and
a sober citizen—make the best of all the good his
poor little country possessed, and cover the bad
with the cloak of charity. Other friends told him,
plainly, to be a man, shake off his morbid broodings,
and take up his pen again, so that both his country
and his acquaintances might have reason to congratulate him on his return. And, in fact, on
arriving at Copenhagen, he was agreeably surprised
to find everywhere outstretched hands and smiling
faces. The Collins received him like a son and a
brother. There were tears in the eyes of Jonas
Collin when he welcomed him back, and Edward,
in his white jacket, and with his inseparable pipe in
his mouth, was the same as ever. People even
stopped him in the street to ask him how he was;
and when he went up to the palace to thank the
King for his goodness his Majesty was most gracious,
and two Ministers of State invited him to call again.*
His spirits revived at once, and if the memories of
his beloved Italy still coloured all his thoughts, he

* Yet in *M. L. E.*, pp. 181, 182, and *seq.*, he speaks as if there had
been a determined attempt to crush him altogether, and insinuates that
for a time all his friends fell away from him.

now felt able at the same time to do justice to his own country also, and even apologise for his former ungraciousness. No doubt, he said, Denmark was really his best friend; but then Italy was his mistress, and surely a man was not expected to love his friend as much as his mistress! And in making allowance for Andersen's melancholy forebodings, we should never lose sight of the fact of his extreme poverty at this time. It is true that with his small stipend, which still had eight months to run, and surrounded as he was by excellent friends, he had no fear of actual want; but, on the other hand, he was always very sensitive about money matters, and it was galling to his proud and independent spirit to accept pecuniary assistance even from Jonas Collin, who stood to him in the place of a father. During the last three months of 1834 * and the first six of 1835, he had the utmost difficulty in making both ends meet. It was as much as he could do to pay his way (he had a horror of running up bills), and with only sufficient money in hand to last him a week, and little prospect of making any more, he was often at his wits' end what to do. At the end of 1834 he vainly applied for the post of Assistant Librarian at the Royal Library; and as late as May, 1835, when *The Improvisatore* had already spread his fame throughout the length and breadth of

* He had returned home in August of that year.

the land, when the first part of the immortal *Fairy Tales* was in the hands of the public, and he was sure of some hundreds of rix-dollars from these and other sources by the end of the year, even then he was obliged to write to Jonas Collin as follows: "I am *poor*, and feel my poverty more grievously than the most miserable street beggar; and it crushes my spirit and courage. . . . . I see a wretched future before me which I have scarcely the courage to contemplate. The time will come when I shall be obliged to seek my livelihood as a poor country tutor, or try to get a place on the coast of Guinea. . . . . Many a want, which some would call petty, lies heavily on my heart. . . . . Reitzel has no money, and therefore will not publish just yet the next volume of the " Fairy Tales " which I have all ready. . . . . I have no clothes; I have to pay my rent every month, and have other indispensable wants. . . . . 'Can you on this security [*i.e.*, the security of his expectations] get me a hundred rix-dollars [£12 10*s*.] from the public funds or any other source ? . . . . I feel deeply your goodness towards me, your gentleness, the delicacy with which you have always treated me; and it is just this feeling which makes me so unhappy at being obliged to be a constant annoyance and burden to you. . . . ."*

* Collin, pp. 241, 242. Collin replied the same day : " Pray be easy this evening, and be sure you have a good night ; to-morrow we'll have

Fortunately, this wretched state of things was soon to cease. In the beginning of 1835 appeared his first novel *Improvisatoren* ("The Improvisatore"), which was an immediate and decisive success. Andersen, usually so communicative as to the begetting of his "spiritual children," had been mysteriously reticent about his "Italian Son," as he called it. The bitter experiençe of *Agnete* seems to have somewhat shaken his self-confidence, and he hesitated to advertise beforehand what might only prove to be another failure. He had gone about with the idea of this new work in his head long before he ventured to set it down on paper. For one thing, he had so many places to see that he had little time for anything else. His pencil, too, during the earlier part of the Italian tour, was much busier than his pen; and he filled his portfolio with sketches, which he either gave away to his friends or kept beside him as memory's landmarks for future use. He did, indeed, attempt to write two tragedies at Naples, but they both expired in the opening scenes. As he prettily expressed it, his Muse had gone to sleep beneath the orange trees, but was sure to awake on the other side of the Alps. And awake she did, sooner than he

a talk together about ways and means." Collin and his son Edward were the only persons who ever knew of these bitter troubles; Andersen himself was very reticent about them. There is no mention of this in *M. L. E.*

expected. At Rome, on his return journey, he began
*The Improvisatore*, which he continued at Munich,
and completed amongst the groves and gardens of
Söro.   He offered it to the well-known publisher
Reitzel, for £25, one-half to be paid on the delivery
of the MS.; but Reitzel would not take the risk
unless Andersen guaranteed a certain number of

SKETCH BY ANDERSEN OF THE SHOP OPPOSITE HIS HOTEL AT ROME

subscribers, which, with the assistance of the
Collins, he managed to do.   The book came out,
people read and liked it, and soon there was such
a demand for it that the first edition was sold
out in a few months, and a second appeared
before the end of the year.   It was indisputably
the book of the season, and the author's reputation was made.

I

The hero of *The Improvisatore* is a youth named Antonio, the only son of a poor widow living at Rome, who is adopted by a nobleman whose life he saves, and educated for the church. But his talents lie rather in the direction of the operatic stage, and when the lovely vision of the great prima-donna Annunziata, crosses his path, he sacrifices the favour of his patron, and all his prospects along with it, to follow his natural bent, and win fame as an improvisatore, with the secret hope that the hand of Annunziata, who is as virtuous as she is beautiful, may one day be his ultimate reward. His platonic affection leads him at first into all sorts of difficulties. He quarrels with his bosom friend Bernardo, whom he wrongly suspects to be his favoured rival, and, in the belief that he has killed him in a duel, escapes from Rome only to fall into the hands of bandits, from whom he is mysteriously ransomed by an unknown friend. Finally Antonio makes his *début* at Naples as an improvisatore with such brilliant success that his offended patron is easily persuaded to forgive him. The prodigal is brought home to Rome again by his patron's daughter Francesca and her husband Fabian, at whose house he studies for the next six years to qualify himself for a more honourable calling, though his poetic soul is revolted by the severity of scholastic restraint, and his lofty aspirations meet with little

sympathy from his irritatingly prosaic patrons. His
susceptible heart, moreover, yearns after a love com-
mensurate with his own, and he is haunted continually by the recollection of the beloved Annunziata.
He meets her again, and the encounter is full of
sorrow for them both. Whilst staying at Venice,
curiosity draws him into a squalid little theatre, and
in the wan and withered features of one of the minor
actresses there he recognises his Annunziata, the
miserable wreck of her former glorious self. Antonio,
who is the soul of chivalry, reveals himself, and offers
the poor lady an honourable protection. But it is
too late. Annunziata, with equal magnanimity,
refuses the noble sacrifice, and dismisses the tearful
Antonio with the cold consolation of a future meeting
in a better world. Shortly afterwards she sends him,
from her death-bed, a letter recounting her mournful
story, and declaring that he alone had ever been her
ideal, though the force of circumstances had separated
them. Antonio, after shedding many bitter tears over
the affecting letter, consoles himself by marrying the
bearer of it, a pretty Venetian girl, Maria by name,
a chance acquaintance of former days, who has ever
since occupied a place in his very susceptible heart.
Most of the characters of this novel are taken from
life. Antonio is transparently Andersen himself,
old Dominica is Andersen's mother, Malibran gave
him the first idea of Annunziata, and Maria, whom

he restores to sight, is the development of a little ·blind beggar girl he met near Pæstum.

Such a novel as *The Improvisatore* would, I fear, have little chance of success nowadays. The plot is too improbable, the characters are too super-ficial, and our *fin de siècle* cynicism would be horribly bored by the all-pervading sentimentality which sixty years ago was considered its crowning merit. But in the thirties things were different. Despite the sarcasms of Heine, the Romantic School still dominated continental *belles-lettres*, and the sentimental romance was everywhere the reigning favourite of fiction. The charm of the book lies in its vivid and picturesque descriptions of Italian life and scenery; the naïve enthusiasm with which they are given is even now contagious. *The Improvisatore* was the literary event of the year in Denmark, and Andersen suddenly found himself the object of a universal enthusiasm. His friends were astonished and delighted, his critics silenced, his enemies converted or confounded. He received congratulations from the most unexpected quarters. One of his most gratifying conquests was the exactingly conscientious poet, Johannes Carsten Hauch, who six years before, when every one was praising the *Fodreise*, had had the courage to call it empty child's play, and express a doubt whether its author possessed any real talent at all. *The Improvisatore* convinced him that his former judgment had been over-hasty, and in a manly apologetic letter to Andersen he admitted he had formed a wrong opinion of him, and desired to be considered henceforth as an admirer. But the fame of the new book soon spread far beyond the narrow limits of its native land. Before the second Danish edition had yet come out, the book was translated into German by Professor Kruse, and within the next ten years Swedish, Danish, English,* Russian and Bohemian versions followed each other in rapid succession. Chamisso, who was one of the first to receive a German copy of the book, wrote the author a letter of congratulation, which caused Andersen to weep for joy, and made his heart overflow with gratitude to God and man. Every one now assured him that he had found at last his true vocation, and that it was as a great novelist that he would go down to posterity. Andersen believed them with his whole heart, but both he and they were utterly mistaken. Judged by the very high standard to which Danish fiction has attained in our own days, *The Improvisatore* must be pronounced a rather poor performance. Even in its strongest points, its descriptions of Italian scenery and manners, it falls far below many Danish novels of a later day. Vilhelm Bergsoe's

* The best English translation is Mrs. Howitt's, 1845. Another (anonymous) English edition appeared in 1857 ; Lockhart spoke very highly of it.

enthralling story, *Fra Piazza del Popolo*, for instance, is immeasurably superior. No, Andersen was to find his way to fame, not by the royal road of the novel and the drama, in the footsteps of far greater than he, but by a new and unfrequented by-path which he, who was the first to explore it, stumbled upon by the merest chance. " After a long fumbling about," a great critic has finely said,* " after many years of aimless wandering. . . . . Andersen found himself standing, one evening, outside a little unpretentious but mysterious door, the door of Fairy Tale ; he touched it, it flew open, and he saw sparkling inside there in the darkness, the little tinder-box which was to be his Aladdin's lamp. He struck fire with it and the spirits of the lamp—the dogs with the eyes like tea-cups, like mill-wheels, and like the Round Tower—stood by him, and brought him the three huge chests full of all the fairy copper money, silver money, and gold money. The first fairy tale was there, and it drew all the others after it. Happy the man who finds the right tinder-box." And now let us see how the first fairy tales came to be written, and what the Danish public thought of them.

* G. Brandes, *Kritiker og Portraiter.*

ANDERSEN, ÆTAT 30

# CHAPTER VI

## THE FIRST FAIRY TALES—MORE NOVELS

How the Fairy Tales came to be written—The first little volume of
"The Tales as told to Children"—A sympathy with the childlike
in nature, and an insight into the supernatural the chief causes of
the success of the Tales—Andersen's poor opinion of the Tales—
Stupidity of the Danish critics with regard to them—The reviewer's doubt whether they are even fit for children—Opinions
of Andersen's friends—Cattiva Danemarca—"The Isola Fortunata" at Lykkesholm—The mischievous hoydens—Andersen's
second romance, *O. T.*—Andersen's injustice towards his critics
—His correspondence an infallible barometer of his varying moods
—First tour to Sweden—Intimacy with Mad. Bremer—Andersen's
third and best romance, *Only a Fiddler*—Opinion of the critics
—Andersen's exorbitant vanity—Popularity of Andersen in Sweden
and Germany—Xavier Marmier's description of Andersen—"*Vie
d'un poète*"—Pecuniary embarrassments—Receives a small pension
from the State—Andersen a dandy—Cannot afford to marry—
Famous and Fashionable—Discontented.

IT is commonly supposed that Andersen was very
fond of children, but his intimate friends assure us
that such was not the case. On the other hand,
they all agree that he had a wonderful knack of
ingratiating himself with little people. Himself a
child in heart and mind for all his genius, he could
thoroughly enter into the feelings and fancies of
children, and when in a good humour delighted to

make them his playmates (especially if they were
well-behaved and nice-looking), and tell them fairy
tales, of which he possessed a perfectly inexhaustible
store. And he had his own peculiar way of telling
these tales, which quite enchanted his wee friends.
Giving free play to his humour and fancy, he would
rattle on without stopping, using childish words and
baby language by preference, and emphasising his
narrative by all manner of comic antics and grimaces.
He could put life into the most ordinary things. For
instance, instead of saying "The children got into
the carriage and drove off," he would say : "So they
got into the carriage. Good-bye, father ; good-bye,
mother ! Crack, crack, went the whip, and off they
dashed, helter-skelter. That was something like a
gallop." Edward Collin tells us that those who
only heard Andersen read his Fairy Tales in public
(though that of itself was a privilege), can form but
a faint idea of his peculiar sprightliness and vivacity
when he had a circle of children round him. Oddly
enough, it never seems to have occurred to Andersen that he might use this unique talent for something more than keeping a mob of children quiet,
till some one suggested that specimens of the tales
should be put into print just as he was in the habit
of telling them *viva voce*, so that they might in that
way be made known beyond the narrow circle of his
private friends. The idea seems to have been that

while the elder children were left to read the tales for themselves, their parents should learn them by heart and then tell them as nearly as possible in the Andersenian manner to the younger ones. So the attempt was made, and at the beginning of 1835, a few months after the appearance of *The Improvisatore*, a tiny volume in 16mo, entitled "Fairy Tales * as told to Children," was offered for sale in the Copenhagen bookstalls at the modest price of 4½d. It comprised "The Tinder-box," "Little Claus and Big Claus," "The Princess and the Pea," "Little Ida's Flowers," and was followed early in 1836 by a second part containing "Thumbelisa," "The Naughty Boy," and "The Travelling Companion." A third part ("The Little Mermaid," † and "The Emperor's New Clothes") appeared in 1837; and these three parts together made up the first volume of the Tales.

* I call them "fairy tales" for want of a better word. The Danish "Eventyr" is really untranslatable. The word is derived from the German word "Aventure," which was itself borrowed from the romance *Adventura* towards the end of the twelfth century, when it began to be used along with the indigeneous *märchen*. The Danish word "Eventyr" comes from the low German form of this word, and first appears in writing towards the end of the sixteenth century. It is used as an equivalent for the German *märchen*, and therefore, of course, means "folk-tale" rather than "fairy tale," though not exactly synonymous with it. In Andersen it nearly always means a fairy tale ; non-supernatural stories he generally calls "Histories." Hence his collected tales are called *Eventyr og Historier*.

† "The Little Mermaid" was written in emulation of Fouqué's "Undine." Of all his works, Andersen tells us this affected him the most.

Little as he suspected it, Andersen had now laid the foundations of his future fame. At last, though he himself would never admit as much, he had discovered his own peculiar domain in literature, where none will dare to dispute his sway. The very limitations of his fancy, its excessive delicacy, flightiness, and instability, its trick of perpetually hovering around a thousand objects without fastening on any, its superficiality, which made him but an indifferent dramatist, and not much more than a second-rate novelist, were in their proper element among the ever-shifting phantasmagoria of fairyland. He had, too, a child's imagination, which personifies and vivifies everything, whether it be a plant, a flower, a bird, a cat, a doll, or clouds, sunbeams, winds, and the seasons of the year. The determining quality of Andersen's art, therefore, was sympathy with the childlike in the widest sense—with children first of all, and then with everything that most nearly resembles children ; with animals, for instance, who may be regarded as children who are never anything but children ; and with plants, who are also like children, but children who are always sleeping.* Nay, even his defects, mental and moral, that sensitive shrinking from all that is disgusting or distressing, that disinclination to look the uglier facts of life fairly in the face, defects that are

* Brandes, *Kritiker og Portraiter*.

responsible for so much of the indefiniteness and mawkish sentiment of his novels and plays,* do but lend an additional charm to his fairy tales, and make them suitable above all others for children. What is mawkishness elsewhere here becomes simply sweetness. Hence it is that all, or nearly all, the children in his fairy tales are good children, and all the animals friendly domestic animals, who may sometimes be stupid and snobbish, but are never savage or brutal. Finally—and here we hit upon the real secret of Andersen's unique art as a teller of fairy tales—he possessed the rare gift of fashioning, or rather evoking supernatural beings of every sort and kind, elves, gnomes, nixies, trolls, dryads and mermaids, who are always true to the characters he gives them. It is impossible not to believe in Andersen's fantastic creations ; he had as keen an eye for the oddities of the elfin race as Dickens had for the oddities of human nature. Andersen is the only story-teller who has succeeded in inventing fairy tales which are as fresh, natural, and spontaneous as a genuine *märchen*. All other workers in this field are either mere collectors, like Grimm and Asbjörnsen, or clever adaptors, like Madam d'Aulnoy. Andersen also drew largely from the common stock, and such little masterpieces as

* " So tremulous a hand could never anatomise a rogue."—Brandes, *Kritiker og Portraiter.*

"The Tinder Box" and "The Wild Swans" are living instances of the inimitable skill with which he could transform a good old story into a new one, and even improve it in the process; but he is at his best when he is original—he never wrote anything finer than "The Shadow" or "The Little Mermaid."

In his autobiography, published nearly twenty years later, Andersen, somewhat querulously begs his readers not to imagine for a moment that the "Fairy Tales" were favourably received or highly thought of at first; quite the contrary. This is true; but he would have been juster and more indulgent to his critics if only he had called to mind that he himself had had but a poor opinion of them at first. He was so full of the triumph of *The Improvisatore* that he had no thought for anything else, and his sole ambition was to become the greatest of Danish novelists. The Fairy Tales he looked upon as mere bagatelles. Still, the fact remains that the Danish public as a whole, critics and all, so far from regarding the first Fairy Tales as a unique and precious addition to the national literature, scarcely condescended to look at them. The critic of the *Dannora* reluctantly admitted that children might perhaps get a little fun out of "The Tinder Box," "Little Claus and Big Claus," and "Little Ida's Flowers"; but, he added, was

that a sufficient reason for allowing them to read
what could not edify, and might even harm them ?
Surely, he urged, nobody would pretend that a
child's sense of decency could be improved by
reading about a princess who, after being carried
from her bed on a dog's back to a soldier who
kissed her, told fibs when she got home, and said
she dreamed it all ! Again, was it the right way
to teach a child respect for the sacredness of human
life by describing to him such painful incidents as
Big Claus killing his grandmother and Little Claus
killing Big Claus, with as little conscience as if it
were a mere matter of felling an ox ? He concluded
by imploring "the talented author" not to waste
any more of his time in future in writing tales for
children. The critic of *Literaturtidenden* complained that Andersen's tales were too colloquial,
and had the grave additional fault of' pointing
no moral whatever. For both these reasons he
expressed his preference for the volume of Fairy
Tales which Molbech had published almost simultaneously.* Most of Andersen's own acquaintances

* Molbech's book was entitled *Julegaver for Börn* (1835) "Christmas Gifts for Children," and was continued every year until 1839. It
is an excellent collection of fairy tales from the most various sources,
including a great many of Grimms' and a few of D'Aulnoy's. In the
preface to a later edition (*Udvalgte Eventyr eller Folkidigtinger*)
there is a handsome recognition of Andersen's superiority in this *genre*,
and "The Steadfast Tin Soldier," which Molbech considered one of
Andersen's happiest efforts, is included in the collection.

didn't know exactly what to make of the tales.
One lady positively couldn't bear them.   Ingemann,
who had little sense of humour, and whose own
novels are saturated with false sentiment, disliked
the comical ones—in other words, the best ones.
Andersen's Swedish friend, the novelist, Madam
Bremer, was more discerning and appreciative, but
even her admiration was a trifle perverse.   She considered "The Little Mermaid" full of the deepest,
most lovely poetry, but scarcely down to the mental
level of a child.   "It has a depth of anguish," she
writes, "almost beyond human comprehension." *
"The Wild Swans" she liked for its charming
descriptions, but her favourite was "Thumbelisa,"
which she pronounced a perfect jewel of its kind.
Yet this gifted lady would have had Andersen leave
fairyland, with all its gnomes and nixies and goblins,
quite out of the question, and draw his inspiration
direct from life and Nature.   Carsten Hauch saw
more in the tales than Madam Bremer, but even he
was not quite satisfied, and some of his criticisms
read comically enough nowadays.   Thus he thought
the conduct of the soldier to the old witch who had
done him a service downright repulsive, and predicted that such "moral indifference" would do the
stories harm.   "Little Ida's Flowers" struck him as
too much in Hoffmann's manner, but "The Princess

* Bille og Bogh : *Breve til Andersen*, pp. 54, 55.

and the Pea" delighted him. There were only two of Andersen's friends who recognised the superlative merits of the Fairy Tales from the first, but they were the clearest heads in Denmark. Hans Christian Örsted wrote to Andersen that while *The Improvisatore* would make him famous, the Tales would make him immortal; and J. L. Heiberg, with the eye of a true critic, placed the latter immeasurably above everything which their author had yet written. Andersen was pleased, but not convinced, by what seemed to him an exaggerated enthusiasm; and the public seemed to hold the same views that he did. The Tales did not take very well at first, and the sale was slow; but they gradually found their way into many a Danish home, and a year or two later, when Andersen was everywhere a welcome guest, he found that the children, at any rate, were his fervent admirers, and that there was scarce a nursery where his Fairy Tales were not known by heart.

Meanwhile he was busy with a new novel, which took up so much of his time that his friends complained that he had clean forgotten them now that he had become famous. He had moved into new lodgings on the second floor of a house in the *Nyhavn*, which were larger and more comfortable than his old quarters, but had their inconveniences also, for overhead was a mob of squalling children,

K

while below him dwelt a violin teacher, who gave
him concerts *gratis* all day long. " So you see," he
wrote to a friend, " I live in the midst of harmonies
and dissonances, as I suppose one must do in this
world." * However, he considered himself more
than compensated by the prospect from his windows.
One of them looked out upon the harbour, where he
could see the wind playing among the sails of the
ships, and from the other he had a fine view of the
Botanical Gardens, stretching out before him " like
a green Lombardy plain," where the trees in the
moonlight looked as black as the " dear dark
cypresses" that he had left behind him. It will be
seen from this that his thoughts still ran constantly
upon his beloved Italy, for which he yearned so
much that he declared he was willing to put up
even with Molbech himself as a travelling companion, if there was no other way of getting there.
His complaints against the villainous climate of
*Cattiva Danemarca* are also loud and long. He
heads his letters to his Italian friends " Rain, Sludge,
and Fog," instead of Copenhagen, " whereby you'll
see," he adds, " that I am back again in my own
dear native land." He suggests that engaged
couples in Denmark should pledge their troth with
umbrellas instead of rings. He complains that the
Danish climate will always prevent him from being

* Bille og Bogh : *Breve fra Andersen*, i. p. 260.

a true poet, and rails against the hard fate which condemns him, a Southerner by temperament, to spend his days in a Scandinavian cloister whose walls are the mists, whose *flagellum* is the winter storm, and whose chain is want of money. He wants to be patriotic, he says, but how is it possible to be enthusiastic about a country with a climate that really belongs to Lapland? "If we had a prince who really loved art," he adds, "I should now be on my way to Greece." But no: he is no longer a fluttering bird, but only a pot-bound plant that has a little water poured over it now and then. He supposes he can't expect more than that ; there are so many other plants to be looked after, both cabbages as well as daisies ; and then, of course, the cabbages are such useful plants. He would be glad if he could sell half his life to a wealthy man, so as to be able to live the other half in Italy ; and he bitterly envies those who are better off than himself in this respect. Even Byron was lucky amidst all his torments, for he could fly about, and was rich enough to despise men, and sing and enjoy life in his own way.

But a Scandinavian winter does not last for ever, and even in *Danemarca Cattiva* Andersen now discovered an " isola fortunata," as he calls it. This was the beautiful old country mansion of Lykkesholm in Funen, which he first visited in the summer of 1835, and where he was to pass some of the happiest days of his life. Never had he been so hospitably entertained before. His hostess, old Madam Lindegaard, treated him like a prince. He was consulted as to his favourite dishes—I may mention, by the way, that he was just a little bit of a gourmand—if he wanted anything he had only to ask for it, and everything he said was considered witty and clever, for was he not the author of *The Improvisatore*, and *The Improvisatore* was a book which the good folks of Lykkesholm positively adored. "For the first time in my life," he tells Collin, "I feel the *agreeableness* of being an author." * He is enthusiastic about everything, from his own "interesting room" in one of the large turrets, with its huge old-fashioned tester bed, with red damask curtains, where he lay awake waiting in not unpleasant trepidation for the appearance of the family ghost, and gazing at the tapestry on the walls, where all Olympus was represented, down to the dishes and drinks he had for dinner. "I have acquired a many-sidedness you will certainly admire," he writes. "I can be as enthusiastic about a splendid meat-soup or beef-steak as about black eyes and Bellini's melodies. I prefer white churn milk to the most beautiful red sunrise, and champagne is the stream which ripples most pleasantly through

* Collin, p. 272.

THE ACTOR FOERSOM

my poetic grove." He had meant to stay only a couple of days at Lykkesholm, but "the beautiful scenery and the sweet cream" made such an impression on his senses, and the delicate attentions of his hostess and her family, who "flattered the *poet* and gave the *man* the best meats," so touched him that he was easily persuaded to extend his visit first to ten, and finally to seventeen days. The young ladies, as he mischievously told Louisa Collin, flocked around him in bevies; and innumerable were the practical jokes the wicked hoydens played upon the poor confiding poet. They put live cocks under his bed and hard peas inside it, and hung paper boxes full of cockchafers on the bed-curtains; but he discovered everything beforehand, and was magnanimous enough not to revenge himself. It is true that one night, when he found a large, life-size doll between his sheets, he had the idea of paying his fair tormentors off in their own coin by dressing himself up *as a ghost* and lying in one of the young ladies' beds, but he had scruples about it at the last moment, and his hostess, whom he took into his confidence, also opined that the joke, though ingenious, was perhaps a little too practical. A fellow guest with him at Lykkesholm was the actor Foersom, a man with a great sense of humour, but no manners to speak of. Thus, once, he scandalised the whole company at table by improvising a scantily attired ballet-dancer out of his two middle fingers and a dinner napkin. The only accident that befell Andersen during his stay at this hospitable old country-house was when he accidentally sat down upon a pair of scissors which had strayed by accident into his tail-coat pocket, of which mis-adventure he gives a most graphic account to Collin : " I was bathed with vinegar; Paulli held the cup, while Foersom closed up the wound. It was a brilliant scene !" Otherwise absolutely nothing occurred to disturb him.

On his return from Lykkesholm to Copenhagen, Andersen completed his second romance, *O. T.*, the title of which is taken from the initial letters of the hero's name—Otto Thostrup. *O. T.* has little or no plot. It is a series of character sketches grouped around the central figure, with a vivid and picturesque background of Danish scenery which is the best part of the book. The descrip-tions of Jutland, indeed, though good, are greatly inferior to Sten Blicher's ; but the quaint and tranquil beauty of Funen, "the granary of Den-mark," Andersen's own native isle, with its ancient churches unspoiled by Puritan hands, its old-fashioned country-houses, rich pasturages, smiling cornfields, and bright beech-woods, is reflected from these pages as from a magic mirror, while the picture given of the old market-place of Odense is

equal to the best descriptions in *The Improvisatore*.*
Very felicitous, too, are the sketches of life and
character which reveal the true humorist, and sometimes (as, for instance, the comical family circle at
Lemvig) have such a strong Dickensian flavour that
we should suspect an imitation did we not know
that it was an anticipation of Boz. Most of these
characters, moreover, are taken from life, and it is
interesting to know that the bluff and hearty Kam-
merjunker is meant for Edward Collin. Unfortunately the book is heavily handicapped by the dead
weight of an insufferably tedious hero. *O. T.* is
a sort of invertebrate, modernised, middle-class
Hamlet whose life has been mysteriously blighted
(it is never satisfactorily explained how) by the
malign influence of a vagabond juggler called
German Henry, combined with an anxiety as to the
disappearance of a beloved sister whom, however, he
never makes the slightest effort to discover. At
least one half of the book is taken up by the moralising and philosophising of this tiresome young
pessimist, who is finally rewarded (far beyond his
merits) by having his long-lost sister found for him,
and receiving, besides, the hand of the nicest girl in

* Andersen was justly proud of this fine piece of word-painting, and
used to say the Odensers ought to be very grateful to him for making
their market-place so famous. *O. T.* has been excellently translated
by Mrs. Howitt. Thostrup is transparently Andersen, though Baron
William is the character that he *intended* for himself.

the story, after allowing *her* sister, for whom he had
a sort of sentimental preference, to be snapped up
before his very eyes.

Andersen was, as usual, enthusiastic about this
his latest work ; he felt, he wrote to a friend, that
he had now scrambled several hundreds of feet
higher up the mountain of Fame.  The critics, too,
were on the whole very favourable.  Even the
*Maanedsskrift for Litteratur*, which he feared
the most, placed it far above *The Improvisatore*
both as to style and characterisation.  The reviewer
expressed his astonishment at the author's " wealth
of fruitful, poetic ideas " and the facility with which
he adapted them to his purposes, especially praising
his sketches of popular life, and his descriptions of
nature.  He rightly observes that * Andersen's
strong point is his fancy which, always vivid,
natural and alert, is swift to seize upon and make
the most of those superficial traits of character,
those outward phenomena, which strike the eye
at once, but is less successful with the total impression, the inner man.  In his autobiography,
Andersen, characteristically enough, does not so
much as mention a word of the praise which is here
bestowed upon him with no niggard hand, but
indulges in a bitter diatribe against the "malignant
injustice of his anonymous critic."  No wonder then

* Collin, pp. 291-3.

if those readers who only know Andersen from his autobiography run away with the impression that his life at this time was made utterly wretched by the neglect and disparagement of his countrymen. His correspondence, however, shows us that the thirties were among the happiest years of his life. And here I may mention, by the way, that Andersen's correspondence is an infallible barometer of his perpetually shifting moods. As a rule, the correspondence of eminent men, especially if they be men of letters, are self-painted portraits, which show us just as much or just as little of the writer's character as he chooses. Andersen's correspondence, on the other hand, is a faithful mirror which reflects his character down to the very smallest minutiæ, and by looking into it at any given moment, we can tell, at a glance, how the world is using him. Speaking generally, the five years which elapsed from the success of his first original novel to the failure of his first original drama, were very joyous years for " the long poet," and in 1836 he assured his friends that he had never felt so well for a long time. " If only you could see me in my comfortable home," he wrote to one of his lady acquaintances, " lying alone in my glory on my sofa in my beautiful new dressing-gown, amongst my books, papers, and drawings ! I have never begun any year with such bright and happy prospects as this one.

Heiberg, Oehlenschläger, all our so-called leading
men, are particularly friendly and respectful. Sometimes the whole thing seems a dream to me when
I think of my childhood and all my poverty. The
poor washerwoman's son, who used to run about in
wooden shoes in the streets of Odense, is now
treated as a kinsman by many of Denmark's most
celebrated men."* And indeed he himself was
becoming a celebrity. About this time his portrait
was painted for the Danish Art Exhibition by
Professor Jensen, and it was with a thrill of delight
that he beheld groups of acquaintances flocking
around it, eyeglass in hand. People too began to
look at him as he walked up and down the fashionable Ostergade, and ladies nudged each other as he
passed, and whispered: "There's the poet!" His
letters of this period are jocose, not to say frisky,
a sure sign that critics are kind, and things are
going on well. He regales his lady friends with
quaint conceits, innocent *double-entendres*, and
comical adventures of which he himself is the hero,
and humorously threatens his beloved but irritating "brother" Edward with a cudgelling if he is not
more affectionate and attentive in future. It is true
that on hearing of Collin's wedding, the memory of
his now blighted love makes the water come to his

---

* Bille og Bogh : *Breve fra Andersen*, i. pp. 64, 65.

eyes again, and he compares himself to Moses standing on the mountain, and gazing at the Promised
Land into which he himself was not to enter; but
he quickly recovers himself, and gives the bride a
sort of inventory of her future husband's good and
bad qualities, with elaborate directions how to
manage him.*

Shortly after the publication of *O. T.* Andersen
set out on a short tour to Sweden, which he was to
describe six years later in that beautiful little book
*I Sverrig* (In Sweden). Andersen was charmed
with what he saw on the other side of the Sound.
He had started with very strange notions of the
sister kingdom. At the beginning of the nineteenth
century Sweden and Denmark were still comparative
strangers to each other. Centuries of hostility, only
comparable to the old hostility between England
and France, had unnaturally divided two nations
who came of the same stock, and spoke pretty nearly
the same language, and if Danes and Swedes met at
all as friends, it was at some foreign capital. Stockholm was far less familiar to educated Danes, than
Paris or Rome. Andersen had expected to find
Sweden semi-barbarous, and the Swedish capital

---

* Collin, p. 286. He adds: "God has given me much in this world,
but what I lack is perhaps the best of all. One has a home for the
first time when one has a faithful loving wife, and sees oneself born
anew in one's dear children."

two hundred years behind the age,* but he speedily came to the conclusion that living and travelling in Sweden was not only far cheaper, but also far more comfortable and luxurious than in his own country, and he was profoundly surprised by the beauty and grandeur of Stockholm, the situation of which he declared to be fully equal to that of Naples. Indeed, for a moment, despite the greyish-green water, and the dark pines, he was doubtful whether he was in the North or South. And if he was charmed with the country, still more delighted was he with the people. Everywhere he was received with open arms, and in the Swedes he speedily found some of his most enthusiastic admirers. The Swedish novelist Madam Bremer, the Jane Austen of the North, whom he romantically met for the first time on the deck of a steamer in the middle of Lake Wener, at two o'clock in the morning, became his friend for life. The lady, whom he describes as " a very quiet but amiable character, profound and womanly, but over forty,"† was a little stiff at first, it is true ; but he presented her with a copy of *Impro-visatoren*—he seems to have always carried an assortment of his own books about with him—which she read the next day and pronounced it the best book she knew, so an intimacy was at once established.

* Bille og Bogh : *Breve fra Andersen*, i. pp. 373, 374.
† *Ibid.* i. pp. 372, 373.

At Upsala the Professors drank Andersen's health in champagne on Odin's grave, and but for its being vacation time, the students of the University would certainly have serenaded the Danish poet by torch-light, a fact he regretted the more deeply as there was a beautiful balcony outside his window from which he could have returned thanks with dignity and effect. Amongst the new friends he made were such men as the Poet Atterbom, the founder of the romantic school in Sweden, and Bernard von Beskow, the chivalrous apologist of Gustavus III.

In the course of 1837, Andersen published a third romance, *Kun en Spillemand* (Only a Fiddler*), which had kept him busily occupied during the winter and spring, and was to mark the highest point he ever reached as a novelist. In "Only a Fiddler" we find a depth and intensity of feeling, and a vividness both of characterisation and descrip-tion which we shall look for in vain in *O. T.* and *The Improvisatore.* This, however, was only to be expected, as, making due allowance for poetic licence, *Only a Fiddler* is mainly autobiographical ; it is not merely founded on fact, it is actual fact. Of course, in pursuance of the plan of the story, not only are Christian's troubles multiplied and exaggerated, but from him are subtracted most of the saving qualities which enable the fittest to survive in the battle of

* There is an excellent translation of it by Mrs. Howitt.

life; such, for instance, as virility, determination, self-reliance, and mental elasticity, so that, in spite of all his gentleness and goodness, he is but a poor creature at best. But, nevertheless, nearly all the details of the life of the Odense tailor's miserable little son, whose passion for music proves his ruin instead of his salvation, are to be found in Andersen's own autobiography which he wrote nearly twenty years afterwards. Skilfully inter-woven with these autobiographical reminiscences is the sinister story of the gipsy girl Naomi, a Heinesque heroine of the Mademoiselle Lawrence type,* beautiful, brilliant, and seductive, but a mere animal without a grain of conscience. She is the next-door neighbour of the poor tailor's son, and the account of how they first become acquainted in their infancy is one of the prettiest things that Andersen ever wrote, and a striking instance of how thoroughly he could enter into the minds of little children. Naomi is finally adopted by a count, who ulti-mately turns out to be one of her putative fathers (he divides the honour with a gipsy and a Jew), and is brought up as a great lady. The irony of circum-stances frequently brings the old playmates together, and the poor fiddler soon learns to love the girl desperately, despite the lofty scorn with which she invariably looks down upon him. His chance

---

* The heartless and sensual heroine of *Florentinische Nächte*.

seems to come at last when her Bohemian instincts
assert themselves, and she elopes with a circus rider
who is as handsome and conscienceless as herself.
Christian now looks forward to the day when
necessity will drive the poor ruined creature home
again, and he may take her to his heart when
all the world cries shame upon her. It is this
thought that sustains him during the twelve years
of her disappearance, and by that time he has laid
up a little silver hoard which will enable them to
keep house together in a humble way. And at the
end of the twelve years tidings come that Naomi *is*
coming home, not, as he had anticipated, a poor, foot-
sore, beggared outcast, but as a rich and noble lady,
the wife of a marquis, and therefore more likely
than ever to regard him as so much dirt beneath her
feet although her own career has been as false and foul
as his has been pure and loyal. This last blow from
outrageous Fortune is too much for the poor fiddler.
He meekly bows his head beneath it, and dies of a
broken heart. On the very day when his rude coffin
is being carried to the little churchyard on the
shoulders of a couple of peasants, a grand carriage,
drawn by four horses, comes dashing along. It is
the French marquis with his lady, the beautiful and
superb Naomi. The road is narrow, so the coffin-
bearers step aside into the ditch, and uncover as
the grand carriage passes. The gracious lady nods

L

carelessly to the peasants. How could she expect
to feel much interest in such as they! It was
a poor man they were burying, " only a fiddler."

Thus the whole plot turns upon the heart-breaking
sorrows of an unrequited love, and yet, for all that,
*Only a Fiddler* is by no means a depressing story.
Its humour is as deep and genuine as its pathos,
and in both respects it shows a remarkable advance
upon *O. T.* Most of the minor characters are as
delightfully comical as in the former romance, while
the humour is again, in many cases, so thoroughly
Dickensian that we are sometimes tempted to
believe that we are reading a Danish version of
a lost original by the author of Pickwick.

There is not one of Andersen's works concerning
which such a difference of opinion prevails among
critics at home and abroad as *Only a Fiddler*.
In Denmark, despite the just and generous appreciation of Hauch and Oehlenschläger, it met with
but a cool reception, whereas in Germany and
Sweden (and, later on, in England and France) it
was welcomed with enthusiasm. Many reasons have
been given for this difference of opinion, but one
reason has been quite overlooked, which, nevertheless,
seems to me to be the right one, and it is this. The
story of Andersen's life was so well known in Copenhagen, that *Only a Fiddler* must have seemed to
most Danish readers the damnable iteration of a tale

that had been told often enough already. Andersen was of course much hurt by the comparative indifference of his countrymen, and his indignation became hotter still when Molbech's paper, the *Maanedsskrift*, which hitherto had taken no notice whatever of his romances, now published a severe criticism of *The Improvisatore*—certainly rather late in the day, as that romance had now been before the world for more than two years. Yet although severe, this criticism could not have been altogether unjust, for Andersen himself says the Collins approved of the gist of it. But his vanity was deeply wounded, and it must be admitted that he was inordinately vain. Not only did he always trumpet his own fame in the ears of his friends and acquaintances, but he was positively offended with them if they did not rejoice with the same childish joy as he did on all such occasions. Once he bawled to a friend on the other side of the street : " Well, what do you think ! I am read in Spain now. Good-bye ! " and this is only one instance out of a hundred.* Andersen was well aware of this weakness of his, and made not the slightest effort to conceal it. He naïvely argued that praise was as necessary to him as sunshine is to a plant, and solemnly protested that it made him humble of heart, and grateful to God and man, while blame destroyed his better

* Collin, p. 470.

nature, and filled him with thoughts which no
Christian should have. No doubt praise did soothe
him for a time; but it acted upon him not as a
healthy stimulant, but as a sort of mental morphia.
The dose had to be continually repeated in larger
and larger quantities, and at last not only exaggerated the complaint, but injured the organism. We
see this in the way in which he speaks of this
criticism of the *Maanedsskrift*. Hitherto he had
regarded his critics as merely perverse or malignant;
but now their conduct seems to him actually
blasphemous. He accuses them of setting themselves up to deny the gifts that God has given him,
and hopes that someone will intervene, and put
a stop to such wickedness. Then his old grudge
against his ungrateful country revives, and he rails
against her most bitterly, contrasting her step-
motherly conduct towards him with the generous
behaviour of Germany. This, however, was only a
passing paroxysm, and he found an ample compensation in the fame that he was rapidly winning
abroad. In Sweden, where the Romantic school had
been dominant for the last twenty years, so romantic
a writer as the author of *The Improvisatore* and
*Only a Fiddler*, was bound to be popular.
Madam Bremer had been charmed with *The
Improvisatore* and *O. T.*, but her favourite was
*Only a Fiddler*. She could not praise sufficiently

the originality of Andersen's conceptions, the fidelity
to nature with which he reproduced them, and the
skill with which, like a mighty alchemist, he ex-
tracted the purest poetic gold from coarse and
even foul incidents which only disgust one in real
life.*   His letter to her seems to have been written
in one of his melancholy discontented moods, for in
her reply she gently takes him to task for it. " You
ought not," she writes, " to be gloomy or discontented with your lot, indeed you should not. . . .
Is there a nobler or more beautiful mission in this
world than to be able to do good to the hearts of
men, and even after one's death to have the power
of passing through this earthly life of ours like
a vivifying spring breeze." Then she tells him, for
his encouragement, that his books are largely read
in Sweden, and are to be seen on the tables "in
front of the sofas" in all the fashionable drawing-
rooms of Stockholm and Upsala, a piece of intelli-
gence which was certainly even more acceptable to
Andersen than the lady's kindly counsel.

Germany, too, had been completely won by *The
Improvisatore* and she remained Andersen's devoted admirer to the last, or, as he expresses it in
his Autobiography, " from Germany came the first

* An allusion to Steffen Kareet, a woman of the same class and
character as Dickens's Nancy, whose tragic fate is one of the pathetic
incidents of the story.

strong recognition of my authorship, and I turned towards it as a sick man turns towards the sunshine, glad and thankful." *    Ziersdorff, in his Review, placed "The Fiddler" above the best novels of Novalis, and on a level with Tieck's earlier master-pieces. All Andersen's romances were translated into German within a few months of their appear-ance in Denmark, ran rapidly through half-a-dozen editions, were everywhere devoured with avidity, and praised enthusiastically in all the critical journals. They were even republished in special editions of foreign classics, and presently there was a large demand abroad for the author's portrait. From Germany Andersen's fame quickly spread to France. *The Improvisatore* was translated into French, the first Danish romance that ever enjoyed that distinction; † a critique of "The Fiddler" appeared in the *Revue du XIX Siècle* the year after its publication, and the *Revue des Deux Mondes* mentioned Andersen with respect, and expressed the wish to know more about him. England indeed had not yet heard of him, and her recognition Andersen seems to have valued most of all. "What would I not give to be translated into English," he cries. To Bulwer Lytton, whose *Pilgrims of the*

* *M. L. E.*, p. 197.
† Andersen himself tells us this, adding, "I feel as happy as a child." Bille og Bogh : *Breve fra Andersen*, i. p. 390.

*Rhine* was one of his favourite books, he sent a German version of *O. T.*, but received no reply. "If I don't hear from him," he writes, "I shall con-clude, either that he does not know German or has not read the book, in which case I shall let him go his own way, though I am sure that in the next world we shall be good friends and brothers."*

But though still unknown in England, Andersen could nevertheless rejoice in a reputation that was already European. Even this, however, was not enough for him, and when the French novelist₁and traveller, Xavier Marmier, stopped at Copenhagen on his northern tour in 1838, Andersen made it a point of calling upon him and making his acquaint-ance, with the view apparently of being advertised still further.† Marmier describes his visitor‡ as a tall young man, whose timid and embarrassed manners and awkward bearing might not perhaps have found favour with a "*petite maitresse*," but whose "caressing looks" and open honest counte-nance inspired sympathy and confidence at the first glance. They soon became very intimate, and one evening, after one of those long conversations ·which "expand the heart and invite confidences."§ Ander-sen gave the young Frenchman a sketch of his life.

* Bille og Bogh : *Breve fra Andersen*, i. p. 453.    † *Ibid.*
‡ *Histoire de la Littérature en Danemarc et en Suède*, Paris 1839. pp. 238-52.
§ Marmier.

"But may all Europe know of it?" asked Marmier. This, of course, was just the very thing that Andersen wanted, and he at once replied: "I belong to the world! Let them all know how I think and feel." * Marmier took him at his word, and this sketch duly appeared in the *Revue du XIX Siècle*, under the title of "Vie d'un poète," and was regarded as the standard authority on Andersen till the appearance of *Mit Livs Eventyr* in 1855. Andersen, in his correspondence, alludes to this "Vie d'un poète" again and again with childish glee. It amused him vastly to hear himself made to talk such elegant and correct French, but he peevishly protests against the conclusion which represents him as so contented, so happy! About this time also he received a friendly greeting through the Marquise de Bonnay from Lady Byron, who had read the "Vie d'un poète" in one of the French Reviews; "and you know," writes Andersen to a lady friend whom he duly informs of the event, "le poète c'est moi." †

And now too fortune befriended him still further by relieving him of a burden that had always weighed very heavily upon him—his pecuniary difficulties. Despite the successes of his books, the hospitalities of his friends, and his own really wonderful

* Bille og Bogh : *Breve fra Andersen*, i. p. 384.
† *Ibid.*, i. p. 470.

thrift and economical ingenuities, Andersen had found it no easy matter to make both ends meet. The *honoraria* he received from his books were very small. From the first edition of *The Improvisatore* he seems to have made but £19, and this he could only get in driblets and after repeated dunning. When, years afterwards, Andersen told Dickens this, the English novelist could scarcely believe it. "You mean £19 the printer's sheet, I suppose?" said he. "No," replied Andersen, "£19 for the whole work." "Ah! I see we misunderstand each other," insisted Dickens; "you don't mean to tell me you only got £19 for *The Improvisatore* that is to say for the whole work; you must mean £19 a sheet?" Andersen was obliged to contradict his friend, and assure him that such indeed was the lamentable fact. "Good Heavens!" cried Dickens, "it would be perfectly incredible if I didn't have it from your own lips." "It is a fact," adds Andersen, "that my translator (Mrs. Howitt) got more than I the author did." * And yet in those days he considered himself fortunate to get even what he did; indeed, for many of the earlier Fairy Tales he was glad to receive part of his *honorarium* in books† instead of cash. He always bore these privations very bravely, being

* *M. L. E.*, p. 211.
† Bille og Bogh : *Breve fra Andersen*, i. p. 369.

extremely reticent on money matters, even to his
most intimate friends, and never complaining except
so far as his poverty prevented him from taking his
longed-for flying visits abroad, and on this score he
could be bitter enough. "Wretched the author
who is born in a small country," he exclaims. "If I
were French or English, I should have no need of
begging from door to door" [for travelling stipends].
"I should then be rich and independent enough
to go whither I would."* "'Tis a strange poetic
position," he says on another occasion,† "to have
one's features stuck into copper-plates, to be turned
into French and German, to read one's own
biography in one of the leading periodicals of
France, and yet for all that to remain a poor lonely
fellow without any prospects, a sort of Scandinavian
Camoens in fact." He began to feel older too.
Many of the little children he had nursed on his
knee were now engaged or married. He was
inclined to think life a weary business. He began
to dread the winter more and more every year, and
yearn for the summer, that Danish summer, "drawn
by tortoises," that was always so slow to arrive and
so quick to depart, a mere Fata Morgana, as he calls
it. Oh for a whiff from the South! That was the
medicine he wanted. His friends suggested that
he should apply to the King for an annual pension,

---

* Bille og Bogh : *Breve fra Andersen*, i. p. 337.    † *Ibid.* i. p. 395.

and Hauck even drafted a petition for him to copy and present to his Majesty ; but the fear of disappointment kept him back. He liked the idea, but thought it might be carried out some better way ; and presently another of those lucky accidents, or providences, as he preferred to call them, which were always happening to him, brought him at last to the goal.

One day, to his great surprise, Andersen received an invitation to breakfast from Count Rantzau Breitenberg, a minister of State, and one of the most influential men in Denmark. The Count, who knew Italy well, had been so charmed with the descriptions of Italian life and manners in *The Improvisatore*, that he determined to make the acquaintance of its author, took a fancy to him, and inquired if there was anything he could do for him. Andersen at once replied that it was his dearest wish* to go to Italy again, or, failing that, obtain an annual pension. The Count considered both requests reasonable ; promised to think the matter over, and represent the case in the proper quarter, and delighted Andersen by informing him that the attention of the Count had been attracted towards him by the biographical sketch in the *Revue des Deux Mondes*. Months and months passed away, and still Andersen heard not a word about his

* The best account of this is in Andersen's letter to Henrietta Hauck. Bille og Bogh : *Breve fra Andersen*, i. pp. 373, 374. Compare also *M. L. E.*

pension. At last he began to fear that Rantzau's promises were only the usual empty compliments of "such great folks," and meant nothing at all. He did not make due allowances for the diplomatic circuities of a Court, especially such a Court as the Danish, where pensioners were many and money was scarce. However, he jogged the memory of Rantzau in a very skilful letter, which shows that there was a strong ingredient of shrewdness mixed up with his simplicity, and he followed this up by, at last, sending in his petition to the King. He bases his claim on the impossibility of living upon the little that his writings bring him in, and lays great stress on the hardship of being obliged to write for money to the detriment of his art. His friends, Jonas Collin and H. C. Örsted, also used all their efforts on his behalf, and finally, on 26th May, 1838, a Royal resolution granted him a yearly pension of 400 rix dollars (£50) less 12½ per cent. for the widows' fund and the prison tax.* This was not very much, but anyhow it was a certainty, and considerably diminished his anxiety about the future. "I have now a little bread-fruit tree in my poetic garden," he wrote to Ingemann, "so that I no longer need to knock at every one's door for a bit of bread." Shortly afterwards he moved into a breezy attic in the Hôtel du Nord, from whence he had a view of Holmens canal,

* Bille og Bogh : *Breve fra Andersen*, i. p. 433.

the theatre, the market-place, and could just catch a glimpse of the sea, "the dear heaving sea," above a stack of chimneys. He now aspired to be fashionable as well as famous. He sported an expensive frock coat with a velvet collar, and a hat as big as an umbrella,* became a little more particular about the company he kept, and thought twice before accepting an invitation to dinner. His lady friends jokingly complained that he had grown so foppish, that there was no recognising the dear old Andersen who had once been so charmingly original. He could now, they said, be scarcely distinguished from a Court flunkey, or an officer in the Guards. Henrietta Hauck believed, or pretended to believe, that a secret engagement with some unknown fair one was at the bottom of the business; but Andersen protested that he couldn't undertake to fall in love, even to oblige his friends, on less than 1000 rix dollars (£125) a year, or marry on less than 2000 (£250), and before such an impossibility as that took place, the girl he had his eye upon would certainly be carried off by some one else, and he would have to remain a dry old bachelor all his days. There does indeed appear to have been one young lady whom Andersen at this time "thought more than well of," and whom he describes as "pretty, clever, good, amiable, and

* Bille og Bogh : *Breve fra Andersen*, i. p. 421.

belonging to one of the best families." "But," he adds, "I have no means, and don't intend to fall in love. . . . Heaven be praised, she treats me like an elderly gentleman whom she has known all her life."* The truth seems to be that, although Andersen was very fond of the society of ladies, and, as a rule, got on with them much better than he did with men, his attachments never meant anything serious. He was an enemy of all dangerous emotions, and a gossip was much more to his taste than a flirtation. He was perfectly content to find half-a-dozen homes in the families of his intimate friends, instead of making a home of his own, and had quite a host of god-children, who loved him almost as much as their own fathers. His special favourite was his little god-daughter Minni, Edward Collin's child, whom he visited every day if only for a minute.

Thus the dearest wish of Andersen's heart had been gratified at last; he had become a celebrity. "Oh, the joy of life is in my heart," he exclaims. "Every day I feel more and more how much I am appreciated!" Even former adversaries and persecutors now began to extend the hand of fellowship. During the Christmas of 1837, his old rector, Simon Meisling, stopped him in the street; apologised for having treated him so badly at school; admitted that he had

* Bille og Bogh : *Breve fra Andersen*, p. 391.

been mistaken, and begged him in the humblest terms to forgive him, whereat Andersen was moved to tears. On another occasion, at a dinner-party at Heiberg's, who should be his *vis-à-vis* but Molbech, who made himself particularly friendly and agreeable, so that by the time the repast was over they were shaking hands warmly, and on the most intimate terms imaginable. Still, this was no more than a truce, and something must also be allowed for the splendour of Heiberg's hospitality, for Andersen remarks that the guests swam in a perfect sea of costly wine; he would never have believed it possible that a Danish poet could have had such an excellent cellar. Andersen's company, indeed, was now in great request; he moved in the best society, and took a conspicuous part in nearly every public function. Thus on the return of Thorvaldsen to Denmark in 1838, an event celebrated as a national festival, when a splendid banquet was given in honour of the renowned sculptor at the Hôtel d'Angleterre, which was thronged with poets, artists, statesmen, diplomatists, and the *élite* of Danish society, Andersen was chosen, as one of the representatives of Danish literature, to greet the great man, and had composed a poem which he recited on the occasion before an immense and enthusiastic audience. His joy, however, was considerably damped by what he calls the "devilish" conduct of Heiberg, who said to him when he had finished: "You were in such a hurry that nobody could follow you, and I'm sure only a very few could understand the poem; but it doesn't signify a bit; true poetry is *not* understood by the many!" "At the moment," adds Andersen, "I positively hated him." *

And here perhaps it is worth noting that, despite his awkwardness and timidity, Andersen was anything but shy, and never seems to have known what nervousness meant. On the contrary, he was rather pushing than otherwise, and had quite an enviable knack of ferreting out the persons most likely to be useful to him, and engaging their sympathies and assistance, and this too without any officiousness or offensiveness on his part. It would be grossly maligning him to insinuate for a moment that he had anything of the snob about him. He was never ashamed of his lowly birth; he never ran after the rich or the noble; he was always particularly gentle and generous to the neglected, the suffering, and the oppressed. But at the same time he loved to move in the highest circles; he hated to be overlooked; was very exacting in his demands upon his admirers and colleagues, and had quite a horror of being confounded with the vulgar herd. I will give an amusing instance of this refinement of vanity, if I may call it so, which shows how easily a trifle could upset

* Bille og Bogh : *Breve fra Andersen*, i. pp. 445, 446.

him. He went to the theatre one evening towards the end of November 1838, and there saw his friends Thorvaldsen, Oehlenschläger, and Ole Bull in the stalls, while he had to be content with a seat in the pit behind. He was at once aggrieved. "I am not big enough to get there yet," he wrote to Henrietta Hauck, "but 'tis sure to come. Yet it annoys me to be excluded by an iron bar from the place where are nearly all my acquaintances and society friends, while I am obliged to sit by the side of the man who trims my hair." * The fact is that Andersen, despite his wonderful successes, was still dissatisfied, dissatisfied with everything, and most of all with himself. Even his own works did not altogether please him now. He declared that he would willingly destroy, and destroy for ever, one half of what he had hitherto published. A couple of his poems, *The Improvisatore*, and *Only a Fiddler*, a selection of the best scenes from *O. T.* and a few of the Fairy Tales, was all that he cared to preserve, and he even affected to look upon his pet works, *The Improvisatore* and *Only a Fiddler*, as merely tentative essays. As for the "Fairy Tales," he contemptuously dubs them "a mere-sleight-of hand with Fancy's golden apples." It is true that he condescended to add to them from time to time ; but it was only to keep his hand in till he had devised

* Bille og Bogh : *Breve fra Andersen*, i. p. 460.

some masterpiece worthier of him. It was a strange blindness that thus led him to almost despise what the whole world has admired ever since, and just at this very time he was writing some of the most exquisite of these unique little masterpieces. In the summer of 1838 appeared "The Goloshes of Fortune," and during Christmas of the same year: "The Daisy," "The Steadfast Tin Soldier," and "The Wild Swans,"* which were followed at the close of 1839 by "The Garden of Eden," "The Flying Coffer," and "The Storks." The public was now getting accustomed to these stories and beginning to like them, while Örsted, Hauck, and a few other far-seeing men had recognised their unique beauty from the first. But Andersen was not content to be the first of story-tellers. He longed to write something imposing and magnificent, before which even such lustrous stars as Oehlenschläger and Heiberg would pale their ineffectual fires. He felt, he said, that there was a hidden treasure within him which he despaired of ever raising to the surface. Thousands of ideas were blossoming in his heart, and hundreds of images were sweeping through his brain.†
He thought at first of writing an epoch-making romance, with no less a person than the great Napoleon for its hero;‡ but gradually his thoughts

* He got the idea of this beautiful story from a folk-tale in Matthias Winther's collection of *Eventyr*.

† Bille og Bogh : *Breve fra Andersen*, i. p. 422.    ‡ *Ibid.* p. 426.

turned towards the drama, which had always had a fatal fascination for him.  What cared he for the critics ?  They had prophesied that he would never make a great novelist, and he had confuted them with *The Improvisatore*.  He now meant, he said, to show the good folks at home that he was a great dramatist also.  He would compel them, yes, *compel* them, to acknowledge God's own gifts.

# CHAPTER VII

Andersen's passion for the stage—Dramatic tinkering—His first
original drama, "The Mulatto"—His extraordinary enthusiasm
about it—Description of the piece—Molbech's opinion of it—
Fury of Andersen—He appeals from Molbech's verdict—"The
Mulatto" accepted—Death of Frederick VI.—Success of "The
Mulatto"—Andersen congratulated by Christian VIII.—Causes
of "The Mulatto's" success—"The Moorish Girl"—Criticisms of
the dramatic censors—Andersen's silly preface to "The Moorish
Girl"—Failure of "The Moorish Girl"—Heiberg satirises
Andersen in "A Soul after Death"—Andersen on his travels
again—Liszt at Hamburg—First experience of railway travelling—Comical adventures on the road—The brutal Englishman—Andersen ill at Naples—Departure for Greece—The
Persian and the little bird—"Yes, sir, verily, verily!"—Impressions of Athens—Riding lessons—Constantinople—The dancing
dervishes—Muhammad's birthday—The mists of the Euxine—
A dull journey down the Danube—In quarantine at Orsova—
Ainsworth his fellow-prisoner—His description of Andersen—A
lecture on locomotion by steam—Andersen's jaundiced state of
mind on his return—"En Digter's Bazar"—Opinions of the
critics.

ANDERSEN had a perfect passion for the stage. Next
to writing a comedy, it was his greatest pleasure to
see one acted; the theatre was always the most likely
place to find him in of an evening, and he knew as

much about plays and playwrights, actors and actresses as any man living. It was the ambition of his life to shine as a dramatist of the first rank, on a stage which could boast of one of the noblest *réper-toires* in Europe, and this ambition, though never realised, was never abandoned. No amount of snub-bing could turn him from his purpose, and he stuck to his hopeless task with a tenacity that was truly heroic. The last four years had been the busiest of his life, and yet he had found time to do a little dramatic tinkering, or, as he himself more poetically expresses it, "to rest for a while in the ascent of the mountain of art and weave a light little wreath of Alpine flowers."* In plain English, between 1835 and the beginning of 1839 he had translated or adapted from German, French, and Italian sources no less than seven operettas, or vaudevilles,† every one of

* Bille og Bogh: *Breve fra Andersen*, i. p. 320.

† (1) Jan. 1835, " Liden Kirsten " (Little Kirsten), a two-act operetta; (2) June 1836, " En Rolig Aften" (A Merry Evening), one-act vaudeville ; (3) same month, " Renzo's Bryllup " (Renzo's Wedding) ; (4) April 1836, " En rigtig Soldat " (A real Soldier), one-act operetta ; (5) Feb. 1837, " Souffleuren's Benefise " (The Prompter's Benefit), one-act vaudeville ; (6) May 1836, " En Odeland " (A Prodigal) ; (7) " Jabo de Veres," one-act dramatic freak. Molbech said of No. 1 that it was less insipid, but thinner and poorer than former works by the same hand ; of No. 2, that it had no dramatic or scenic interest whatever; of No. 3, that it made him pity the Danish composer who was reduced to accept Mr. Andersen's libretto ; of No. 4, that it was written for schoolboys by a schoolboy ; and of No. 5, that it was hopelessly out of date ; No. 6 he rejected without comment ; while No. 7 he called " trivial, witless nonsense." As regards No. 7, however, this Aristar-

which was ruthlessly massacred in turn by the cruelly unflinching Molbech in his most approved style. Andersen's feelings may be imagined. He frequently complained that he would have starved to death long ago, if the success of his career had depended upon Molbech. But what supported him through all these disappointments was the stern resolve to put the churlish censor to silence by producing a dramatic masterpiece, the grandeur of which all but the spiritually blind would be forced to recognise at the very first glance. Hitherto he had given only the fag ends of his time to the drama, now he would devote himself to it entirely. So he set to work with a will, and during the best part of 1838 could think and talk of nothing but his new work. This time he went all the way to the West Indies for an inspiration (the hero of the play being a mulatto from Martinique), and read a whole library of books about Africa and America to get up the proper quantity and quality of local colouring. He jubilantly informed

chus was much at fault, or Andersen must have greatly improved it, for on being re-cast and sent in again in Sept. 1839, under the title of "Den Usynlige fra Sprogö" (The Invisible at Sprogö), it was accepted, and Foersom played the principal part with such comic originality, that the whole house was in roars of laughter from beginning to end, and it had a run of twenty-one nights. In 1855 it formed part of the Casino's *répertoire*, and had a run of twenty-eight nights. L. Möller said of it, that for unity of action and general perfection, it was superior to anything Andersen ever wrote for the theatre.

his friends that he was now quite at home among niggers and ostriches, and dreamt every night of slimy anacondas wriggling in the rank grass, and of transparent skies full of meteors. As the work grew beneath his hands, he became more and more enthusiastic. It was to make as great an epoch in his life as ever *The Improvisatore* had done. "There is not a trace of Andersen about it," he exclaims,* "and the hero will be portrayed with a fiery energy which more than makes up for the alleged flabbiness of the heroes of my best novels." He is certain that it will be accounted his most original and perfect work. The tropical sun which burns in his breast all the time he is writing it, makes him, he says, absolutely insensible to the severity of the Danish winter outside his study, nay, the cold rather does him good than otherwise. His friends, especially his lady friends, to whom he read long extracts from the play as it proceeded, seem to have been equally delighted with it, and the actor Nielsen and his wife predicted for it a tremendous success. The writer of these lines frankly admits that it was with great expectations that he began to read a play heralded with such a flourish of trumpets; but he laid it down after a careful and conscientious perusal with the feeling that he had been grossly deceived. *Mulatten* (The Mulatto), for such was the ultimate title of this

* Bille og Bogh : *Breve fra Andersen*, i. p. 477.

strange production, is in fact the sort of thing which
might perhaps be honourably mentioned in the
reports of an Aborigines Protection Society, but
certainly does not rank very high as literature. The
hero, Horatio, is a mulatto of Martinique, who wins
the gratitude of two white ladies, Eleonora and
Cecilia, the wife and ward respectively of a planter,
by saving them from a revengeful runaway slave who
has suffered severely from the planter's tyranny.
The ladies are surprised to find classical tastes and
romantic aspirations in a young man of colour, and
both of them, especially the ward, fall in love with
him before they are well aware of it. The interven-
tion of the planter, La Rebellière, a demon of the
Legré type, threatens to turn an idyll into a tragedy.
Horatio is shot down, and only not killed outright
because La Rebellière, partly from jealousy, partly
from sheer brutality, has reserved him to be whipped
to death on the morrow; but at the very moment
when the unfortunate mulatto is about to be delivered over to his hideous fate, Cecilia, who happens
to come of age on that very day, first manumits
and then marries him, to the joy of all the
negroes and half-breeds, and the utter confusion
of the fiendish planter. Such, spun out into five
acts of very commonplace rhyming verse, is the
plot of "The Mulatto," without doubt one of
the feeblest of Andersen's works. Even *Agnete*

which, with all its faults, contained some really fine lyrics, is far superior to it. It may seem almost incredible that an author of Andersen's great poetic gifts, should have written no less than 106 pages of verse which contain not a single line worth remembering, but such is the simple fact. A piece at once so poor and so pretentious, was of course fair game for a censor like Molbech, and it suffered severely from his vitriolic pleasantry. After briefly epitomising the plot, he proceeds to show (not a very difficult task) that "this sketch," as he calls it, is trivial, bald, and without any real dramatic interest or true poetic life whatever. The characters he considers wrongheaded, affected, and vaguely incoherent abstractions, who talk nothing but bombast, and the plot forced and unnatural. Finally, he sees no difference between this play and the crude vaudeville, "The Spaniards in Odense," that Mr. Andersen wrote five years before (indeed if he, Molbech, *had* to choose between two such sour apples, he would prefer a bite from the latter), and he declares that in common justice to other rejected pieces he cannot conscientiously advise the Directors of the Royal Theatre to accept "The Mulatto."

It is not to be supposed that Andersen actually *saw* Molbech's censure, but he heard of it in due course, no doubt through Jonas Collin, who was one of Molbech's co-censors, and his first emotion was not so much grief, or even rage, as sheer amazement. He had such a high opinion of this new piece himself, that he could scarcely believe his ears. Molbech had dared, actually *dared*, to set himself up against the performance of "The Mulatto."* But Andersen did not mean to let matters rest there. He was no longer the poor-devil author of five years ago. He now had influential patrons on his side, and an admiring public behind him, so he determined to defy Molbech. "He would tread me into the dust," he wrote to Henrietta Hauck, "but I mean to live in spite of him, live when he stands like a dead name in an old folio. God is with me, and they shall bow down before me, as the sun and moon did in Joseph's dream." To his friend Edward Collin he addressed himself in a still more peremptory style. "I am not going to be trodden down by a tyrant," he exclaims. "My piece *must* be played. I cannot and *will* not put up with this injustice. My friends must either take my part or give me up."† And his friends did take his part. The play was referred to Holstein, the chief director of the Royal Theatre, whom every one regarded as a sort of High Court of Appeal in such matters, while Andersen bet the actor Nielsen a bottle of champagne that "The Mulatto" would create a furore such as no other piece had done for the last twenty years, and prove

* Bille og Bogh : *Breve fra Andersen*, i. p.482.   † Collin, p. 311.

the deathblow of the detested Molbech's critical reputation.*

Holstein read "The Mulatto," and on the whole liked it. He agreed, indeed, with Molbech that it had no particular dramatic interest, that it very often sinned against good taste, and that its hero was a mere phrasemaker ; but, on the other hand, it seemed to him to have many interesting characters, exciting incidents, piquant situations, and novel striking ideas ; he gave it as his opinion that, despite its defects, it would take with the public, and prove a paying concern—and it was accordingly accepted.†

It was in April 1839 that Holstein recommended "The Mulatto" to the Directorate of the Royal Theatre, but it was not till December of the same year that the rehearsals began. Andersen assisted at the final dress rehearsal, and was delighted at the

* *Apropos* of "The Mulatto," Collin tells us an anecdote which shows us how obstinately Andersen could hold his own when his " spiritual children " were concerned, and how adroitly he could resort to repartee. A Danish West Indian objected, somewhat coarsely, that a love affair between a white woman and a man of colour, as described in Andersen's play, was impossible, because the mulatto had such a nasty smell. " Ah ! " said Andersen, " but I can insert this line in the proper place : Thy smell is foul, and yet I love thee still."

† Holstein, moreover, was rather surprised that Andersen should have borrowed the idea of this play from a second-rate French novel, *Les Épaves*. " 'Od's death," said he to Andersen, " I cannot understand why it is that you, who write romances yourself, do not make a comedy out of one of your own romances. Nobody can prevent you from doing that." Both Molbech's and Holstein's reports are in Collin, pp. 305-9.

way in which the actors played their parts. It went off brilliantly. Madame Heiberg,* in particular, who took the *rôle* of Cecilia, transported every one by her interpretation of the planter's ward. That night Andersen was absolutely feverish with excitement, and could not sleep a wink. He was haunted, besides, by the apprehension that the old King would die before the piece was fairly launched, for his Majesty had long been ailing, and the latest report was that a change for the worse might be expected at any moment. However, he was up again at dawn, although it was mid-winter, and posted at his window watching the machinists carrying the palm-trees, the mulatto's bed, and the booths for the slave-market scene into the theatre, until late into the day. The posters were all up, crowds of people began assembling at the doors to wait for the box-office to open, and every one was agog with expectation, for the play had now become the talk of the whole town. Then mounted *estafettes* dashed through the streets, the gates of the city were closed, sorrowful groups gathered at the street corners, and the melancholy tidings spread that

---

* This beautiful and accomplished woman, whose maiden name was Johanna Louisa Pætges, did almost as much for the Danish stage as her gifted husband, who married her when she was only nineteen. Andersen himself has said of her that if she had been born in France or Germany instead of little Denmark, she would have been accounted one of the greatest actresses in Europe.

King Frederick VI. had died at half-past eight that
morning.* For the next month Copenhagen was
like a huge house of mourning, and all the theatres
were closed. The old King had been so beloved
that his death was looked upon as a public calamity.†
In his bitter disappointment, however, Andersen
forgot for the moment that Frederick VI. had been
his benefactor also, and almost took it as a personal
grievance that he should have died at such an
inopportune moment. For the next few days he
was quite sick at heart, and could take no interest
in anything. But the month passed more quickly
than he had anticipated, and at last, early in February,
the long-deferred first night of "The Mulatto"
arrived. Andersen was in his usual place in the
theatre in a dreadful state of suspense, which almost
grew into agony as the piece proceeded. During
the first act the audience was "horribly quiet," even
the best scenes failed to rouse them, and the poor
author began to feel very angry. But when the
fourth act was reached, "a little southern blood
came into their veins," and by the time the fifth
act began the temper of the house was wound up to
a positively tragic pitch.‡ The curtain fell amidst a

* Bille og Bogh : *Breve fra Andersen*, i. pp. 518, 519.
 † His last words were characteristic of the man. On feeling the
chill of death creeping over him he exclaimed : " It is getting cold ; we
must see that the poor folks have fuel."
‡ Bille og Bogh : *Breve fra Andersen*, i. 526, 527.

perfect tempest of applause. Andersen had never
heard any piece clapped so enthusiastically before;
he was positively frightened. A few days later the
new King, Christian VIII., sent for him, and warmly
congratulated him; he obtained the long-coveted
distinction of a place in the Court stalls alongside
Oehlenschläger and Thorvaldsen; all the papers
lauded the new piece and its author to the skies, and
a whole string of counts and excellencies waited
upon him with their congratulations. It is true that
a few of the best judges still held back. For instance,
Oehlenschläger did not take quite so enthusiastic a
view of the play as the more impulsive Thorvaldsen,
who clapped his hands sore; the critical Heiberg,
whose opinion Andersen valued most of all, remained
discreetly silent; while Molbech never showed his
face in the theatre at all; still it was the greatest
public triumph that Andersen had yet experienced,
and he was proportionately grateful. On the second
and third nights the theatre was so crowded that not
a place was to be had for love or money, and
the whole audience seemed enchanted with the play
from beginning to end. Then the King again sent
for Andersen, and presented him with a breast-pin
set with nineteen diamonds as a souvenir of the late
monarch, a token of his own royal favour, and a
recognition of the young author's talents. The conversation naturally turned upon "The Mulatto," and

Christian VIII. said he meant to come and see the piece himself.* He was as good as his word, for on the eleventh night he was present in the Royal box, and, in the interval between the acts, looked across to the stalls, and nodded to Andersen. As such a thing had never been known to happen before in a Danish theatre, Andersen could not conceive that the Royal greeting was meant for him till his Majesty repeated it so often, and so emphatically, that there could be no doubt about it.†

"The Mulatto" had a run of twenty-one nights, an extraordinary success in those days, and therefore more than justified Holstein's prediction that it would pay. Andersen must have cleared more than the 1000 rix dollars (£125) he had originally looked for, and was able to put by something towards that tour to the East on which he had been bent ever since he returned from Italy. On the other side of the Sound "The Mulatto" also caught the popular fancy. It was speedily translated into Swedish, and received with applause at the Royal Theatre at Stockholm. When Andersen, to escape the dulness of Holy Week, skipped over into Scania in 1840,‡

* It is characteristic both of Andersen's vanity and his _naïveté_ that at both audiences he told the monarch, in confidence, of some petty attacks that had been made upon the play by a portion of the Press. The King, who no doubt knew his man thoroughly, condoled with him, and sent him away comforted on both occasions.

† Bille og Bogh : _Breve fra Andersen_, i. p. 551.

‡ The southernmost province of Sweden.

the students of the University of Lund gave him a perfect ovation, and the Rector, in a congratulatory address, alluded to "The Mulatto" as beautifully illustrating the triumph of mind over circumstances.

It may seem odd that such a very poor play should have won the public favour so easily, but "The Mulatto" owed its success partly to the excellent acting of Madame Heiberg and the Nielsens, and partly to the just and noble sentiment underlying it—viz., that true merit is independent of race and colour, which was so completely in unison with the liberal ideas of the day. Andersen, however, made the very natural mistake of supposing that the success of his play was entirely due to its own intrinsic merits, and at once set about increasing his reputation by a fresh dramatic masterpiece. At the very time when "The Mulatto" was drawing crowded houses he was already at work upon another play, entitled *Maurerpigen* (The Moorish Girl), which he assured his admiring and sympathetic lady friends would be even better than "The Mulatto." Miss Hetty Wulff declared that this was impossible. "Nay," replied Andersen, "it *is* better, ever so much better, or else I should despair of myself." In seven months "The Moorish Girl" was finished ("The Mulatto" had taken eighteen to write), and its author was more than satisfied with it. The idea of it, too, was entirely his own; no one could reproach him, as they had done with regard to his former "original drama," with stealing it from a French novel or from anywhere else. "It is far, far above 'The Mulatto,'" he exclaims; "and, for the first time in my life, I feel certain that I am a dramatic author."*

"The Moorish Girl," it must be admitted, is not only more original, but more interesting than its predecessor. It is the story of a heroic Spanish peasant-girl, Raphaella, with whom the King of Cordova, whose life she has saved in battle, falls in love. Raphaella, however, flies from the dangers of a Court to her native mountains, where she throws herself away upon a worthless young Spanish hidalgo, Zavala, who, soon tiring of her, seeks fresh amatory distractions in the Court of the Moorish king. Adding treason to treachery, Zavala presently leads the Moors against his own native city of Cordova by secret mountain paths, but is interrupted by Raphaella and her brave peasants, and shot dead. The Moorish king, who turns out to be Raphaella's father, is released, while her own king, who now owes his crown as well as his life to her, takes her back to his capital to be his bride. But the Princess of France, to whom he has been affianced, has already arrived there, and the Archbishop will not consent to marry the king to a mere peasant-girl (especially

* Collin, p. 320.

N

as she has Moorish blood in her veins) at the risk of a war with France. The King of Cordova, indeed, is bent upon marrying Raphaella, and none else; but the heroic damsel, with the connivance of the Archbishop, contrives to palm the princess off upon the king, in the very bridal robes that had been made for herself, and then simplifies matters by hurling herself off a rock into the abyss below. There are some fine songs in " The Moorish Girl"; the local colouring is natural and picturesque; a faint odour of orange-blossoms seems to hang about it from beginning to end, yet it is but a slight poetic toy, which has nothing of a drama about it save a division into acts and scenes. The *dramatis personæ* are mere abstractions without the least individuality; there is not material enough in the plot to have made a couple of acts, to say nothing of five; and the strained and violent *dénoûment* is only explicable on the hypothesis that the author was at his wit's end how to get rid of his heroine. That the piece abounds with solecisms and anachronisms goes without saying.

" The Moorish Girl " was finished early in August 1840, and the same month it was sent in to the theatrical censors. Molbech declined to give any opinion whatever as to its merits. It is evident from his curt memorandum * that the recollection

* Collin, pp. 321, 322.

of "The Mulatto," which had succeeded in spite of his verdict, was still a sore point with him. He simply observed that there was no moral or political objection to the new play, but advised the directors of the theatre to consider very carefully beforehand whether it was likely to repay the very heavy expense (especially in the Alhambra scenes) which would have to be incurred in mounting it properly. Jonas Collin, on the other hand, predicted for "The Moorish Girl" a success equal at least to that of "The Mulatto," and therefore strongly advised its acceptance. There can be no doubt whatever that it was Collin's sympathy with and fatherly solicitude for Andersen that made him, as one of the theatrical censors, vote in favour of "The Moorish Girl" on this occasion ; but he took the precaution first of all to consult J. L. Heiberg on the matter, whose authority on all things theatrical was then regarded as absolutely infallible. That sharp-sighted critic, himself the leading dramatist of the day, shook his head doubtfully over "The Moorish Girl." He said that he had expected something much more satisfactory from the author of "The Mulatto." Did the author himself know what he was about when he wrote it ? Why had he written it at all ? What was there in it that had made him so enthusiastic about it ? What was there in it that could rivet the attention of the public, or excite its sympathy ?

Nothing, so far as he could see. The whole poetic intention of the piece seemed to him vague and unsettled. It was called a tragedy, but he could see no necessity at all in it for a tragic *dénoûement*. It bore marks of extreme haste, and both the style and versification left very much to be desired. In fine, he declared the play had not got what every good acting play ought to have—a point, or if it had, the point was so cunningly concealed that the public would never find it out. Such an opinion from such a critic was an absolute sentence of death,* and Andersen felt this himself. He was infinitely chagrined that Heiberg, of all persons in the world, Heiberg, whom he had always looked up to and admired, should have turned " cold and hostile " towards him, as he expressed it, but he durst not question the verdict of such an authority. " The Moorish Girl " instantly fell at least fifty per cent. in his own estimation. The masterpiece from which he had expected the greatest joy, had now lost all worth and interest in his eyes. Then his friends, the Collins, Örsted, and Oehlenschläger, thought the best thing they could do with him was to pack him off abroad again. They saw that he was in a morbidly irritable state, which made everything at home intolerable and abominable to him, and they bade him in Heaven's name to be off. He did not need twice

* Collin, pp. 323, 324.

J. L. HEIBERG.

telling, but left his unhappy piece to its fate, and departed with the firm conviction that æsthetic cliques and envious cabals were bent upon compassing his ruin.* To die abroad, he said, was now his dearest wish. Before leaving Copenhagen, however, he did one of those foolish things which he always regretted so bitterly immediately afterwards. He had "The Moorish Girl" printed and wrote a preface to it, which even his friend Edward Collin is obliged to call a whining recapitulation of all his sufferings past and present. It certainly is a perfect monument of childish boastfulness, wounded vanity, and tearful expostulation.† In this preface, after alluding to his "hard childhood," to the mocking and derision that had ever been his portion at home, the malice of critics, the wickedness of those who pursued him abroad with malignant poems in unfranked letters, he proceeds to recount all his triumphs also. His romances, he says, have been translated in Sweden and Germany; in the German papers he is regarded as one of the foremost of Danish notabilities; his life has been sketched in various foreign languages; he has won recognition in Germany, and no doubt his fame will have preceded him to Constantinople. Then he adds that "two kings have encouraged his

* See *M. L. S.*, p. 233, which must not, however, be taken literally.

† See preface to *Maurerpigen* first Danish edition, in British Museum; the book is rather a curiosity. The preface was suppressed in later editions.

talents," that he has found "upright friends among
Denmark's noblest and greatest," and that while only
"a few solitary individuals" are against him, the
public, as a whole, is on his side. The critics were
not slow to take up this silly challenge.   "As now,"
said one of them, "as now he has summed up all his
receipts and expenditure (carefully booked they are
no doubt), and finds, on striking a balance, that kings,
and great men, and the public are on his side, it is
surely pretty plain that on the whole he has not so
very much to complain of, and perhaps had no great
need to travel all the way to Turkey to forget a petty
slight." *   Then dropping his bantering tone, the
same writer proceeds to take Andersen to task for
that "literary vanity" which destroys all true inspiration.   "In Andersen's dramatic poetry," he concludes, "there reigns an eternal self-obscuration, for
between the light of poetry and the poetising individuality, the person of Andersen himself intrudes
like an unbidden guest, and refracts all the rays."
Bitter as it was, this was sound and salutary advice ;
unfortunately, like most good advice, it was absolutely
ignored by the person to whom it was addressed.

Meanwhile preparations were being made for producing "The Moorish Girl," but that unlucky piece
seems to have been born beneath a malignant star.
Madame Heiberg, whom Andersen had counted

* Collin, pp. 325–327.

upon to play the principal part, would not so much
as look at it. Andersen became urgent, and the
actress refused again so emphatically, that the author
went away deeply wounded, and bitterly complained
to his private friends that she had used him hardly.
But Jonas Collin, and Andersen's other friends, with
whom it had now become a point of honour to see
the piece through during his absence, still persevered
with it. No expense was spared in mounting it;*
and on December 18, 1840, while Andersen was at
Rome, "The Moorish Girl" was acted in the Royal
Theatre in Copenhagen for the first time. The
handsome decorations and the beautiful dresses
were applauded, Hartmann's music gave satisfaction,
and Madame Holst did all that could be done with
the principal part, and yet the piece proved a complete failure. It failed to excite any interest, and
the frequent interruptions of the action by the
endless songs, dances, and processions, which formed
part of it, were more than the public could stand.
It was only acted twice and then withdrawn,† it
must have cost the theatre a pretty penny.

* Yet Andersen ungratefully complains in his Autobiography that
the scenery was inadequate, and one of the causes of its failure.

† Compare J. Collin's affectionate letter of condolence in Bille og
Bogh, *Breve til Andersen*, pp. 114, 115, and Collin, p. 328 : "I need not
assure you, my dear good Andersen," wrote J. Collin on this occasion, "how much this result has grieved us all, especially as you had
promised yourself so much from this piece, and partly based the plan
of your tour upon it."

Nor was this all that poor Andersen had to put up with, for he was now to receive a fresh flout, of itself indeed trifling enough, but exceedingly hard to bear because of the hand that gave it.

Early in 1841 Heiberg published a volume of poems which contained some of that brilliant and accomplished writer's happiest inspirations. The principal piece in this collection was the equally witty and profound poetico-satirical comedy *En Sjæl efter Döden* (A Soul after Death), the fundamental idea of which was the assumption that existence in Hell is absolutely identical with the frivolous aimless, sort of life which the majority of well-to-do idle people actually live on this earth. The leading personage is a selfish superficial philistine with a tincture of modern liberalism, who, rejected alike from the Christian Heaven and the heathen Elysium, finds rest at last with the rogue Mephistopheles, who pronounces him perfectly qualified to continue his earthly existence amidst the trivialities of Hell. Mephistopheles takes his *protégé* the round of the infernal regions, and shows him its curiosities, accompanying his explanations with a running commentary that has well been called "a perfect shower-bath of satire," on the political, dramatical, and educational follies of the day. Andersen is among the exhibits in Heiberg's Hell, not Andersen the tale-teller, indeed, (*him* the clear-sighted critic had been the first to recognise), but Andersen the dramatist, whose theatrical platitudes the brilliant inventor of the Danish vaudeville naturally regarded as so many buffets on the cheek of good taste. Mephistopheles, therefore, is made to point "the long poet" out to the soul that he is chaperoning, and after a few words of introduction thus hits him off :*

"In Constantinople he means to increase
His fame by achieving a fresh masterpiece.
The Seraglio amidst, free from critics' vexation,
He stands like a long note of interrogation,
And while the chief eunuch his temples doth crown,
And the tag-rag and bob-tail right humbly bow down,
His "Mulatto" he reads the Harem to content,
And his "Moor Girl" to those whom the Turks would torment."

It will be seen that, after all, there was much more of mirth than of malice in these lines; but Andersen's friends the Collins, well aware of the irritable state of mind he was in just then, were anxious, if possible, to prevent him from seeing this *jeu d'esprit* till his return, and took all imaginable precautions accordingly. As it turned out, they would have done very much better to have sent him a copy of the book instead, for some of Andersen's lady friends, who made it their business to keep him well posted up with the gossip of the town, duly informed

* Of course any translation of these witty lines must be merely tentative. Very much of the point is necessarily lost in the process.

him, without going into particulars, that Heiberg
had given him a good jacketing ; that all the town
was in roars of laughter over it, and that they
themselves were equally indignant and annoyed at
the insult thus inflicted on him during his absence.
Andersen, who justly remarks that it is doubly painful to be laughed at when one does not know what
one is being laughed at for, at once jumped to the
conclusion that something absolutely outrageous had
been said about him, and what would have seemed
little more than a cold *douche* to him if he had
actually had the book in his hand, now affected him
like "molten lead dropped into an open wound."*
He fired up at once,† and in his first fury sat down
and scribbled off a doggerel epistle against Heiberg,
full of gall and venom, which the poet Holst, who
was his fellow-traveller at the time, fortunately
prevented him from sending.   Then he overwhelmed
Heiberg with torrents of billingsgate, and turned
savagely upon Holst for taking Heiberg's part, and
admiring a poem that was an attack upon himself,
so that it very nearly came to a quarrel between
them.   However, his wrath subsided as quickly as it
had arisen, and it must also be borne in mind that
he was suffering at the time from a combination of
neuralgia and dyspepsia which would have tried the

* *M. L. E.*, p. 240.
† See Holst's amusing letter to Edward Collin (Collin, pp. 330, 331).

patience of Job. Nevertheless he seems to have had
an inkling throughout that Heiberg was in the
right about his play after all, and certainly for
Heiberg, both as a poet and a critic, he always
entertained an extraordinary respect. At any rate,
though he deeply resented his criticism, he could
never regard him as he did the crabbed and
morose Molbech. There was something about the
serenely urbane and delicately trenchant Heiberg's
personality, which both charmed and awed Andersen,
and to the very last Heiberg's house possessed a
peculiar and irresistible attraction for him that no
other place ever could have.* So Andersen gradually
consoled himself. The failure of "The Moorish Girl,"
he said, was, after all, only a single drop in the
bitter cup he had to swallow. As time went on he
could even be merry at his own expense. He jocosely
observed, for instance, that while his sons, *The
Improvisatore*, "The Mulatto," and "The Fiddler"
did him credit, his daughters, on the other hand,
*Agnete* and "The Moorish Girl," had hitherto been
more of a burden than a comfort to him, which made
him a bit anxious about future daughters, for he
foresaw that more daughters there would certainly
be. Nay, when on his return he read Heiberg's
poem through for the first time, he admitted that

* Heiberg, too, liked Andersen, and did the fullest justice to his
genius.

there was really nothing in it to take offence at, and that if he had been an occasion of wit to so great a satirist, both Heiberg and Denmark ought to be grateful to him for it.

But now let us follow Andersen on his travels.

ANDERSEN, ÆTAT. CIRCA 35

It was in the autumn of 1840 that he quitted Copenhagen, and after a few days' stay at Count Rantzau's castle in Holstein, where he was treated in princely style, proceeded to Hamburg.*    Here

* By far the best account of this tour, which lasted eight months,

he saw and heard for the first time the world-
renowned Liszt, whose fantastic rhapsodies greatly
impressed him. There seemed to him to be something demoniacal about this lean young man with
the long dark hair hanging about his pale face;
but it was a suffering demoniac, who had to play
his soul free at the piano. At Magdeburg,
where he arrived after a wearying thirty-six hours'
journey in a dusty diligence, he took a railway
ticket for Dresden, though not without considerable misgivings. Railway travelling was quite
a new experience to him, and the din, bustle,
and confusion of the station so overwhelmed him
that he scarcely knew whether he was standing
on his head or his heels. He stared at the vans
and engines ("itinerant chimneys" he calls them)
with stupid amazement, and when he did pluck
up sufficient courage to get into his compartment, it was with the intimate persuasion that
he would either be blown up or dashed to pieces
at an early stage of the journey. The starting
signal seemed to him to have much in common
with " the swan-song of a pig at the moment when
the butcher's knife cuts its throat;" but his confidence gradually revived when he perceived that

is to be found in *En Digters Bazar.* Compare also Bille og Bogh,
*Breve fra Andersen,* ii. pp. 1–46 ; Collin, pp. 329–35 ; and *M. I.. E.*,
pp. 234–52.

the train glided as easily over the rails as a sledge over frozen snow, while the swift rate of progression absolutely delighted him. It was just the mode of travelling he had been longing for all his life, and he had now, he says, a capital idea of what the flight of birds of passage must be. He had some amusing experiences on the way which he takes care to record. At one place he caught sight of some planking which seemed to contract into a single stake, so rapidly did it flash past, and the next moment a man sitting beside him said: "Did you see that? That was a boundary mark. We are now in the principality of Cöthen!" and offered him his snuff-box. Andersen bowed, tried the snuff, sneezed, and then enquired: "How long shall we be in Cöthen?" "Oh!" replied the man, "we had already got out of it while you were sneezing!" Andersen took to this new mode of locomotion from the first; thought it in every way vastly superior to the old coaching journeys, and ridicules the notion that railways are likely to destroy the poetry of travel in terms which would not, I am afraid, meet with the approval of Mr. Ruskin. When they reach Leipsic, Andersen stopped to make the acquaintance of Mendelssohn, who had been so fascinated by the perusal of his *Only a Fiddler* that he had sent him a general invitation, and, although very busy now, received him with open arms, and wrote him a "Lied ohne Wörter" in his album. At Munich Andersen saw on a bookstall a German edition of his *Improvisatore* forming part of a "Miniature Library of Foreign Classics." He at once stepped into the shop, and asked for the book, whereupon the young shopman gave him the first volume of it.

"But I want the whole work?" said Andersen.

"That *is* the whole work," replied the young man; "there is no more of it. I ought to know, for I have read it myself."

"But don't you think then that it ends a little abruptly, and that there is no *dénoûment?*" asked Andersen.

"Well, yes!" admitted the other; "but it is in much the same style as the French romances, you know. The author just *suggests* a conclusion, and leaves the reader to fill it up in his own mind."

"At any rate that is not the case here," interrupted Andersen; "this is only the first part that you have given me."

"I tell you," cried the shopman, getting angry, "that that is all. I have *read* it!"

"But I *wrote* it!" retorted Andersen.

He reached his beloved Italy early in December, and it was all as familiar to him as if he had only been away from it a single day. All the way from Florence to Rome, which he travelled by car, he

o

had as one of his fellow-passengers a stout, sandy-whiskered Englishman, encased in wraps up to the very eyes,* whose conduct was so intolerably boorish, that long afterwards Andersen's blood used to boil at the very thought of him, though, at first, the very coolness of the fellow's impudence was an amusing novelty. The other passengers were a pale young English priest of the Camaldulense order, who did nothing but read his hours, cross himself, and close his eyes in silent prayer from morn till night; a young Italian priest, who was a little more sociable, and a Roman signora with a little spindle-shanked husband who dressed like an *abbate*. The first night they put up at a lonely inn, where they arrived wet to the skin and half frozen. They had to shiver for an unconscionable time in the bare stony guest-chamber, before a few twigs and sticks could be found to make an apology for a fire, and just as it was at last beginning to burn up, in came the Englishman with his wet clothes over his arm, which he hung up forthwith on a screen round the fire. "I want 'em to have a good steaming," he condescended to explain. As the rest of the company put up with this impudence, Andersen had to put up with it too, and so the Englishman's wet clothes got all the little warmth there was. That

* Andersen says of him elsewhere that he had the self-assurance of a flunkey and the bearing of a tallow-chandler.

night Andersen and the Englishman had to share
the same bedroom, but the latter took care to slip
away first, and when Andersen entered the room,
he found this son of Albion standing on his
(Andersen's) counterpane which he had spread out
on the floor, and engaged in making his bolster a
little higher with two of Andersen's pillows which
he had coolly appropriated.

"I don't like lying low!" said the Englishman,
by way of explanation.

"Neither do I!" replied Andersen, restoring the
pillows to their proper place, to the infinite amazement of the Englishman.

The next day they stopped at Castellone to dine.
Here the Englishman made such a racket, and
chivied the people of the inn about so unmercifully,
that every one was convinced he must be a prince in
disguise at the very least, and in the fond expectation of a really royal largess from him, allowed themselves to be kicked and cursed, ran all his errands,
and smiled and bowed at everything he said and did
—and after all he didn't give them a farthing.
"For I am very dissatisfied," said he; "I am
dissatisfied with the food, the house, and the
attendance—with everything, in fact." And the
crestfallen domestics bowed still lower, and both
the priests were so impressed that as he got into
the car again, they took off their hats to him. At

Assisi, where they visited the church Dei Angeli, the Englishman insisted upon having the guide all to himself, as he could not see things properly in company, and the monk who acted as his *cicerone* got neither money nor thanks for his pains. "These fellows have nothing else to do," said he. This was too much for the Roman Signora, who up to this time had been very friendly with him, and she reproached him for his stinginess. Henceforth a coolness sprang up between them. They no longer sang duets together, nor did she, as heretofore, feed him with sweet biscuits in the short intervals between his enormous meals. At Atricoli, where the "pavement seemed to have been laid while an earthquake was going on," and the inn was so luxuriantly filthy that Andersen preferred to eat his dinner in the stable, the Englishman's ever increasing rudeness contributed still further to make this pleasure tour a sort of penitential pilgrimage. He made a raid upon the food of another party of travellers, insulted the good-natured priest, and even began to talk uncivilly to the Signora. At Civita Castellana Andersen positively refused to share his bedroom with the brute any longer, so the priest, the Signora, and the Signora's husband made him a sort of couch on a couple of chairs, in the midst of which operation the Englishman came rushing in as red as fire, and boiling over with rage

at Andersen's refusal to keep him company.
"What," he cried, "would you have me lie. and be
murdered in this den of thieves, all by myself?
You're not a good comrade, and I won't speak
another word to you all the rest of the way." "For
which," says Andersen, "I thanked him from the
bottom of my heart." But the climax was reached
when they came to La Sterta, and the Englishman,
making his way incontinently to the fireplace,
began taking what he liked best from the pots and
pans that were simmering there, which brought the
landlady down upon him, and a battle-royal ensued.
She rushed upon him with her kitchen knife, while
he defended himself with a chair, till just as every-
one fancied murder was about to be done, the landlady's husband came to the rescue by catching his
irate spouse round her ample waist, and lifting her
bodily off her feet. She, however, took it out in
abuse, while the Englishman revenged himself by
eating for three and paying for one, besides grossly
insulting the Signora and her husband ; whereupon
the whole company put him into coventry and
would have nothing more to say to him. "Never,"
says Andersen, himself the soul of courtesy "never
have I met a man with such a—what shall I call it
—such an unconscious shamelessness. Everything
existed only for him, every one had to give way for
his convenience. He never tried to utter a com-

pliment which did not turn to rudeness in his mouth. At last, while in his society, I could not help thinking of the wicked stepmother who, after her husband's daughter had come back from the well into which she had thrown her, and gold and roses fell out of the girl's mouth whenever she talked, cast her own wicked daughter into the well, thinking it would fare the same with her; but when she came up she was worse than ever, for at every word she uttered a frog or a lizard sprang out of her mouth. The more I saw of the Englishman, the more I heard him talk, the more certain I became that he must be a veritable brother of the stepmother's wicked daughter."

At Rome Andersen had rather a miserable time of it. The weather was cold and wet, he suffered severely from toothache,* he missed Thorvaldsen and his other artist friends, and he spent his Christmas Day alone in his room, where he dined off grapes and bread and cheese, and passed the time by reading the Bible, Goethe's "Faust," and Becker's "History of the World." The news of the "Moorish Girl's" fiasco naturally depressed him still further, and when he got to Naples he was so feverish that, following the advice of a Neapolitan

---

* It was while he was in this condition that he wrote the clever comical sketch *Mine Stöyler* (My Boots), which is not generally included among his tales.

doctor, he consented to be bled. "Death looked in
at my door," he says, "but my time had not yet
come, so he went away again." He also had
financial difficulties to worry him. He had counted
upon his second play paying most of the expenses of
his tour to the East, and now it was doubtful
whether he would be able to proceed beyond Naples.
But the King now sent him 300 specie dollars (£75)
through Collin, and this, with the 200 rix dollars
(£25) he had saved from the proceeds of "The
Mulatto," enabled him to continue his tour with a
joyful heart, and henceforth we find both his health
and his spirits improving. A stream of oblivion, he
tells us, now seemed to flow between him and all
his bitter morbid reminiscences, and he was able to
raise his head proudly and confidently once more.

On the 15th March Andersen quitted Naples in
the French steamship *Leonidas* for Greece, calling
at Malta on the way, where he landed with a Russian
officer, and, as usual, saw everything that was to be
seen. He was much impressed, too, by the sight of
Etna from the sea. It was like an amphitheatre for
the high gods themselves. Vesuvius seemed to him a
mere sand-hill in comparison. His fellow-travellers
consisted, for the most part, of Spanish pilgrims, Italian
priests, and various Orientals. There was nobody on
board with whom he could exchange a word in Danish
or German, and when he talked French he was taken

for an American. He made friends, however, with a Persian from Herat, whom he had noticed sitting on a carpet on the deck, dressed in a green caftan and a white shawl, and amusing himself all day long by playing with his earrings and his scimitar. One day, as Andersen was passing him, the Persian caught him suddenly by the arm, laughed, nodded, and pointed at the rigging. "The long poet" looked in that direction, and saw a little bird which had dropped exhausted upon the ship. A crowd of spectators immediately gathered round it, and Andersen got quite angry when a portly Roman priest proposed that the bird should be cooked, and eaten, because it looked so plump. "Our little winged pilgrim shall not be eaten," cried he, and, taking it under his protection, he fed it till it was strong enough to fly away again. This little incident cemented his friendship with the Persian, and they used to exchange fruit, and talk in pantomime together. On one occasion, Andersen felt that he must really say something articulate, and determined to try his Eastern comrade with the first line of Genesis in Hebrew, in the belief (he was no philologist) that Hebrew was a sister-tongue to Persian, though, for the matter of that, he might just as well have addressed him in Danish. So, pointing to the stars, he exclaimed : " Bererchit barah Elohim et haschamaim

viet ha arets." The Persian smiled, nodded, and
animated, no doubt, by an equally amiable desire to
say something in the only European language he
knew anything about, replied in English : " Yes,
sir ; verily, verily."          .

At the end of March, 1841, Andersen arrived at
Athens which it had long been the desire of his
heart to see, though he was considerably disillu-
sioned when he did see it. It reminded him, he
said, of Fairyland fallen to pieces. However he
made the best of it, and soon felt perfectly at home
there, even cheerfully putting up with the suffocating dust because it was "classic dust." He was
particularly struck by the picturesque contrasts of
this "sublime wilderness" as he called it. The
steps of the Parthenon covered with a luxuriant
growth of wild gherkins ; tortoises* crawling about
in the bushes over the torsos of marble lions ; the
unburied skulls of Turks and Greeks scattered
among mortars and culverines from Venetian times ;
the skeleton. of an ass in the middle of a devastated
mosque which had been built over the ruins of the
temple of Erectheus—all these were sights which

---

* Here may be mentioned an anecdote which illustrates Andersen's
extraordinary fondness for animals of all sorts. As he was driving to
the marble quarries of Pentelikon, he saw a little tortoise in the road,
and dismounting picked it up and took it into the carriage both to
prevent it from being run over, and also to "help it on in the world a
bit."

brought the tears to his eyes. His stay at Athens, which lasted a month, was an extremely pleasant one. He found many of his own countrymen in high positions there, and they went out of their way to make him comfortable. It had been arranged that he should spend his birthday (April 2) on the top of Parnassus, but a heavy fall of snow making that famous mountain inaccessible, he had to be content with a banquet in town, when the best champagne flowed in streams, and two famous Greek rhapsodists were specially hunted up to do honour to the occasion. He was also presented to the king and queen, and took riding-lessons under the personal supervision of the Austrian Consul-General Prokesch-Osten. "And I only wish you could see me on horseback, in my tall Greek hat with the long fluttering tassel," he writes to E. Collin. "The first day I was, naturally, horribly nervous, and when the beast strayed a little way out of the path—I confess it freely—I bellowed with all my might, but I bellow no more now."

And now Andersen had the choice before him of returning to Germany, and prolonging his stay there till October, or of going on to Constantinople, and returning home thence in July. After a long and severe struggle he chose the latter alternative. A whole series of unpleasant adventures awaited him however. In the Archipelago he experienced a

violent storm for the first time in his life, when the
ship "shivered like a sparrow in a whirlwind."
Andersen made up his mind that he himself, and
every one on board was about to die, and felt a
strange composure at the thought; but the next
morning, when he awoke, the vessel was safe and
sound in Smyrna harbour, and at six o'clock on the
following morning, was steaming through the Dardanelles. The first view of Constantinople impressed
him as nothing else had ever done before. The
situation of the imperial city struck him as vastly
superior to that of Naples, but somewhat akin to
that of Stockholm, though more fantastic and picturesque—a chaos of red.roofs, black cypresses and
snow-white minarets. Here he enjoyed "eleven
interesting days." His evenings were spent in the
salons of the Danish Minister Baron Hübsch, or the
Greek Minister Chrystides to whom he had letters
of introduction, and all day long he wandered about
the bazaars with a guide who cost him five shillings
a day, which he considered quite enough, though he
certainly seems to have had his money's worth in
sight-seeing. In a mosque at Scutari he witnessed
the performances of the Dancing Dervishes, which
filled him with horror and loathing. Andersen's
guide, mistaking the cause of his emotion, whispered
to him : " For Heaven's sake don't laugh, or they'll
certainly murder us." " Laugh ! " exclaimed Ander-

sen; " I'm nearer to crying. It is terrible, it is ghastly, and I can stand it no longer." And out he went without more ado.

A more attractive sight was the procession of the Sultan and his Court to the Sophia Mosque, on Muhammad's birthday, which he was fortunate enough to witness from a coigne of vantage. The splendid caparisons of the imperial chargers in particular called to mind the wonders which the Spirit of the Lamp conjured up for Aladdin. The Sultan Abdul-Medjed, then only nineteen years old, rode a magnificent Arab steed, surrounded by a host of youths on foot, as handsome as houris, with green fans in their hands. The Padishah himself wore a green frock-coat buttoned across the breast, and had no other ornament but a large jewel, and a bird-of-paradise feather fastened together on his red fez. He looked very pale and haggard, had a bored expression, and his black eyes were fixed steadily on the spectators, especially on the Franks. They all took off their hats to greet him, but he made not the slightest response. " Why doesn't he nod back to us?" asked Andersen of a young Turk by his side, " he saw us take off our hats I suppose." " He saw them," replied the Turk, " you may be quite sure of that. He saw them and took particular notice of them too." And he seemed to think that the demands of courtesy had thereby been amply satisfied.

The only inconvenience which Andersen had to
complain of during his pleasant stay at Stambul,
was the raw coldness of the atmosphere, due to the
heavy wet mists from the Black Sea. He couldn't
have been worse off in Denmark itself, he says
These same fogs, moreover, caused him some alarm
on his departure for Kustendje, whence he was to
proceed overland to Czernawoda, and there take
another steamer for Vienna. As however the Black
Sea had already swallowed a couple of steamers
during the preceding spring, he hoped it would be
satisfied with this mouthful, and let "the poet" go
free. No sooner were they fairly on the Euxine,
than down the mists came so thickly as to hide
the coast, and compel the captain to lay to repeatedly. The deck and rigging got as wet as if
they had been at the bottom of the sea, and so
chilly was the temperature that Andersen imagined
himself on an expedition to Spitzbergen instead of
on a pleasure trip off the Turkish coast in the month
of May. But the sun came out at last, and they
reached the Dobrudscha without any accident.

From Kustendje Andersen proceeded by ox-waggon
through a dreary wilderness to Czernawoda, the
nearest steam-packet station on the Danube, where
the Austrian-steamer *Argo* was waiting to take him
to Vienna. And now began a journey so dull and
monotonous that he positively wished himself back

in Copenhagen. For thirty days he saw on both
sides of him a coast that made him fancy he was
sailing among asparagus tops, while beyond there
was nothing but "flat green-cabbage scenery." The
climax of this "soul-wearing" journey was a ten days'
quarantine detention at Orsova, where he and his
companions were locked up like criminals in damp
rooms with prison fare and marshy water. In the
day-time he dreamt that he was in the leaden dun-
geons of Venice, while at night he seemed to be
living in Hell, Heiberg's Hell. At last they all
grew sick, and the doctor ordered them medicine
which Andersen thought might have been excellent
for Wallachian horses, but was scarcely fit for
human beings with weak stomachs. Poor Andersen's sufferings, were, moreover, not a little accen-
tuated by the perverse enthusiasm of some eccentric
musical virtuosos, who would persist in playing Bul-
garian flutes morning, noon and night. They always
played the same tune, which was strictly confined to
two, or, at the most, three notes pitched at a very
high key, and he tells us that it sounded just as if
some one were blowing down a tulip stalk, and
treading on the tail of a cat at the same time.
Still he had at least one consolation in his cap-
tivity—the consolation of an agreeable companion.
This was William Francis Ainsworth, the cousin of
the novelist, who was returning home from a

missionary journey in Kurdistan, and shared Andersen's room with him in quarantine. Ainsworth has
left us a very interesting account of Andersen.* He
describes him as a tall, pale, delicate-looking young
man of prepossessing appearance, with brown hair
and sharp features, a very slight slouch in his gait,
and the sideling movement of an abstracted man.
He found him friendly and cheerful in conversation
although restless and preoccupied, but with an
extreme simplicity in his manners, and a trustful-
ness in others that "made it impossible not to
entertain feelings of regard and interest for him at
once." Ainsworth thought himself particularly
fortunate in securing such a pleasant, and in every
respect gentlemanly companion, while in durance
vile. "I use the word gentlemanly advisedly,"
he adds, "for his manners were in every respect
those of a person of cultivated intellect and refined
feelings." At dinner time, when they generally
met together for the first time every day (the
morning being mostly occupied with correspondence),
Andersen was always ready with some quaint
conceit or comic story. At Pest they lost sight of
each other, for Andersen had provided himself with
letters of introduction, whereas Ainsworth was a
mere bird of passage.†

* *Literary Gazette*, No. 1551, p. 877.
† Ainsworth could not help being struck by Andersen's skill in cutting

On resuming his journey from Orsova, Andersen was pleased to observe that there was considerable improvement in the scenery. The Hungarian side was like a vast garden, where the orchards were covered with such myriads of white butterflies, that Andersen fancied the fruit trees were blooming a second time, while on the other side were the endless oak and chestnut forests of Servia, which wearied the eye at last. Unfortunately for the comfort of the passengers, the steamer now became so crowded (owing to the concourse of folks to the great fair at Pest) that there was scarcely room to move. The people almost stood upon one another. Many of them made a point of sitting down all day on benches, or on the corners of tables, so as to have a place to lie down upon at night, when the whole steamer resembled a huge family bed full of brothers and sisters, and you couldn't move a step without treading on some one's face. There was one nervous lady on board who expected that the steamer would explode every moment, and could not be made to understand the principle of locomotion by steam. At last Andersen, who rather plumed himself on his

figures out of paper, and it is interesting to observe that the drawings of the Mewlewis, or turning dervishes, in his *Travels and Researches in Asia Minor* (vol. i. p. 149) are from cuttings by Andersen. He observes, too, that Andersen was naturally of a pious turn of mind and observed the Sabbath strictly by putting by his papers and doing no work on that day. Andersen, curiously enough, makes much the same remark about Ainsworth.

power of popular exposition, undertook to make
matters clear to her. " Just suppose, Madame," said
he, "that you have a pot upon the fire, and it
is boiling very fiercely. Suppose again that a large
lid is on the top of this pot. If this lid be screwed
down tightly, the pot might burst because of the
pressure of hot steam inside it. But if it be but
loosely put on, it will only bob up and down,
the steam will ooze out, and the pot will not burst."
" But Heaven help us ! " cried Madame, " if the lid,"
and with these words she pointed down to the deck,
·" if the lid here over the steam engine bobs up and
down, as you say, we shall all be pitched into the
Danube ! " and she clung convulsively to the railing
of the steamer. "I am sure she would have fainted,"
adds Andersen slily, "if only she had been quite sure
the vessel would not have blown up in the meantime."

It was with a sigh of unspeakable relief that
Andersen at last stepped ashore near the Prater
whence he drove into Vienna, visited his old friends,
made new ones, and then set off homewards *viâ*
Prague and Dresden. At the *table d'hôte* at Hamburg he met a number of his countrymen, and while
he was discoursing to them about beauteous Greece,
and the gorgeous East, an old Copenhagen lady, who
was sitting by his side, turned to him and said :
" Now tell me, Mr. Andersen, during all your long

P

and numerous travels, have you seen *anything* so
pretty as our little Denmark?" "I should rather
think so," replied Andersen, "and much prettier
too." "Fie!" exclaimed the old dame, "you are no
patriot, I see!"

On his arrival at Copenhagen he was welcomed by
his friends with an enthusiastic affection which, for
the moment, drove away all bitter and melancholy
thoughts.  His whole time, for weeks to come, was
taken up with paying and returning calls ; he had a
special audience of the King and Queen, and at the
Collins' there was quite a family *fête* in his honour.
If he had been a son of the house he could not have
been greeted more warmly.  And yet the failure of
"The Moorish Girl" still weighed upon his mind,
and made him take a jaundiced view of things in
general.  Copenhagen struck him as peculiarly cold,
*triste* and stale.  He complains that there is nothing
to see in it but the rain pattering perpetually against
the windows, and nothing to hear but petty tittle-
tattle, and spiteful critic-cackle on every side of him.
"These people have no enthusiasm for anything," he
cries ; "they can only grin."  Even his interest in the
theatre seemed to flag, and he is very sarcastic about
plays and players.  The new prima-donna at the
Italian Opera, with whom every one else was enrap-
tured, he calls a shrimp of a thing ; she reminds him
of a little black coffee-can.  The Royal Theatre

pleased him even less. The poet Christian Winther had dramatised the old Danish legend which Andersen himself subsequently expanded into the delightful story of "The Marsh-King's Daughter," and Andersen went to see it. The false sisters who treated the fair Egyptian so badly, were represented by life-size dolls which, according to Andersen, "hung together like a bundle of radishes," and when, by some blunder of the machinist, one of these dolls, in its flight through the air, suddenly faced round and regarded the audience with an idiotic stare, it looked, he says, for all the world like "a vision of Molbech going to Heaven." It was about this time too that he wrote that unworthy letter to his French friend Xavier Marmier, obviously for the purpose of advertising himself, in which he is so scandalously unjust to Heiberg and his wife.* It seems however to have relieved him of most of his accumulated venom. He found his principal consolation in working away at his new book (largely a record of his travels), which appeared early in 1842 under the title of *En Digter's Bazar* (An Author's Bazaar).† It contains three of the prettiest of the Tales, viz : "The Metal Pig," "The Compact of Friendship," and "A Rose from Homer's Grave," together with the humoresque " My Boots," which is better than all three. Örsted

* Bille og Bogh : *Breve fra Andersen*, ii. 54.
† Translated fairly well into English by Beckwith in 1846.

and Oehlenschläger were delighted with it, and even those critics (the severe P. L. Möller for instance) who complained of its occasional lapses into bad syntax, were filled with admiration by its beautiful, vivid, nay, ravishing series of landscape and genre pictures, and its luxuriant, often glowing colouring. Andersen sent a copy of the book to the King of Sweden, through the poet and historian Bernhard von Beskow who was himself so charmed with it that he translated some of the best episodes into Swedish, "that others may enjoy this beautiful gift with me," although an authorised Swedish version was already in course of preparation. In Germany also it was received with enthusiasm, and we shall see when we come to speak of Andersen's visit to England, that there also the reviews greeted it with an unanimous chorus of praise.*

* When it first came out in Denmark some amusement was caused by its being dedicated piecemeal to no less than nine different distinguished people. Some put this eccentricity down to vanity; I think myself that it was merely effusive gratitude towards the persons so honoured. Anyhow a book with nine dedications seemed as odd a monster as a seven-headed dragon or a dog with two tails, and people laughed a good deal, and not always good-naturedly. The nine dedications vanish from subsequent editions.

# CHAPTER VIII

## PROGRESS OF THE FAIRY TALES—DRAMATIC TRIUMPHS AND DISASTERS—"THE LONG POET" A EUROPEAN CELEBRITY

The second series of the " Fairy Tales "—Their growing popularity in Denmark—Third series establishes the reputation of the tales once for all—Thorvaldsen's fondness for them—Popularity of "The Ugly Duckling"—The *Billedbog uden Billeder*—Success of " The Tales " in Germany—Andersen's new dramatic ventures, " Kongen Drömmer " and " Den nye Barselstuen "—Reasons why Andersen could never become a really great dramatist—His infatuation in this respect—Sends in two dramas anonymously—Andersen's new play, "Lykkens Blomst," rejected by Heiberg—Andersen remonstrates with his censor—Heiberg's amusing reply—The comedy " Herr Rasmussen " and its miserable collapse—Andersen's second visit to Paris—Andersen lionised—Victor Hugo—Heine—Balzac—De Vigny—Alexandre Dumas—Rachel—The purple *salon*—Mlle. Déjazet—Grisi—Andersen's French—Hysteric outburst—Four months' tour to Germany—Meets Grimm at Berlin—Andersen the guest of Christian VIII. and his Consort at Wyk, in Föhr—An instance of Andersen's delicacy in money matters—His triumphal progress through Germany—Oldenburg—King of Prussia decorates him with the Red Eagle—Andersen and Jenny Lind—Court at Dresden—"The Tales " all the rage—Friendliness of the Duke of Weimar—Affecting news—Home grievances—His daily bread almost too sweet for him—Third visit to Italy—The Sirocco-like heat—Return to Denmark.

MEANWHILE "the little Fairy Tales,"* as their author half contemptuously calls them, had, like

* In *M. L. E.* Andersen insinuates that he always believed in the

invisible but indefatigably benevolent little house-
elves, been stealthily but steadily building up his
reputation for him.    In Denmark, as I have already
said, they had, at first, been somewhat coldly received, relegated to the nursery, and only just
tolerated even there, in striking contrast to the
enthusiasm with which they were welcomed in
Germany and Sweden.    It was only when the great
actors and actresses of the Royal Theatre took to
declaiming them at fashionable afternoon entertain-
ments, that they began to come into vogue.    It was
felt that if Phister did not disdain to recite "The
Naughty Boy" and "The Swine-herd," and if
Madame Heiberg had "The Matches" written expressly for her, there must be very much more in
these pretty trifles than had at first been suspected.
People ceased therefore to sneer at the Tales, and
began reading them instead, though it was not till
1845, when the third series of the Fairy Tales came
out, that they became as popular in Denmark as out
of it.    The second series, which went on from Christmas 1838 to Christmas 1842, had consisted of "The

"Fairy Tales," and was much grieved at their hanging fire at first. In
reality he regarded them with comparative indifference—*e.g.*, the following contemporary extract from his correspondence, which is only
one of many such : "The Vaudevilles and the children's fairy tales
are the only things I have written since 'The Mulatto,' and that is as
good as nothing.    Consequently I have only been vegetating for the
last two months."—Bille og Bogh : *Breve fra Andersen*, i. 489.    This
was in 1839.

Daisy," "The Steadfast Tin Soldier," "The Wild
Swans," "The Garden of Eden," "The Flying
Coffer," "The Storks," "Oli Lockeye," "The Rose-
Elf," "The Swine-herd," and "The Buck-Wheat."
Of these "The Daisy," "The Steadfast Tin Soldier,"
and "Oli Lockeye," are quite original, the others
are adaptations of stories that Andersen himself had
heard when he was a child.* This series was grace-
fully dedicated to Madame Heiberg as one of the
few who had always appreciated the Tales ; indeed
Andersen tells us that it was her encouragement,
together with H. C. Örsted's frequently-expressed
delight at the humour of these charming stories,
which encouraged him to proceed with them despite
the disparagement of critics.† Still it must never
be forgotten that, even in Denmark, all those whose
opinion was worth anything at all, had always been
the sworn champions of "The Tinder Box" and its
companions, and, as the poet Carsten Hauch told
Andersen, so long as the big men were for him, it
did not matter much about the little men who
would be bound to follow suit in the long run. In
1845 began a third series entitled *Nye Eventyr*
(New Fairy Tales), the first volume of which contained "The Angel," "The Nightingale," "The

* Except "The Flying Coffer," which is taken from the *Arabian
Nights.*

† Preface to the complete collection of the "Tales" in 1874.

Sweethearts," and "The Ugly Duckling." This volume may be said to have established the success of the Tales once for all. "The Ugly Duckling" in particular became a general favourite.* "I think 'The Ugly Duckling' one of the best of your tales, and classical of its kind," wrote Hauch, "I congratulate you. Mind you give us some more of the same sort."† Hertz, too, the terrible "spectre" of bygone days, emphatically declared that Andersen's *Eventyr* were superior to the general run of the German *Märchen*, and even equal to Grimm's, at a time when such an expression of opinion was considered by many a dangerous heresy. What Hertz liked best about them was their good humour, and their "comical, entertaining satire."‡ The more romantic Ingemann on the other hand, whose own sense of humour was somewhat defective, was more attracted by the sentimental side of "those divine tales," as, he called them. The great sculptor Thorvaldsen took a positively childish delight in listening to them. "Won't you give us wee ones another tale?" the genial giant would frequently say. Once (it

---

* *Apropos* of "The Ugly Duckling," one of Andersen's German translators made a blunder over the name which had comical consequences, rendering the Danish "*grimme*" (ugly) by the German "grönne" (green), whereupon a French translator, following suit, gave the title as Le petit canard *vert*, no doubt imagining that *verdant* was the dominant colour of Danish ducks.

† Bille og Bogh : *Breve til Andersen*, p. 667.    ‡ *Ibid.* p. 245.

was during the summer of 1846) while• he and
Andersen were staying together at Nysö, and the
latter had been reading "The Sweethearts" · and
"The Ugly Duckling" aloud, Thorvaldsen said to
him : "Come now, write us a new and comical
story. I wonder if you could make one up about a.
darning needle !" And that is how "The Darning
Needle" came to be written. In the summer of·
1846 "The Snow-Queen " and "The Fir-Tree"
appeared, and the series was completed by a little
volume containing "The Elfin Mound," by many
considered Andersen's best *original* supernatural
tale ; "The Red Shoes," which is really a chapter
out of his own autobiography, the playfully sarcastic
"Springing Bucks," "The Shepherdess and the
Chimney-sweep," and "Danish Holger." This little·
volume was dedicated to his old opponent, now his
firm friend, Henrik Hertz, "by way of thanks for the
works his deep poetic soul, and his rich wit and
humour have given us."* Besides these Andersen
had also contributed : "The Elder Mother" to the
periodical *Gœa* and "The Bell" to Gerson and
Kaalund's *Monthly Magazine.* "The Bell," certainly the most sublime of all the stories, is as the
greatest of Danish critics has said, "the one in
which the poet of *naïveté* and nature has reached
the highest point of his poetry." Here too perhaps

* Appendix to complete (Danish) edition of Tales, 1874.

is the place to mention an exquisite little masterpiece which, under the title of " What the Moon
saw," is very often included in English editions of
the Fairy Tales, though it is more of a connecting-
link between them and the travel-books.  I mean
of course the inimitable *Billedbog uden Billeder*
(Picture-book without Pictures), that " Iliad in a
nut-shell," as an English critic has well called it,
which appeared in 1840.  Andersen himself was
rather doubtful about it while he was writing it.
" Although I dare not call it my best work," he
says, " it is still *something* I fancy, and certainly
the book that has interested me most. . . . . I
hope that it will work its way into popular
interest." *  His hope was more than realised, for
none of his other works, not even excepting " The
Tales," has been translated so often.  It was Andersen's original intention to have expanded the three
and thirty evenings of " The Picture Book " into
one thousand and one, and it is an irreparable loss
to literature that he did not carry out his intention.  Still he has given us some little compensation
in that other very similar, faultlessly beautiful
collection of poetic genre pictures and humoresques,
*I Sverrig* (In Sweden).  Andersen was always
intensely grateful to Germany for her prompt and
generous recognition of his genius from the first, and

* Bille og Bogh : *Breve fra Andersen*, i. 514. ·

I believe that it was the swift and decisive success of the " Fairy Tales " in that country which first opened his own eyes to their superlative merit. Seven German editions of the earlier Tales appeared within nine years after their publication in Denmark, and it was in Germany too that they were first illustrated.   In 1839 Vieweg published a translation of the first series of the " Tales " adorned with three steel engravings, and an elaborately engraved title page in which was Andersen's name enclosed in a wreath with representations of little Ida, the Student, the Witch, the little Mermaid, and the other chief characters grouped around.*   Andersen was almost beside himself for joy at this great event, and took care to describe all the pictures to his friends in full.   Latterly it was always a great point with him to have his Tales illustrated, and illustrated well.

From Andersen's point of view the *Fairy Tales* were all very well, but they did not adequately represent his genius, or anything like it.   No, he would not be content till he had approved himself an even greater poet than Oehlenschläger, and an even greater dramatist than Heiberg.   He had already, after four years of labour, composed the best part of a great, or rather a long, epic poem, entitled *Ahasuerus*, of which more anon, but it

* Bille og Bogh : *Breve fra Andersen*, i. 472.

was towards the stage that he continued to look most longingly, though here unfortunately there was a lion in the path, of whom Andersen was terribly afraid. This was none other than the illustrious Heiberg himself, who had superseded Molbech as chief dramatic censor, and Andersen always imagined that he had lost rather than gained by the change. Heiberg indeed was never so rough and rude with him as Molbech had been ; but on the other hand, though Molbech's taste was, generally speaking, correct, dramatic criticism was not altogether his forte, and his decisions could be and had been successfully appealed against, whereas nobody in his senses would have thought of questioning Heiberg's verdicts. Now, according to Andersen, the great censor's otherwise infallible critical faculty was vitiated by one serious defect : an utter inability to recognise anything good in any play to which his, Andersen's name, happened to be appended. How then, he argued, was a poor Heaven-born dramatist like himself to get his just due ? At last he hit upon a saving expedient. In November 1843 he sent in his new one-act tragedy, *Kongen Drömmer* (The King Dreams) to the theatrical censor *anonymously ;* in January 1845, he repeated the experiment with his one-act comedy *Den nye Barselstuen* (The New Lying-in Room),

and on both occasions, just as if "the imp of the
perverse" had had some hand in the matter, he
was signally successful. This success did him
more harm than good in the long run, because it
thoroughly convinced him that professional jealousy
was really, after all, the main cause of his former
ill-treatment at the hands of the dramatic censors.
This of course was simply nonsense. It is quite
within the bounds of possibility for a clever man of
letters, with a strong liking for the stage, to give
dramatic shape to a happy inspiration, and yet be
anything but a born dramatist. This was exactly
Andersen's case, as a very little consideration will
show. He had always failed hitherto as a dramatist, and was always bound to fail, simply because
he lacked those faculties of the true dramatist
whereby he is able to diagnose his characters,
marshal and combine his incidents, and weave
both characters and incidents into a harmonious
whole or plot, proceeding gradually and naturally
to an inevitable dénoûement. In a word he lacked
concentration, and psychological depth. A regular
five-act drama was quite beyond his powers.
It was much too complicated and elaborate for
him. On the other hand he had a keen eye for
the salient superficial traits of character, an intimate
knowledge of stage effect, born of long experience,

while we have only to look at his fairy-tales, especially the shorter ones,* to see what an original use
he could make of *simple* situations whether comical
or the reverse. Thus a one-act drama, provided it
had a really good and original idea at the bottom of
it, was well within his capacity, and the leading
ideas of both the tragedy "The King Dreams," and
the comedy, "The New Lying-in Room" are distinctly good and original.

"The New Lying-in Room" caught the public
favour instantly, and was acted no less than forty-
seven times. Strange to say, nobody, not even
Heiberg, guessed that Andersen was its author,
though the peculiar humour of the piece might have
given them a clue. Those friends who were in the
secret, H. C. Örsted and the Collins, vowed that if
the piece did succeed, Andersen would never be able
to hold his tongue about it. Nevertheless, he heroically resisted the temptation under the most provocative circumstances. Thus Privy Councillor Adler
said to him, after a disparaging allusion to another
play of his, *Lykken's Blomst* (The Flower of
Fortune), which had proved a failure : "Now there's
'The New Lying-in Room.' It is an excellent play.
If only you could write something in that style. But

---

* The longer ones are less happily contrived. Take for instance
one of the longest, "The Marsh King's Daughter." Here it is quite
plain, I think, that Andersen was at his wits' end how to terminate the
story.

it is quite outside your talent. *You* are a lyric poet, and have not the humour that man has." Again, on the evening after the first representation, a rising young critic came rushing into Andersen's rooms with such a glowing account of the new piece, that Andersen was afraid his voice or his face might betray him, so he said at once : "I know who the author is." "Who is it?" cried the critic. "It is yourself," replied Andersen, "I can see it by your agitation." The young man grew quite red and protested with his hand on his heart, that it was not he. "I know what I know," added Andersen smiling, and pleaded another engagement to slip away.

"The King Dreams," and "The New Lying-in Room" are Andersen's best, or rather his only good plays, his other dramatic efforts scarcely deserving the name of plays at all. But he thought differently, and the more or less contemptuous rejection of all his other essays in this direction, by the politely sarcastic Heiberg, was a source of the most bitter vexation to him. One play of which he was particularly enamoured was the two-act drama *Lykken's Blomst* (Flower of Fortune), already alluded to, which he sent in during 1844, apparently unconscious that it was a plagiarism from one of Heiberg's finest masterpieces "Syvsoverdag ("Seven-Sleepers' Day"). "However much it may flatter me to see my poor works taken as patterns," says

Heiberg in his report to Jonas Collin on this play,
" it can surely afford me very little pleasure to see
them give occasion to such utter absurdities." The
play was accordingly rejected. Andersen was
furious. The conduct of Heiberg seemed to him
utterly inexplicable on any other hypothesis than a
deliberate intention to exclude his pieces for ever
from the stage. " A heavy sea has gone over my
head," he cried, " and I shall not be able to hold
out much longer." He stormed and raved to no
purpose, and at last rushed off to Heiberg's private
house to argue the matter out with the censor himself. Heiberg received his visitor in the most
friendly manner and explained, at great length, his
reasons for rejecting the play, reasons so just and
cogent that Andersen could not possibly confute
them, so he fell back upon recrimination. He had
come to have it out with Heiberg, and to wipe off
all old scores, and his memory was as retentive of
injuries, real or imaginary, as the memory of an
elephant. " Why," he asked, " did you years ago
deny me originality ? I suppose my romances at
any rate are original, and you told me yourself you
had never read any of them." " Yes," replied
Heiberg, " that's true enough. I have not read
them yet, but I am going to read them." " And
then," pursued Andersen excitedly, " you ridiculed
my 'Bazaar' in your 'Danish Atlas,' and talked about

my enthusiasm for the lovely Dardanelles.* Now
it so happens that I *never* thought the Dardanelles
lovely.   It was the *Bosphorus* that charmed me so,
but apparently you never noticed that, or perhaps
you have not read the ' Bazaar ' either, you told me
once you never read big books."   " Oh, the Bosphorus was it ? " said Heiberg with his peculiar smile,
" I didn't remember, and you see other people
didn't either.   I suppose I wanted to have a little
fling at you, that's about the long and short of it."
" This   confession,"   adds   Andersen,   " was   so
natural and so peculiar, that I couldn't help laughing, and when I looked .into his wise eyes, and
recollected how many beautiful things he had
written, I couldn't bear him any grudge or ill will."†
So the fierce debate gradually meandered into a
friendly conversation.   Heiberg spoke up hand-

---

* The verses Andersen complained of were these :—
                Or you're such a fool, may be,
                (For, indeed, such fools there are)
                Who devour with ecstasy
                All that Andersen now tells
                Of the lovely Dardenelles
                In his Ottoman Bazaar,
                While oppressed with dull ennui,
                You heedlessly pass by
                The scenes that charm the eye
                In our own dear Sound as fair
                (If you'd only learn to know it)
                And we're spared the wailings there
                Of the much misconstrued poet.·

† *M. L. E.* p. 338.

somely for " The Tales " which he *had* read, and they
parted amicably enough, though so long as it was
Andersen's delight to write dramas, and Heiberg's
duty to censure them, they were bound to be more
or less of belligerents.  In the beginning of 1846
Andersen again tempted Fortune by sending in
another comedy, *Herr Rasmussen,* which Heiberg
disapproved of.  But unfortunately the Collins
liked the piece, and it was put upon the
stage while Andersen was abroad.  The result
was simply disastrous.  It did not receive a
single clap, and when the curtain fell after the
first Act, there was a frightful hissing.  Edward
Collin, who was among the audience in a feverish
state of excitement, at once departed.  He could
stand it no longer, and felt that the piece was past
praying for.  During the last Act, the public freely
took part in the dialogue amidst universal hilarity :
never had been known such a miserable collapse.
" If," wrote Edward Collin to Andersen on this
occasion, " if you see in this another proof of Danish
misappreciation and perhaps animosity . . . . you
are very much mistaken.  There is certainly nobody
you can better believe on this head than myself.
You recollect how good I thought the piece, how
comical I found it.  I went to the theatre with
the fullest conviction that it would succeed, and
provoke roars of laughter from beginning to end.  I

went to the theatre I say and—I was bored, I was
embarrassed, I found it so vapid, so completely
wanting in comic situations and characters, that I
can assure you I never saw anything like it—I am
intimately persuaded that had you seen the piece
yourself, you would have had the same feeling. . . . .
The only person I am really sorry for is father, for
he will naturally have a bad time of it for forcing
the piece on against the will of so many other
persons."*

Of course Andersen regarded the conduct of the
Danish public on this occasion as an abominable
outrage that cried loudly to Heaven for vengeance,
but he got ample compensation for this slight rebuff
in the extraordinary, not to say extravagant ovations
which he received abroad during the years 1843–46.
In March 1843 he visited Paris for the second time
under very different conditions to those of his first
visit nine years before. Then he was nobody, now
he was indisputably one of the best known writers
in Europe. It is true that he never was, or could be
so popular in France (or, for the matter of that, in
any of the Latin countries) as he was in the Ger-
manic lands,† but his reputation had preceded him,

* Bille og Bogh : *Breve til Andersen*, pp. 97, 98. Such a letter from
such a man should of itself effectually dispose of Andersen's insinua-
tions in his autobiography, that his career as a dramatic author was
ruined by a clique.

† This has been well pointed out by Dr. Brandes in his *Kritiker*

and during his stay at the gay capital he was
lionised to his heart's content.  His descriptions of
the great authors who paid him compliments, and
the great actresses who entertained him in their
*salons*, are very vivid and entertaining, though in
describing them he (indirectly and unconsciously of
course) tells us even more about himself.*  He now
renewed his former acquaintance with Victor Hugo
and Heinrich Heine, both of whom were very
amiable, though the grand manner of "the proud
poet-king," as he calls the former, a little overawed
him.  Hugo took him to see *Les Burgraves* which
had just come out, but Andersen thought it
rather dull, and was somewhat embarrassed how to
express himself on the subject to its distinguished
author.  Heine on the other hand was delightful.
Andersen's opinion of him had changed considerably
during the last ten years.  He had begun by
admiring and imitating him, then he had been
half ashamed of his own admiration, as if it were
a species of devil-worship, and had consequently
avoided him during his first visit at Paris.  But
now he had learned to know the world a little better,
and to take men as he found them.† and on this

*og Portraiter.* Andersen was "un peu trop enfantin" for the French.
There are even fewer French, Italian and Spanish translations of his
Tales than there are Hungarian and Slavonic.

* For Andersen's second visit to Paris, see Collin, pp. 341–6 ; Bille
og Bogh : *Breve fra Andersen*, i. pp. 65–86 ; and *M. L. E.*

† Andersen's definitive opinion of Heine as a writer is expressed in

occasion, too, Heine was so natural and affectionate that Andersen quite loved him, especially after he had been informed that Madame Heine absolutely doated on "The Steadfast Tin Soldier," which her husband had read to her in French. Shortly afterwards Heine introduced Andersen to his wife. He found her playing with a whole flock of children whom, as Heine comically explained, they had borrowed from a neighbour because they had none of their own, and while the author of the *Lieder* sat down in a side-room to write a "beautiful deeply melancholy poem" in Andersen's album, Andersen himself helped Madame Heine to amuse the children.

Amongst Andersen's new acquaintances may be mentioned Balzac, Lamartine, De Vigny and Alexandre Dumas *père*. Andersen was introduced to Balzac at a soirée at the Countess Prasse's. His hostess, after making him sit down beside her on the sofa, with Balzac on the other side, took each of them by the hand, and exclaimed : " Lucky creature that I am ! I feel quite shamefaced to be sitting here between the two most famous men in Europe ! " " Mais, Madame la baronne ! " modestly protested

a letter to Collin, in 1865, as follows :—" Heine is a glittering firework : it goes out and dark night surrounds us. He is a witty babbler, impious and frivolous, and yet a true poet. His books are elfin girls in gauze and silk which swarm with vermin, so that one cannot let them move freely about the rooms of respectably dressed people."— Collin, p. 108.

Andersen, and he was proceeding to explain his own
insignificance in as good French as he could muster
on the spur of the moment, when he chanced to
catch sight of Balzac's face behind her back, distorted
into a satiric grin.    Andersen describes the author
of *La Comédie Humaine* as a fairly well dressed man
with very white projecting teeth, and a trick of half-
opening his mouth.    The "elegant" Alfred de
Vigny he met at the same place, and that "amiable
personage" quite won his heart by clambering the
many stairs of the Hotel Valois, right up to Andersen's little attic under the roof, with all his works
under his arm, as a parting present.    "I cannot tell
you," writes Andersen on this occasion, "how
intently he gazed at me, how hard he pressed my
hand.    I am sure he is a great, a noble soul."    But
"the dearest of them all," the one whom he would
have chosen for a comrade, was the jovial Dumas
whom he generally found lying in bed, even late
into the afternoon, with pen, ink and paper, writing
away at his latest novel or drama.    One day when
Andersen caught him like this, Dumas gave him a
kindly nod and said: "Sit down a bit, I am just
having a visit from my Muse, she will be gone
directly."    It was Dumas who introduced him to
the great Rachel.    He first made her acquaintance
in her little room behind the scenes, where she was
waiting her turn to go on the stage in the character

of Phædra, and he was quite surprised to find her
so "young looking" and "royally noble." He also
spent an afternoon in her purple salon where everything was rich and splendid, though perhaps "a
little too *arrangé*." Rachel "who was dressed in
black, and in the highest degree gracious," made him
sit down beside her, while she poured out tea, and
give her an account of the Danish literature. Whenever he was at a loss for a word she encouraged him
with the most delicate compliments, and at his
parting visit wrote these words in his album :
"L'art c'est le vrai ! J'espère que cet aphorisme ne
semble pas paradoxal à un écrivain aussi distingué
que Monsieur Andersen." Déjazet he was also introduced to behind the scenes, but she didn't please
him. He saw her in " Mlle. Déjazet au Serail" which
he considered simply horrible. " I cannot understand," he writes, "how such a vaudeville can be
tolerated, still less how such a gifted nature as
Mlle. Déjazet can find any pleasure in exhibiting the
very lowest brutishness." He heard Grisi in "Othello"
and " Semiramis," and thought her a mere shadow of
Malibran. He therefore went to hear her in " Norma,"
prepared to be critical, and came away enthusiastic ;
there was a power, a grandeur, " an ocean of melody "
in her wonderful voice which completely overwhelmed
him. Altogether his second visit to Paris was one
of his most delightful experiences. He wrote to

Collin that he was reading up for his examination in
knowledge of human nature, and hoped to pass.
Every one was killing him with kindness, every one
thoroughly understood him.  They were all so kind,
so good.  The difficulties of the language too had
been much exaggerated, or else the linguistic standard of the Collins' was much too severe.  Even
those of his countrymen who spoke the language
better than he did, envied the agility with which
he could "vault through a conversation."  He had
ventured to converse with Rachel, who spoke the
purest French of all, for, argued he, "good French
she can hear every day, but my French is at least
original."  And Rachel, according to Andersen, took
a positive pleasure in listening to him, and declared
that there was wit and soul in what he said.  In
short his whole sojourn there was a spiritual recreation.  Yet the most trivial contretemps at home was
sufficient to disturb his felicity abroad, and it is
rather startling in the midst of these enthusiastic
effusions and joyful pæans, to suddenly come across
such a harsh dissonance as the following: "The
Danes are evil-minded, cold, satanic.  They exactly
suit their wet, mouldy-green islands.  I hate and
loathe my country, just as much as my country
hates and bespatters me."*  And all because his old
play *Agnete*, in which he himself professed to have

* Bille og Bogh: *Breve fra Andersen*, ii. p. 83.

lost all interest, had failed to please the public at Copenhagen. It is only fair to add, that this was an isolated outburst of which he himself seems to have been ashamed, for he told his correspondent to destroy the letter in which it occurs.

Andersen returned to Denmark in 1843, and in March 1844 he was away again for four months, this time in Germany. It is from henceforth that his intimacy with the Grand Duke of Weimar and his family begins. A comical adventure befel him at Brunswick. An enthusiastic lady admirer there said to him: "I do not honour thee, I love thee." "She was pretty, but married," adds Andersen; "so I hardly knew what to reply; but I kissed her hand, and then pressed the hand of her husband, so that he also might not be left out in the cold."* Still funnier was his first encounter with Grimm whose collection of fairy tales was to be the only serious rival of the Andersenian stories. Grimm was the only person of distinction in Berlin whom he did not yet know, so he called upon him though he had no letter of introduction. "Considering the importance my name has in Germany, I was persuaded," says Andersen, "that he must know of me. I came, gave in my name, and fancy—he did *not* know me, absolutely knew nothing at all about me; I felt

* Collin, p. 365.

quite stupid when he asked me what I had written. At last I got a little angry, especially when I found out that he knew Danish. He confessed that he had never heard my name." Andersen's Berlin friends consoled him with the assurance that Grimm was at least thirty years behind the age.

On Andersen's return to Denmark he received an invitation from the King and Queen to stay with them at Wyk in Föhr, one of that strange low-lying group of little Frisian islands off the south-west coast of Denmark, the peculiar scenery of which has been so vividly described by Biernatzki in "Die Hallig" and "Der braune Knabe," and less success-fully by Andersen himself in his later novel *The Two Baronesses*. Andersen was soon made to feel quite at home. He took all his meals with the royal family, and shared in all their excursions. Every evening he read to them a couple of the Fairy Tales. The King appeared to like "The Nightingale" and "The Swineherd" best, and Andersen therefore recited them several evenings running. These were "beautiful bright, poetic days which could. never come again." Here also he spent the 5th of Sep-tember, which he always kept as a season of thanks-giving, for it was on that very day, twenty-five years ago, that he had come up to Copenhagen for the first time, a poor friendless lad with his little bundle in his hand. Count Rantzau, who knew what that day meant to Andersen, told the Queen all about it, and she told the King. After dinner their Majesties congratulated Andersen on having overcome so many difficulties, and late the same evening, Christian VIII. had a long conversation with him, in which he asked for further particulars of his early struggles, and said how pleased he was to hear from foreigners of the high appreciation of his Tales in Germany. The King next inquired how much he had to live upon, and when Andersen replied 200 specie dollars (£50) besides what he made from his works, Christian exclaimed, " and little enough too ! " Count Rantzau told Andersen afterwards that the King had meant by these words to put a wish into his mouth, so to speak, and had fully expected him to petition there and then for an increase of his pension; but this Andersen could not find it in his heart to do. It seemed to him shabby to ask his host for more in such a blunt, downright fashion. The King waited for some time to give him a chance of speaking, and then said : " If at any time I can help you on in your literary career, you must let me know." "At present," replied Andersen, "I have nothing to ask. I can only tell your Majesty that I am very thankful and happy." In telling Collin this Andersen admits that, perhaps he behaved like a fool, but declares at the same time he would not act against his feelings.

In October 1845, Andersen again quitted Denmark for a tour in Central and Southern Europe, and was absent nearly twelve months. With him to live was to travel. His tour through Germany on this occasion resembled a triumphal progress. Poets and philosophers flocked around him, publishers fought over him, and princes held out their hands to him. The first Court that honoured him was Oldenburg. He was presented to the Grand Duke on the day after his arrival, read " The Snow Queen," " The Tin Soldier," " The Nightingale," and " The Swineherd," *in German,** and went away with a costly ring on his finger. At Berlin, too, he found that the Fairy Tales were all the rage, and he himself was looked upon as a society lion, a sort of " masculine Jenny Lind," as he expresses it. The King invited him to dinner as soon as he arrived, and decorated him with the Order of the Red Eagle of the third class ; the Crown Princess gave him a blue velvet album ; he took tea at Potsdam with the King, Queen, and Humboldt ; Prince Radziwill protected him ; three painters insisted upon his sitting to them, and Ministers haled him off to their houses, not to hear him read, but to make much of him, and to say they had spoken to him. Here also he found his friend Jenny Lind, whom he had learnt to know six years before

---

* Andersen was prouder of this than of anything. " What does my little friend think now of my German ? " he wrote to Collin.

at Copenhagen, and they spent Christmas Day together, and had a little Christmas tree all to themselves. Fröken Lind was one of the most thoroughgoing admirers of the "Tales," and always looked upon Andersen as a brother; they certainly were kindred natures. As for Andersen, he was so enthusiastic about the Swedish Nightingale, that some of his lady friends began to think whether they ought not to make haste to congratulate him. He soon undeceived them. "Jenny Lind," he writes, "is a pearl. She is not so great a singer as Malibran, but a better actress. She is the most amiable child I have ever known. In private life she seems to me an ennobled Cinderella. Don't misunderstand me. She is already engaged."* In another place he says that nobody could see her in "La Sonnambula" without going away a better man.

From Berlin he proceeded to Dresden, so exhausted by social civilities, that the railway-carriage seemed to him a delightful haven of rest. At the Saxon Court he was received with equal heartiness. By special request of the King and Queen, he read to them "The Fir Tree" and "Danish Holger," and was delighted to find that the children of Prince John of Saxony knew all the Tales by heart. But it was at the Court of Weimar that his happi-

* Bille og Bogh : *Breve fra Andersen*, ii. p. 97.

ness reached its culmination. He describes the month he stayed there as the most blissful of his existence. He was lodged in sumptuous apartments full of rococo furniture, he had a gorgeous lackey to wait upon him,* and all the ducal family treated him like "a dear, dear friend." Indeed, if his narrative be absolutely trustworthy, the Court of Weimar at that time must have been the most sentimental spot in Europe. We hear of the young Hereditary Grand Duke sitting with him on the same sofa, hand-in-hand, and when Andersen told him how deeply moved he was at his noble conduct, the expansive Prince pressed "the long poet" to his breast, and begged him to stay with him for ever. On another occasion, the Hereditary Grand Duke took him to the Countess Radern's where they found Jenny Lind, and she sang a Swedish hymn so touchingly that every one was quite upset. The young duchess fell upon Jenny's neck, Jenny herself burst into tears, the Hereditary Grand Duke pressed her hand to his lips and Andersen was deeply affected. "How lovely is life!" he exclaims. "All men are good at bottom, I trust them all, and have never been deceived in any."

Nevertheless, now and again, "a little gall apple catches in the point of his pen," and he feels that he

* It was here that he wore a sword, a court-dress, and a three-cornered hat for the first time.

must have some slight aggravation, or his daily bread
would be too sweet for him. It sometimes seems to
him that he really must suffer a great deal of injustice at home, or else great Germany must stand very
much below the intellectual level of little Denmark.
He is quite angry when Jonas Collin insinuates that
all this hob-nobbing with princes and potentates may
unsettle him, and Edward Collin's sensible suggestions that Carsten Hauch's recently published criticism of his (Andersen's) works at Copenhagen, should
give him far more grounds of encouragement than
"all these German laurel leaves," Andersen contemptuously scouted as an empty tirade. But his
greatest grievance was the necessity of obtaining his
own Sovereign's permission to wear the Order of the
Red Eagle conferred upon him by the King of Prussia.
He could not understand this at all, and expressed
himself surprised in the highest degree to find himself
so dependent.* It was only with the utmost difficulty that Jonas Collin could make his "dear Semper
Idem, otherwise H. C. Andersen," comprehend that
this was a matter of etiquette to which every Dane
must submit.

The delicate attentions of his German friends followed him even to Rome. Goethe's widow sent him
bouquets of roses all the way to the Eternal City,

* He was also rather hurt that a foreign Sovereign should have
decorated him before his own Sovereign.

and he had so many choice flowers in his room there, that their fragrance made him feel quite faint. It had been his original intention to proceed to Spain, but the sirocco-like heat which prevailed throughout Southern Europe during the summer of 1846, prevented him. During his stay at Rome, he had to lie on the sofa every day from 11 to 4; lived on four or five portions of ice a day, and was seized with vertigo every time he ventured into the street before sunset. At Naples, it was even worse. The air seemed to be impregnated with the sand of Africa, and he felt like a fish cast ashore in the hot sunshine; by the time he had reached Marseilles, he was worn down to a mere shadow. A brief stay at Vernet in the Pyrenees enabled him to resume his homeward journey, and after just " peeping " across the Spanish frontier, and addressing the natives in their own language which they would not understand as spoken by him, he crawled painfully through France to Geneva, and after recruiting there for a while returned to Copenhagen through Germany, paying, *en route*, a visit on the Hereditary Grand Duke of Weimar at Ettisheim, where he was again received with open arms. Contrary to his usual custom, he seems, this time, to have quite longed to see his native land again. " I come flying home with a full heart," he writes to Collin, " a little spoiled with the homage of princes and great intellects, but dear

Ingeborg * will soon put her mental bridle upon the snorting steed."

And yet, in a little more than six months, the restless creature was eager to be off again. England this time was the goal of his desires, and in the following chapter we shall see what he thought of us, and what we thought of him.

* E. Collin's sister, whom Andersen loved the most of them all, and who could always do most with him.

# CHAPTER IX

## ANDERSEN IN ENGLAND

English translations of Andersen—The critics—*Literary Gazette--Examiner—Athenæum—Spectator*—Andersen's first impression of the Thames. London-traffic—The reception at Lord Palmerston's—The London Season—Prince Consort—Lady Morgan—The lady who kissed his hand—His bust by Durham—Meets Dickens at Lady Blessington's—Delight at his reception in London—Violent diatribe against his critics at home—Fêted to death—His ignorance of English—Andersen and Mrs. Howitt—Cause of the misunderstanding between them—Jenny Lind—Andersen visits her at Brompton—Taglioni—Andersen's general impression of London—In Scotland—Edinburgh—Amusing incident at the Heriot Hospital—The Highlands—A Scotch Sabbath—Visits Bentley—And Dickens—Andersen's second visit to England—Correspondence with Dickens—Stays at Gadshill—Miss Burdett Coutts—Avoids London—Bitter moments—Sympathy of Dickens—Departure from England.

ANDERSEN was already pretty well known in England. Mrs. Howitt had, as early as 1845, translated *Only a Fiddler* and *The Improvisatore;* in the course of 1846 there were no less than four independent translations of the Tales, of which Mrs. Howitt's " Wonderful Stories " * is indisputably the best, and Miss Peachey's " Danish Fairy Legends " decidedly

---

* For a critical estimate of all the English versions of the Tales, see Appendix No. 3.

·the worst, while Mr. Beckwith, in the course of the same year, produced a somewhat indifferent version of *En Digters Bazar*. In 1847 we find three fresh editions of the Tales, and a translation from the German of *A Picture Book without Pictures*, while Mrs. Howitt contributed under the title of "The True Story of My Life," a version of *Das Märchen meines Lebens*,\* which Andersen had prefixed to the German edition of his collected works. All the English critics were charmed with the "Tales" and the "Bazaar," but rather more doubtful about the novels. The merit of being the first to introduce Andersen to the English reader belongs to William Jerdan, the editor of the then moribund *Literary Gazette*,† who had communicated with Andersen in 1846, sent him a copy of his paper, and courteously invited him to extend his travels to England. The "long poet" had responded in a characteristically effusive epistle, expressing his unbounded devotion to all his English friends male and female in general, and to Jerdan in particular.‡

* This, therefore, was the second Andersenian autobiography, "La vie d'un poète" being the first. The first part of the definitive and voluminous *Mit Livs Eventyr* did not appear till 1855, and has never been Englished.

† Founded by Henry Colburn and William Jerdan in 1817, it was from 1820 to 1830 the leading literary Review of London, but declined rapidly in the thirties, and was superseded by the *Athenæum* and *Spectator*.

‡ Bille og Bogh : *Breve fra Andersen*, ii. pp. 156–9.

This outburst was largely due to Andersen's gratitude for the very flattering but altogether uncritical
notices of the "Bazaar" and the "Tales" which had
already appeared in the *Literary Gazette.** Andersen
evidently regarded that periodical as the leading
literary paper of the day in England, and lost no
opportunity of flourishing it defiantly in the faces of
adverse critics at home. But the other journals
were also favourable to him. The *Examiner*, in its
notice of Miss Peachey's version of the Tales,† declared that it had never met with any production
" so given up to a sense of the variety of being that
exists in the universe." One's consciousness as a
human being, it said, ran the risk of being lost
altogether in the crowd of swallows, storks, swans,
mermaids, slugs, cuttle fish, ducks, *and green peas*
(for Mr. Andersen's very vegetables have as much
conversational power as his ducks and geese), all of
which were always talking in character, but without
the slightest confusion of ideas, whilst even his balls
and peg-tops had an astonishing individuality all
their own. The *Athenæum* warmly praised "the
rich and graphic beauty" of the descriptions of Italy
in *The Improvisatore*, pronouncing them to be as
full of colour as the poems in prose and verse of
Byron and Beckford, Goethe and George Sand. The

* February 20, June 13, and October 10, 1846.
† July 4, 1846.

same review described "A Poet's Bazaar" as a
treasury of pictures absolutely perplexing from the
variety and richness of its contents, and parted from
it reluctantly after expressing its enthusiasm in ten
columns.* As to the Fairy Tales, the *Athenæum*
frankly avowed that no amount of criticism was
adequate to do them justice. "Fanciful though it
seem," said the reviewer, "we could defend our
crotchet that the most fitting review of this volume
would be a strain of elfin music such as Weber wove
for his mermaids in ' Oberon,' or Liszt can whisper
when in a mood of gentle improvisation. Common
Cheapside paragraphs are too square and hard and
ungraceful to invite gentle readers to pages so full
of enchantment as these." † But the ablest of all
Andersen's English reviewers, and the one that on
the whole took his intellectual measure best, was the
critic of the *Spectator*. He rightly regarded the
" exquisitely beautiful " " Tales and Stories written
for children " as among the Danish author's most
successful efforts, and pronounced "The Ugly Duckling " as " unsurpassed by anything of its kind we
have ever seen." Everything in " A Poet's Bazaar,"
too, pleased the *Spectator* except its quaint and
inappropriate title suggesting an assortment of showy
gimcracks ostentatiously displayed, whereas the

* November 7 and 14, 1846.
† *Athenæum*, June 6, 1846.

genius of Andersen, opines the reviewer, is above all things "cordial and kindly, winning our love rather than commanding our admiration." Towards the novels, *Improvisatore, O. T.*, and *Only a Fiddler*, on the other hand, the *Spectator* was less indulgent, fastening at once upon Andersen's cardinal defects as a novelist. The following opening paragraph of the review of *The Improvisatore,** for instance, might have been written by Molbech himself: " H. C. Andersen is a Danish celebrity who seems to us to be rather characterised by poetical temperament than by poetical power, and to possess the superficial brilliance and fluent rhetoric that belong to the gifted improvisatore, rather than the sound judgment, deep thought, and regulated imagination which distinguish the great genius." †· The reviewer goes on to observe, very pertinently, that the plan of the story is not badly construed for the exhibition of Italian character and scenery, but that the personages are altogether exotic.‡ The *Spectator* considered *Only a Fiddler* a far superior

* *Spectator,* March 15, 1845.

† Note, however, that at the time when this was written the " Fairy Tales " were still unknown in England.

‡ On the other hand, the reviewer is quite wrong in imputing the artless *naïveté* which runs through the story to "an affectation of sentiment and morals " borrowed from the modern French school. Andersen, when he wrote *Improvisatoren,* knew little French to speak of, his sentiment and sensibility is, and always was, entirely his own.

work* to *The Improvisatore*, and acutely recognised it as an idealisation of the author's individual experiences. Andersen's endeavour in the episode of Noemi and Christian to "depict the innermost feelings of children," receives its due meed of praise, while his attempt to inspire sympathy with the outcasts of society in the later parts of the story, draws forth the remark that "the philosophy of the case is beyond H. C. Andersen's cast of mind." *O. T.* is curtly dismissed with a few contemptuous lines, and most people will agree with the reviewer that the plot of that story is false, absurd, and melodramatic. On the other hand, no mention is made of its truly Dickensian humour, and its noble description of Odense market-place.

In concluding its review of "A Poet's Bazaar," the *Athenæum* reviewer had confessed to a more than ordinary curiosity as .to the impressions which England would be likely to produce upon a pilgrim so artless yet so wise, so national and yet so enthusiastically large in his views and catholic in his sympathies as the Danish author.† As that curiosity has, so far as I am aware, never yet been gratified,‡ I will devote the remainder of this

* *Spectator*, August 30, 1845.

† *Athenæum*, November 14, 1846.

‡ *Das Märchen meines Lebens* was written prior to Andersen's visit to England. *Mit Livs Eventyr*, published eight years afterwards, has never yet been translated.

chapter to the description of Andersen's experiences of England.

In the middle of June, 1847 after making what can only be described as a triumphal progress through Holland, Andersen quitted Rotterdam for London in the night-packet, *Batavian*.\* The following morning when he came on deck the English coast lay before him. It is thus that he describes his first impressions of the Thames :—" The Thames is sufficient of itself to persuade you that England is the mistress of the waves. Her slaves are for ever flying out of it on her errands ; countless swarms of ships ; steamer after steamer, like so many couriers with heavy smoke-gauze in their hats, and a fiery red flower blazing atop. Like lordly, full-breasted swans, one great vessel after another glided by us, then there were pleasure-yachts with rich young gentlemen on board . . . . and the higher up the Thames we got, the more and more crowded it became. I had begun to count the steam-boats to see how many we should meet, but very soon had to give it up. At Gravesend it looked as if we were about to plunge into a huge smoking bog-fire, but it was only the smoke from the steamers and the chimneys that lay before us . . . . and still, although it scarcely

---

\* The chief authorities for this, Andersen's first visit to England, are : *M. L. E.*, pp. 421–463 ; Collin, pp. 420–5 ; Bille og Bogh, *Breve fra Andersen*, ii. pp. 170–191 ; " Mary Howitt, an Autobiography," pp. 182–184.

seemed possible, the traffic grew thicker and thicker,
till it became a perfect muddle of steamers, boats,
and sailing-ships, a sort of blocked-up moving street.
I absolutely could not understand how these countless masses of vessels could move in and out without
running into each other every moment. Presently
there were traces of the ebb-tide, the miry, slimy
bottom appeared near the banks ; I thought of Quilp
in Dickens' 'Nelly and his [sic] grandfather ;' I
thought of Marryat's sketches of life by the river
here."

On landing at the Custom House he took a cab,
and kept driving on and on through "this endless
city of cities," till he began to despair of ever
reaching the modest Hôtel de Sablonière in
Leicester Square, which his friend Örsted had recommended to him. The bustle and traffic, the
ceaseless throng of the foot-passengers, the multi-
tude and variety of the vehicles, filled him with
astonishment and consternation. It seemed to him
as he looked out upon the crowded thoroughfares as
if one half of the whole population of London were
pouring to one end of the town, and the other half
to the other end, or as if there were some great
event going on in every corner of the town simultaneously which accounted for the endless flow of
wave after wave of omnibuses, cabs, and cars in this
human Mælström. He wrote to his friends in

Denmark that of all the towns he knew, only two, London and Rome, deserved the name of metropolis. Paris seemed to him quite contemptible by comparison. He had come to London without any letters of introduction, but the Danish Minister, Count Reventlow, whom he waited upon next day, told him that he didn't require any, as his novels and stories were the best recommendations he could possibly have. The same evening he accompanied the Ambassador to a reception at Lady Palmerston's. There he made his *début* in London society with not a little trepidation, for he had heard " frightful things " about the haughty reserve of the English aristocracy, and was therefore delightfully relieved to find himself a social star of the first magnitude. One of the first persons he met at Palmerston's was his friend the Duke of Weimar, who introduced him to Lady Suffolk, and he was speedily surrounded by a bevy of noble dames who knew " The Top and the Ball " and "The Ugly Duckling " by heart, and were very attentive and agreeable. Then the Duke of Cambridge came up and talked to him about Christian VIII., while the Prussian Ambassador, Bunsen, whom he had met before at Rome, compared notes with him about the Scandinavian artistic colony there, so that in a very short time he felt perfectly at home. A few days later he was present at the ball at Lady Palmerston's on the

Queen's birthday, where a mob of notabilities were pressed as close together as "rose-leaves in a vase," and the heat and crush nearly made him faint. For the next three weeks, indeed, he lived in a constant whirl of excitement which tickled his vanity perhaps, but was very trying to his nerves. The Prince Consort invited him to Marlborough House, and greeted him so affectionately that Andersen felt that he should love him ever afterwards from the bottom of his heart; Lords Castlereagh and Stanley also entertained him; Bulwer Lytton sent him a greet- ing from the country where he happened to be canvassing votes at the time; he dined at Roths- child's, where there was such a profusion of silver plate that he felt quite "drawn towards mammon;" and was taken by Reventlow to see Lady Morgan, whom he describes as a very lively and merry old lady, but quite French, and tremendously rouged. In short, English society chose to regard him as "one of the most remarkable and interesting men of the day," and he had to pay the penalty of a society lion at the height of the season. Every day was taken up by invitations to breakfast, dinner, and supper, followed by balls lasting far into the follow- ing morning. It was, he tells us, one long day and night of festive humming and buzzing in hot saloons and on crowded staircases, lasting for three weeks, of which he only took away a confused impression of beautiful shapes in velvet and gold lace flitting about splendid saloons festooned with roses. He has therefore very few adventures to record during his visit to London, but occasionally we come across a comical incident. Thus at one great mansion, where everything was "silk and silver," the lady of the house, as he was about to take leave, pressed his hand to her lips instead of shaking it, and exclaimed: " I must kiss this precious hand that has written joy and consolation for so many." Andersen, who tried to withdraw his hand in vain, could think of nothing better to do in his confusion than to seize the lady's hand and restore her kiss tenfold. Other distinguished ladies were equally enthusiastic, though a trifle less demonstrative. Some of them assured him that he was a thousand times handsomer than his last portrait, which they disparaged as altogether too stiff and gaunt. Much more to his and their taste was the bust which the sculptor Durham did of him. It must have been considerably idealised, for he describes it as like in a high degree, but so ennobled, so handsome. "Yes," he exclaims, " that is how I should like to look. That is how my face *will* look in a higher world ! "

At Lady Blessington's, whither he was taken by his friend Jerdan, he met the man he most desired to see, Charles Dickens, whose novels he knew well, and greatly admired. This meeting must be told in

Andersen's own words: "I was yesterday at Lady Blessington's. . . . . And can you guess now who was my neighbour at table? Wellington's eldest son? Before we sat down to eat, Lady Blessington gave me the English edition of '*Das Märchen meines Lebens*,' and bade me write my name in it. Just as I was writing, a man came into the room, just like the portrait we have all seen, a man who had come to town for my sake, and had written : 'I *must* see Andersen!' He had no sooner saluted the company than I left the writing desk, and rushed towards him; we took each other by the hand, looked into each other's eyes, and laughed for joy ; we knew each other so well, although this was our first meeting—it was Charles Dickens. He quite comes up to my highest expectation of what he would be like.* Outside the house is a pretty verandah which runs along its whole length . . . . here we stood for a long time and talked—talked in English, but he understood me, and I him." Dickens talked, among other things, about "The Little Mermaid" which Lady Duff Gordon had just translated in *Bentley's Magazine*, and praised "A Poet's Bazaar" and *The Improvisatore*, which he had also read. He also drank Andersen's health at table, and the

---

* Elsewhere Andersen describes Dickens as "young, handsome, with a shrewd and amiable expression, and beautiful long hair falling down on both sides."

Marquis of Douro followed his example. Dickens
came up to London a second time on purpose to see
Andersen, and on this occasion brought him a
beautifully bound edition of his works, in every
volume of which he had written " To Hans Christian
Andersen, from his friend and admirer, Charles
Dickens."

Andersen was charmed, delighted, almost overpowered by his reception in London, although,
characteristically enough, he seems to have regarded
it not so much in the light of a personal triumph, as
of a crushing rebuke to his less appreciative countrymen.  Thus his letters from London to his friends in
Denmark are a curious jumble of gratitude and
spite, ecstatic joy and bitter exasperation.  The
English are described as the most sterling, amiable
and moral people in the wide world.  Thanks to
them, he has reached the apex of glory and recognition.  He cannot hope for more than this metropolis
of the world has already given him.  " Here," he
exclaims, " I am regarded as a Danish Walter Scott,
while in Denmark I am degraded into a sort of
third-class author far below Hertz the classical, and
Heiberg the infallible."  His anger is especially
hot against the Danish newspapers for taking not
the slightest notice of the honours paid to him in
England.  Such contemptible meanness, as he calls
it, deeply wounded him.  It made him feel " fever-

ishly ill " to be "eternally set at nought " in his own country. His dark moments are all owing to the people at home—God forgive them !—it was they who always "spat upon the glow-worm *because* it glowed." "Oh!" he exclaims, "I suffer so to-day that I could weep, and now I must set off with a sick heart to take part in joyful festivals where every one bows down before me." Yet, despite these feverish outbursts, gratitude to God and man was Andersen's predominant feeling during his visit to England, and it is due to him to say that the more he was fêted and flattered by the great world of London, the more humbly and modestly he expresses himself. On the other hand, all this excitement and dissipation was too much for his naturally delicate physique, and he became positively ill before the season was well over. Another considerable draw-back to his happiness was his ignorance of the language. Andersen could read English fairly well, and could even write it a little, though not without considerable trouble ; but to talk it with any degree of fluency he never could manage, and though he made a marvellously good use of his little stock of words, and dexterously helped himself out with pantomime when words failed him, it was a secret vexation to him that he could never get any further.*

* Of course his English friends tried good-naturedly to persuade him that he was making immense progress, and some of the ladies

It was possibly because she was unaware of Andersen's state of health, and did not suspect the
inadequacy of his colloquial English, that Mrs.
Howitt has been, I think, somewhat hard upon him
in the description she has given us in her autobiography of his visit to Dr. Smith and the Gillies'
family at Hillside, Highgate.* Mrs. Howitt, as
already mentioned, had been the first to translate
Andersen into English, and with his usual effusiveness
he had then and there claimed her as a friend, and
enrolled her among his numerous literary sisters.
The accomplished lady was evidently much gratified
by this attention, and a week before Andersen's
arrival in England, a very flattering, not to say
gushing, notice of " this extraordinary man, this
genius," appeared in *Howitt's Journal*, accompanied
by his portrait and a memoir.  Immediately upon
his arrival Mrs. Howitt and her daughter called upon
their Danish friend, and invited him to their cottage
at Clapton.  Andersen went, was very hospitably
entertained, and promised to go again and stop for
a few days, although the long journey there and
back in a stuffy omnibus in the dog-days, tried him
severely.  During his second visit at the Howitts',

even went so far as to praise his accent.  But although Andersen half
believed them at the time, and never failed to repeat these and similar
compliments to his friends at home, he was too well aware of his own
deficiencies in this respect to be long deceived.
    * Howitt, " Autobiography," pp. 183-4.

a trip to the pleasant villa of Dr. Southwood Smith at Highgate was planned, and the whole party set out in a one-horse carriage. The pace was slow, the vehicle was crowded, the heat was suffocating, and again poor Andersen seems to have suffered severely. Nevertheless, Highgate was reached at last, and there, in a hayfield, a number of people were assembled in honour of the distinguished guest, together with a group of children whom Andersen took to be a school or *pension*. They were dancing round a large beech-tree when he arrived, but at once crowded about the stranger, who was introduced to them as Hans Christian Andersen who had written the Fairy Tales. Now Andersen, who never had that fondness for children which is popularly attributed to him, and was doubly embarrassed on this occasion because he could not speak to the little ones in their own language, nevertheless did his best to amuse them by making them a pretty device of flowers, an art at which he had always been an adept. The children, however, were naturally shy in the society of the gaunt, awkward, and silent stranger, so they, one by one, slunk off to their games while Andersen remained with the company in a sultry little summer-house, in the full heat of the sun, where he felt half baked, casting longing looks at the shady trees in the hayfield. At last he could endure it no longer, and was obliged to take

s

refuge in a cool little room at the back of the house, where he remained till the sun had set and there was a little fresh air to breathe.* This is mainly Andersen's account of the matter, which I take to be substantially true. Mrs. Howitt, on the other hand, insinuates that Andersen withdrew from the company through jealousy of the American writer, Henry Clarke Wright,† who happened to be present on the occasion, and entered heart and soul, "without any suggestion of condescension," into the glee of the children who felt somehow that the stiff and silent foreigner was not kindred to themselves. Then she adds : "Soon poor Andersen, perceiving himself forsaken, complained of headache, and insisted on going indoors, where Miss Mary Gillies and I, most anxious to efface any disagreeable impression, accompanied him ; but he remained irritable and out of sorts." The fact seems to be that Mrs. Howitt, when she wrote this portion of her autobiography, had a grievance against Andersen, which made it almsot impossible for her to regard him in a very favourable light. It arose in this way.‡

---

* *M. L. E.*, pp. 427-8.

† Best known in England from his moral story-book, "A Kiss for a Blow," four editions of which appeared in England between 1851 and 1874. It is a useful little infantile manual, but of no literary value whatever.

‡ Compare Howitt, "Autobiography," pp. 182-3, and *M. L. E.*, pp. 517-20.

Andersen, it appears, had been assured in Germany *
that the Howitts were making a fortune out of his
translations, and was naturally anxious on his
arrival in London, poor man as he was, to come to
an advantageous money arrangement with them.
With his usual delicacy in such transactions, he
wrote to Mrs. Howitt, expressing his gratitude to
her for the able manner in which she had Englished
him, at the same time declaring that as he could
not bear the thought of discussing money matters
with friends, he would prefer to arrange the
business through his countryman the banker, Hambro.
Hambro saw the Howitts accordingly, and very
soon persuaded both himself and Andersen that the
Howitts' gains had been much exaggerated, though
it seems to me they could scarcely have received less
for translating than the author had originally
received for writing his novels and tales. Andersen
expressed himself perfectly satisfied, and shortly
before his departure from England very generously
invited Mrs. Howitt to translate the whole of his
fairy-tales, at the same time placing at her disposal
the beautiful woodcuts of the Leipsic edition. Mrs.
Howitt " foolishly," as she herself admits, " let the
proposal drop," whereupon Andersen, who was now
in a position to pick and choose among the London

* To be perfectly fair, I here follow entirely Mrs. Howitt's account
of the matter.

publishers, applied to Bentley. This Mrs. Howitt
seems to have deeply resented ; at any rate, in a
work subsequently published by Mr. Howitt and
herself, entitled " The Literature and Romance of
Northern Europe," we find that not only are *all*
Andersen's later works indiscriminately depreciated,
but he is himself described as an egoist and a *petit-
maître*. Andersen keenly felt the injustice of this
attack at the time, but readily forgave it when,
some years later, his Swedish friend, Madam Bremer,
who had visited the Howitts* as she passed through
London on her return to Sweden from America,
informed him that "good Mary Howitt" had spoken
so kindly of him, and lamented, with tears in her
eyes, that he would now have nothing more to do
with her.

Another of his "sisters," in whose society Andersen always found inexhaustible happiness, was Jenny
Lind. She was the rage of the town just then, but,
for the sake of quiet and fresh air, she had hidden
herself in a little house at Old Brompton. This was
all that Andersen could find out about her at the
hotel where he was staying, but the police, "always
my surest help," directed him to the cashier of the
Italian Opera, as the person most likely to give him

---

* Mrs. Howitt, who, by the way, knew Swedish much better than
Danish, had translated some of the best of Madam Bremer's novels
into English.

further and accurate information. He forthwith left his address for her at the Opera, and the next morning received an affectionate letter from Jenny, inviting her "brother" to come and see her. As he drove up, Jenny saw him through the window blinds, and rushed to the garden gate to help him out of his cab, sublimely indifferent to the gaping crowd which used to besiege her little cottage from dawn till dusk, on the off-chance of seeing her come out, and led him into the house, where, he tells us, everything was " nice, elegant, and cosy." On the table lay an elegantly bound copy of "The True Story of My Life," which Mary Howitt had dedicated to Jenny Lind, and a caricature of Jenny herself, representing her as a big nightingale with a girl's face, with Lumley standing beside her strewing sovereigns on her tail to make her sing. She promised him a ticket for the Opera every night she appeared, but would not hear of his paying for it, because it was "so absurdly dear." " You shall read me a 'fairy-tale' instead," said she. He was only able to hear her twice: once in " La Sonnambula," and again in Verdi's "I Masnadieri." It was on the latter occasion that he also saw the famous Taglioni for the first time, in " Le Pas de Deésses." " Before she came in," he tells us, " my heart quite throbbed with expectation, which is always the case with me when I am expecting something great and splendid. She came—and I saw before me an elderly, somewhat sturdily built, and very comely woman ; she would have made a handsome hostess at a reception, but as a young goddess—fuimus Troes! I thought—and the elderly lady's graceful dancing left me quite cold and indifferent. 'Tis only youth that can dance such dances, and that was the charm of Cerrito ! *  *Her* dancing was inexpressibly beautiful, just like the flight of a swallow."

Andersen's general impression of London was a pleasant one. " London," he says, " is the city of courtesy, and the police, in this respect, set the example. You have only to apply to one of these officials in the street, and they show you the way, and put you right at once ; in every shop you enter, too, you always get the most courteous replies. As to the eternally grey atmosphere and the coal-smoke of London, they have been very much exaggerated.† There is lots of smoke, it is true, in the old and densely populated parts of the town, but the larger part of it is just as airy and free of smoke as Paris itself. I have seen many beautiful sunshiny days

---

* Francesca Cerrito was born in 1821 at Naples, where she made her *début* at the Carlo Theatre. She danced in London with Grisi, Taglioni, and Fanny Elsler, during the season of 1840-5. Andersen no doubt saw her at Vienna.

† We shall see that as to this he changed his opinion after his second visit.

in London, and many starry nights. . . . . To my
mind, London is the metropolis of all cities, without
prejudice to Rome. Rome is a bas-relief of the
world's night, in which the very carnival revel is
but a noisy, roystering dream. . . . . London is a
bas-relief of the world's day, all busy bustle, life's
rapid, lightning-like loom."

It was a great relief to Andersen, however, when
the London season came to an end, and he set out
for Scotland, where he was to be the guest of the
Danish banker, Hambro, at Lixmount, near Edinburgh. The rapid speed of the English expresses,
and the dark, mile-long tunnels, were new and
terrifying experiences to him. " Formerly," he says,
" we used to travel through valleys and over mountains, now we go through mountains and over
valleys." English scenery struck him as very much
like the scenery of his native isle, Funen, but fresher,
greener, and on a far grander scale, " as, indeed, is
everything in this splendid country." At York
station a gentleman greeted him, and introduced
him to two ladies ; it was the Marquis of Douro,
whom he had met at Lady Blessington's. Andersen
stayed a night and a day at York, whose fine
cathedral and picturesque old gabled houses he
greatly admired. Edinburgh he compared at first
sight to Naples in a setting of Greek scenery, the
formation of the mountains reminding him very

strongly of the country round about Athens. " The
spectacle of the old town, seen from the new," he
says elsewhere, " is inspiring and splendid, and
places Edinburgh, from an artistic point of view, on
a level with Constantinople and Stockholm. . . . .
Where the town slopes down towards the sea, stands
the hill, Arthur's Seat, known from Walter Scott's
romance, ' The Dungeon of Edinburgh ; ' * the
whole of the old town, in fact, is a sort of commentary upon these mighty romances for all lands.
It is befitting, therefore, that Walter Scott's handsome memorial should stand just where one can
survey the whole panorama."

The famous physician, James Simpson, was his
*cicerone* through the town. Holyrood struck him
as a series of long halls and tiresome rooms full
of bad portraits ; the only thing that interested
him there were the blood-stains on the floor of the
little room where Rizzio had been murdered, and
the luxuriance of the ivy in the ruins of the church
hard by, the like of which he had never met with
hitherto except in Italy. At the Heriot Hospital,
which he visited with Hambro, he had an amusing
adventure. They had signed their names in the
visitors' book, and the porter, who acted as guide,
imagining that the jovial, white-haired Hambro was
" Hans Christian Andersen," followed him every-

* He means " The Heart of Midlothian."

where, and paid him the most marked attention. "So *that* is the Danish author," cried he at last. " Well, I always fancied he was like that, with just such a sonsie face and venerable hair." " No," replied a member of the party, " you are wrong. There's the author ! " and he pointed at Andersen. " What, so young as that !" exclaimed the old porter. " Why, I've read him often and often, and got my lads to read him too. It is a remarkable thing to live to see such men ; as a rule they are either old or dead before any one hears anything about them." Andersen was so affected that he went up to the old man and pressed his hand, and then turned aside to hide his tears. After spending a week in Edinburgh, visiting Lord Jeffries at his country seat, and being frequently entertained at Simpson's house, where he was introduced to the leading notabilities of the Northern Athens, such as Wilson, Miss Rigby, Mrs. Crown, and others, " the Danish Walter Scott," as his Scotch friends now persisted in calling him, accompanied Hambro on a tour through the Highlands. He saw Kirkcaldy, Stirling Castle, the field of Bannockburn, Callender, Loch Katrine and the Trossachs, Loch Lomond and Dumbarton, at which place he took leave of Hambro, and proceeded by steamer up the Clyde to Glasgow, returning thence by train to Edinburgh, very much grieved that he had no time to visit Abbotsford to see Lockhart, whose acquaintance he had made at London. His three weeks' visit to Scotland had been exceedingly pleasant, but not quite the repose that he had anticipated. He also considered travelling in England and Scotland very dear, "but," he adds, " you get something for your money. Everything is excellent, the people really look after you ; there is real comfort everywhere, even in the smallest village inn." But with every disposition to be delighted with everything, there was nevertheless one thing in the " land of brown heath and shaggy wood " that he could by no means reconcile himself to, and that was the Scotch Sabbath. He experienced the full force of it during his stay at Dumbarton. Let us hear his own account of the matter : " It was Sunday, and that means something in Scotland, I can tell you. Everything is then at rest, even the railway trains dare not run. In fact, the only thing that, to the great offence of the rigidly righteous Scots, does not stand still is the express from London to Edinburgh. All the houses are closed, and the people sit inside and read their Bibles or drink themselves blind drunk—for so I was everywhere told. It is quite contrary to my nature to sit indoors all day, and see nothing at all of the town, so I proposed a promenade. I was told it would not do at all, as the people would be sure to take offence. Towards evening, however, we all went out for a turn in the country, but there was such a stillness, such a peeping out of windows, such a spying after us, that we soon turned back. A young Frenchman I had a talk with assured me that he and his friends had recently gone out one Sunday afternoon with fishing rods, when they met an old gentleman, who upbraided them most angrily and in the hardest terms for their ungodliness in thus amusing themselves on Sunday, instead of sitting at home over their Bibles ; at any rate, said he, they shouldn't scandalise and seduce others. Such Sun-day piety cannot, as a general rule, be sincere ; where it is so I respect it, but as an inherited custom it is apt to become a mere mask, and only give occasion to hypocrisy."

On returning to London he found it deserted by the polite world, and most of his society friends abroad, or at the seaside. He now longed after Denmark again, and all his " dear ones " there ; but before leaving England he spent a few days with his publisher, Richard Bentley, at Seven Oaks,* and on his way to Ramsgate to catch the Ostend boat, accepted an invitation to dinner from Dickens, who was then staying with his family at Broadstairs. It

* Andersen was much impressed by the wealth and comfort of the London publisher's èstablishment. " He has a nice residence," he wrote to a friend at Copenhagen, " with such elegance. Lacqueys in silk stockings wait upon us,—that's something like a bookseller for you ! "

was not till late in the evening that Andersen could regretfully tear himself away from his genial host, but little as he expected it he was to meet him once more before his departure, for Dickens walked from Broadstairs next morning to bid him a final good-bye on Ramsgate pier, and promised to correspond with him regularly. "We pressed each other's hands," says Andersen, "and he looked at me so kindly with his shrewd, sympathetic eyes, and as the ship went off, there he stood, waving his hat, and looking so gallant, so youthful, and so handsome. Dickens was the last who sent me a greeting from dear England's shore."

Andersen's first visit to England was not without results from a literary point of view. Within the next five years Bentley published two * more small collections of the Fairy Tales, besides a translation of a new novel, *The Two Baronesses*, of which more anon, while a third independent † version of

---

* *A Christmas Greeting to my English Friends*, containing seven, and *A Poet's Day Dreams*, containing fourteen new stories, both dedicated to Dickens. In his preface to the former work he says, " I feel a desire, a longing to transplant in England the first produce of my poetic garden as a Christmas greeting, and I send it to you, my dear, noble Charles Dickens, who by your works had been previously dear to me, and since our meeting have taken root in my heart." This preface is a good specimen of Andersen's English at its best, revised and corrected as usual, of course, by one or other of his Danish friends, perhaps Edward Collin.

† *The Dream of Little Tuk, and other Tales*, containing seven stories. Mr. Boner's version is but indifferent.

the Tales translated by Charles Boner was brought
out by Grant & Griffith.

Andersen paid a second five weeks' visit to
England in 1857, during the whole of which time he
was the guest of Dickens* at Gadshill. At first,
indeed, he had been very doubtful whether he
should accept Dickens' invitation. "There is one
thing you will observe at once when we meet," he
writes, "I talk English very badly, yes, even worse
than when I was in your family circle last time, for
then I had been nearly three months in England,
but now I have not been there for ten years, have
no practice in speaking English at home, and shall
come straight from my Danish Fatherland over to
you." Finally he declared that he would not come
to England at all, unless he were sure of finding
Dickens there. "My visit is to you alone," he says,
"and unless I hear from you I shall go to Switzerland." But Dickens was not to be put off, and sent,
by return of post, a reply brimming over with
cordiality. "I hope," he writes, "that my answer
will at once decide you to make your summer visit
to us. . . . . We shall be at a little country house I
have. . . . . You shall have a pleasant room there
with a charming view, and shall live as quiet and

* The sources for Andersen's second visit to England are : Bille og
Bogh, *Breve fra Andersen*, ii. 362–80, and Bille og Bogh, *Breve til
Andersen*, pp. 122–6, containing three letters from Dickens.

wholesome as in Copenhagen itself. If you should
want at any time you are with us to pass the night
in London, this house,* from the roof to the cellar,
will be at your disposal. . . . . So pray make up
your mind to come to England. We have children
of all sizes, and they all love you. You will find
yourself in a house full of admiring and affectionate
friends, varying from three feet high to five feet
nine. Mind, you must not think any more of going
to Switzerland. You must come to us."

This letter removed Andersen's last scruples. In
the beginning of June he appeared at Gadshill Place,
and was received literally with open arms. Looking
back upon this visit, he used to say it was the
happiest period of his life. He did not feel in the
least as if he were in a foreign land ; it was just like
being at home, he said. In a letter to the Queen
Dowager of Denmark, he describes Dickens as the
most amiable man he had ever known, with a heart
equal to his mind. Nay, with his usual affectionate
exaggeration, he was inclined to place Dickens above
every one in everything ; declared seriously that he
preferred his acting to the acting of Ristori, and was
very indignant when his host's benevolent efforts to
raise a subscription for Douglas Jerrold's widow were
put down to base or petty motives.

The Dickenses certainly did their very utmost to

* Tavistock House, London.

make his visit a happy one, and throughout his stay
he did exactly what he liked. He went to hear the
Handel Festival at the Crystal Palace, was present
at the private view of the Academy, and spent a day
and a night at Miss Burdett Coutts' town house *
with Walter Dickens. As a rule, however, he was
very chary of accepting invitations, and avoided
London like the plague. The heavy smoke and
oppressive heat of the place made him quite ill every
time he went there, and not even the satisfaction of
walking through its leading thoroughfares arm-in-
arm with Dickens, could reconcile him to it. What he
liked best of all was to roam about the green Kentish
lanes with the dogs, or to roll about in the clover
fields with the children The whole landscape
around Gadshill seemed to him a beautiful garden,
and he is perfectly enthusiastic about the fresh hay
and the wild roses. Yet even at Gadshill he had a
few dark and bitter moments. It was while he was
staying there that the news reached him from
Copenhagen of the unfavourable reception there of

* Andersen seems to have been astonished by the magnificence of
Miss Coutts' establishment. " It is," he says, " the most elegant house
I have ever seen. Miss Burdett Coutts is said to be one of the richest
ladies in England. Dickens said that her fortune was incalculable,
and Hambro put her yearly income at such a figure that I really don't
understand it. . . . I was at her house last night, and had a bedroom
such as I never had before, with a bathroom close to it,—costly carpets
. . . . and a view over Piccadilly . . . . the whole of this vast house
was more than kingly.

his last novel, *To Be, or not to Be*, and for a time
it completely upset him.  He wept and wrung his
hands for rage and grief, and was only with difficulty
comforted at last by the sympathy of Dickens, who
embraced him, spoke to him like a brother, and
affectionately reminded him of the eternal compensation he possessed in a world-wide reputation, and
the precious gift of genius that God had given him.
Then writing something with his stick in the sand,
Dickens pointed to it and said : " Such is criticism
in general!"  Then he blotted it all out with his
foot, and added : " Now it is gone, but the author's
work remains."  "And," exclaims Andersen, "when
this great author, perhaps the greatest author of our
times, thus exalted me highly, at that very moment,
I say, I felt myself so small, so humble, thankful
and grateful in God's sight.  Every time I am
exalted by praise, I have the feeling of humble
devotion to God.  Oh, that men would only understand this ! "

In the middle of July Andersen quitted England,
which he was never to see again.  His parting with
the Dickens family was heartrending, and he was
so full of the memories of English hospitality, that
Paris, whither he went next, seemed quite strange
and dismal by contrast.  " Poor Paris ! " he cries,
" thou art but a beehive without honey ! "  So unendurable indeed did he find it, that he left the

place in two days for Germany, where, next to
England, he felt himself most at home. Andersen
always preserved a grateful recollection of Charles
Dickens,* and advertised his works largely in Denmark ; but the enthusiasm he felt for him in 1857
was too perfervid to last very long, and Dickens'
very natural hesitation to foregather indiscriminately
with all the Danes whom he was in the habit of
sending from time to time with letters of introduction, seems at last to have somewhat offended
Andersen ; anyhow during the last fifteen years of
his life we meet with no mention whatever of
Dickens in his correspondence.

* He sent a full account of his visit to Dickens to the *Berlinjske
Tidende* of Copenhagen, 1860.

# CHAPTER X

*Ahasuerus*—Description of the poem—Never finished—*The Two Baronesses*—A mere repetition of *O. T.*—Criticisms—Fresh Fairy Tales—Andersen's "Fairy-dramas" at the Casino—"The North Star" and "The White Falcon"—The Schleswig-Holstein War of 1849-51—Andersen's ignorance of politics—His patriotism —Reflections on peace and war—Kindness to a wounded soldier— Visit to Sweden—Presented to King and Queen—Reads his tales to them—Bernard von Beskow—In the Dales—Leksand —The gingerbread-patterns—The midden-beauty—A rainy day in the Sæther Valley—The lonely inn—A midnight alarm— Hospitality of the Swedes—The whole tour "a beautiful poem"— *I Sverrig*—Received enthusiastically.

"IF," wrote Andersen to his friend Miss Henrietta Wulff, in May 1848, "if my residence in London last summer was the brightest point of my life, this winter and spring in Copenhagen have been the most bitter ones I have ever experienced. I feel just as if I were jostled and chivied about in every direction, just as if all the poetic fire in me were being extinguished day by day " *—which signifies, being interpreted, that his last works, the epic poem *Ahasuerus*, and the novel *De to Baronesser* (The Two Baronesses) had fallen perfectly flat.

* Bille og Bogh : *Breve fra Andersen*, ii. p. 187.

After nearly six years of protracted labour, the long-
advertised epic that bears the name *Ahasuerus*
was given to the world.* Begun with an enthusiastic *élan* which carried the author triumph-
antly through the first, and not altogether infelici-
tously through the second, part, it unmistakably
hangs fire at the commencement of Part III., and
breaks off abruptly without ever coming to a conclusion at the end of Part IV. *Ahasuerus* was
to have been the crowning proof of its author's
poetic talent; it had the unexpected, yet equally
beneficial result of convincing every one, himself
included, that poetry on a grand scale was quite
beyond his powers. After *Ahasuerus* even Andersen had not the courage to write any poetry beyond
a few lyrics. Henceforth he devoted himself almost
entirely to his Fairy Tales, so that, in a. negative
sort of way, the world has reason to be grateful
to him for attempting this apology for an epic.
Still it is only fair to admit that even *Ahasuerus*
begins well, and that the first two parts are full
of promise. The opening couplets describe the
fall of Lucifer. Amongst the rebel host is Ahas
the angel of doubt, weakest of those who spurn and
reject what they themselves do not understand.

---

* He finished it towards the end of 1846, and on his departure for
England entrusted its publication to Edward Collin. It appeared
during his absence from Copenhagen in 1847.

No sooner does his foot touch the earth than he
loses with his wings every recollection of his former
state. Here the author takes a bold poetic leap
of some six thousand years or so across the centuries.
At the very same time that Christ is born in Beth-
lehem, Ahas lies a weeping new-born babe on the
breast of a human mother; thus the spirit of doubt
becomes incarnate at the same time as the Saviour,
only his name is now not Ahas, but Ahasuerus.
Thus it seems to have been Andersen's original
intention to have exhibited in a series of historic
tableaux the mortal struggle that has been going
on between faith and doubt ever since the world
began. The first part of the poem opens at Jerusalem, where the poor cobbler Ahasuerus chains the
people to his threshold by the stirring tales he
tells of the judges of the people, the holy prophets,
and of Jehovah's power and glory in the olden times.
Even the Scribes and Pharisees linger near his
humble workshop to converse with the hardy patriot
who, with the insulting pomp and splendour of
the Roman legions before his eyes, can yet take
comfort in the thought that :

> "The rustiest nail in God's high temple door
> Is more than all the gold that decks an idol."

Among his listeners is the Jewish maid Veronica,
who though, as a good daughter of Israel, she looks
up to the doctors of the law, cannot get from them

the comfort and assurance she finds in the new
prophet, the Nazarene whom the common people
gladly follow. From his friend, Judas Iscariot,
Ahasuerus also hears of this teacher of strange
doctrine, but remains neutral till the triumphal entry
of the Nazarene into Jerusalem, when he also bears
his palm in the procession, and cries Hosannah,
convinced at last that this is indeed the Messiah
who has come to put an end to the Roman rule.
Judas has joined the Master partly out of hatred
of the empty pretensions of the Pharisees, partly
from a real admiration of the wondrous man who
is as wise as a serpent, yet as harmless as a dove.
But the entry into Jerusalem takes place, and
nothing comes of it. Was it only to overturn a few
hucksters' stools in the forecourt of the Temple, only
to heal a few sick, and irritate the priests, that this
great triumph was brought about ? This will never
do. A first blow has been struck, the Sanhedrim
has been infuriated, it is for Judas to hasten on
the coming of the Messiah's kingdom now that
the Messiah himself seems to falter. If the
Nazarene be the Messiah indeed, legions of angels
will surely surround him at the critical moment ;
if not, let him fall as he deserves to fall for so de-
ceiving the people. Thus soliloquises the traitor :

> " No fear have I.
> Ha ! Moses needed once an Aaron's help.
> Messiah needs his Judas, and our names

Together knit, twin stars conjointly standing,
Shall shine o'er David's realm now born on earth.

&ast;  &ast;  &ast;  &ast;  &ast;

I'll go, I'll go to Caiaphas."

Then follows the catastrophe. Judas kills himself from remorse, but the more evil Ahasuerus, in his rage against the false Messiah for disappointing his hopes, roughly repulses Him from his door,* where He would have rested in His weariness on the road to Golgotha, and thereby draws down upon his own head the curse of perpetual unrest till Christ shall come again.

Part II. opens at Rome under Domitian. Ahasuerus, who has been captured at the siege of Jerusalem, where he sought death in vain, now regains his liberty by his unconquerable valour as a gladiator in the arena, becoming finally the executioner and torturer of the Christians, whom he hates with an uappeasable hatred. So far the interest of the subject is well sustained, but Part III. flags terribly. Indeed, it is only by the most extravagant expedients, such, for instance, as making Ahasuerus the avenger who brings Attila first, and then the Mahommedans, down upon the Christian world, that the epic can be made to move on at all. Then, too, the narrative is repeatedly inter-

* It should be remarked, however, that Andersen, with excellent taste, has *not* brought our Lord forward as a *dramatis persona* at all. The procession to Golgotha is related incidentally.

rupted, and even obliterated, by irritating lyrical interludes. We have choruses of wood-doves, church nixies, ravens, flaming towns, hurricanes, and other personifications. It would almost seem as if Andersen's guardian-genius, the Muse of Fairy Tale, impatient of his long desertion of her, had chosen this way of reminding him that *his* Pegasus was no fiery heroic charger with mighty pinions capable of carrying him far above the clouds into the sublimest regions of poetry, but a sort of gorgeous butterfly only properly at home in earth's sunlit-gardens. In Part IV. the poem simply collapses. Ahasuerus ceases to be a personage, and becomes a mere passive spectator of the various events described, which range from the humiliation of the Emperor Henry IV. at Canossa to the discovery of printing at Mayence. Finally Andersen, who by this time is at his wits' end what to do with his own hero, sends him with Columbus on the caravel, *Santa Maria*, to discover America, and simply leaves him there with the *naïve* admission* that he cannot finish the poem himself, but hopes that another and a better poet will at some time or other do it for him.

Andersen's fourth novel, *The Two Baronesses*, was written after his return from England, completed

* "A better poet in a better way
Will tell us of the wanderings that follow."

at Glorup in Funen, in the autumn of 1848, and first appeared in London at the end of the same year, and subsequently in Copenhagen during 1849. This fact, together with an ambiguous expression in the author's preface * to the English edition, naturally led the English critics to believe that Andersen himself had written the book in English first of all, and the *Spectator* even complimented him upon his diction, remarking that it did him credit as a linguist. But to write even half a dozen lines of perfectly correct English was a feat far beyond his capacity, and it is most probable that his Danish MS. was Englished for him by or through Edward Collin, or perhaps one of the Örsteds. Another curious feature of the book which excited much merriment at the time was its sentimental dedication to its publisher, who was addressed in the preface as " dear friend," and thanked effusively for first taking under his

---

* " To you (*i.e.*, Bentley) I dedicate this my new romance, the first that I myself have sent into the world in the English language." (Preface to *The Two Baronesses.*) This preface, by the way, is a translation of Andersen's own Danish letter to Bentley of 5th September, 1848. In a previous letter to Bentley (24th May, 1848), *also in Danish*, he writes : " I am busy fair-copying the last chapters of my romance which is now ready. It is a month since the English MS. was composed (*udarpeidet*). . . . I hope to send you the rough MS. of the first part shortly." From this it would appear that Andersen meant to convey the impression that he himself had written the English MS. But Andersen would certainly not have written ordinary business letters to his English publisher in Danish, if he had been able to write a novel of 600 pages in English.

protection "a young, foreign, and unknown author." Andersen, as usual, thought very highly of this his latest production. He expressed his belief to Bentley that it was certainly his best and most finished work, and hoped the public would think the same. Judging it on its merits, however, *The Two Baronesses* is little more than a somewhat pale and stale repetition of the novel *O. T.*, written eleven years before. Like its predecessor it has no plot, and the frame or background (in this case a description of those curious sandy islets, the Halligs, lying off the south-west coast of Denmark,* and supposed to be the remains of a submerged Frisian continent) is much more effective than the picture or narrative. The characters, the incidents, and the general plan of the two books are strikingly alike, there is even a somewhat similar mystery with an equally unconvincing solution. Andersen himself is unmistakably present throughout in the character of "the poor gentleman." *The Two Baronesses,* moreover, lacks the spontaneous freshness of the earlier story, and is in every way inferior to it. It not only tells one nothing new, but gives one the impression that Andersen, as a novelist, has nothing new to tell. Even the original descriptions of the Halligs cannot be compared with Biernatzki's treatment of the same subject, while the episode of the

* Since 1866 they have ceased to be Danish.

childish loves of Elimar and Elizabeth, although very charming, has not the peculiar witchery of the Christian and Noemi idyll in *Only a Fiddler*.

Still *The Two Baronesses* did not prove such an utter *fiasco* as *Ahasuerus*, and even had a sort of *succès d'estime* both in England and Denmark. Carsten Hauch went so far as to promise it a prominent position in the national literature, and much admired the description of " The Halligs," but thought the character of the heroine too unwomanly.   Madame Bremer had no doubt that it would be one of " the pyramids in his poetic realm," but added significantly, " if you want to know what are the marvels in that realm that especially attract me, those marvels, I mean to say, which revive, refresh, touch and charm me most, I tell you plainly they are your Fairy Tales, those oases in life's desert with their fresh bubbling springs, lofty palms and laughing flowers, those pious roguish children of yours that lead us sportively into the kingdom of heaven before we really know where we are ; " * and she invites him to her dear Aavesta,† where he will find old memories, young roses, and warm hearts that will give him fresh ideas for no end of charming stories.

* Bille og Bogh : *Breve fra Andersen*, p. 670
† Her country-house in Sweden.

Andersen needed no outward stimulus to make him persevere with what had now become his most congenial work. Between 1847 and 1848 he had brought out two more little volumes of the " *Nye Eventyr* " (New Fairy Tales), as he now called them, containing "The Old Street Lamp," "The Neighbours," "The Darning Needle," "Little Tuk," "The Shadow," by many considered the best of all the tales, "The Old House," "The Water-drop," "The Little Match-girl," "The Happy Family," "The Story of a Mother," and "The Collars." Most of these stories are based on personal reminiscences. The little boy who visits the old gentleman in the old house, and makes him a present of a tin soldier, that he may not "feel so terribly lonely," and the little girl in the same story who couldn't help dancing to every kind of music, sacred or profane, are real persons, children whom Andersen actually knew. The satirico-scientific "Water-drop" was written for H. C. Örsted. The story of "The Little Match-girl" was suggested by a picture in Herr Flinch's Almanack, for which Andersen was invited to write something. To the fat white snails which Andersen observed among the luxuriant dock leaves at Glorup in Funen, we are indebted for "The Happy Family." It was jotted down during his visit to London. The idea of "The Story of a

Mother" occurred to him suddenly as he was walking in the street. This tale is said to be a special favourite with the Hindus.*

Another species of composition closely connected with the Tales, and quite as successful, were the "Eventyr-Comedier," or Fairy Tale Plays, which, from 1849 onwards, Andersen began to write for the newly opened variety theatre, the Casino, at Copenhagen. The first of these plays, entitled "Meer end Perler og Guld" (More than Pearls and Gold), had a run of 114 nights, and was followed by "Oli Lockeye," which was acted 66 times † amidst enthusiastic applause. Henceforth Andersen turned his back altogether upon the Royal Theatre and the regular drama, and continued, almost to the end of his life, to supply the Casino with these sparkling poetic trifles from Fairy Land.

In the course of 1848 Andersen received two marks of distinction from foreign potentates; the King of Sweden sent him the Order of the North Star, while the Duke of Weimar conferred upon him the Order of the White Falcon. Andersen had a peculiar, one is almost tempted to say childish, fondness for such decorations, and eagerly seized upon every opportunity of displaying them. He

---

* See *Bemerkninger* til *Eventyr og Historier*, suffixed to the popular Danish edition of the collected Fairy Tales, 1887.

† Collin, pp. 427-8.

was particularly gratified by the Weimar Order as binding him all the more closely "to the home of Goethe and Schiller, and the great names of German literature." On the other hand, the black ribbon of the Swedish Order struck him as of rather sinister augury, its arrival coinciding with the death of his royal friend and patron, Christian VIII.

A great political event now occurred, which for the next three years was greatly to disturb Andersen and turn his thoughts altogether away from the pursuit of literature. The new King of Denmark, Frederick VII., had scarcely ascended the throne when the Duchies of Schleswig and Holstein, secretly encouraged by Prussia, renounced their allegiance to the Danish crown, appointed a pro-vincial government, and convened a Schleswig-Holstein parliament at Rendsburg ; then, assisted by German troops, they rose against Denmark, defeated her in three pitched battles, and drove her troops out of the Duchies (April–June, 1848). But the Danish statesmen were not idle. After obtaining friendly assurances from England and Russia, and inducing Sweden to offer her mediation, which was accepted by Prussia, the prime mover of the revolt, thereby gaining a seven months' respite in the shape of an armistice which enabled her to effectually use her diplomacy abroad and concentrate her forces at home, she found herself at the beginning of 1849 in

a position of decided advantage.   In the spring of
that year the war was resumed, and the Prussians
under Prittwitz occupied Schleswig, while the
Schleswig-Holsteiners invaded South Jutland, defeated the Danes at Kolding (April 23), and sat
down before the fortress of Fredericia, but were
utterly defeated there (July 5 and 6) by the Danes,
and compelled to raise the siege.   Four days later
Prussia concluded a fresh armistice with Denmark,
leading ultimately (July 2, 1850) to a definitive
peace between the two Powers which practically
left the Duchies to settle their quarrel with Denmark
alone.   At first they attempted negotiations, but,
finding Denmark inexorable, determined to try
the fortune of war once more, and their army,
30,000 strong, under General Willesen, largely re-
inforced by German volunteers, assumed the offensive, and invaded North Schleswig, but was utterly
routed by the Danes at the two days' battle of
Idstedt (July 24 and 25, 1850) and driven beyond
the Eyder.   The Danish General Krogh then re-
occupied the whole of Schleswig, and Willesen, after
two fresh defeats, resigned his command to General
von der Horst (December 7, 1850).   But now the
other European Powers, who had in the meantime
become convinced that the integrity of the Danish
monarchy was a matter of European interest, inter-
fered, compelled the Schleswig-Holsteiners to disarm

and disperse, and by the London Convention of
May 8, 1852, practically handed them back to
Denmark.

It was a great triumph for little Denmark to have
prevailed single-handed against the German Bund ;
a triumph due, moreover, quite as much to her own
energy and courage as to the political vacillation of
Prussia, and the military incapacity of the Schleswig-
Holsteiners. Nevertheless, the three years during
which the struggle lasted had been a very serious
time for every patriotic Dane, and Andersen had
not been without his share of anxiety. Of politics,
properly speaking, he neither knew, nor cared
to know, anything. The subject did not interest
him in the least. There is scarcely a reference
in his voluminous correspondence to such epoch-
making events as the revolutionary movement of
1848, the Crimean, the Austro-Prussian, and the
Franco-German wars ; and this is somewhat curious
in one who took such an intense interest in the
progress of humanity, saw more of the world than
most men, and was always an acute observer with
catholic tastes and cosmopolitan sympathies. But
though no politician, Andersen certainly was an
ardent and devoted patriot. His frequent and
offensive invectives against his country must not be
taken too seriously, or judged too harshly. His
bark, be it remembered, was always much worse than

his bite, and in these instances it was the wounded vanity of the author, and not the real sentiments of the man, that spoke. Whenever the honour or safety of his native land was concerned, none could be more loyal and self-sacrificing. At such times he felt that Denmark was his proper home, and his enthusiasm for her knew no bounds. It was, however, a great grief to him that the strife should be with Germany, which had always shown him so much kindness, and where there were so many persons who possessed his gratitude and affection ; he frequently longs in his correspondence for the time when " the powder-smoke " will disappear, and the sun of peace shine forth again upon the nations ; and he feelingly alludes to his collaboration of an opera text with the musician Glaser, as an instance of how it was possible for Germans and Danes to work amicably together in the realm of art at the very time when their respective nations were standing face to face on the battle-field. Still his patriotism is unswerving and unmistakable ; as a Dane, he suffers severely when he hears or reads of the falsehoods circulated by some of the least scrupulous German papers, and he expresses the conviction that Germany herself will, in the long run, recognise what a great injustice has been done to little Denmark.*    In the progress of the war he took a deep

* He is never abusive, however, and took no notice of the advice of

interest. The courage, the steadfastness, the cheerfulness with which the Danish soldiers endured their manifold hardships, filled him with unbounded admiration. There are moments when he feels that even war has a religion of its own. Every noble trait of personal devotion sends "a shiver of enthusiasm" through him; he cannot read of a deed of heroism without the tears coming to his eyes. The Danish common soldier seems to him worthy to be mentioned with Napoleon's Old Guard.* Nay, the tidings of such glorious victories as Fredericia gives him, the least pugnacious of men, momentary accesses of martial ardour. He hopes the Swedes will "have a go at the enemy," and that "our Lord will also move His little finger in the matter, which would be quite worth 5000 men at least." He declares that if he were only made of different stuff, he would shoulder his musket, and be off to the front himself. "You may smile," he writes to a friend, "but I solemnly assure you that run

that more fervid and indignant patriot, his friend Ingemann, to send back to the King of Prussia "his bloody eagle," *i.e.*, the Order of the Red Eagle conferred upon him.

* He caught an occasional glimpse of the army, as, for instance, when after the evacuation of Schleswig, in the earlier part of the war, the Danish forces were concentrated in "fat, green Funen," his own native island, which became for the time a sort of huge camp. Andersen on this occasion moved freely about among the soldiers, and quite won their hearts by his warm sympathy and frequent hospitality. He also composed some patriotic songs for them to sing round their camp-fires.

U

away from the foe I would *not*. I might perhaps feel timid, horribly timid, but recollect that to be timid is not to be a coward ; timidity one cannot always help feeling, but it depends upon a man's own will whether he be a coward or not." But these martial transports were very casual. At the bottom of his heart Andersen utterly abhorred war, and ardently desired peace. " Every day," he writes to another acquaintance,* "I listen to the thunder of the cannon ; every evening I reflect with the most heartfelt emotion, how many eyes have this day closed, what dear ones we have lost ! I know indeed that there is something grand and beautiful in falling [on the battle-field], but how about those who live and languish ! There is something horrible and unnatural in thus being maimed and mangled. War is indeed a terrible monster who feeds upon blood and burning towns." The tragic death of his young friend Lieut. Læssoe, who fell at Fredericia, makes it impossible for him to think calmly of "this great victory." His thoughts turn again and again to the many who have sacrificed life and limb there, and above all to Læssoe's aged mother in the agony of her bereavement. At such moments he is inclined to regard *all* war as apostasy from God. " When will men learn to understand each other properly," he cries. " I believe so firmly in the native nobility

* Bille og Bogh : *Breve fra Andersen*, ii. p. 199

of my fellow-creatures that I am sure that when they do so, every [relation of life] will blossom into friendship."* He was jubilant at the final conclusion of peace, and it was a supreme satisfaction to him to be entrusted with all the arrangements for a patriotic festival in honour of the home-returning soldiers, which his friend Count Moltke gave on a magnificent scale at Glorup, his country-house in Funen.

Andersen had no actual experience of the horrors of war, but he felt some of its inconveniences. So far as his literary productiveness was concerned, the years 1848–1851 were almost entirely barren. He had neither the heart nor the will to occupy himself with anything serious. Another effect of the war, moreover, was for a time to completely cut him off from the continent, but he found ample compensation on the other side of the Sound in Sweden, which charming and picturesque country he explored during the five best months of 1849.†

* On the return of the soldiers to Copenhagen, after the first campaign, Andersen had a public opportunity of testifying his respect for the defenders of his country. He was watching the procession from a window by the side of the composer Gade, when he saw in the crowd below a wounded soldier who had lost his right hand. Andersen, moved with pity, flung the veteran a bouquet, which he picked up and stuck in his wounded arm. This so touched the warm-hearted poet that he begged Gade to allow him to give up his place in the window to the poor man, rushed down into the street, piloted the soldier through the crowd, and ensconced him comfortably in a chair among the ladies at the window, while he himself went down into the street.

† *I Sverrig* (In Sweden), published at Copenhagen in 1851. See

On Ascension Day, 1849, Andersen set foot in Sweden, in the loveliest spring weather. After a short stay at that "half-Dutch, half-English" city Gothenburg, where he was somewhat taken aback, at a grand banquet given in his honour, to find that he was the only distinguished person present who did not wear "decorations" on his breast; and after a brief visit to the Trollhättan Falls, which he invites his Copenhagen friends to see as soon as possible before they have been utterly spoiled by the factories growing up around them, he proceeded through the great lakes Wener and Wetter to Stockholm. The rare beauty of Stockholm impressed him more than ever, and the winding waters of Lake Mälare looked so genuinely Turkish from his lodgings in the city, that, but for the absence of the minarets, he would have fancied himself at Constantinople, with a bit of Pera right in front of him. But his delight was considerably damped by the wretchedness of his rooms at the hotel, with their nasty wooden furniture and old and musty wall-paper, which compelled him to have his windows open night and day. He expresses his astonishment that Stockholm should not possess a hotel fit for human habitation, and declares that in this respect she is as far behind Copenhagen as

also, Bille og Bogh, *Breve fra Andersen*, ii. pp. 210-228 ; *M. L. E.*, pp. 490-516 ; and Collin, pp. 434-5.

Copenhagen is behind London.* His old friend, the poet and historian Baron Beskow, with whom he stayed part of his time, presented him to King Oscar, who received him so very heartily that Andersen half fancied they must have met before. The King twice invited him to dinner, and presented him to the Queen and the Crown Prince, when by special request he read to them "The Flax," "The Ugly Duckling," "The Shirt-collar," "A Mother," "The Fir Tree," "The Little Match-girl," and "The Darning Needle." He saw tears come to the eyes of the royal consorts as he read "The Story of a Mother," and on his departure the Queen gave him her hand, which he gratefully pressed to his lips. Beskow also introduced him to the historian Fryxell and the other literary celebrities of the Swedish capital, and with him Andersen stood on the very spot in the Opera House where Gustavus III. was shot by Anckarström at the famous midnight *bal masque* on March 16, 1792.† A banquet was also got up in his honour,

* Yet during his first visit Andersen was quite delighted with his accommodation at Stockholm. Can London and Paris have spoiled him? At the present day the Stockholm hotels are inferior to those of no other European city.

† This Opera House has lately been pulled down to make way for a larger one. It stood close to the Hotel Rydberg, and opposite the Palace. Beskow wrote the chivalrous apology of this brilliant and much maligned monarch, entitled *Gustaf III, som Konung och Menniska.*

on which occasion a band of prettily dressed little
girls strewed flowers in his path. The "long poet"
was a little embarrassed at first, but he pretended
to take it all as a joke, so he kissed a couple of
the prettiest children and then managed to slip
away.

After a short visit to Upsala, where he was
serenaded by the students of the University, he set
out for the Dales, as the Swedish Highlands are
called, and traversed that romantically beautiful
region right up to the very borders of Finmark.
Wild and grand scenery had always a peculiar attraction for Andersen, and he was astonished and
delighted by what he now saw. He describes the
Dales as a veritable Switzerland. The costumes of
the country people struck him as even more gorgeous
and picturesque than the costumes of "the motley
South," and here too, instead of the "suffocating odour
of jasmine and orange-blossoms," he had the "fresh
fragrance of the young birches." He drove through
forests leagues and leagues in length, where there
was no sign of a human habitation but an occasional
wreath of blue smoke curling upwards among the
wooded heights. The Dal river, that "transparent
lake flowing through eternal woods," with its swift
broad current and frequent foaming waterfalls, he
considers far superior to the Rhine. The whole
journey, in fact, was "a beautiful poem," with a

strong human interest too, for it abounded with
comical adventures and amusing experiences.
Leksand, in the very heart of the Dales, he
reached in time to see hundreds and hundreds
of peasants, from all the villages round about,
come to the picturesque old church, in their gaily
decorated boats across the Siljan, in costumes of
every imaginable shape and colour, with their
hymn-books carefully wrapped up in silk pocket-
handkerchiefs.* "I was sitting in my room"
[at the inn, after service], he continues, "when
in came the landlady's little granddaughter, a
pretty little child, to whom the sight of my parti-
coloured knapsack gave great delight ; I rapidly
clipped for her, out of a sheet of paper, a Turkish
mosque with minarets and open windows, and off
she rushed in great glee. Shortly afterwards I
heard a lot of loud talking in the yard outside, and
the idea struck me that it had something to do with
my clipping. So I stepped softly out on to the
wooden balcony, and saw grandmamma standing in
the garden below, and lifting my clipping high in
the air, with a beaming countenance. A whole
crowd of Dale lads and Dale lasses stood round
about, all in an artistic ecstasy over my handiwork,
but the little one—the wee, blessed little one—was
shrieking, and stretching out her hands towards her

* See *I Sverrig*, pp. 126-128, one of his very best descriptions.

lawful property, which she was not allowed to have because it was too pretty. Highly flattered and amused, I crept softly back again, but the next moment there came a knocking at the door; it was the grandmother, and she came with a whole plateful of gingerbreads. ' I bake the best gingerbreads in the Dales,' said she, ' but they are all in the old patterns from my grandmother's time; now couldn't you, sir, who clip out so well, clip us some new patterns ? '

"And there I sat the whole of that midsummer evening, clipping patterns for gingerbreads; nut-crackers with spurred boots, windmills that were both men and mills, with slippered feet and doors in their stomachs, and ballet-dancers who pointed one leg at the Pleiades. I gave the whole lot to the old grandmother, but she turned the ballet-dancers up and down, and did not know what to make of them. She thought their legs were too high, and took the poor things to be one-legged and three-armed in consequence.

" ' These shall be the new patterns,' said she, ' but they're rather different from the old ones.' " *

"I hope," adds Andersen, "that I shall live in the Dales in my gingerbread patterns."

As usual, his observant eye was quick to note the comic and the picturesque sides of things in these

* *I Sverrig,* p. 189.

out-of-the-way parts. Take, for instance, this description of an inn in the Dales :—" We came to the inn, which seemed to have been turned inside out, for everything was in the wrong place. In the living-room the flies had so bedaubed the whitewashed walls that they might have passed for paintings ; all the pieces of furniture were confirmed invalids with thick coverlets of dust. The road outside came to a dead stop in the middle of a midden, and on this midden the daughter of the house was gambolling. She was young and well-built, all white and red, with bare feet, but large gold earrings in her ears ; the gold shone in the sun, and was set off by her rosy red cheeks. Her flaxen yellow hair had come loose, and fluttered round her bonny shoulders. If she had had any idea of her own loveliness, she would certainly have given herself a good washing."

The weather was unusually, even oppressively, hot for that northern clime, but when the rain did come down, it rained as if it would never stop, and one such rainy day was one of the most amusing of Andersen's experiences. The Lord Lieutenant of Upsala had lent him a car, to make an excursion to the beautiful Sæther Valley, but this car gave him so much trouble, that, long before he had done with it, he had learnt enough to make his living as a carman for the rest of his life. A strap was always bursting here, or a cord was always snapping there, the wheels required constant greasing, and he had to dismount scores of times to make sure that other parts of the mechanism were in proper working order. Under these circumstances progress was slow, and, to add to his troubles, the rain came pouring down till the highway was quite navigable, and gave him a perfect idea of the beginning of the Flood. At last he came to the Sæther Valley, but instead of proceeding to that famous vale, Andersen preferred to direct his course to the little wayside inn close beside it. Everything in the inn-yard, manure and market garden stuff, sticks and straws, were floating together in a state of "chaotic happy-go-luckiness." The hens sat close together, washed down to mere shadows, and the ducks crouched against the wet wall, sated with moisture. The ostler was cross, the chamber-maid still crosser; it was difficult to get a word out of them; the staircase was steep, the floor aslant, and looked as if it had been lately washed, thick sand was strewn all over it; the air was cold and moist; yet out of doors, scarcely twenty steps on the other side of the road, was the famous valley, that garden of Nature's own laying out, whose beauty consisted in trees and bushes, springs and bubbling brooks! It was a deep hollow with the tree-tops appearing above it, while the rain threw its thick veil across them. The whole of that long

afternoon Andersen sat there, gazing at intervals in
the direction of the beautiful valley, while the revivi-
fying rain poured steadily down. It seemed to
him as if Wener and Wetter, and a couple of other
lakes besides, were pouring through a huge sieve
from the clouds. He had ordered meat and drink,
but not a vestige of food appeared. There was a
running upstairs and a running downstairs, a roast-
ing and basting over the fire, the chattering of
wenches, the gobbling sound of country bumpkins
over their soup—and travellers arrived, were comfortably entertained, and got both roast and boiled
to their hearts' content. Several hours elapsed, and
then Andersen, losing all patience, called the
waitress, and gave her a severe lecture for keeping
him waiting so long. "Why, sir!" replied she
phlegmatically, " how *could* you eat while you were
sitting there, and doing nothing but write, write all
the time ?" It was a long evening, but it came
to an end at last. All the other travellers
had departed to find a better night's lodging at
Hedemora. Down in the dirty bar-room—Andersen
could see them through the half-open door—sat
a couple of rough-looking fellows playing with
greasy cards, while a big dog lay under the table,
and glared at him with large red eyes. The kitchen
was empty, the rooms deserted, the floor was soak-
ing, the storm roared, the rain splashed, so Andersen

went to bed. He had slept one hour, maybe two, when he was suddenly awakened by a loud hubbub in the road outside. He sprang up in bed. It was pitch dark. The time was about one. He listened and heard a violent hammering at the door, and a deep guttural voice shouting with all its might. Fancying that some lunatic had broken loose, Andersen got out of bed, carefully locked his door, got in again, and listened once more. This time he heard a banging at the house-door, the shrieks of terrified women, the lowing and bleating of sheep and kine, the clattering of wooden shoes over the stones in the yard below—every moment the racket grew louder and louder. What could it all mean? Out of bed he got again, and rushed to the window, but there was nothing to be seen, and it was still raining. Presently he heard a heavy tramp! tramp! tramp! coming up the stairs. The door of the apartment next to his was thrown violently open, then there was silence. He listened intently, and glanced nervously at his own door, but was reassured to find it protected by a long and strong iron bolt. The next instant there came a kick at *his* door, and a gruff voice cried : " Is there anybody in here? The house is on fire ! " Andersen needed no more. In a second he had his clothes on, and was out of the room and down the stairs ; but as he could see no smoke below, he returned, quickly packed up his traps, and came down again. By this time tongues of flame were shooting out of all the windows. The fire-engines arrived in time to extinguish the burning walls, but Andersen had had enough sleep for that night, and left the place at six o'clock the next morning. He had not gone very much further when his car broke down altogether, but he fortunately found a hospitable refuge hard by at Tuna parsonage, which he calls "the most comfortable place on the whole journey."*

This was the only misadventure, if misadventure it can be called, that befell him during his Swedish tour. From first to last he enjoyed himself thoroughly, and the people pleased him quite as much as the scenery. He also made the delightful discovery that he was better known in Sweden than in any other country but his own. His books kept on turning up in the most out-of-the-way nooks and corners. He came across the *Fodreise til Amager* in one place, and *The Two Baronesses* in another, "so there you have Andersen from first to last!" he writes exultantly. Never had he been welcomed so heartily anywhere else, both by high and low, as in Sweden. The towns feasted and serenaded him, the nobility and gentry entertained him at their country-seats, the farmers and villagers placed their

* Compare *I Sverrig*, pp. 118-124, and Bille og Bogh, *Breve fra Andersen*, pp. 218-19.

carts and horses at his disposal, and turned out in hundreds to shake hands with him; young ladies strewed flowers in his path, and he frequently found bunches of the most beautiful roses on his plate at breakfast-time.

Andersen was not ungrateful, and he has recorded his pleasant experiences in a book which, after "The Tales," must certainly be regarded as the most beautiful and poetical of all his works—I mean *I Sverrig* * (In Sweden), which was received with unqualified admiration on both sides of the Sound. This masterpiece is not so much an itinerary like *En Digters Bazar*, or the subsequent *I Spanien* (In Spain), as a series of exquisite minia-ture *genre* pictures much in the same style as, and in no way inferior to, the *Billedbog uden Billeder* (Picture-book without Pictures). It is, in fact, a unique collection of poetical gems artisti-cally strung together on a cord of blue and gold.†  In such exquisite descriptions of the wilder sort of Swedish scenery as "Trollhättan," "Kinnikulle," and "I Skoven," such masterly *humoresques* in Callot's manner as "Tiggerdrenge," such touching remi-niscences of the grim and cruel Past as "Wadstena,"

---

* It is also the most carefully written of his works.  He recast it again and again before finally giving it to the public.  There are two English versions, of 1851 and 1852 respectively, both of them very indifferent.

† The national colours of Sweden are blue and yellow.

where the great magician compels History to surrender her hidden and half-forgotten secrets, or in such vivid and richly-coloured pictures of popular customs and costumes as " Midsommerfesten paa Leksand," and " Ved Siljan-Söen," we have the humour, the pathos, the fancy and the imagination of Andersen at their very best. It is in this little volume, moreover, that we first meet with five of the finest of the immortal " Tales," namely, " The Grandmother," "The Puppet Showman," "A History," " The Dumb-book " and " Bird Phœnix."

# CHAPTER XI

As already said, Andersen's Muse between 1849 and 1851 was almost entirely silent, and this silence was due in great measure to the agitation arising from the Schleswig-Holstein war and its con-sequences. But there was another, and perhaps even more operative cause. From 1850 onwards Andersen began dabbling with philosophy, and this new occupation engrossed a great deal of time, which, from a literary point of view, was so much time wasted.* His interest in scientific and meta-

* This is what Andersen's intimate friends feared from the first,

H. C. ÖRSTED

physical subjects generally was first awakened by
his friend Örsted's work, *Aanden i Natur* (Spirit
in Nature).   This remarkable book, which appeared
in 1849, was a republication in volume form of a
series of discourses composed at various times, and
expounds its distinguished author's theory of existence in a singularly lucid and attractive form.   Its
fundamental idea is that the only two permanent
principles in nature, invariable amidst all her varying moods, are her elemental forces (*Krafterne*),
which can be traced back to a fundamental force
(*Grundkraft*), and her laws which, in their ultimate
expression, point to a universal, all-embracing
Reason.   According to this theory, corporeal sub-
stances (*legemerne*) are only so many moods or
expressions of living activities, body and spirit are
inseparably bound together in one and the same
principle.   In the process of thought creative nature
wakes to consciousness within us, and that is the
reason why we are able to comprehend nature at all.
Between God's will, which must not be assumed to
be like the human will, and Nature's essence, there
can be no question of strife, for they are one.
" Spirit in Nature" made a great stir in Denmark
during the fifties, and elicited a good deal of

although he assured them that their fears were groundless, as "the
human heart was the only lamp of poetry" he ever meant to
hold to.

enthusiasm, but also a good deal of criticism, especially on the part of the clergy. Jacob Peter Mynster, by far the ablest Bishop of Denmark, and her metropolitan from 1834 to 1854, acutely foresaw that, in the hands of shallow or dishonest disputants, it might serve as a weapon against the supernatural element in religion, and he at once engaged in a vigorous but perfectly friendly polemic with Örsted, who defended his views as quite compatible with a complete and sincere acceptation of Christian dogma. Andersen watched the contest with keen interest. His sympathies were entirely with Örsted, who had been one of his best friends for more than twenty years, and for whom, as the discoverer of the influence of the electric current on the magnetic needle,* which led to the invention of the electric telegraph, he had the most profound admiration. Then, too, he bore a secret grudge against the Bishop (of which more anon), and did not scruple to accuse him of using dishonest arguments.† Indeed, the controversy led him to plunge still deeper into scientific investigations. He was greatly interested in the progress of the age ; believed with incurable optimism in the rapid amelioration of the human

* Örsted first made known his great discovery in a Latin dissertation, dated July 21, 1820.
† Bille og Bogh, *Breve fra Andersen*, ii. p. 257. Not publicly, of course, but in letters to private friends.

race, and rapturously hailed each new discovery and
invention of the nineteenth century as a fresh stride
towards that devoutly to be wished for consumma-
tion. " I feel," he once wrote to his friend Hauch,*
" I feel and see another proof of God's infinite love
in every new insight He grants us into the laws of
nature, and the sublime power He thereby gives to
humanity. I know there are many who say that
the progress of our times is only a material progress.
I do not admit that they are right, but, even if I did,
I should say that the material good we win is a
scaffolding, as it were, on which the spiritual edifice
is to be built up. . . . . My interest in science has
grown upon me so much of late that I am sure that if
I had been as filled with the idea of her glory twenty
years ago as I am now, I should certainly have
chosen another path . . . . or rather I should have
acquired knowledge which would have led me in a
different direction, and my productivity as an
author would have borne a different bloom." He
never would allow that there was or could be any
antagonism between Science and Poetry. Nay, in
opposition to his friend, the ultra-romantic Ingemann,
he even refused to concede that poetry was higher
than science, and many were the debates they had
on this subject. Ingemann admitted that the age in
which they lived was the age of great inventions;

* Bille og Bogh : *Breve fra Andersen*, pp. 291-2.

but he held at the same time that modern progress was on purely material, mechanical, prosaic lines. Believing as he did that the advance of science threatened to rob life of all its poetry, he naturally regarded it as almost demoniacal, and half playfully, half reproachfully upbraided Andersen for allowing himself to be led astray by Örsted's sophistries. But this did not damp Andersen's enthusiasm in the least. Steam, photography, electricity, each fresh invention of the age, filled him with rapture; he declared that life in the nineteenth century made him feel as if he stood beneath "the flapping pinions of an infinitely powerful spirit," and the reflection that all these inventions tended to bring men closer together, and combine towns and nations into one enormous family, had, he said, a more elevating effect upon him than the most sublime song that poet ever sang.

Nor did the advance of science make him feel in the least anxious about the future of religion. Without doubt Andersen was a deeply religious man, but his religion was eccentric and peculiar. Like most of the clever young men of his age, he had passed through his sceptical *stadium*. In these early days, too (and, indeed, for some time afterwards), although never anti-Christian, he was decidedly and demonstratively anti-clerical. The cause of his bias against the parsons is not quite clear, but I

shrewdly suspect it had something to do with the
snub he received from Bishop Mynster, just before
he went to Slagelse.   The Bishop was one of those
to whom  he had applied for assistance in those
miserable days, and  Mynster seems to have used his
influence in the young man's behalf.   When, however, Andersen came to bid the prelate farewell, and
thank him for his kindness, Mynster, somewhat
injudiciously, sought to improve the occasion by
lecturing the lad, reminding him how much he had
cause to be thankful for, and expressing the hope that
he would prove grateful to all who had befriended
him.   It is clear, from  Andersen's correspondence,
that  he deeply resented this patronising tone ;
never quite forgot it, and for at least twenty years
afterwards had as little to do with the clergy as
possible.   It is noteworthy, too, that the peccadilloes
of parsons were for a  time a favourite subject for
satire in his letters to his intimate friends ; that he
loved to hear anecdotes representing the clergy in a
ridiculous light, and in his earlier novels—*O. T.* and
*Only a Fiddler*, for instance—the odious and contemptible characters are invariably parsons.   It may
also be remarked that Andersen was never a very
regular church-goer.   He had nothing to say against
church services in general, and the hymns always
appealed to him strongly ;* but he could not concen-

* Especially in England, where he thought them beautiful.   On the

trate his attention on devotional exercises for any length of time, and used frequently to say that he felt much more religious under God's free heaven than in a stuffy church. During such penitential seasons as Lent, when the services of the church were longer and more frequent than usual, he generally went abroad for a holiday. On the other hand, he always had a vivid sense of the presence of God, an unshakable confidence in His providence, and a deep gratitude for the many mercies of which he believed himself to have been the unworthy recipient. Now and again, indeed, when things do not turn out exactly as he wishes or when gainsayers (especially critics) are unusually malignant, he petulantly upbraids his Maker, much in the same way as the African or Polynesian savages have been known to beat and abuse their idols for inattention to their supplications; but such outbursts, even in his youth, are very rare, and cease altogether as he grows older. His obedience to the dictates of conscience, which he always took to be the voice of God, is very remarkable, and this especially in the matter of sexual morality. He would, however, have been the last man in the world to have posed as a moralist. He had seen too much of unregenerate human nature to expect impossibilities from it, and

other hand, the length of the English church service positively appalled him.

was possessed by a deep sense of the world's beauty
and joyousness which made his philosophy of life
large and liberal. His humour, though always
sound and healthy, could be free and almost broad
at times, and his sprightly wit, especially in his
correspondence, is full of sly suggestiveness, and loves
to hover, with harmless gaiety and perfect tact, round
a *double entendre*. As he grew older and wiser, and
his religious views gained in clearness and consist-
ency, he began to be sensible of the growing
estrangement on the Continent between faith and
science, and the visible progress that materialism
was making in Germany saddened but did not
alarm him. Intimately convinced that there could
be no real antagonism between these two voices of
God,* he became anxious to make this as clear to
others as it was to himself, or, as he expresses it,
"to bring about peace and concord between science
and the Bible," and, characteristically, he felt quite
confident in his own abilities "to give the deathblow to materialism, that monster that would devour
everything divine." He proposed to do this in a
new novel which, naturally, was to be his "most
important work," and he proceeded forthwith to

* "To my mind it is just science that throws light upon divine reve-
lation. I go with open seeing eyes towards the goal that others
fumble for blindly. God can surely endure to be looked at with the
little bit of sound sense He has put into our heads." (Bille og Bogh :
*Breve fra Andersen*, ii. p. 336.)

equip himself for the performance of so momentous a task. Besides thoroughly mastering Örsted's *Aand i Natur*, though that in the opinion of many was anything but an orthodox book, he diligently attended the lectures that Counsellor Eschricht was delivering at that time against materialism which appealed to him strongly. He also studied all the literature on both sides of the question that he could lay his hands upon, and, even when he went to the country for a holiday, he armed himself with such books as Dr. Friedrich Fabri's *Briefe gegen den Materialismus,** which, he says, "cast fresh light into his soul," and the anonymous German romance, *Eritis sicut Deus.†* He also concientiously read the chief works of Strauss and Feuerbach, which, so far from unsettling, only confirmed him in his religious belief. He declares again and again that all his reading strengthens within him more and more the conviction that religion and science are not hostile empires, but neighbouring states which have no visible boundaries, but glide into each other imperceptibly.‡    The result of all this diligent

---

* First published in Stuttgart in 1856.

† 1854.

‡ Bille og Bogh : *Breve fra Andersen*, ii. pp. 349–50. " It interests me to see," he goes on, " how the worst materialists trace everything back to a dead original matter existing from eternity, and recognised by them as eternal, only they say that it lacked motion, and they cannot discover how it first began to move. Why, the whole thing appears so

research was Andersen's last romance, this time a romance with a purpose, *At være eller ikke være* (To Be, or not to Be), which occupied him off and on for nearly four years, and appeared in 1857 at Copenhagen and London * simultaneously.

The hero of *At være eller ikke være* is a poor boy, Niels Bryde, the son of one of the watchmen of the "Round Tower," who is adopted by a charitable old country clergyman, Japetus Mollerup, resident among the heaths of Jutland. Obstinate and passionate, the lad nevertheless has a good heart, his parts too are excellent, and by the time that he is able to go up to the University as a theological student, his delighted old foster-father has the very highest hopes of him. But the infidel works of Strauss and Feuerbach destroy his faith; he renounces theology for medicine, and by the time he has obtained his doctor's diploma, settles down as a confirmed and contented atheist. There is sorrow and anger in the quiet old parsonage among the Jutland heaths and sandhills. The pastor, after fruitless remonstrances and still more fruitless arguments, renounces the reprobate altogether; but in the pastor's wife and her daughter, the gentle loving Bodil, who has always been more than a sister to

clear to me. Surely this is nothing else than the chaos of the Bible when God moved upon the waters—from Him comes motion."

* The English translation, a fairly good one, is by Mrs. Bushby.

him, he still possesses affectionate friends who continue to hope the best of the truant from the fold.
But Niels, who is blessed with a resolute energetic
character, continues to knock about town happily
enough, making his living as a doctor. His
atheism becomes more and more rampant and dogmatic as he grows older, and he especially prides
himself on possessing a higher and more consistent
theory of life than the ordinary run of professing
Christians around him. He is especially incredulous
as to the doctrine of a future state, which he considers quite inconsistent with the latest develop-
ments of modern science. " To Be, or not to Be " is,
to his mind, the question on which all else depends.
In the course of his wanderings Niels makes the
acquaintance of an interesting and amiable Jewish
family, Aron by name, and from the very first is
much struck by the intellectual depth and acumen
of the youngest daughter, Esther. A closer acquaintance reveals to him that this girl is as pious as she
is profound, and henceforth it becomes his greatest
joy to argue with her about the faith which he
himself has lost, but she has found. For, though
born and bred a Jewess, Esther has always been
attracted by the beauty and tenderness of Christ's
teaching, and ultimately she herself is baptized.
Her arguments with Niels continue. He is not
convinced, but gradually forsakes his dogmatic

atheism for a tentative agnosticism : he has shifted
his position without being quite aware of the
fact himself. Then the Schleswig-Holstein war
begins, and, like a true patriot, he hurries to
the front. He is present at the great battles
of Fredericia and Istedt ; Esther's brother, who
serves as a volunteer, dies almost in his very
arms ; he himself is wounded, and only saved from
death by the devotion of a faithful dog, and finally
returns to Copenhagen a wiser and a sadder man :
by this time his agnosticism has deepened into Deism.
Shortly after his return to the capital the cholera
breaks out there, and, with a heroic fidelity to duty,
he remains at his post among the dead and dying.
Then occurs the great sorrow of his life, which
brings him back at last to his former faith. Esther,
whom he has learnt to love with all the intensity of
a strong nature, is carried off by the epidemic, and
the impossibility of conceiving that such a nature as
hers could perish utterly, converts him at last to the
long doubted doctrine of a future state and a clearer
perception of the Christian faith.

Such is the bare outline of *To Be, or not to Be*,
and I may say at once that as a religious romance
with a purpose, it is utterly unsatisfactory and in-
conclusive, though not more so than works of the
kind are bound to be. It is remarkable, however,
for a complete absence of theological bitterness,

and the arguments in favour of the materialistic standpoint are set forth with singular frankness and fairness. On the other hand, the author never seems to be quite certain of his own standpoint, and finally, as we have seen, it is not sound argument, but mere sentiment, that converts the stubborn materialist, Niels Bryde, into a believer—a most lame and impotent conclusion. But although it fails of its immediate purpose as an antidote for unbelief, *To Be, or not to Be* stands, as pure literature, on a much higher level than either *The Two Baronesses* or *O. T.* The fine descriptions of the peculiar scenery of Jutland, the stirring episodes from the Schleswig-Holstein war (Andersen visited the principal battle-fields immediately after the peace), the humorous account of Copenhagen,* and its plague of dogs, to take only a few instances, are in the master's best manner. All the principal personages, too, are drawn with unusual boldness and distinctness. The good old clergyman, Japetus Mollerup, whose one weakness was an inordinate fondness for bad tobacco, so that tobacco smoke was the first impression of him you took away with you; his worthy wife, who had a perfect passion for turning bad boys into good Christians; the lady

---

* We also learn a good deal about the famous "Round Tower" and the "sugar-pigs" which the "Fairy Tales" have made so famous.

who talks *staccato* like Jingle ; the amiable Bodil,
and the intense Esther, two of Andersen's best
female characters—all provide excellent entertainment ; whilst among the minor characters are whole
groups of those human oddities, Nature's waifs and
strays, that had as much fascination for Andersen
as for Dickens. Unfortunately, the controversial
element in the book is so predominant, and was
so largely advertised beforehand by Andersen himself as by far the best part of it, that *To Be, or
not to Be* was criticised in Denmark rather from a
theological than from a literary standpoint, and
criticised very severely. The philosophers and theo-
logians were particularly hard upon the author for
trespassing so presumptuously on their domains, and
even a personal friend like Professor Sibbern could
write to congratulate him on the *failure* of his book,
and counsel him not to mix up polemics with literature in future. Andersen was, of course, greatly
incensed at what he called the ingratitude of his
countrymen, but he found some consolation in the
assurance of some of his German friends that the
book had been a great help to them in their religious
difficulties, and in the sympathy of Charles Dickens,
to whom he ventured to confide his troubles. " I
was always afraid," he writes, " that you would grow
tired of the foreigner who could not speak your
language properly, and with such a feeling one

always has eyes and ears in the very tips of one's fingers." Then he goes on to say how little pleasure he had got out of his new book at home, and how an inexpressible weariness and indifference to everything has settled upon him in consequence. Dickens is, as usual, sympathetic and appreciative, and praises *To Be, or not to Be* as " a very fine book —full of a good purpose, admirably wrought out—a book in every way worthy of its great author." *

We have seen that the disturbances arising from the Schleswig-Holstein war practically excluded Andersen from the Continent for four years. He amply indemnified himself, however, during the ensuing five, for from 1851 to 1856 he visited South Germany no less than four times, besides taking flying visits to France, Italy, Switzerland, and Bohemia. There is no need to follow him step by step over ground traversed and described by him before; but it may be observed that during these years he seems to have lost something of his former zest for foreign travel. For this there were several reasons. First of all, that strong anti-Danish feeling which prevailed largely in Germany during the fifties was not without its effect on the keenly sensitive Dane,† and he had to refuse many invitations for

* Bille og Bogh : *Breve til Andersen*, p. 125.

† " I don't mean to expose myself to any unpleasantness," he wrote to a friend, " it is mournful to see what lies issue from the German papers." (Bille og Bogh : *Breve fra Andersen*, ii. p. 265.)

purely political reasons. Then, too, he had already passed the meridian of life, and, though wonderfully young for his years, was more easily fatigued and more exposed to climatic influences. He now begins to suffer from the heat of the south, for instance. Even the familiar palms and cypresses could not reconcile him to the "flame-like" atmosphere of Italy, and he was glad to fly for refreshment to the falls of Schaffhausen, "that huge green billow ever rolling forward and changing suddenly into whirling clouds." Finally, he was not so much disposed now, as formerly, to accept everything with *naïve* enthusiasm. Universal homage had given him an "unco guid conceit" of himself. He was inclined to be critical and fastidious. Thus Liszt's playing which, after an interval of nearly twenty years, he heard again at Cassel in 1857, no longer excited his admiration; on the contrary, it rather annoyed him. " This wild-ness is a little beyond me," he writes,* "and once when there came a clash of cymbals I thought a plate or two had been broken somewhere. Yet the public was charmed, and there was a perfect rain of wreaths. 'Tis a ridiculous world!" At Weimar he was disgusted to find the son of the great Goethe officiating as Kammerherr to the Grand Ducal family, and ladling out the soup at dinner-time. Nevertheless he had the satisfaction, such as it was,

* Bille og Bogh : *Breve fra Andersen*, ii. p. 379.

Y

of adding another monarch to the circle of his
acquaintances. This was that popular prince, Maxi-
milian II. of Bavaria, whose acquaintance Andersen
first made in 1852, and whose guest he was two
years later. On the second occasion they sailed
together on the Bavarian lakes, and drove together
into the most romantic parts of the Tyrol. The
King, who had read *Das Märchen meines Lebens*,
and was an enthusiastic admirer of the *Fairy
Tales*,* was never tired of hearing about Andersen's
early struggles from his own lips. As for Andersen,
the fact that he, "the son of a poor cobbler," should
be flying across the mountains with a king for his
companion, seemed to him like a chapter out of a
fairy tale more wondrous than any he had ever told.

In 1853 Andersen had his first, I will not say
encounter, for he prudently took care to keep out
of its way, but his first experience of a new and
terrible enemy—the cholera, which visited Copenhagen during the summer of that year, and carried
off thousands of victims. Andersen fled to Jutland,
where he remained in a state of dire trepidation till
the epidemic was over. And here I may mention
that Andersen had a peculiar horror of all manner
of sickness, a horror due, not so much to natural

---

* *The Elder-mother* was a great favourite of his, and on one of
their excursions he plucked a branch full of elder flowers, which he
presented to Andersen with a graceful compliment.

timidity, as to his extraordinarily vivid imagination. What he suffered from the tyranny of his
imagination almost passes belief. Take only one
of many instances. A doctor, who knew him
very intimately in his later years, tells us how he
one day met Andersen trembling all over with
anxiety simply because a friend, with whom he was
about to make an excursion, happened to arrive
half an hour late. What he endured during that
half-hour no tongue but Andersen's could ever tell.
He was quite certain that his friend must have come
to a violent end, been run over, perhaps, smashed
in a collision, or blown up by an explosion, and he
pictured him as expiring amidst the most unspeakable torments. Nay, his mind's eye had actually
seen the corpse carried home on a stretcher, all
crushed and bleeding, with foaming mouth and pro-
truding eyeballs. He would have escaped from
the horrifying sight, but he could not. His feet
seemed rooted to the spot. He was obliged to stay
and see the body of his dead friend put in a decent
coffin, and consigned to its last resting-place. Then
he pictured himself sitting down with streaming
eyes, and writing letters of condolence to the
sorrowing relations—and, at that very moment, who
should come up with smiling face and outstretched
arms but the very friend whose death he had so
vividly realised, and who, on perceiving poor Ander-

sen's terrible state of agitation, was not only abject
in his apologies, but registered a mental oath never
to keep him waiting five minutes again.*

These involuntary excursions with his tyrant fancy
were frequent and distressing. If any epidemic
were raging within fifty miles of him, he was
intimately persuaded that he would be the first
victim. If a cat scratched him, or a dog snapped
at him, he would go in terror of hydrophobia for
days together. Nay, he had a physical perception
of the symptoms of every disease that his fancy
saddled him with. If he had a pain in his extraordinarily long neck, he at once jumped to the conclusion that he had swallowed a nail, and was
suffering from internal hæmorrhage. If he struck
his bony knee a little harder than usual, he was
certain the injury would end in dropsy ; and if he
discovered a pimple above his eye, he gloomily
resigned himself to its growing and growing till it
blinded him altogether. It was therefore a peculiarly anxious time for him when the cholera broke
out in Copenhagen in the course of 1853. The bare
anticipation of its coming was sufficient to drive
him away, and long before it actually made its
appearance he had flown to the little town of Silkeborg amidst the highlands of Jutland, from whence

* See W. Bloch : *Om H. C. Andersen. Bidrag til Belysning af hans
Personlighed.* No. 364 of *Nær og Fjern.*

he kept an observant and troubled eye upon the capital. Throughout the summer and early autumn of 1853, the disease continued to rage in Copenhagen with terrible severity. It was, as Andersen said, a worse plague than war; "for war," he adds, "has a dash and a swagger about it, it brings with it glory and enthusiasm; but this cholera is a foul bat with poison-distilling wings, and tortures its victims before killing them." He lost many of his acquaintances during this visitation, and a dread came upon him every time he began a letter lest he should be writing to a dead man. He felt so uncomfortable the whole time, that he could settle down to nothing, and the tears came to his eyes when he thought of all his dear ones in Copenhagen, and of Death going from door to door. It was in one of these anxious moments, when his thoughts "hovered between the grave and God," that he composed his beautiful little hymn, *Som Bladet der fra Træet falder.** As the autumn progressed the epidemic abated, and Andersen was able at last to surrender himself entirely to the enjoyment of the beautiful scenery around him.

Silkeborg is situated on the picturesque Guden river, at the head of Langsö (Lake Long), in the heart of Jutland, midway between Aarhus on the east

---

* "Like as the leaf falls from the tree."

and Ringkjöbing on the west coast. In Catholic
times it belonged to the demesne of the Bishops of
Aarhus, who built a manor-house there,* which, after
the Reformation, was appropriated by the Crown.
In 1845 the brothers Drewsen got a licence to build
a paper factory there, and round this factory rapidly
grew up the youngest of the Danish towns, which,
though it has not yet attained the magnificent pro-
portions which Andersen in his enthusiasm promised
it, is now a flourishing place of some three thousand
inhabitants. Andersen was deeply interested in the
progress of the little town which he had seen grow
up beneath his very eyes, and it enabled him to
realise how towns in America are able to spring up
so rapidly. Then, too, the singularly wild and
romantic scenery for miles and miles round Silkeborg
was after his own heart. The lakes, the hills,† and
the long stretches of heather there reminded him of
the "land of Rob Roy," especially of the parts round
Stirling and Loch Lomond, although the Silkeborg
district had the advantage of being more thickly
wooded. Here, too, it was that he saw *coal-black*

* A legend says that as Peter, Bishop of Aarhus was sailing on Lake
Long, his silk biretta was blown off his shaven head, and fell into the
water. He straightway vowed to build a manor-house on the spot
where his silken cap fell, and Silkeborg (*i.e.* Silk-burg) rose on the
spot.

† He was asked to give his name to these heights, and he called
them "The Andersen Highlands," because they reminded him of
Scotland.

storks for the first time, " spanking about " in the tarns and marshes, and living quite wild in the trees, whilst, in the depths of the forests, huge eagles were still to be found. A young eaglet that was brought to Andersen as a curiosity, measured three ells across the wings. From his window, too, he had a beautiful view over a garden that teemed with roses, and in the middle of the large green grass-plot was planted a couple of juniper-berry trees that looked just like Italian cypresses. Old elder-berry trees "bowed to each other across the River Guden," which fell into Lake Long just in front of the house ; high banks of ling and drift sand rose on the other side of the water, and beyond them, as far as the eye could reach, stretched the dense black woods. Silkeborg was one of the few places that Andersen never tired of, and he returned to it again and again with ever fresh enthusiasm. We also have some cause to love it, for it suggested some of his most characteristic and peculiarly Danish stories, such, for instance, as *Ib and Little Christina, The Marsh King's Daughter, Waldemar Daae and his Daughters,* and *A Story of the Sandhills,* which might well be classed together under some such title as " Jutland Tales."

# CHAPTER XII

BETWEEN 1852 and 1862 Andersen published nine little volumes of fresh tales (fifty-five in all), to which he gave the name of *Historier* to distinguish them from the previous *Eventyr*. This new series seems to me to be slightly inferior to the earlier one. Some of the tales * show traces of the author's growing fondness for philosophising and moralising, and are not improved thereby. Others †️ are little better than fill-ups, and a few—a very few —are positively wearisome. But many of these *Historier* are excellent ; for instance, *The Story*

---

* *E.g., Svanereden, Om Artusinder, De Vises Steen, Det nye Aarhundredes Musa, Psychen.*

†️ *E.g., Et Billede fra Kastelsvolden, Fra et Vindue i Varton, Bispen paa Börglum.*

*of the Year* (1852), *Ib and Little Christina*, and *The Money-Pig* (1853), *Soup on a Sausage-Peg* (1857), *The Marsh King's Daughter*, and *The Racers* (1858), "that pearl of a story," as Brandes enthusiastically calls it, *Valdemar Daae*, and *The Pen and the Inkstand* (1859), and the universally admired *Ice Maiden* * (1861). With some half-dozen exceptions, † belonging, like *The Tinder-Box* and *Little Claus and Big Claus*, to the category of nursery-tales re-told, all these stories are original, and many of them possess considerable biographical interest.‡ *There's the Difference* resulted from a visit to Christinelund near Præstö in Zealand, where a blossoming apple-tree standing near a moat, the very image of Spring itself, " so shone into and scented my thoughts," says Andersen, "that I could not get rid of it till I had transplanted it into a tale." *Five from a Peas Pod* is a reminiscence of the home of his childhood, where his whole garden consisted of a wooden box full of earth, with some chives and a single pea in it. The kernel of *She's no Good* is to be found in some words which Andersen heard his mother say when he was a little boy. One day he saw a lad running along the street of Odense, on his way to

---

* Its original title was *The Eagle's Nest.*

† Such, for instance, as *The Wicked Prince, The Girl that trod on the Loaf, Bumpkin Hans,* and *The Bell-deep.*

‡ See *Bemerkninger til Eventyr og Historier.*

the river, where his mother, a washerwoman, was rinsing clothes. As the lad passed by, a widow noted for the sharpness of her tongue threw up her window, and cried : " So you're taking some more brandy down to your mother, eh ? Fie, fie, for shame ! Don't you let me see you turn out like your mother, for *she's* no good." Andersen at once ran home and told his family what he had seen and heard. " Yes," said they all, " the washerwoman *does* drink, and she *is* no good." Only his mother took her part. " Don't judge so harshly," she said. " There the poor wretch is toiling and moiling all day in the middle of the cold water, and sometimes she does not get any warm food for days together ; she must have something to keep her up. It's not the right thing for her to take, I know, but she has nothing better. I know she is an honest creature, who has gone through a lot, and anyhow she always keeps her little boy tidy." *The Marsh King's Daughter* is one of Andersen's most carefully elaborated stories. The idea of it, he says, came suddenly into his head like the remembrance of some old melody. He immediately told the whole story to some friends, and wrote it down forthwith ; but although he cast it and re-cast it three or four times over, it still seemed to him to lack vividness and actuality. So he set about diligently studying the old Icelandic Sagas, so as to catch something of the spirit of the remote age in which the story is laid. Some modern books on African travel supplied him with all he wanted to know about the land of Egypt, while a couple of scientific works on the flight of birds gave him the requisite characteristic traits of bird-life. Then he sat down to the tale again, and worked away at it till he was quite satisfied he had done his best with it.

*The Child in the Grave* and *The Story of a Mother* are, by Andersen's own confession, the stories which gave him most pleasure, because, as he tells us, so many a deeply sorrowing mother found comfort and consolation in them. The latter tale is said to have been an especial favourite in India. *A Story from the Sand-hills* had a very curious and interesting origin. Andersen was talking one day with the poet Oehlenschläger on the subject of "eternal life," and in the course of the conversation Oehlenschläger remarked : " Are you really certain that there is a life after this life ? " Andersen replied that he felt perfectly certain of it, adding that he founded his certainty on God's justice. " Why, man can demand it ! " he hastily exclaimed in the heat of debate. " What ! " cried Oehlenschläger, " is it not a piece of presumption on your part to demand an eternal life ? Has not God given you no end of good things in this world? I know what a boundless measure of benefits He has given me already, and when I close my eyes in death I shall thankfully praise and bless Him for it.    If after that He still grants me an eternal life, I shall accept it from His hands as an *additional* mercy." " That's all very well," replied Andersen. " I know that God has given you no end of good things in this world, and I can say the same of myself; but what about those who have a very different lot, those who are cast upon the earth with sick bodies and feeble minds, or are the victims of the direst sorrow and need, through no fault of their own ? Why should they suffer so much ? Why should things be so unequally distributed ?  That would be an injustice, and God cannot be unjust, so He will give compensation, and lift and loose what we cannot." From this conversation sprang the pathetic *Story from the Sandhills.*

*The Muck-beetle,* one of the most delightfully humorous of all the tales, was due to a playful suggestion of Charles Dickens.  In one of the numbers of *Household Words,* Dickens had brought together a number of Arabic proverbs and sayings, laying particular stress upon the following aphorism : " When the Emperor's horse was shod with gold shoes, the muck-beetle stuck out his foot for a gold shoe also." " We recommend," said Dickens in a note, " Hans Christian Andersen to write a tale about this." Andersen would have liked nothing better, but at first, try as he would, no story would come. Nine years later he chanced to read Dickens' words again, and then the tale of *The Muck-beetle* suddenly sprang into life. *The Ice Maiden* was written in Switzerland. The episode of the eagle's nest was an absolute fact, related to Andersen by the Bavarian popular poet, Koppel.

By the beginning of the sixties the *Tales* had, even in Denmark, come to be generally regarded as classical, although many of their admirers intensely offended the author by the critical airs they gave themselves, and their irritating preference, freely expressed, for the earlier stories.* He might have consoled himself for this insidious disparagement by the solid financial success of the later *Eventyr* and *Historier*. A very large sale could not, indeed, be reasonably expected in so small a country as Denmark, yet from four to five thousand copies of the stories were sold there between 1853 and 1858, and his share of the proceeds not only enabled him to undertake his long desired and often deferred tour to Spain (a description of which will be found in the next chapter), but also to begin to lay by

---

* "I have frequently heard people say 'Now, what I like best, you know, are your original good *old* stories ; and when I have asked which are they? I received as often as not the reply : " Oh, *The Butterfly, It is Quite Certain, The Snow Man*, which really belong to the *new* ones, the very *newest* in fact." (*Bemerkninger til Eventyr.*)

some money against sickness and old age. Abroad, too, the tales continued to grow in favour year by year. He frequently received invitations from German publishers to write them fresh stories on his own terms, and it was a great satisfaction to him to learn from one of the Ministers of State at Dresden that a volume of selections from his *Eventyr* was used as a text-book in all the schools of Saxony. In France, too, the *Tales* were by this time pretty well known, though there they never met with any very general recognition, and were even considered by some people *un peu trop enfantin.* Andersen also frequently complains of the ignorance and carelessness of his French translators, and their persistent misinterpretations.*    In England, on the other hand, his stories had long become household words, and he followed their progress there with intense interest and delight.    He had all the notices from the *Athenæum, Saturday Review,* and other English papers, clipped out, and sent to him regularly ; and the following amusing anecdote will show how he treasured up the opinions of his English critics.    A friend in Copenhagen had written to tell him that there was a shopman there who had absolutely *never heard* of Andersen.

* The best French version appeared five years after Andersen's death, and is entitled *Les Souliers Rouges, et autres contes,* Paris, 1880. It is translated by Gregoire and Moland, and illustrated by Jan D'Argent.

"How frightful!" he replies. "I suppose that by this time the unhappy man has been sent to some idiot asylum, where at least he will learn that the first letter in the alphabet is A, and that A stands for Andersen, and that Andersen is king in his own realm, as an English critic so finely puts it."*

The universal popularity of the Tales encouraged Andersen to extend his practice of reciting them in public. The "children's poet," who rarely and reluctantly read to children, was always delighted to see a grown-up audience before him. His afternoons now became quite an institution in the Danish capital, and he drew large and fashionable audiences, who were, I am afraid, not altogether uninfluenced by the fact that the *Tales* had now become fashionable at half the Courts of Europe. Andersen was not a good elocutionist; but his highly characteristic antics, and his strongly marked style, fitted in so well with his peculiar personality, that every one felt at once that his way, and no other, was the proper way of reading the *Eventyr;* and, generally speaking, it was a real pleasure to listen to him, especially when there was something new to be heard. But this was by no means the case always. Andersen had his own favourite tales which he persisted in reading over and over again, till most people knew them by heart.

* Bille og Bogh : *Breve fra Andersen*, ii. p. 450.

Thus he sometimes rather abused the patience of the
public, though they dared not rebel against his
tyranny, for tyranny was the only name for it.
Even the timid expression of a preference for this
story, or that, was sufficient to offend him, and he
would express his displeasure by wrinkling his nose,
giggling sarcastically, and pulling faces, so that it
was sometimes very difficult to preserve one's
gravity. When he began to read he demanded the
most intense, the most absolute, attention. The
ladies had to cease knitting, the gentlemen had to
put down their cigars, in order to hear him read
what they had heard a hundred times before.
Sometimes human nature revolted against such
rigorous discipline, and the death-like silence that
prevailed was not always a sign of attention. " I
remember," says Dr. Bloch,* " a comic scene which
occurred at an At Home, where all the guests had
been gathered together to hear Andersen read. I
cannot remember now which story it was he chose to
read, I only know that it was a sad subject, and
grew sadder and sadder as the recitation proceeded.
Amongst the audience was an elderly, white-haired
gentleman, who seemed to be following the story
with the deepest interest. Leaning back in his
chair, with folded arms and closed eyes, he was

* *Om H. C. Andersen. Bidrag til Belysning af hans Personlighed. Nær og Fjère,* No. 363.

listening with an expression of the most rapt attention, whilst now and again he would give an
approving nod. When the recitation had lasted
for some time, a young and lively lady suddenly
attracted the attention of every one present by her
extraordinary conduct. She began to smile, sternly
checked herself, smiled again, this time more
broadly, whipped out her handkerchief, stuffed it
into her mouth, and then lay back on her chair, and
laughed without uttering a sound, till all the blood
rushed to her head, and the tears trickled down her
cheeks. The looks of amazement which were
directed towards her from every quarter only made
her laugh the more, whilst by way of explanation
she pointed energetically at the above-mentioned old
gentleman. There he sat, just as before, with one
hand stuck under his waistcoat, his head a little on
one side, his eyes closed, and with an expression of
the deepest interest and sympathy on his features.
But, on regarding him more curiously, a soft regular
breathing could be heard proceeding from his lips :
he was asleep. The comicality of the situation, the
contagion of the young lady's silent laughter, was
too much for the whole audience—in a very short
time every mouth was stuffed full with a pocket-
handkerchief, every face was purple, and every eye
was running over. It was useless for the hostess to
frown, and gently whisper : "Hush! hush!" And

z

all the while the unsuspecting Andersen read on and on, and, when he had come to the end of his story, he had the triumph of seeing every eye full of tears."

But Andersen's most appreciative audiences were the artisans and mechanics of Copenhagen. His popular readings began in the winter of 1860, and were continued at irregular intervals for some years. The younger professors of the University of Copen-hagen had about this time begun to lecture three times a week at the Workman's Institute on various subjects. They wanted to see what effect poetry would have upon the men, as interpreted by Ander-sen, and the result was brilliant. There was quite a rush and a crush to get into the hall: it would only hold seven hundred, but the crowd outside insisted that the windows should be thrown open, so that they also might be able to hear. Andersen had been very nervous about this reading, a rather un-usual thing with him, and his anxiety during the six days and six nights immediately preceding it had been terrible. He quite expected he would break down, or faint; but the moment he began to warm to the work, all his fear left him, and he proved a decided success. By way of introduction he delivered a short lecture on the utility of poetry, pointing out how it appears in the Bible in the shape of parable and allegory. Then he read four of his own tales, ending with *Something*, which profoundly impressed the audience ; there was such a stillness in the large hall that one could have heard a pin drop. The comical *It is quite certain* amused them vastly, and they seemed to thoroughly appreciate every detail.*

Andersen's fondness for reciting his own stories induced him to even give readings in Germany occasionally, although German was a language that he knew but indifferently.† All the more precious, therefore, were the successes with which his audacity on these occasions was generally rewarded.

In 1859 Andersen visited North Jutland and the Scaw, the most peculiar part of Denmark, which always had a great fascination for him, and which he has so graphically described in *A Story from the Sandhills*. It is a wild and desolate region, where the German Ocean and the Cattegat meet, and strive together for the mastery, where the monotonous expanse of the vast ling-clad heath, haunted by the Fata Morgana, is only broken here and there by an ancient funereal tumulus, or by sylvan oases where the eagle still builds his nest, or the wild black stork dwells. Here, too, are churches dating from the tenth century, which look like lumps of rock

* Bille og Bogh: *Breve fra Andersen*, ii. pp. 414-15.

† He could speak it with tolerable fluency, but he always got Edward Collin to revise and correct the German versions of his tales.

for the West Wind and the North Sea to battle over,
or lie three-quarters buried in the sand, and over-
grown with thorns and dog-roses. Here Andersen
spent most of the summer, wandering among towns
that had neither streets nor roads, and "with houses
lying higgledy-piggledy among billows of sand."
The neglected, half-submerged churchyards not only
deeply interested him, but gave him much to do.
Like "Poor John" in his own beautiful story, *The
Travelling Companion*, Andersen had an especial
veneration for the dead, and was never weary of
performing various pious little offices in their behalf.
So here, too, he put to rights, as best he could, a
grave in which a young Dutch sailor, who had been
cast ashore, was buried, and placed a wreath of
flowers at each of its four corners. In another little
churchyard, close to the sea, he was shocked to find
heaps of human bones bleaching in the sunshine, and
took the trouble to dig a fresh grave, and cover them
up decently; "so you see," he wrote to a friend,
"that I have been doing something up here, if not
for the living, at least for the dead."

At the end of the year Andersen had a stroke
of luck which was at the same time a tribute of
the national respect: the Danish Folkething, or
House of Commons, raised his pension to 1000 rix
dollars.*    "I can now let the bird fly about a bit,"

* £116 3s. 4d.

he cried on hearing the good news, and accordingly
in the course of 1860 and 1861 he took tours through
Germany, Italy, and Switzerland, which would serve
him, he said, as a spiritually rejuvenescent Medea-
potion. In spite of occasional unpleasantness,* owing
to the still continuing tension between Germans and
Danes which was shortly to culminate in the second
Schleswig-Holstein war, these fresh excursions
abounded with pleasant experiences and comical
adventures. At Munich he sat for his photograph
by special invitation of the well-known artistic
connoisseur, Hofrath Hanfstüngl, who wished to add
Andersen's portrait to his illustrated work on celebrated personages of the day. Andersen was astonished at the result. " Never," he exclaims, " have I
seen such a beautiful portrait of myself, and one so
like me too ? I was altogether amazed that the
sunlight could make such a thing of beauty out of
my face. . . . . It is the only portrait of me that
my vanity would like to go down to posterity."
Dresden, during his visit there, seems to have been
suffering from a plague of authoresses,† " who
swarmed in and out of the houses like so many flies ; "

* At one place he abruptly quitted the *table-d'hôte* because something disrespectful to Denmark was said in his presence. He also
avoided visiting the various German Courts, though he laments his
hard fate—to be obliged to keep away from those who had been kind to
him.

† 365 of them, according to Andersen.

and Andersen comically complains that he wore out
his pen through writing verses in the albums of
these "ancient Sapphos." One gifted lady talked
learnedly to him about the resemblance between the
English and Danish languages ; and, by the time she
had finished, it became perfectly plain to him that
she knew very little about either. " The difficulty
about the English is the pronunciation," she said in
conclusion, " for the words are written one way and
pronounced another, so that you have no clue at all.
Thus you spell the name of the celebrated English
novelist D-i-c-k-e-n-s, but you pronounce it B-o-z."
At Nice, Andersen met for the first time Björnstjerne
Björnson, whom he thought one of the most amiable
Norwegians he had ever encountered. Björnson was
at that time engaged upon his famous tragedy,
*Sigurd Slembe.* The intimacy, thus begun, ripened
gradually into friendship. In Switzerland, Andersen
had many opportunities of studying the manners and
customs of the English tourists, whose insular ex-
clusiveness and solemn taciturnity amused him
mightily. They seemed to have taken a solemn oath
of silence to speak to nobody at *table-d'hôte* except
the waiters, whom they addressed in a language that
was neither French nor English.* Occasionally

---

* At the same time Andersen confesses that his own French was
not very much to boast of. He used to "chatter with shameless
rapidity," that people might not notice his blunders, and at *table-d'hôte*
he was occasionally guilty of a gross impropriety when he meant all

Andersen made a sally or two in English, in
order to draw them out, but they remained absolutely stiff and dumb till they found out who he was,
when their faces brightened at once, and the ladies
even went the length of presenting him with posies.
One English girl, indeed, was so taken up with him
at dinner-time that she lost her boat; and another
declared privately to a friend of his that she
would like to travel all over the world with him.
Andersen was much flattered, and inwardly resolved
that he would never laugh at the English again.

At Geneva he came across many Americans who
pressed him to visit the United States, assuring him
of a hearty welcome there. Of that he had not the
slightest doubt, for by this time he was as much known
and admired in America as in England itself, and he
was always particularly grateful to the mother country,
" the land where our dear Dickens dwells," for " so
lovingly " bearing his name across the great ocean.
But not all the eloquence of his friends could ever
persuade him to go to America. " There is that
endless ocean between us," he wrote, " that long
fortnight of raging sea, and I am quite sure that
for very many days of that fortnight I should only
get sea-sickness for my money. . . . . The great

the time to be engagingly gallant. " But what does it matter if it be
said in all innocence ?" he adds. On the other hand, he boasts that
he could build up an intelligible if somewhat audacious conversation
in French with thirty words and a half.

ocean is a terror to me, and yet I love it so much—
when I am safely on dry land." *

Still, perhaps, he might have been ultimately
persuaded to make the venture but for a shocking
catastrophe in which, about this time, one of his
dearest friends, Miss Henrietta Wulff, mysteriously
perished. In the autumn of 1858 this lady, who
was a great invalid, had left Hamburg for New
York, for the benefit of her health, in the steamship
*Austria*, which was burnt at sea about a day's
journey from the American coast. The fate of Miss
Wulff was for a long time doubtful, and Andersen
hoped against hope in a perfect agony of suspense.
The vision of the poor defenceless creature being
burnt to death, haunted him night and day, and
quite unsettled him. At last, on New Year's Day,
1859, he received a letter which at least gave him
the comforting assurance that Miss Wulff's last
moments must have been comparatively painless,
as she had been suffocated in her sleep. But her
tragic fate was ever present with him, and the
Atlantic had now fresh and invincible terrors.

During the ten years that elapsed between 1851
and 1861, death had been very busy with Andersen's friends. His first serious loss was that of
H. C. Örsted who died in 1851, only a few months

* Compare Bille og Bogh : *Breve fra Andersen*, ii. pp. 259 and
273.

after the celebration of his Jubilee by the University of Copenhagen. The old man (he was 73) was in high spirits on this occasion, and when, in the evening, the students held a torch-light procession in his honour, Örsted went down to them, and invited the whole two hundred up in batches to drink a glass of wine with him. Up they all ran forthwith, to the no small consternation of worthy Madame Örsted, who cried to the students : " No, no ! this is too much. My husband really cannot drink with the whole lot of you ! " " I mean to go with my merry friends as far as I can, anyhow ! " replied the genial old man with a smile, as he raised his glass. Nearly nine years later (1860) died Heiberg, who, together with Andersen, had taken a prominent part at the Örsted festival, leaving behind him one of the greatest names in Danish literature. Andersen had not always been on the best of terms with the famous dramatist, but latterly, especially after Heiberg had gone out of his way to praise Andersen's *Fairy Tale Operettas*, the relations between them had become very friendly, and the news of Heiberg's death, which reached Andersen at Geneva, deeply affected him. " God has granted our little country so much that is splendid," he cried, "but alas ! He calls it back to Him again. Only fancy ! I shall see Heiberg no more ! " Exactly twelve months later Andersen was to suffer a far heavier bereavement, for it was then that his second father, the noble-minded Jonas Collin, departed this life in his 75th year. Andersen was abroad when Collin died, but got home in time to attend his funeral. At the end of the same year he had to mourn another life-long friend, the poet and novelist Ingemann, in whom he had always found a most indulgent (some think a too indulgent) sympathiser and defender. Such an affectionate nature as Andersen's naturally suffered severely at every such bereavement. "All the old friends are going," he cries, "and the new ones are never like the old." "It is odd," he says in another place, "to see the ranks marching off like this, one after the other. The rank in which I am is coming to the front now, so I suppose that will march off next." Yet the intimate belief that he would shortly meet all his dear ones again in another and a better world always acted as a check upon his grief. He never sorrowed as those must who have no such hope, he only redoubled his attention to the survivors, especially if they were poor and friendless. Madame Ingemann, now very old and infirm, henceforth became the chief object of his tender concern, and the troubles and cares of her last days were not a little lightened by his loving sympathy.

# CHAPTER XIII

## *IN SPAIN*

In Spain—The Perpignan stage coach—Spanish crinolines—La Señorita —Barcelona—Valencia—Alicante—Murcia—A Spanish diligence —Malaga—Horrors of a bull fight—Granada—The Alhambra— Spanish courtesy—The blues—*En route* for Gibraltar—The wakeful children and the candle—Tangiers—The surf boat and the six sages—Drummond Hay—The Moorish *Märchen* of the Ravens—The poor Jew and the rich Jew—Tea with the Pasha of Tangiers—Cadiz—Seville—Madrid—The physiognomy of cities— Toledo—Burgos—Nearly asphyxiated—Homeward with the birds of passage.

In 1862 Andersen was able to undertake his often contemplated, and as often postponed, tour to Spain, which was to introduce him to quite a new world. He was accompanied by young Jonas Collin, the grandson of his benefactor, and has recorded his experiences in that vivid and entertaining book, *I Spanien*,\* one of his most successful works, although, from a literary point of view, this southern itinerary is certainly inferior to the northern one, *I Sverrig*, already mentioned. At the very outset, Andersen,

\* "In Spain." It was translated into English in 1864 by Mrs. Bushby. It was compiled, immediately after his return, from the diary he kept on the occasion. The following narrative of the tour is mainly taken from it.

who was never a *laudator temporis acti*, and hated
roughing it, was very much disgusted to discover
that the railroad broke off abruptly at Perpignan,
and that consequently he would have to resume
once more " that tortoise-like torture-box on wheels "
ironically misnamed a *diligence*. He was prepared,
however, to suffer something, for Spain had been
described to him in the most harrowing terms. He
was given to understand that Protestants in that
strictly orthodox land were treated worse than the
heathen ; that travellers were habitually exposed to
the attacks of bandits and highwaymen, and that
the food was uneatable. All this he had heard and
read before he set out, so that it was with something
like a sinking heart that he mounted the diligence
which left Perpignan at 3 o'clock on a fine afternoon
in the beginning of September 1862. The vehicle
was heavily laden with passengers and luggage,
twelve horses covered with jingling bells · were
harnessed to it ; crack went the whip, and off they
started full tilt through narrow streets and picturesque surroundings, which could have furnished
the stage decorations for a mediæval drama, till the
broad open highroad with its alleys of pines and
platanes, and a sporadic cypress standing out in the
distance like a note of exclamation, lay before them.
In the same compartment with Andersen sat two
Spanish ladies, mother and daughter, with uncon-

scionably huge crinolines. Andersen was quite persuaded that, if they had paid a visit to the Scaw, the mother alone would have sufficed to cover the whole of Denmark's northernmost promontory, and he had the uncomfortable sensation of a man sitting on the corner of a balloon which he every moment expects to feel inflated. Early next morning he caught a glimpse of the sea, and turning to the younger lady, remarked : " el mar ! " " Ingles ? " she inquired, " Danès " said he, and so the ice was broken, and a sort of conversation began, or rather, Andersen always gave the cue, and the lady took it up. Thus he began with a mere string of names—" La Poesia de España, Cervantes, Calderon, Moreto "—upon each of which in turn La Señorita waxed so voluble that mamma woke up, and was told by her daughter that their fellow-passenger, the Danish gentleman, had been eloquently expatiating on the glories of Spanish literature.

Barcelona, the Paris of Spain, as he calls it, was the first great Spanish city Andersen came to, and here he found sights sufficient to fill a whole fortnight. The Cathedral, wedged in as it was between tall houses so that one ran the risk of passing it by without knowing it was there, dis-appointed him, and he was glad to quit its dim, incense-clouded interior for the pleasant orangery outside, where God's sun shone again, where fountains plashed into marble basins from the mouths of bronze horses, and gold-fish sported among the succulent water-plants. On the other hand, he was never tired of strolling on the Rambla, the fashionable promenade of Barcelona, where the elegantly curled dandies, with their cigars and eyeglasses, looked just as if they had been clipped bodily out of the latest French fashion books, and the graceful mantilla alternated with French caps and shawls. The splendour of the cafés astonished him. They were far superior to anything of the kind he had seen at Paris, and he was also very agreeably surprised by the excellence of the Spanish cuisine. The only thing that tormented him at Barcelona was as to how he should get to Valencia, which he proposed to visit next. He had the choice between a long and difficult journey by road in a hot and stuffy diligence, with the possibility of being attacked by bandits at a certain place among the mountains, and a voyage on a roughish sea in a small steamer the look of which he did not like at all. He hesitated up to the last moment, but as all his acquaintances at Barcelona advised him to go by sea, he decided to take the steamer, though not till after he had quite satisfied himself that her engines were in good working order and her captain was really an able seaman. He sat on deck all night with the wind whistling about his ears, and the vessel swaying beneath him "like a rocking-chair," but his troubles were speedily over, for when the sun rose next morning, pouring a flood of light over the dark mountains, the weather was so calm that it seemed to him as if he were gliding over a transparent watered-silk carpet.

A huge bridge, a dry river-bed, old walls, and a city gate made of freestone were his first impressions of Valencia. The dark, vine-covered staircases and passages, the lofty but sparsely furnished rooms, the whole character of the accommodation and attendance told him plainly enough that he was no longer in semi-gallic Barcelona, but in genuine Old Spain. Break-fast was ready for him when he landed. There were good meats, grapes as large as plums and of aromatic flavour, melons that melted on the tongue like snow, while the wine glowed, and the air was hot enough to bake the Northerners through and through. Valencia itself Andersen found rather dull, and so sultry that he felt half tempted to improvise a hat out of a fresh green pumpkin and lie in the shade all day long. Once or twice, in the early morning, he sallied forth with book and pencil to sketch something, but nothing worth sketching could he discover.

Alicante proved depressing. Andersen describes it as a collection of white-washed, flat-roofed houses with projecting balconies, and a promenade that looked as if it had been snipped off the Paris Boulevards, but so tiny that nobody there would ever have missed such a trifle. Murcia, with its picturesque gipsy colony, its fine cathedral that had once been a mosque, its shady *alameda* or poplar walk, and its comfortable Casino, was a little more tolerable, but both the Danish tourists were glad to turn their backs upon it in four days, and take the diligence to Cartagena, whence they were to go by boat to Malaga. Andersen's description of this particular Spanish diligence is so characteristic that I must give it in full :

"The diligence we were to get into seemed to consist of a couple of wooden booths that had been hammered together. Collin and I shared the front booth with an old priest ; the partition between us and the hindmost booth was broken down at starting, so that we had a fresh current of air playing on our necks the whole way, and six persons by way of ballast. There was an affected coquette of a serving-maid whose tongue ran on like a coffee-grinder ; there was an elderly madam, fat and coarse, a piece of sleeping flesh in fact, and in the furthest corner sat a person in an incredible patchwork of clothes, one might have guessed the most difficult conundrum sooner than have made out to which of the clouts in his coat and trousers the original pattern belonged. There were three other persons besides, one of whom belonged to the better dressed classes. He had a

frilled shirt and a sparkling breast-pin, but his linen
was so filthy that I could not help fancying that if
this was his usual everyday. get up, he must certainly have hired his dirty underclothes from the
unwashed stock of some laundress. Tobacco smoke
and the smell of leeks was the atmosphere of the
diligence. I perceived it just as I had put my foot
on the wheel to mount up ; I had to turn round to
get a mouthful of less blended air. I looked up
towards the balcony of the nearest house where
stood a crowd of women beckoning to their de-
parting friends, and right in the front row stood a
pretty little child, a girl of about two. I nodded to
her, and she was so embarrassed that, in her innocence, she pulled her little smock, her sole garment,
right over her head. So now let nobody ever tell me
that little Spanish ladies are not modest."

After an exhaustingly hot journey by steamer
from Cartagena the travellers reached Malaga, whose
beauty and luxurious comfort more than made up to
them for the dreariness of Alicante and the dulness
of Murcia. The first thing the waiter brought them
at the hotel was a glass of English ale, which seemed
to them a heavenly beverage after the hot wine and
the lukewarm aniseed water they had hitherto been
accustomed to. In no other Spanish town did
Andersen feel himself so much at home as in Malaga.
All the indispensable requisites of an ideal foreign

2 A

tour, from his point of view, such as picturesque
crowds, fine scenery and the open sea, he found
here in endless variety, and, which was of scarcely
less importance, he was hospitably entertained at
the house of the Danish Consul, Scholtz, who had
married a Swedish lady, a friend of Jenny Lind, so
that Andersen found "a little bit of Scandinavian
domesticity" transplanted on the very coast of the
Mediterranean. It was at Malaga, too, that he saw,
"in all its crude hideousness," a bull fight, which he
thus describes : "Twelve bulls were to attack the
wretched half-blinded horses, one after the other.
The first bull immediately thrust his sharp horns
into the horse's flanks, and tore it so that the bowels
gushed out; some fellows stuffed the intestines in
again. The animal sustained another attack, but
after staggering about for a few moments, literally
lost in the arena pieces of torn intestine fathoms
long. The next horse fared little better, for it got
one of the bull's horns in its hinder quarters, so that
the blood spurted right over the railings. It
managed to go a few steps further, and then col-
lapsed. A third horse was cast high into the air
with its rider; only with the utmost difficulty did
the *Bandarilleros* save the horseman, while the
horse was gored and worried by the infuriated bull.
Such a sight was almost too much for me; water
absolutely gushed out of my finger tips. Horse

upon horse lay like carrion in the arena, and only after the bull, amidst the applause of the public, had received his death-stroke from the *Espada*, came a couple of draught-horses and dragged the butchered animals out of the arena amidst a burst of wild and furious music. I saw a horse that was not quite dead raise its head as it was being carried off; its teeth gnashed together, and then its head sank down again. It was shockingly painful ; almost unendurable, in fact. I was very near fainting, and yet I could not prevail upon myself to quit the bull fight which I was now really seeing for the first, and possibly for the last time. There was something so interesting and attractive in the suppleness and strength, the alertness and dexterity with which the *Bandarilleros* and the *Espada* gambolled about in the arena—it is just like a studied game, like a dance upon the stage." Thus Andersen's fondness for dramatic effect for once got the better of his soft-heartedness.

From Malaga, Collin and he proceeded to Granada, which struck Andersen as one of the most interesting places in the world. The Alhambra, however, at first disappointed him. It was very pretty, but surprisingly small. He had looked for something far vaster and grander ; yet as he wandered through its colonnades, halls and courtyards, they appeared to expand before him, and it seemed as if he were walking through " Fancy's bazaar of petri-

fied lacework." The fantastic splendour of the
"Sala de los Embajadores," where the Moorish
kings were wont to give audiences to the envoys
of foreign powers, fairly took his breath away ; any
attempt to describe it in words seems to him absurd.
"What is the use of saying," he exclaims, "that the
parapet consists of green porcelain flagstones, that
the walls appear covered along their full length
with tulle hung over gold brocade and purple, and
that this tulle is a mass of hewn stone lit up by
the ærially arched horse-shoe windows. . . . . no
mere words ; photography alone can reproduce the
picture."

Spanish courtesy lent an additional charm to the
delight of a pleasant visit, and Andersen gives an
amusing instance of its polite exaggeration. One
day he wanted to buy some drawing paper, and was
accordingly taken by his Malagan friend and host,
Colonel José Larramendi, to a paperseller, and
introduced as a stranger from Denmark ; but when
Andersen took out his purse, the shopkeeper politely
informed him that the paper was paid for already !
Larramendi had signalled to him that the stranger
was his guest. "I knew," continues Andersen,
"that I should never get leave to settle the score
when Larramendi was with me ; but when, a week
later, I went by myself to the same shop to buy
some more paper, I got the same answer as before :

'It is paid for.'   'Nay,' said I, 'that is not possible.
To-day I am alone ; nobody is with me !'   'Yes, I
am with you,' said the paperseller ; 'my house is
yours.'   Naturally I never went to 'my house' again,
but I must tell the story to give an idea of Spanish
courtesy and attention."

Nevertheless, Andersen's stay at Granada was not
altogether a pleasant one.   To begin with, the
Spanish sun proved a little too hot for him ; then,
again, living was much dearer there than it need
have been, thus ultimately compelling him to greatly
restrict his travels, and finally both young Collin
and himself were sick and irritable and quarrelled
frequently.   Worst of all, Granada was the scene
of one of those chronic outbursts of vexation and
wounded pride which had embittered his happiness ever since he had first begun to travel some
forty years ago.   What it was all about this time
is not quite clear, but that it had something to do
with his less successful literary essays (possibly his
Casino plays) there can be no doubt.

On October 20, Andersen and Collin quitted
Granada for Gibraltar.   The diligence this time was
a sort of omnibus with seats on both sides crowded
with people, though most of the room seems to
have been taken up by an old grandmother with
a crinoline so large that it could have served the
whole company for a tent.   At Laja, which they

reached at midnight, they were rid of some of their noisier travelling companions, but got in exchange a whole family, whom Andersen thus hits off in one of his masterly little sketches : " The husband was tall, dark, solemn, and full of Spanish *grandezza*; he looked very learned, and was called *Catedratico*, or, as we should say, Professor ; his wife was a dainty child, she did not seem more than sixteen, and had large gentle eyes, and three children. We took the whole lot into the carriage, and the children did all that only children can do in a carriage, and absolutely *would* not go to sleep without a light. So the young mamma had to sit with a large dazzling wax-candle in her hand, which very nearly blinded me, and when *she* wanted to sleep papa had to hold the light, and when papa wanted to sleep the waiting-maid had to hold it, and when she also went to sleep, and all but lost both the candle and baby too in consequence, her neighbour put the light out at last, and we all sat in a delicious sleep-inviting darkness. Suddenly the smallest of the little ones uttered a piercing shriek, and then the second one took it up, and then the third. There was a general commotion—and again the candle was lit."—After that, sleep was impossible for the remainder of the night, and every one, especially Andersen, got very cross and uncomfortable. The air was cold and clammy. the wet mist lay over the mountains like a veil, the waggon threatened to go to pieces every moment in the villainous roads, the young mamma was very sick, and all the men began to smoke in silence. But next morning, when the sun came forth, a beautiful expanse of smooth blue sea lay right in front of them, and the white flat-roofed houses of Malaga and her splendid cathedral welcomed them in the distance. Never had Malaga *la Hechicera* seemed more of an enchantress than she did now.

Early on November 2, a little steamer, which pitched tremendously, left Gibraltar for Tangiers with Andersen and Collin on board. Africa had always been the object of Andersen's fervent long-ings, and he was now at last to catch a glimpse of it. The low coast near Tangiers, with its green hillocks, reminded him, at first, of the northern coast of Zealand, but behind the town there seemed to have been cast "a little specimen of the yellow sand of the desert, over which a train of loaded camels was moving." The steamer lay-to a good way from land, and a couple of boats, full of half-naked, sunburnt Moors, rowed rapidly out to meet it, forced their way, shrieking and howling, up the ship's ladder, took forcible possession of Andersen and Collin and their luggage, and dashed off again ashore amidst the rolling breakers. "Here," says Andersen, "half a score or so of caftaned Jews sprang into the

surf and waded out to us. One snapped up a
trunk, another a knapsack, a third ran off with the
umbrellas; it was a perfect raid. They paid no
attention whatever to words or shouts. One caught
me by one leg, another by the other, and, before I
knew where I was, I was hoisted on to the head
of a third, raised aloft, and carried ashore. . . . .
There we stood as if we had been spirited away to
Damascus, or some other of the cities mentioned in
the 'Thousand and one Nights.' In an open hall
before us, with turbans and long beards, sat people
who looked very much like the Seven Sages, though
here there were only six, and as to their sageness I
cannot say, for I didn't understand their language."

During their stay at Tangiers, Andersen and
Collin were the guests of the English Minister, Sir
Drummond Hay, who had married the daughter of
the late Danish Consul-General Carstensen, so that
the travellers had the satisfaction of hearing their
mother tongue spoken on the African coast. Andersen was equally astonished and delighted to discover
that the pretty daughters of the house were enthusiastic admirers of the *Fairy Tales*, English
and French translations of which he found in their
father's library. Drummond Hay even suggested to
him the idea of a fresh story by telling him the
amusing Moorish *Märchen* of the Ravens, which
Andersen thought so good that he made no attempt

to improve it. The Moors believe that ravens, when
they come out of the egg, are white, and they say
that the poor raven-father was terribly shocked
when he first saw the fledglings creep out quite
snowy looking. " Why, what's the meaning of this ? "
cried the raven-father. He looked at himself, but
not a single white feather could he find upon his
own body—and yet the youngsters were white.
Then he looked at the raven-mother, but not a
single white feather was to be found on her either,
so he naturally addressed the mother, and asked for
an explanation. " I don't understand it at all,"
replied she, " but, depend upon it, time will put it
all right." " I'll fly away," said he, " away, a-wa,
a-wa, wa, wa ! " and away he flew, leaving the mother
sitting with the young ones. But after flying about
a little time, he began to think : " I couldn't have
looked straight, I must go back and have another
look ! " and when he came and looked, behold ! the
white fledglings had become grey. " Anyhow, grey
is not white ! " cried he ; " still you can't call it black
either ! Neither mother nor I look like that ! " So
off he flew again, and when he came back the fledglings had become black. " Leave everything to
time and it will come right ! "

Andersen, who thoroughly explored Tangiers and
its environs, always considered his sojourn on the
Moroccan coast the most interesting part of his tour.

He wandered about town and country without a guide, and everywhere met with civility and attention. Once, as he was exploring a lonely part of the coast, suddenly, between a little pine wood and the sea, he came upon a large yellow beast which, at first sight, he took for a lion, and was terribly frightened till he saw that it was only a dog. This, however, was the most exciting adventure he had in Africa. On another occasion a poorly-clad Jew, smiling all over his face, invited him into a side street. Andersen naturally asked him what there was to be seen there, and with many friendly nods and humble gestures the man replied " A Jew's house." Andersen's curiosity was aroused, and although he had money about him, and the place was lonely, and the man a stranger, he resolved to trust him, and followed him down a labyrinth of narrow alleys, till they stopped before a low door in a wall into which the Jew disappeared, beckoning to him to follow. Andersen was by this time very much inclined to suspect that his guide was an assassin, but the adventurous character of the whole thing had such a piquant attraction for him that he determined to see it out. So he followed and found himself in a little paved courtyard where a very dirty Jewish girl was bustling about, and from whence a broad staircase led up to a little open chamber. Here lay a pale young woman with a carpet spread

over her and a little child at her breast. "Jew
woman! Jew baby!" cried the man, hopping and
skipping about. Then he took the child and held it
towards Andersen, that he might see for himself
that it was a true son of Abraham. The woman
then took the cushion on which she was lying and
gave it to Andersen who sat down, while the man
kissed his pale, delicate wife and child in turn,
and looked very happy. The whole furniture of the
place seemed to consist of a few rags and a water-
jar.

In striking contrast to this poor habitation was the
mansion of the rich Israelite whom Drummond Hay
took him to see. Viewed from the outside, indeed,
the house did not look very imposing, for all that
could be seen of it was a square hole in the wall
with a grating over it and a low door; but no sooner
had they crossed the threshold and entered the
little forecourt, than everything had a very different
appearance. The floor and steps were inlaid with
porcelain slabs, the walls appeared to be of brightly
polished stone, the rooms were lofty and airy, with
an open colonnade leading into a garden. Here sat
the young wife, a pretty woman with coal-black hair
and shining white teeth, dressed in a rich, open, gold-
embroidered, green velvet kirtle over a white silk
undergarment, a long red silken scarf, trousers of
brocade with many buttons, each button being a

pearl, while her fingers were covered with costly
rings. Her hair, after the Jewish fashion in Morocco,
had been shaved off, but artificial plaits hung down
from the blue silk turban on her head. Her earrings
were so massive that they looked like "small
stirrups." Her husband was evidently very proud of
all this splendour, and turned his wife round and
round on the floor, so that Andersen might survey
her from all sides. The visitor was then regaled with
cakes and orange liqueur, whereupon the Bible in
English and Hebrew was produced, and Andersen
created quite a sensation by reading aloud the whole
of the first chapter of Genesis in Hebrew, a feat that,
by the way, as he himself admits every Danish Latin
schoolboy could have done just as well. He was also
presented by Sir Drummond Hay to the Pasha of
Tangiers, and tea was brought in cups "as big as bathroom warmers." Two of these Andersen managed to
drink, but when the hospitable pasha would have
sent for a third he begged to be excused, explaining
through Drummond Hay that it was contrary to the
precepts of his religion to drink three cups at once,
a plea admitted as valid by the pious pasha.

Cadiz, which Andersen visited next, surprised him
by its extraordinary cleanliness, but did not otherwise interest him. Here there was no picture gallery,
no Moorish antiquities of any importance, and, fresh
as he was from the Morocco coast, the place seemed

to him jejune and prosaic, and presented nothing that was in any way novel or peculiar. It also made him reflect that Spain had hitherto not suggested a single idea for a fairy tale,* so that he was afraid he would not be able to redeem his promise to his circle of dear little people at home. Seville, on the other hand, with its mangificent churches, its Moorish Alcazar, and its incomparable collection of Murillos,† struck him as one of the most interesting cities in Europe, but for the want of the sea, it would have been absolutely perfect. " If only Seville lay where Cadiz lies," he says, " it would be a Spanish Venice, aye ! and a living Venice too ; a prodigy of the first rank, full of poetry and beauty, and superior to all the other cities of the world."

From Seville, Andersen proceeded *via* Cordova and Santa Cruz de Mudela to Madrid. Here the weather

---

* Nor are Andersen's tales much read in Spain. The only Spanish translations of Andersen I am aware of are : *Los Cisnes En-cantados* (The Enchanted Swans), Madrid, 1871; a very poor version of *The Wild Swans* by Julio Nousbela ; a small anonymous collection entitled *Un Manojo de Cuentos* (A Handful of Stories) Madrid, 1872, containing an unconscious parody (I can call it nothing else) of *The Little Match Girl* and Fernandez Cuesta's admirable *Cuentos Escogidos de Andersen*, Madrid, 1879, containing twenty-two of the best stories, rendered with great spirit ; *El Intrépido Soldado de Plomo* (The Steadfast Tin Soldier), and *La Niña y los Fosferos* (The Little Match Girl), being particularly good.

† Andersen gives a most enthusiastic description of Murillo's paintings. He preferred the great Spaniard to any of the Italian masters.—*I Spanien*, pp. 163-6; 198-9.

was raw and inhospitable, and he was surprised to find that winter had arrived there before him, and all the housetops were covered with snow. With the city itself he was much disappointed. It did not appear to him to have the character of a Spanish town at all, still less could he understand why it should ever have been made the capital; but he was bound to admit that it possessed one precious pearl, to see which it was quite worth the trouble of travelling all the way from the north, and that was its magnificent picture gallery, which he considers one of the first in Europe. "But," he exclaims, summing up his impressions, "it is with cities as it is with men; there is something about them which attracts or repels us. Paris I should never choose for my home; Venice has never pleased me, it has always made me feel as if I were on a wreck out at sea; to me Madrid is as a fallen camel in the desert; I was now sitting on its hump and looking around me far and wide, but it was an uncomfortable seat, and a dear one too." It was quite a relief to him to quit the Spanish capital, and Old Toledo, "mediæval, romantic, and full of poetry," seemed to him at first quite refreshing by comparison. But the utter loneliness of the place,*

---

* "I know of nothing more lonely than the broad, cut-up highway just below Toledo's ancient walls, and the view from thence; the aspect of the place is so mournful, the dark and distant mountains stand out so theatrically; everything inspires me with awe and melancholy. I felt as if I stood beside a bier whereon a dead grandeur lay outstretched."—*I Spanien*, p. 208.

the intense cold, and the very indifferent food which, though cheap enough, was the poorest they had yet tasted in Spain, very soon set the travellers moving again, and they went on to Burgos.

At Burgos the snow lay deep in the streets, and the wind blew bitterly cold through all the crevices of the crazy old inn where they put up. From the balcony door Andersen watched the people in the street below, struggling through the snowdrifts, while the air was full of larger and heavier flakes than are usually seen in Denmark, even at Christmas time. It was so freezingly cold that Collin and he sent for a *brasero,* and while they were warming their hands and feet over it, two unfortunate tortoises that Collin * had brought with him all the way from Africa, crept right under the stove and were baked to death. That same evening had like to have been the travellers' last. In the middle of the night Andersen suddenly awoke with an oppressive feeling in the pit of the stomach and a racking headache. He shouted to Collin, but got no answer. With a great effort Andersen got out of bed and staggered like a drunken man to the balcony door. It was fast closed. An agonised feeling of heaviness came

* Young Collin was an amateur geologist and entomologist, and seems to have somewhat annoyed Andersen by his scientific zeal, which went the length of collecting living specimens of the insects and minor fauna of the country, so that Andersen at last complains that they were carrying about a whole menagerie with them.

over him, but, putting forth all his strength, he got
the door open at last, and the snowflakes came in
with the fresh, vivifying air. They had nearly been
suffocated by the fumes of the charcoal in the
*brasero*.

All the way back from Burgos, through the
Spanish Basque provinces, the travellers felt winter
in all its severity. It was only when they had
crossed the French frontier that they found the
sun shining warmly, and the trees covered with
vernal buds. "And now," concludes Anderson joy-
ously, "I was flying homewards with the hosts of
the birds of passage, to see the beeches burst forth,
to hear the cuckoo and all the twittering birds, to
walk in the tall, fresh, green grass, to listen to that
Danish music, my mother tongue and see faithful
friends, and within my breast I brought back with
me a whole treasure of reminiscences."

# CHAPTER XIV

## DARK DAYS—AT HOME—GROWING OLD

The second Schleswig-Holstein War—Andersen's patriotic anguish—
—More tales—In Holland—At Paris—In Portugal—Settles
down in a house of his own—Lamentations—" Rolighed "—The
happiest period of Andersen's life—Distinctions—Receives the
freedom of Odense—His literary Jubilee—Popularity—Birthday
presents—The story of the clover-leaf—Andersen's lady admirers—
His grotesque ugliness—And foppishness—The lady who made
love to him—Cessation of criticism—George Brandes and Andersen—Andersen comparatively well off in his old age—Economy
and generosity—Andersen's peculiar method of dealing with
servants—The aggrieved *soubrette*—Visit to Norway—The last
*Eventyr og Historier.*

ANDERSEN tells us * that he returned home from his
Spanish tour so thoroughly renewed in intellectual
vigour, that the forcing power of his imagination
was able, in the course of the following year, to
make the dry sticks of his Iberian diary burst forth
into the flower and foliage of a new book,† and he
found time besides to compose an original two-
act comedy for the Royal Theatre,‡ and a four
act drama § for the Casino. But the year after that

* Bille og Bogh : *Breve fra Andersen*, ii. p. 500.
† *I Spanien.*
‡ *Han er ikke født* (He is not Born).
§ *Paa Langebro* (On Long Bridge).

came a great change.   Dark political storm-clouds
gathered over the horizon of his native land, and
just as the sudden death of King Christian VIII. in
1848 had been the immediate occasion of the first
Schleswig-Holstein War, so now, too, the sudden
death of Frederick VII. in 1863 led to the second
Schleswig-Holstein War in which little Denmark,
attacked or abandoned by the very Powers who had
guaranteed the integrity of her dominions fifteen
years before, was forced, after a resolute resistance,
to submit to the terms of her mighty antagonists,
and suffer a cruel amputation which to many, in the
first moment of bitter agony, seemed likely to prove
mortal.   There is no necessity to dwell upon the
melancholy story:   how, in December, 1863, the
forces of the German Bund, in support of the claims
of the Prince of Augustenberg, occupied Holstein
and Lauenburg, how, on January 16, 1864, Austria
and Prussia demanded autonomy for Schleswig-
Holstein, and how the Danish Government, vainly
relying on the support of England, refused to grant
it, and prepared for war; how, in February, the
Austro-Prussian forces crossed the Eyder, and compelled the Danes to retire behind the Düppel
entrenchments, which were stormed by the Prussians,
while the Austrians simultaneously invaded Jutland;
how Denmark indignantly, perhaps foolishly, rejecting every offer of mediation, heroically continued the

war till the fall of Als, the total occupation of
Jutland, and a threatened descent upon Funen,
compelled her (July 18) to accept an armistice,
and ultimately a peace (October 30), whereby the
Duchies of Schleswig-Holstein and Lauenburg were
ceded to Austria and Prussia—all these events are
much too recent to need recapitulating. We know
how the tiny kingdom recovered from the shock, and
proceeded with unexampled energy and astonishing
success to turn even her terrible adversity to good
account, wisely husbanding her now diminished
resources, and gallantly endeavouring to win that
eminence in literature which was denied to her in
politics; but, for the moment, the blow was
crushing, and every patriotic Dane thought of his
dismembered mother country with a bleeding heart.
Andersen also suffered intensely. Naturally san-
guine, he thought at first that Denmark would still
be able to hold her own, despite the fearful odds
against her; there was, he said, a spiritual energy
and freshness about the old country, sufficient to
shake off the heavy billows that were rolling over
her, and he was confident that God would never
desert little Denmark. But when the *Dannevirke**
had to be abandoned by the exhausted and out-

* The famous ancient boundary wall of the Danes against the
Germans in Schleswig, extending from the North Sea to the Baltic
along the line of the Eyder.

numbered Danish army, when it became more and
more evident that this was not a war of ruler
against ruler, but of a great nation against a small
nation, the image of dismembered Poland began to
sweep before him, and he even lent an ear to those
alarmists who declared that peace could only be
obtained by an absolute submission to Germany.
Then an anguish almost too grievous to be borne
came upon him. " What ! " he exclaims, " shall our
rich and beautiful language, for the next hundred
years to come, be only known through the medium
of Norway ! " He declares that it is only the
strained recollection of all the favours and blessings
that God had bestowed upon him during a long life,
that gives him strength to drain to the dregs this
bitter cup of humiliation. The events of the terrible
months of April and May made him feel quite old.
The supply of youthful freshness that he had brought
back with him from Spain was now, he said, quite
drained out of him. He refused an invitation to
Norway because he could not enjoy himself while his
country was suffering, and when he wandered,
melancholy and pensive, through the woods in April,
and saw for the first time that year the budding
trees, and the cowslips and buttercups in the fresh
green grass, and the note of the cuckoo struck upon
his ear again, he was half surprised, and almost
offended that spring, which he had clean forgotten

all about, should visit the land just as if there were
no such thing as war and disaster, and national
humiliation. "I feel," he cries, "that it is high time
for me also to march off now, and yet I have done so
little. I am as heavy and weary as after a day's
march in the hot plains."

But Time, that great consoler, consoled even
Denmark and her sons, and Andersen was among
the first to recover his mental and moral equilibrium.
He began to feel that poetry and art were now to
be Denmark's *Dannevirke*, and, after a twelve months'
interval of silence, he brought out (1865-6) two
more little volumes of the "Tales," thirteen in all,
of which the most notable are *The Silver Penny*,
*The Snowdrop* and *The Toad*. The desire for
foreign travel also came back to him, with all its
old force. In 1865 we find him in Sweden again.
In 1866 he visited Holland where he was met by
his admirers and translators,* who insisted upon
entertaining him in their houses so long as he
stayed in the country. His hosts, with exquisite
courtesy, brought together Danes and Danish-
speaking Dutchmen to meet him in their drawing-
rooms, and he was thus frequently able to read to
them his stories in his mother tongue, to their and

---

* Perhaps the best of his Dutch translators is Nieuivenhuis.
Professor Van Kate turned some of the tales into beautiful verse. As
a rule the Dutch versions are quite equal to the German.

his infinite delight. At a banquet at Amsterdam a
splendid cake was especially prepared for him,
covered with small sugar storks (every one knew
by this time that the stork was his prime favourite),
while Fortune stood at the top of it with two flags
in her hand, a Danish and a Dutch, and on the
Danish flag was Andersen's name in gold letters,
with a lyre beneath it. From Holland he proceeded
to Paris where he went to the Vincennes races
with the Danish Crown Prince Frederick, and had
a place reserved for him in the Emperor's box, "and
there," he says, " a *Lorette*, dressed like a princess,
gave me a look as if I were an old gold-fish worth
angling for. Poor child, poor child !" He was glad
to quit Paris, which he now liked less than ever ;
yet, his visit there had its bright points too. Thus
a writer of vaudevilles, a collaborateur of Scribe's,
asked his permission to dramatise "The Goloshes
of Fortune ;" the firm of Hetzel made arrangements
with him for the publication of a select edition of
his works in French ; and Jules Sandeau paid him a
graceful compliment by calling him the Haydn of
poetry. It was during his visit to Paris, moreover,
that he received the Order of Our Lady of Guade-
loupe from the Emperor of Mexico. From Paris he
proceeded, *via* Bordeaux, to Portugal, where he
stayed nearly four months. During part of the time
he was the guest of Carlos O'Neil at his country

house near Setubal, in a romantic valley surrounded
by groves of orange and citron trees, with the ruins
of ancient monasteries peeping picturesquely forth
from among the wooded hills around. One of the
most beautiful of these ruins, Brancanas, Andersen
visited every evening, and it was one of his greatest
delights to sit in the midst of the peaceful sylvan
solitude, watching the swarms of fire-flies around
him, and the thousands of stars above his head, and
listening to the murmuring of the great ocean hard
by.* He frequently rambled about among the
mountains, too, on the back of "a sensible ass who
knew his way about much better than I did;"
watched every evening the rustic lads and lasses
dancing to the music of flutes in the illuminated
orange gardens, and was present at a bull-fight, which
was a comparatively bloodless affair, compared with
the bull-fights of Spain. With the O'Neills he also
visited the famous University of Coimbra, and at
Cintra he made the acquaintance of Lord Lytton
(Owen Meredith), whom he was to meet again at
Vienna.

On his return home in 1867, at the earnest solicit-
ations of his friends, but greatly against his natural
inclinations, he started an establishment of his own.

* For Andersen's visit to Portugal, see Bille og Bogh : *Breve fra
Andersen*, ii. pp. 552-4. There is also a short account of it, "*I Port-
ugal*," in his collected works, which has not yet been translated into
English.

Hitherto he had been very loosely attached to his native soil. His incessant wanderings up and down Europe, his visits, longer and more frequent every year, at the country houses of the gentry in Zealand, and Funen, had prevented him from even thinking of making a fixed and comfortable home for himself against old age, and he always had a perfect horror of tying himself down to any particular place. The sort of abode he liked best was an attic in a large hotel, or a couple of small furnished rooms in some central part of the town, with plenty of flowers and evergreens in the windows, and a few good prints or paintings on the walls. A good prospect, especially a view of the sea, was also a great desideratum of his, and quite sufficient to induce him to make a move; indeed, it was mainly to better himself in this particular that he shifted his quarters so often, till finally, for good, in 1866, he settled down, at No. 18, Nyhavn, which he furnished carefully, although, as I have said before, it was very much against the grain for him to settle down at all. " So now I am actually to have a house and a bed of my own," he writes on this occasion. " It positively frightens me. I am weighed down to the earth by furniture, beds and rocking chairs, to say nothing of books and paintings. If I had moved into a hotel, then, at any rate, I should have felt that my wings were free, but now I am saddled with a house at 25 rigsdaler* per

* £2 15s.

month, and yet I know I shall run away from it as
soon as ever the first warm sunbeam pricks me as it
pricks the (other) birds of passage."* To another
friend, a musician, he laments the folly which made
him spend 100 rigsdaler † on a bed, "and my death-
bed, too," he adds, "for if it does not last me till I
die, it will not be worth the money I have paid for
it. If I were only twenty years old, I should put my
ink-pot, a couple of shirts, and a pair of socks on my
back, and, with my stick in my hand, and my goose-
quill by my side, I would go forth into the wide
world. But as Madame (Edward) Collin says : I am
now an elderly man, and must think of my bed—my
death bed!—so I think you had better see about
composing a nice funeral-march for me. The small
school-children (*not* the grown-up Latin scholars)
will naturally follow me to the grave, remember ; so
set the music to the tramp, tramp, tramp of the feet
of little children. . . ... I hope you will come and
see my new abode. There is a good staircase and a
noble corridor. Everything about me is quite handsome. I have nice carpets, many pictures, statuettes
and knick-knacks, so that my rooms are very
comfortable. The windows, too, do not want for
flowers . . . . and the whole of the *Kong's Nytorv*,
with all its life and bustle, lies before me. . . . . I
have had many visits from my lady-friends lately,

* Bille og Bogh : *Breve fra Andersen*, ii. pp. 555-6.
† £11.

and they call it really cosy."* Here, then, he was generally to be found in the winter, especially at Christmas-time, when his table would be covered with all sorts of coloured paper, out of which he clipped, with cunning fingers, knights, ladies, castles, windmills, ballet-dancers, and all kinds of fantastic marvels for Christmas trees, and children's parties; but in the spring and summer, when not abroad, he spent most of his time at a comfortable, prettily situated country house† in the environs of Copenhagen, very appropriately called "Rolighed" (Tranquillity), belonging to his friends the Melchiors, where he could do exactly as he liked, and make himself quite at home.

And now we have come to what was certainly, by far, the happiest period of Andersen's life. The trials and troubles of his earlier life were more than made up for by the extraordinary and manifold triumphs of his latter days. For at least fifteen years before his death he had the supreme satisfaction of feeling and knowing that of all Danish writers he was the most famous abroad, and the most popular at home. Honours and dignities continued to be showered upon him to the very last. He was

---

* Bille og Bogh : *Breve fra Andersen*, ii. pp. 559-60. Compare Bloch : *Om Andersen. Ner og Fjern*, No. 364.

† An avenue of poplars led up to it : "where," says Andersen, "the sun, every evening, strews so much gold among the leaves of the trees, that one might almost fancy oneself in California."

made a Professor by the University, an *Etatsraad*,
or State Councillor, by the King, and was able to
add the red and white ribbon of the Dannebrog, and
the red, white, and blue ribbon of the Norwegian
Order of St. Olaf to his other decorations before he
died. In December 1867 he received the freedom of
his native city, Odense, and the festivities held in
his honour on that occasion almost overwhelmed
him.* He was the guest of Bishop Engelstoft at the
Palace, where all the notabilities of the place came to
pay their respects to him, and at the great banquet
given in the largest room of the old Town Hall, two
hundred and forty guests sat down to dinner.
Telegrams of congratulation were handed to him,
between the toasts, from all parts of the land, and
among them was one from King Christian IX. and
the Royal Family, in the most gracious and affectionate terms. Andersen was deeply moved when this
crowning compliment of the feast was read aloud,
and the whole assembly stood up as one man and
hurrahed.† This banquet was followed by another
at the Burgomaster's, and a grand concert given by
the local musical society, while the students serenaded him and all the school-children had a holiday,
and strewed flowers in his path. When, to show

* See Bille og Bogh : *Breve fra Andersen*, ii. pp. 579-82.

† Andersen was so full of gratitude for this mark of favour, that he
would have telegraphed back on the spot, but he was told that it was
not becoming for a private person to telegraph to his sovereign.

his gratitude, he read some of the "Tales" one evening to the artisans at the Mechanics' Institute, there was another outburst of enthusiasm. Comical incidents too were not wanting to add piquancy to the festival. Thus, an old cabinetmaker paid Andersen a visit, and told him that he had been a school-fellow of his when he was twelve and Andersen was eight. "He seemed to expect that I should know him again," adds Andersen, "but naturally it was impossible for me to recognise a single feature. I could not even remember his name." In the spring of 1868 Andersen again visited Odense, and received another ovation. In the morning he gave a public reading in support of the Institute for poor artisans and their widows, which brought in 220 rigsdalers, and in the evening he was invited to the theatre to see his best play, *The New Lying-in Room*, acted in becoming style. The best box in the house was placed at his disposal, there was a beautiful bouquet ready for him on his chair, and as soon as the piece was over, the Burgomaster rose and proposed three cheers for Andersen, which were given by the whole audience, accompanied by a flourish of trumpets. On his departure he was escorted to the station by a whole host of friends and admirers, who half filled his carriage with bouquets. On landing from the steamboat at Fredericia, he gave his bag to a poor little boy

to carry for him, when the lad begged him to
show him Hans Christian Andersen, who, he had
been told, was on the boat. "I asked him," says
Andersen, "if he had read anything of Hans
Christian Andersen's, and when he said yes, I
told him I was Hans Christian Andersen, whereupon he became fiery red, and tumbled over my
bag repeatedly in his efforts to cast furtive glances
at me." * .

In September 1869 his literary jubilee was celebrated at Copenhagen. The festivities began at the
Students' Club, where he gave a public reading,
and the poet Hansen delivered a congratulatory
speech. His bust was then unveiled, and placed in
a niche in the walls of the club, by the side of
Ingeman's, and opposite Heiberg's, amidst a burst
of hurrahs, nine times repeated. On the following
day a banquet was given him at the Hôtel d'Angleterre, the doors and entrances of which were gaily
adorned with flowers and evergreens, and everyone
there was so kind and good to him, that he considered himself in honour bound to press the hands
of all the 244 guests one after the other, and felt
just as if he were in heaven. Of the many gifts he
received, the one that pleased him most was a large
basketful of roses and laurels, in the midst of which
lay a large and beautiful dock-leaf, with a snail upon

* Bille og Bogh : *Breve fra Andersen*, ii. p. 586.

it, all in silver—as a souvenir of the tale, *The Happy Family.*\* Two days later he visited the King and Queen at Bernstorff. Their Majesties congratulated him on the success of his jubilee, and the King, after showing him over the castle gardens, and plucking for him the most beautiful rose he could find, placed one of the royal carriages at his disposal for the rest of the day.

A less striking, but far more conclusive, proof of Andersen's popularity than all these public demonstrations was what I may call the private intimacy between him and his admirers. His correspondents were innumerable, and he was constantly receiving little tokens of respect and affection from grateful if humble friends, most of whom were quite unknown to him. He has recorded several instances of this appreciativeness. Thus, early in the morning of his fifty-second birthday, he had a visit from his tailor, like himself a native of Odense, who now told him how glad he was that a fellow-townsman of his should have become so famous. Then the good man produced a nice new white atlas-vest, and insisted upon Andersen's accepting it as a birthday-present. Shortly afterwards a poorly but neatly dressed man entered the room, who also wished to bring his congratulations. He was a joiner living in a distant part of the town, who had never exchanged a word

* Bille og Bogh : *Breve fra Andersen*, ii. p. 605.

with Andersen before, but told him now that of late
years he and his wife had been wont to celebrate
"Andersen's birthday," * by indulging in the extravagance of a cup of chocolate, and he begged
respectfully that he might be allowed to christen his
newly-born son Hans Christian Andersen in honour
of the occasion.† Again, at Christmas 1862, he received from a poor student, living on one of the
Danish islands, a dried piece of four-leaved clover
which had its own charming little story. It appears
that, when this student was still a very little boy,
" The Tales " had been his favourite book, and one
day, when he had been more than usually impressed
by them, his mother had told him that poor Andersen had had a hard time, and that people had been
very unkind to him when he was young. The child
wept, and, finding in the fields shortly afterwards a
clover-leaf, the symbol of luck, asked his mother
whether he might not send it to Andersen. His
mother, however, thought that such a gift might be
taken as a liberty, so the leaf was put away in her
hymn-book. Years afterwards, during the Christmas
of 1862, when the little boy had become a student,
he happened to come across *The Ice Maiden*, and as
he was reading it he thought to himself: "I may

* Since the publication of *M. L. E.* in 1855, everybody in Copenhagen knew when Andersen's birthday was.

† Bille og Bogh : *Breve fra Andersen*, ii. pp. 360-361.

surely tell Andersen the story of the four-leaved
clover now, and send it to him, though by this time
he has no need of "lucky leaves." So Andersen
got the dry leaf after all, and valued it even more
than the gold snuff-box set with brilliants, which he
received from the King on the same day.

It was one of the penalties of this extraordinary
popularity that he should be constantly consulted
by all sorts and conditions of men on every conceivable subject, and though this unlimited confidence
in his sympathy and judgment was, no doubt, very
flattering to his vanity, it had its inconveniences,
and even its vexations. He used to receive long
epistles from servant-girls of a literary turn, telling
him the story of *their* lives ; he was overwhelmed
with letters from young men, mostly mechanics, who
wanted to come up to Copenhagen to make a name
as authors, and consulted him as to the best way of
setting about it, "just as if I kept a registry office
on Mount Parnassus, and could get them good places
there." But the most serious nuisance of all was the
misguided enthusiasm of lady admirers which now
and then led him into the most embarrassing
situations.

For Andersen, especially in his later years, *had*
his lady admirers, though, so far from being a ladies'
man himself, his attitude towards the sex in general
had always been one of discreet, not to say suspicious,

reserve. Nor was he precisely the sort of *beau*
women, especially pretty women, might be supposed
to find attractive. His personal appearance, at first
sight, was almost repulsive.* Nature had certainly
not been a generous mother to him, so far as bodily
gifts were concerned. There had always been something odd about him, something limp, awkward and
shambling, which involuntarily provoked a smile.
He was tall and lean, and queer and bizarre in all
his movements. His arms and legs were extraordinarily long and thin, his hands were broad and flat,
and his feet were of such huge dimensions that he
always had to have his boots and shoes made
especially for him. His nose was of the so-called
Roman type, but so disproportionately big, that it
domineered the whole face. His eyes, on the other
hand, were so small and deeply set in their sockets,
as to be almost invisible. He was conscious of his
personal deficiencies,† and did the best he could to
remedy them; but, although he had his hair curled
and his beard shaved every day, though he wore
very high, stiffly-starched collars to conceal his long
neck, and very wide trousers to hide his thin legs,

* Compare this description of Andersen in middle-age, which I owe
to Dr. Bloch, *Om H. C. Andersen*, with Thiele's description of him
as a young man, in Chap. ii.

† Yet Andersen was by no means dissatisfied with his personal
appearance as a whole. He made no claims to being handsome,
but he always fancied he looked distinguished.

though he dressed carefully, not to say elegantly, and never forgot to relieve the sable sombreness of evening-dress by a glittering display of all his decorations, it was impossible to deny that he was grotesquely ugly, and difficult to imagine how any woman could fall in love with him. Yet, as I have said, the " long poet " *had* his lady admirers notwithstanding, devotees who absolutely raved about him, and even pestered him with their attentions. He used frequently to get anonymous letters from these *exaltées*, containing declarations of love in the most gushing terms. On one occasion he received a packet from a mysterious lady enclosing an embroidered sketch-book with a note telling him that he should never know her name, but would he meet; her at a place indicated, that she might see him and speak to him for the first and last time.* But the most alarming adventure of this kind was when he one day received a visit from a young and pretty girl who, without any beating about the bush, confessed her love for him in the plainest and most unmistakable terms in the world, and whom he had to turn out of his apartments by main force. It was an infinite relief to him to learn subse-

---

* Andersen was inclined, however, to regard this as a hoax. " I never let myself in for such trysts," he writes, "and besides it seems to me as if some gentleman was at the bottom of this affair. Let him cool his heels till he freezes." (Bille og Bogh : *Breve fra Andersen*, ii. p. 357.)

quently that this highly provocative young person had gone out of her mind, and was in a lunatic asylum.

Another circumstance which contributed not a little to Andersen's happiness in his later years, was the cessation of hostile criticism, or indeed of any criticism at all really worthy of the name. This was due partly to a pretty general conviction that no amount of the best-meant criticism could do him the least good, and partly to a genuine belief that he had already had more than his fair share of abuse, and deserved a little compensation. Add to this that his country was now really proud of him, and we shall understand, I think, how it was that a time came at last when every one was as liberal with praise as they had before been with blame, and he was petted and fondled like a child on its birthday. We need not suppose that all the incense thus lavished upon Andersen was absolutely sincere. Perhaps it may be taken not so much as a tribute to his talents, great as they were, as a sort of homage paid to the old man who had gone through so much trouble in his time, and could not hope to live much longer. But anyhow it made him very happy and tender-hearted, for he was one of those natures who revolt against adversity, but feel humble and grateful the moment Fortune begins to smile upon them. But that his sensitiveness to criticism was Andersen's sore

point to the very last, is amusingly brought out by
his correspondence with his latest and greatest critic,
Georg Brandes.  In 1869, Brandes had contributed
to the *Illustreret Tidende* the first part of his famous
essay on the Tales, subsequently incorporated in his
now classical *Kritiker og Portrœter*.  Of this essay
I can only say that it is a masterpiece of literary
criticism, which for depth, acumen, subtlety, and
delicate analysis, can be compared with the most
finished performances of Saint-Beuve himself.  No-
where else have the Tales been so brilliantly, and at
the same time so sympathetically, interpreted, and it
must always be reckoned as another striking instance
of Andersen's extraordinary good-luck that he should
have found such a critic during his very lifetime.
Andersen was delighted, as well he might be, with
Brandes' criticism as a whole, and thanked him in
the most grateful and affectionate terms.

Another cause of satisfaction to Andersen in the
decline of life was the consciousness that, relatively
to his simple tastes and modest requirements, he was
now pretty comfortably off.  By dint of careful
economy he had, by 1869, contrived to lay by in the
bank 14,000 rigsdaler *—a hoard he was constantly
adding to almost up to the very day of his death.
It was a fixed principle with him never to let his
banking-account fall *below* 12,000 rigsdaler,† but he

* £1633.                              † £1400.

drew freely upon it so long as it remained *above* that amount, for, though never wasteful, he was always judiciously generous with his money, and it gave him infinite pleasure, when an old man, to take abroad with him one or other of his young friends who might not be overburdened with loose cash, and pay his expenses. Thus, in 1870, he treated young Jonas Collin to a two months' trip through Germany to Italy, Switzerland, and France. The letter in which he privately makes the proposal to Edward Collin, Jonas's father, speaks as much for Andersen's delicacy as for the goodness of his heart. After going very carefully into an estimate of expenses, he continues: " I believe Jonas will be all the better for such a recreation, which will take him away for a few weeks from the squabbling, scribbling, and worry of business. . . . . What do you say about my plan, and what does my money-box say to it? If you approve of my good intention, *but not* otherwise, you may show Jonas this letter or tell him about it. I should be very glad if it could come off, but one request I have to make : it must be *a secret to the whole world* that Jonas is invited by me, and that I pay the piper—*nobody* must know that."— Andersen, therefore, had no reason to be troubled about money any more, yet, only a few weeks before his death, he was suddenly haunted by the nervous fear that there was not money enough in the bank to

bury him with; but Edward Collin jocosely assured
him that, even if he had "only fifty more years to
live," he might comfortably take a foreign tour every
year without stinting himself in any way, and yet
have enough left for a splendid funeral. "Thank
God!" cried Andersen, when this letter was read to
him, "I can be put under the sod now, at any
rate!"*

Andersen was never very robust, although most of
his complaints were purely imaginary; but up to
within five years of his death he enjoyed fairly good
health, and took the keenest pleasure in life. At
thirty he used to complain that he felt sixty at the
very least, but when he had turned sixty he humorously boasted that he was growing younger again,
and hoped in ten years' time to be a fitter comrade
for his friend Jonas, who had always had an old head
upon his young shoulders. But he was now surrounded by lovingly watchful friends, who tried to
make life easy to him, and were quick to note every
slight fluctuation in his health long before he himself
suspected there was any change at all. At the
beginning of 1869 it was plain to many of them that
he was ageing, and when, after the fatigues and
exertions of his literary jubilee, he was about to set
out for Germany and Switzerland, the Countess
Holstein, at whose castle he was a frequent guest,

* Bille og Bogh : *Breve til Andersen*, pp. 101-2.

ventured to suggest that he should take with him a careful and reliable attendant, "So I am as old as all that, eh!" wrote Andersen to another friend, *à propos* of this. "It was nice and kind of them, of course, but I naturally rejected the proposal. I find it dear enough travelling alone." Love of economy, however, was not the sole reason why Andersen would not be bothered with an attendant. Another reason, no doubt, was his curious objection to the ministration of servants, especially men-servants. And here I may mention, by the way, that Andersen's attitude towards domestics in general was amiable but peculiar. He was friendly, sometimes almost familiar, with them, liked to talk to them, and might even, now and then, present them with some of his books; but if there was the slightest suspicion of insolence in their conduct towards him, he instantly became a veritable *grand-seigneur*, who knew how to command respect. Sometimes his irritable temper got the better of him, for the merest trifle was enough to put him out, and then he would say sharp and cutting things. But he was mollified in a moment by the faintest sign of sorrow or regret, and the sight of tears, especially women's tears, was always too much for him. A very good story is told of how an artful *soubrette*, at a Continental hotel, got the better of him in this way. She had neglected to make his bed the way he liked, and he called her attention to the fact that she had not done so. The girl stood him out that she had. He flew into a passion at once, gave her a good talking to, and wound up by pitching the pillows at her head. At this she suddenly burst out crying, and in an instant all his wrath was gone as if by magic. His scowling brow unbent, he looked at the wench for a moment with furtive embarrassment, and then approaching, offered her his hand (which she would not take), and begged her pardon. It was of no use. He grew uneasy; his face had a comical expression of mingled remorse and desperation; it was plain that he absolutely did not know what to do next. Suddenly an idea occurred to him. He faced about a little, fumbled uneasily in his waistcoat-pocket, so that a gentle jingling sound could be heard, and approaching the wrathful damsel, with a deprecating look, again extended his hand towards her (she took it this time), whereupon, to his manifest relief, her tears ceased to flow.*

In 1869 Andersen traversed the greater part of Central Europe from Vienna to Zurich, renewing old acquaintances and making new ones. In 1870 he took the trip with young Jonas Collin above alluded to, and in 1871 he crossed the sea to Norway, which he now visited for the first time. When his friends, anxious about his health, mildly remonstrated

* W. Bloch, *Om H. C. Andersen*, in *Naer og Fjern*, No. 364.

with him about travelling and exerting himself so
much at his age, he vowed he could not help it, and
that it was his destiny to knock about the world so
long as he had the strength to move. "I suppose,"
he says apologetically, "I must have been born
under a star which may be called Pendulum, so that
I am bound to always go backwards and forwards,
tic-tac! tic-tac! till the clock stops, and down I
lie." * But the Norwegian trip was his last great
effort, and the fatiguing festivities held there in the
old man's honour convinced him, at last, that he had
no longer the physical strength to get up at three
o'clock in the morning to see the sun rise, or to sit
up late at night for a week at a stretch to respond
to toasts at banquets.† With the sublimely magnificent land itself he was delighted, and all classes of
the population united to make his visit as pleasant
as possible. During the greater part of his stay at
Christiania he was the guest of Björnstjerne Björnson,
who, at the great banquet given to him in the
Botanical Gardens, recited a beautiful poem he had
composed in honour of the occasion, beginning:

> " Welcome to us from Fairy Land,
> Thou child-like soul with childhood's dreams ! "

A deputation from the dinner-committee escorted

* Bille og Bogh : *Breve fra Andersen*, ii. p. 622.
† " Every day I have been at a banquet, except one day in betwee
when I lay sick in bed." *Ibid.*, p. 644.

Andersen to the gardens, the entrance to which was crowded with people. The table was spread in the open-air, with Andersen's bust in the centre of it. Moe, the celebrated collector and editor of the Norwegian Fairy Tales, made the principal speech, in the course of which he, first of all, mildly upbraided the guest of the day for visiting every country in Europe before coming to Norway, and then wound up with a eulogy that so deeply affected Andersen, that, when he rose to reply, he could not utter a word. "God knows what I said," he adds, "but I managed to pull myself together, and when I had finished I saw tears in many persons' eyes, and Björnson told me that I had never spoken better in my life." Then, by special request, he read *The Snow-man*, and *It is quite certain*, which provoked an extraordinary burst of enthusiasm, all the ladies present throwing to him their bouquets. Next day he was invited to a students' smoking concert, but stipulated beforehand that he should only stay an hour, as he was "now an old man."*

Political feeling was running very strongly in Norway while Andersen was staying there, and both Radicals and Conservatives seemed to have tried to draw him over to their side, and make capital out of him; but he was not to be drawn, and congratulated himself on the dexterity with which he

* Bille og Bogh : *Breve fra Andersen*, ii. p. 641-3.

avoided giving any expression of opinion whatever.
" A great German once told me," he writes, " that I
was the best Danish diplomatist he ever knew. I
follow my heart and my instincts, and they always
pull me through." It was while staying at Christiania
on this occasion that King Oscar sent him the Order
of St. Olaf.

At Christmas 1871, after his return from Norway,
appeared another volume of tales, entitled *Nye*
*Eventyr og Historier* (New Stories and Histories),
dedicated to his Danish publishers, the Reitzels,
containing thirteen stories, most of them reprints
from newspapers and magazines, but all written
during the course of the year. It was followed at
Christmas 1872 by a second volume of four stories :
*What Old Johanna said, The Door Key, The*
*Cripple,* and *Aunt Toothache.* With this little
volume the immortal tales came to an end, for it
was the last thing the old man (he was now sixty-
eight) ever wrote. Of these concluding tales the
first two belong, like *The Tinder Box,* to the
order of nursery-tales retold, while the two last are
quite original. *Aunt Toothache,* a clever phantasy
in Hoffmann's manner, gives a humorous description
of the author's own experiences of neuralgia, from
which he suffered severely throughout life. *The*
*Cripple* he considered one of the most successful
things he ever wrote, " a sort of glorification of fairy-

tale writing," in fact, and therefore " a befitting conclusion to the whole collection,"* which he had begun
exactly thirty-seven years before.†

* *Bemærkninger til Eventyr og Historier.*

† The total number of Tales is 156, not including *The Picture Book without Pictures.*

# CHAPTER XV

## THE LAST DAYS OF "THE GOOD OLD POET"

I AM inclined to think that the beginning of Andersen's last illness should be dated from the accident
which happened to him in the spring of 1872. His
natural elasticity, indeed, enabled him to recover
from the shock, and apparently get the better of it,
but he was never the same man afterwards.

Andersen had set out on a tour through Germany
with his young friend, Herr William Bloch, and all

went well till they reached Innsbruck, and took up
their quarters at an inn there.  In the middle of the
night Andersen awoke, feeling very uncomfortable.
The bed was not made to his liking, and he got up
in the dark to put the under-mattress straight.
Reaching out too far for a chair, he overbalanced
himself and fell prone, dragging a table and a large
candlestick after him.   His fall was so heavy that it
awoke his neighbours, and young Bloch came rushing
in to find him lying on the floor with a bad bruise
on his nose.  They got him into bed again, and
bathed the place with cold water, but presently he
felt pains all over him, and it was found that he had
contusions on the knee-cap, thighs,* shoulders, and
temples.  He was naturally very nervous about the
consequences of this mishap, especially when he
found he could only walk with difficulty, but he
insisted upon returning to Munich, where he could
get better medical advice than in the Tyrol, and
there he stayed four days, driving about to show
Bloch the curiosities of the place, though he himself
was suffering from a severe headache and giddiness.
His bruises soon healed, and he was able to proceed
to Augsburg and Nuremberg, and stay some time at
both places, but the shock he had received was a

* Poor Andersen is very particular about the colour of his knee-cap,
and he tells us it was like an orange surrounded by green, blue, and
black rings.  (Bille og Bogh : *Breve fra Andersen,* ii. p. 653.)

severe one, and in the early autumn of the same
year, after returning to town from a visit to the
Melchiors at "Rolighed," he was attacked by a
severe illness, and it was found that his liver was
very much affected. His complexion grew yellow,
he became very weak, and felt a pressure over the
pit of the stomach. Nevertheless he pooh-poohed
his illness at first, and tried to get about as usual,
but it grew worse instead of better, and he had to
keep indoors in his house at Copenhagen nearly the
whole winter. His numerous friends tried, however,
to make things as pleasant for him as possible, and
he gratefully exclaims more than once that this his
first and indeed only illness was full of the fruits
and flowers of blessing. Amongst these friends were
the members of the Danish Royal Family, and the
old man was much touched and flattered by their
kind and constant attention. The Crown Prince
visited him twice, and one day the King took him
by surprise, and brought young Prince Waldemar
along with him. It was arranged that as soon as he
could bear the journey, he was to travel south again,
and try the goat-milk cure at Glion, near Montreux,
by the Lake of Geneva. The week after his birthday, which was religiously kept as usual by his
friends, who sent him more flowers and books than
he knew what to do with, he set out accompanied
by another young friend, Nicholas Bögh, for without

such help he would have been unable to travel at all. He was too weak to call anywhere to say good-bye, except at the Palace, and, to prevent him from toiling up the lofty staircases, the whole of the Royal Family, children and all, came down to the ground-floor to greet him. In taking his leave, the King presented him with his own new portmanteau, and the same evening, while Andersen was sitting in his little room at home, superintending his packing-up, he was surprised by another visit from his Majesty, who said he couldn't help coming to have another peep at him before he started. His friends insisted that he should stop for a couple of days at the Hôtel Royal in Copenhagen to see how he bore the change ; there was a whole army of acquaintances at the railway-station to see him off, and, travelling by very short and easy stages, he reached Frankfort safely, though during his stay there he was too weak to go out of doors. At Berne he was thoroughly examined by Dr. Dor, who told him that his lungs were perfectly sound, the action of his heart good, and that, in fact, he was a very healthy subject, but extremely nervous. The cough and the giddiness he made light of. He advised Andersen to eat plenty of strengthening food, drink wine, and keep in warm, good air. In a month he hoped to make him quite well again. At Verney Andersen saw another doctor whom he didn't like at all. " He came with

so many prescriptions," he complains, "that half of
them would have been more than enough. . . . I
told him I was better than he fancied, but that it
was his presence and his talk that set my pulse
throbbing."

On the 11th May he moved his quarters into the
Hôtel Righi Vaudois at Glion, and felt wonderfully
better at once in the pure and mild air. He and
Bögh occupied cheerful adjacent apartments, where
they had sunshine from sunrise to sunset, with
splendid views of the Dent du Midi, the Lake of
Geneva, and the Jura Mountains. "The cuckoo is
here too," says Andersen, " but he is silent immediately I ask him how long I have to live, and yet
it is so nice to live, to have friends as I have, and to
be able to live in scenery like this." He began,
shortly after his arrival, to try the goat-milk, which
tasted to him like very thin, weak chicken-broth.
He soon found that on level ground he could walk
very much better than before, but climbing was still
too much for him. His troublesome cough quitted
him entirely, but he now complained of a highly
uncomfortable dryness on the left side of the neck,
just as if it were being "scraped inside." His
appetite, however, was enormous, his digestion perfect, and he slept his eight or nine hours a day.
With the surrounding scenery he was delighted.
"Everything is so beautiful," he writes. "The

2 D

snowy mountains rise aloft in the clear sunshine, there is a fragrance of grass and flowers, the beeches hang their fresh green fringed leaves over me in my wanderings, which, I must say, are not very far ; my strength will not return, and sometimes a faintness comes over me, so that I can scarcely keep my feet, or hold things in my hands." But in truth he was in a highly nervous state, and the least trifle was sufficient to upset him. Thus he was much troubled and annoyed, during his stay in Switzerland, by some ridiculous stories about himself which had got into the American papers. It appears that one of the many Americans who used to call upon him at "Rolighed" to worry him for autographs, had sent a long account of the interview to the *Chicago Times*, freely drawing upon his imagination for his facts. Andersen was made to say that he had been with the Empress Eugénie and the Prince Imperial in Switzerland ; that he was personally acquainted with the Emperor of Germany and the Emperor of Austria ; that he used to dandle the children of the Tsar on his knee ; and, most amusing of all, there was another legend in a widely circulated American monthly, to the effect that his popular name at Copenhagen was "Little Hans," and that whenever he showed himself in the streets there, he was immediately surrounded by a whole swarm of children who pulled him by the sleeve and cried : "Little

Hans! Little Hans! do tell us a fairy-tale," whereupon good-natured Little Hans would sit down upon
the nearest door-step, surrounded by a group of old
and young, who listened with every sign of rapture
to the marvellous stories that flowed from his lips.*
It would have been best, of course, to have taken
no notice of this nonsense, but Andersen was out of
sorts, and took the matter seriously. "I cannot
bear all this falsehood while I am still a sick man,"
he cried. The idea of his being on intimate terms
with the three Emperors struck him as too supremely
ridiculous to need any refutation at all, but he wrote
a pretty sharp letter to the editor of the American
monthly, confuting the " Little Hans " legend, and
received an apology to the effect that the information
had been received from a Dane resident in the
United States, who professed to know him very well.
That he was better in health, however, there could
be no doubt. The goat-milk and the invigorating
air of Glion had a marked effect upon him, and he
progressed daily. Dr. Dor, who saw him again on
his return from Glion to Berne, assured him that he
was now quite another man, with a good colour, a
bright eye, and no end of vivacity. Indeed he felt

* Compare Bille og Bogh, *Breve fra Andersen*, ii. pp. 672-4, and
Bloch, *Om H. C. Andersen.* Another American legend which
amused Andersen very much, described him in his infancy as a lovely
child with long locks, sparkling eyes, and rosy-red feet, chasing
butterflies in the sunshine.

so well at Berne that he ventured to read some of his tales in public (the first time for nine months) though he suffered for it afterwards. His gratitude to his young friend Nicholas Bögh for taking such care of him was unbounded, and he determined to reward him by giving him a peep of Italy which the young fellow had never seen before. So he hired a carriage for a week, and away they flew over the Splügen to Chiavenna. They had intended to proceed as far as Bellagio, on Lake Como, but, on the way thither from Chiavenna, the horse, maddened by the attacks of mosquitoes, nearly kicked the conveyance to pieces, and Andersen, Bögh, and the coachman had scarcely succeeded in dismounting, when back the beast rushed at full tilt to Chiavenna, with bag and baggage, leaving the passengers standing in a blazing sun, on the high-road, with lofty white walls on each side of them, and not so much as a tree to give them shade. There was nothing for it but to trudge back to Chiavenna on foot, where Andersen arrived "like roast man," ready to drop, and had to lie for four hours on his bed. After that they gave up their Italian tour, and visited the Engadine, which neither of them had seen before. An attack of cholerine at Munich deprived Andersen of much of the strength he had gained in Switzerland ; he had frequent fainting fits, and it was only with the utmost difficulty that he contrived to reach

Denmark, more dead than alive, retiring to rest at
" Rolighed," where he remained from the 24th July to
the middle of September seriously indisposed. In
the autumn he rallied, and came to town again;
indeed, he was now so much better that he could
take little walks. Still it is evident from his
correspondence that he felt very poorly and depressed.
" I can't endure the thought of facing another
winter here," he wrote pathetically to the composer
Hartmann, " and yet I have a terror of travelling.
Not to be at home, not to be abroad—where on earth
then am I to be ? . . . . The Melchiors are good to
me beyond all expression, but there are limits to
everything. Since I came back they have given me
a nurse, but my whole nature has always revolted
against such beings. . . . . If I *am* to die, may I
die quickly ! I cannot wait; I cannot lie and roll
up into myself like a withered leaf ! . . . .*

During the winter of 1873-4 his outings were
limited to going backwards and forwards between
his house at Copenhagen and the Students' Union,
and taking walks for half-an-hour every day in the
Haven Street (Havnegade) to breathe the fresh air.
He occupied himself by writing up his correspondence,
which had attained enormous dimensions, and making a large folding screen with nine panels, designed
by himself, and representing characteristic features

* Bille og Bogh : *Breve fra Andersen*, ii. p. 682.

of Danish scenery. His greatest grief was that he
could not go to the theatre, but he knew everything
that was going on there, and saw it all quite plainly
in his mind's eye. At seven o'clock in the evening he
would exclaim, "Now it has begun!" and later on,
"Now they have got to this part, or to that." The
playbills always hung on his walls, and the actors
and actresses looked in regularly to give him the
latest news. His chief amusement, when he was not
going over his letters or keeping his diary, was to sit
at the window and watch the little tugs run up into
the harbour, and tow the big ships after them. He
was unable to visit his friends, because his rheu-
matism prevented him from mounting stairs. Now
and then he drove to the Collins' or the Melchiors'
and stayed to dinner, but a dinner-party now always
meant a sleepless night. It was a weary time, but
he was inexpressibly grateful to the loving friends
who did their best to cheer him up. "Yes," he
writes on one occasion, "life, after all, is the most
lovely of fairy-tales, and I often ask myself, with
heart-felt emotion, Why does God grant me so much
happiness? Where all is given one cannot be proud,
one can only bow the head in humility and thankfulness. . . . . I have now entered my seventieth year,
and that is, according to the Bible, the normal
maximum age for man; at least, I cannot hope for
many more years to come."

In the spring of 1874 he accepted an invitation to Holsteinborg, the country seat of one of his best friends among the Danish nobility, Madame Scavenius, the doctors thinking that rest and quiet and the fine air might give him sufficient strength to undertake another little foreign tour when the weather grew warmer. At Holsteinborg he stayed three weeks, outliving, as he says, a whole generation of flowers. He gives beautiful expression to this thought in a letter to Madame Melchior, which he evidently intended to work up into a new fairy-tale had he lived long enough. "When I came here," he writes, "the lilacs hung in heavy pink clusters, and the laburnums peeped forth from their green cases, presently revealing themselves in the summer-like weather in all their loveliness and fragrance, but now they are paling fast. The lilacs now remind one of shabby cotton dresses; the leaves of the laburnums are of a sickly pallor, and the wind tosses them about the garden-path. *Their* floral life has gone; but a new generation has come upon the scene, the red hawthorn as fresh as if it were dipped in the lovely clouds of sunset. A few more weeks, and its day will also be over; and then the roses will have their turn, and, before we are well aware of it, the dahlias and the asters will be with us in their scentless, dazzling pomp, and when they are gone we shall rejoice in the red hips and haws and the

berries of the woodbine. This is the generation of
flowers—a shorter one than ours; but they rejoice in
the air and the sunshine; it is we who think so much
of the fading away. . . . . And why all this long
story? Well, it passed from my thoughts into my pen.
Perhaps I shall write it all down again another time,
and use it as the introduction to a new fairy-tale.
My latest trip to Fairyland begins to-morrow—I
mean my visit to Bregentved." *

Bregentved was the country seat of the Countess
Holstein. It was beautifully situated, and especially
famous for its old-fashioned garden (one of the largest
and finest in Denmark), which reminded Andersen of
the noblemen's parks he had seen in England. Here
were large green lawns, handsome bosques of noble
trees, and endless avenues of lindens. Swans and
shining white lotuses swam upon the peaceful lakes,
and adds Andersen, joyfully : " The stork-father and
the stork-mother sit here in their nests, with two
young ones, who have not made up their minds yet
whether they can fly or not." Andersen stayed at
Bregentved during the greater part of July, and
rapidly improved in health. He was able at last to walk
for whole hours at a time in the gardens, recovering
much of his good humour and high spirits, and even
making fresh plans for " flying out again into God's
beautiful world." Nay, presuming on his newly-

* Bille og Bogh : *Breve fra Andersen*, ii. pp. 696–7.

recovered strength, he assisted at the festivities on the countess's birthday, wrote thirty cotillon verses for the great ball that was given on the occasion, took a lady down to supper at twelve o'clock, although he felt ready to sink to the ground for fatigue, and stayed up till three o'clock in the morning to hear his verses read, with the natural result of utter prostration on the following day, which he spent in bed or on his sofa. But the countess, anxious about his health, made him prolong his stay, and he rallied once more. His only grief now was that his Muse would not visit him, and reviewing his whole literary career, he comes to the conclusion that his life's work is done. " It is," he beautifully says, "it is as if I had filled up my wheel of life with fairy-tale spokes quite close together. If I go into the garden among the roses, what have they (and even the snails upon them) to tell me that they have not told me already? If I look at the broad water-lily leaves, I remember that Thumbelisa has already finished her journey. If I listen to the wind, it has already told me about Valdemar Daae, and has no better story. In the wood, beneath the old oak, I recollect that the old oak has long ago told me its last dream. Thus I get no new fresh impressions, and that is sad." *

In the autumn of 1874 he returned from Bregentved to " Rolighed," looking much the better for the

* Bille og Bogh : *Breve fra Andersen*, ii. pp. 698-9.

change. He was able now to take long walks in the garden and on the shady side of the country lanes. He also paid frequent flying visits to town, and was present at the opening of the splendid new national theatre, which is still one of the chief ornaments of Copenhagen. This was a day he had long looked forward to, and he enjoyed it thoroughly. He occupied a seat in the front stalls, and was greeted with something like an ovation; but when he rose and bowed his acknowledgments on all sides of him, the audience was scared by his ghastly appearance. He subsequently visited the theatre again once or twice, but only for a very short time. During one of his visits to Copenhagen he waited upon the King, who presented him to the Princess of Wales and " her five pretty children, who all knew the old story-teller." He was also frequently to be met with at the Collins', where he went to consult Edward, now an old man like himself, on money matters, or chaff young Jonas on his absorbing fondness for grubs and beetles. His interest in current literature continued to be very keen, and he is said to have read more during this last winter than at any other time of his life. Mindful of his own early privations, moreover, he always assisted rising talent in difficulties to the utmost of his power, and more than one struggling author owed his or her subsequent fame and fortune to the ready help of " the good old poet." Indeed, in his old age Andersen, with all his peevishness and crotchets, must have been singularly amiable and fascinating. There was nothing crabbed, morose, or pessimistic about him. He always hoped for the best, always looked at the bright side of things ; he was never tired of life, or disgusted with the world ; he looked back on the past with a comical sort of half-wistful regret that it could not be all lived over again. "If I could only go back to thirty," he once said, "and yet retain all my experience, I would turn somersaults all the way down the Ostergade." * Life had always been to him a feast of good things, and he was loth to leave it. Very beautiful are his letters to little children in these latter days. It is quite true, as I have said before more than once, that Andersen was not very *fond* of children ; as a rule they bored and embarrassed him. Children, too, were rather afraid than otherwise of the odd-looking man with the big nose, especially at first sight. But his letters to his little friends are, in their way, quite as fascinating as his tales, and it is much to be regretted that so few of them have come down to us. Take, for instance, this message sent to "Little William," with the obvious intention of teaching him kindness to animals: "Greet my friend William for me, and tell him I hear he aimed a blow at the little fly who only wanted to

* The fashionable thoroughfare of Copenhagen.

know how he was. The fly assures me it was so, and
that she can prove it was William because he had
such a dirty hand. She says she saw the mud on
his hand quite plainly when he drove her away.
Now, whom am I to believe—the fly or William ?
Tell him, too, that the fly was a flying princess ; her
father is still alive and is the fly-king, and reigns
over all roses." * And now compare with this
message to a naughty little boy the following charming letter to a good little girl, " Little Marie," an
especial favourite of Andersen, to whom he wrote
more than once :

"DEAR LITTLE MARIE,—Papa and mamma
can read this letter to you, as you cannot read
it yourself yet; but only wait till this time
four years ; ah, then you'll be able to read
everything, I know. I am in the country now,
like you. . . . it is so nice, and I have had some
strawberries—large red strawberries, with cream.
Have you had any ? One can taste them right
down into one's stomach. Yesterday I went
down to the sea. . . . and sat on a rock by the
shore. Presently a large white bird that they
call a gull came flying along. It flew right
towards me, so that I fancied it would have
slapped me with its wings ; but mercy on us, it
said, ' Ma-ma-ree !' ' Why, what's the matter ?'

* Bille og Bogh : *Breve fra Andersen*, ii. p. 576.

I asked. 'Ma-ma-ree!' it said again, and then of course I understood that 'Ma-ma-ree' meant Marie. 'Oh,' said I, 'then you bring me a greeting from Marie; that's what it is, eh?' 'Ya-ya! Ma-ma-ree,' it said. It couldn't say it any better than that, for it only knew the gull language, and that is not very much like ours. 'Thanks for the greeting,' said I, and off flew the gull. After that, as I was walking in the garden, a little sparrow came flying up. 'I suppose now you have flown a long way?' said I. 'Vit, vit,'* it said. 'Have you been at Petershöi?' I asked. 'Lit, lit, lit,'† it said. 'Did you see Marie?' I asked. 'Tit, tit, tit,'‡ it said. 'Then give my greeting to Marie, for I suppose you are going back?' I said. 'Lit, lit,'§ it replied. If it has not come yet, it will come later on, but first I'll send you this letter. You may feed the little bird, if you like, but you must not squeeze it. Now greet from me all good people, all sensible beasts, and all the pretty flowers that wither before I see them. Isn't it nice to be in the country, to paddle in the water, to eat lots of nice things, and to get a letter from your sweetheart?— H. C. ANDERSEN." ‖

* Far, far!                    † A little, a little, a little.
‡ Often, often, often.              § A little, a little.
‖ Bille og Bogh : *Breve fra Andersen*, ii. pp. 620–621.

Abroad, too, Andersen had many juvenile correspondents, among them Mary Livingston, the little daughter of the great explorer, who wrote to him several times, telling him all about her games and studies, and making quite a friend and confidant of the old man.  He also received, only a few months before his death, a very touching tribute of affection from the children of America.  The tidings of his illness had crossed the Atlantic, and awakened a great deal of sympathy in the United States.  There seems to have been a very prevalent idea there that he was not as well off as he might have been, and a strong desire was felt to supply him with some extra comforts that he might not be able to procure for himself, such as a carriage.  It was therefore proposed that a subscription should be set on foot for the purpose, and that every child in the Union should contribute something.  Touched as Andersen was by this demonstration of good will, he could not help feeling grieved that he should be supposed to be living in poverty in his old age, and he wrote a letter to the editor of *The Evening Bulletin*, of Philadelphia, explaining matters with equal dignity and delicacy.  After thanking the little ones for their affectionate gift, which, under the circumstances, he could not find it in his heart to reject, he proceeds as follows : " I owe it both to myself and to the nation to which I belong to explain a

possible misapprehension. I am still weak from
illness, and shall soon enter upon my seventieth
year, but I am not in want. My country will never
let its authors suffer need. Although not in the
service of the State, I annually receive from the
State a pension which, relatively to our resources,
is a handsome one, and my works also bring me in
something. . . . . My sympathetic friends must not
think of me, therefore, as a poor old neglected author
anxious about his daily bread, and unable to take
proper care of his sick body. God has been very
good to me in this respect also; loving friends
surround me, an endless portion of joy, if not of
wealth, has been granted to me, and it is not the
least part of this joy that I should live to see
many of great America's loving children break
open their money-boxes to share them with the
old author whom they fancied to be in narrow
circumstances . . . . . One thing, however, I must
insist upon. I cannot accept any gift from individuals. However well meant such a gift might
be, it would, I am sure, bear a character offensive
alike to the wish of the givers and to my own
self-respect. What would come to me as an
honour and a testimony of devotion if it were
presented by the youth of America as a whole,
would be but a painful benefit if it were parcelled
out into gifts from single persons, and I should be

liable to feel humiliation where I ought to feel only pride and thankfulness."*

Andersen's suggestion was adopted, and the gift from the youth of America collectively, ultimately took the form of a parcel of handsome and valuable books relating to America, which reached him on his seventieth birthday. He received at the same time a most pressing invitation to visit the States in 1876, when the centenary of the Declaration of American Independence was to be celebrated, and was told that if he came he would have a reception greater than that ever accorded to a monarch. But it was not to be; before the time came he was in his grave.

Another rare and peculiar distinction enjoyed by Andersen at the very end of his life was to see a statue raised to his honour, yet even here he found cause for offence. The sculptor had represented him as a venerable man, sitting with hand upraised, and smiling face, in the midst of a pretty group of listening children to whom he was telling stories. One can scarcely imagine a more appropriate idea, but Andersen objected both to his being depicted as old and to his being surrounded by children. "What sort of an idea is this to make a bust of me as a toothless old man?" he cried indignantly. "Not as such have I laboured and written and read." The

* Bille og Bogh : *Breve fra Andersen*, ii. pp. 710–11.

group of children was even less to his taste. Anybody who knew him at all, he said, knew that he could never have told tales with a pack of young Copenhageners crowding around him, and clambering on to his knees and shoulders. Nay, it even seemed a disparagement to represent him as solely, or even chiefly, the friend of children. "Children alone cannot represent me," he exclaimed.

When the spring of 1875 came round, Andersen, mindful of the benefits he had derived from his visit to Glion the year before, began to think of travelling abroad again. It was his intention to pass the autumn months at Montreux, and then winter at Mentone. "No doubt it will cost a lot," he said, " but then I hope to come back quite well again." So possessed was he by this idea, that he had his furniture stored, bought a new tourist suit, had two hundred visiting-cards printed, saw that his trunk was very carefully packed, and even engaged rooms beforehand at Montreux. But it was evident to those about him that he would never make another long journey in this world. In the late spring he managed, though not without great difficulty, to reach " Rolighed," and occupied two handsome rooms on the first floor, reserved for him there with the verandah outside overlooking the Sound that he was never tired of looking at. Here, till the day of his death(for he was never to quit "Rolighed" again alive)

2 E

he was the object of the most unremitting care and devotion. Madame Melchior and her daughter nursed him in turn (a professional nurse he never could bear the sight of), and a serving-man, to whom he had once been very kind, volunteered to wait upon him night and day.* The doctors had by this time discovered that his complaint was cancer of the liver, but they humanely hid the fact from him, and he was spared the suffering that so often accompanies the disease. He now became very weak. Only once in the course of that summer could he walk in the pleasant and familiar garden of " Rolighed," in which were many wild flowers from wood and field which he had transplanted there from time to time with great taste. He loved wild flowers, and always held that they were very unjustly disparaged. " Flowers know very well that I am fond of them," he used to say. "Even if I were to stick a peg into the ground, I believe it would grow." He was now not even able to make those peculiar and fantastically graceful little bouquets with which he had been wont to ornament the dinner-table. It was an art that he had preserved from his childish days. He had henceforth to let others bring flowers to him from the garden. During the month of July he was entirely confined to his two

---

* I am indebted for this account of Andersen's last illness to the interesting article of Herr Nicholas Bögh entitled, *H. C. Andersen's sidste Dage*, which appeared, a few days after Andersen's death, in the *Illustreret Tidende*, Nos. 830–831.

rooms and the verandah outside them, and amused himself by making fresh plans for the future. He had of late the idea of building a villa of his own, and he thought a great deal about it now. It was to be in the Moorish style, and have a circular glass vestibule full of evergreens and palms, with a large fountain filled with goldfish in the centre of it, and busts of Thorvaldsen and all the great Danish authors round the walls. "There, in the very centre of them, I'll sit and write," he would say, "and I would turn out something worth reading then, I can tell you!" About a fortnight or three weeks before his death, he began to fall into a drowsy, semi-conscious state, but had frequent intervals of his old sprightly vivacity. He suffered very little pain, and used to murmur repeatedly, with half-closed eyes, "Oh, how happy I am! How beautiful the world is! Life is so beautiful! It is just as if I were sailing into a land far, far away, where there is no pain, no sorrow." Sometimes, but very rarely, he would speak of death, and once he asked his friend Nicholas Bögh whether he thought he (Andersen) would be among the lost. "At any rate," he added, "I have never *wished* to do evil. I have always loved what is good, though I know very well that I have often been ill-tempered, bitter, and absurd." Only one thing seemed to weigh upon his mind, and he con- fided it to Bögh. He had always had a great diffi-

culty in accepting the dogma of the Divinity of
Christ, although he wished to and had striven hard
to grasp it firmly, believing all along that it was the
"truest and happiest of things." Bögh comforted
him by saying that where the heart is right, God
will always take the will for the deed, and that he
might humbly hope that this great truth would be
made clear to him in the life to come.

The last entry in Andersen's diary is dated
July 27th, five days before his death. The next
day he sat on his balcony for a short time, but
could neither read nor write. On the 29th he was
obliged to take to his bed, but when Madame
Melchior came to see him that morning and brought
him a beautiful rose, he kissed it, pressed her hand
gratefully, and looked into her face with a happy
smile. "If I were not so very tired," he said, " I
should feel quite well." When he was told that it
was the 1st of August he was quite surprised that
August should have come so soon, but exclaimed
shortly afterwards: "What a lot of trouble I am
giving! How tired you must be of me!" Although
not afraid of death, he had always had a dread of
dying, his vivid imagination associating all sorts of
physical pain and anguish with the process of dis-
solution. But he was spared all suffering; it was as
a friend that Death came to his bedside. During
the last two days he was very drowsy, had to be

awakened to take food, and, when spoken to, gently desired to be left alone. "Don't ask me how I am," he would say, "I understand nothing more." On Wednesday morning Madame Melchior came to see him as usual and found him asleep. At eleven she quitted his room for a short time, and five minutes afterwards the man-servant in attendance came to tell her that the patient, after breathing a soft sigh and moving his tongue a little once or twice, had ceased to breathe.

\*       \*       \*       \*       \*

One day, several years before his death, when Andersen was sitting amidst a circle of intimate friends, the conversation turned upon funerals in general, and Andersen, half playfully, half seriously, began to talk about his own funeral and arrange beforehand all the details of the pageant, for of course a great man like him was bound to have a grand funeral. "And take care, above all things," he said to his listeners, "that you drill a little hole in my coffin, so that I may have a peep at all the pomp and ceremony, and see which of my good friends follow me to the grave and which do not." And, certainly, if he could have peeped he would not have been disappointed with his obsequies. His death was regarded as a national calamity. He was buried magnificently at the expense of the State, and the whole Danish nation stood sorrowing by his grave.

The corpse was followed to its last resting place, amidst the tolling of all the bells in Copenhagen, by a long procession of the highest in the land; the great church of Our Lady,* so nobly adorned by the hand of Thorvaldsen, where the funeral service was held, could not contain a tenth part of the mourners that flocked towards it,† and, for several days after the burial, the grave was visited by multitudes who had not been able to arrive in time for the funeral, many of whom plucked and took away with them, as precious relics, a leaf or a flower from the wreaths that had been placed upon the tomb. And it was only right and just that "the good old poet" should thus be honoured by his mother country, for to none other of her sons does she owe as much as she owes to him. Little Denmark can point, indeed, to a long and illustrious succession of great men. Such statesmen as Griffenfeld, such sailors as Tordenskjold, such philosophers as Kierkegaard, such dramatists as Holberg, and such poets as Oehlenschläger, to take only a few instances at random, must ever be ranked amongst the world's leading spirits, yet beyond the narrow limits of Danish history and Danish literature they are still names unknown to all but a small

* Vor Fru.

† Compare Bögh, *H. C. Andersen's sidste Dage* and Bloch, *Om H. C. Andersen.*

circle of specialists. But there is one man who has made Denmark famous throughout the length and breadth of the round world, and that man is Hans Christian Andersen, the son of the poor cobbler of Odense.

# APPENDICES

# APPENDIX I

"MARCH 25, 1824.—I hope that you will read through my letter, as I promise I will not plague you often with such epistles. You are angry with me, and especially because I am supposed to have smiled upon getting a bad mark ; but I assure you in God's name (and I think I may say you have never found me out in an untruth) that I have never, either at school or after I have gone home, given any sign of self-satisfaction ; such behaviour is altogether foreign to my nature. . . . . I came to school with too great an idea of myself ; this unusual sphere of work, the lack of all previous elementary instruction, made learning all the more difficult for me ; only the goodwill of those set over me could give me the courage to persevere. Have patience with me a little while longer, and should I not show some progress by next quarter, I promise you that I will withdraw of my own accord from a position where I can only excite dissatisfaction. The long mornings will soon be here ; they helped me last year, and then you yourself admitted that I had been diligent ; they will help me this year also, I am sure. . . . I repeat it, have patience with me for a little while longer, and, with God's help, things will be better ; if not, I will gladly be off, and if I should have offended you in any other way, oh, tell it to me and let me defend myself, for I really feel quite easy on that score. Forgive me this once, and I'll show you that I will not abuse your kindness."*

* *Coll.* pp. 10-11.

# APPENDIX II

TⁿE following extracts are from Andersen's earliest work, *Fodrejse til Amager*. In No. 1 we see the first faint suggestion of *The Story of the Year;* in the second, an anticipation of *Olі Lockeye*.

## No. 1.

"It is New Year's Day, and the year is a child in a snow-white garment. The sparrow beneath yon paternal roof twitters so cheerily its simple, naïve song, which strangely touches us. . . . . Strange figures and flowers freeze upon the window-panes, and round the fire sit groups of children and listen to stories and fairy-tales. And now Spring comes, the white garment is cast aside, the earth dresses herself in flowered calico; heigh-ho! what a merry time it is! The springs babble and the woods hold their green heads aloft. Winged dandies in butterfly-skins flutter from flower to flower

*Und Alles haucht den Geist der Liebe.*

Soon a faithful wooer appears. Summer brings with her her splendid dowry of God's blessed corn, and the reaping takes place on the golden acres. . . . . But now Autumn comes, the sky wrinkles its forehead, the forest loses its lovely locks, and Madam is going down hill; the evenings are long and dark; a merry ball is now to end the motley day, the storm blows his trumpet, the sea beats its drum, the yellow leaves circle round in a lively Viennese waltz, and, weary of dancing, Madam lies her down in her little homely sleeping chamber. Winter covers her with his snowy shroud, and those two old journeyman carpenters, Frost and Cold, fasten down the lid—sleep well, thou old year!"

## No. 2.

"I looked up. All the roofs in the whole street, all the houses I could see around me, were swarming like anthills with tiny gossamer-like beings who, with incredible agility, swung themselves through roofs, walls and closed windows. 'They are dreams,' said the old Night-watchman. I could not stare enough at the tiny aërial creatures. What strange scenes did they not enact, and they took mankind itself wherewith to make the marionettes of their motley theatre. Here they placed the bridal wreath on a young girl's head. There some of them, like pretty little angels with white wings, played with the wee slumbering children, and carried them up to the great Christmas-tree in Heaven. Others again came like little thieves and robbed the miser of his money chest, though he had it under his pillow all the time. Now they fed the hungry prisoner on his straw pallet, and now they put a dear departed one back again into the old family circle all radiant with life. But only a few hours does the pretty magic revel last, and then Common Sense comes and drives the old man Sleep out of doors. In a great hurry and fluster he must pack up all his variegated dream shapes (which is the real reason why our night dramas so seldom have a proper *dénoûment*), and then he steals away with all his glittering tinsel." *

* *Samlade Skrifter*, vol. vii. Copenhagen, 1854.

# APPENDIX III

"It [*Dödningen*] begins thus: 'About a mile from Bogense, on a field near Elevdgaard, one comes upon a hawthorn remarkable for its size; it can be seen all the way from the Jutland coast.'—Here we have a pretty and picturesque description of nature, a finished style already.—'The first night he *lodged* in a haystack in the fields, and slept there like a *Persian* prince in his splendid bedroom.'—A Persian prince! a child wouldn't understand that.—Let us put instead: * 'The first night he was obliged to sleep in a haystack in the fields, for he had no other bed. Yet it seemed very cosy to him; no king could have had a nicer time of it.' Any child can understand that.—'The moon [resuming his quotation from *Dödningen*] hung like an *Argantean* lamp under the vaulted roof, and burned with a steady flame.'—Isn't the tone much more familiar when we say: * 'The moon, high up under the lofty blue ceiling, was a splendid large night-lamp, and it didn't set the curtains on fire either.'—The story of the marionettes has been written over again; it is quite enough for us to know (as in *The Travelling Companion*) that the piece was about a king and a queen—Ahasuerus, Esther and Mordecai —who were mentioned in this, the first draft, are too learned names for children. . . . . It swarms, too, with erudite comparisons—*e.g.*, 'The wanderers learnt from the host that they were in the realm of the King of Hearts, a capital ruler, and

* Quoting from *The Travelling Companion*.

nearly related to Silvio, King of Diamonds, who is well enough known from Carlo Gozzi's dramatic tale, *The Three Bitter Oranges.*'—The Princess is compared with Turandot. It is said of John : 'It was just as if he had lately read Werther and Siegwarth ; he could only love and die '—jarring tones in a fairy-tale. The vocabulary is not yet taken from a child's storehouse ; the tone is conventional, and the designations are too abstract, *c.g.,* 'John talked, but he did not know himself what he was talking about, for the Princess smiled so blissfully at him and held out her white hand for him to kiss ; his lips burned, he felt his whole inside *electrified.* He could not enjoy any of the *refreshments* the pages presented to him. He only beheld the beautiful image of his dreams.'—But now let us hear it in the style we all know : * 'She was lovely indeed, and she held out her hand to John, who loved her more than ever. She surely could never be the evil, wicked witch that all the people said she was. They went up into the drawing-room, and the little pages presented them with sweetmeats and gingerbread nuts. But the old king was so grieved that he absolutely could not eat anything ; and besides, the gingerbread nuts were too tough for him.' "

* From *The Travelling Companion.*

# APPENDIX IV

THE ideal translation of the Fairy Tales is Victor Rydberg's monumental Swedish version, but that it should be so, was, apart from the peculiar genius of the translator, only to be expected, considering that the idioms of the two principal Scandinavian languages are almost identical. Most of the German versions (there are twenty at the least) are good, many of them very good. The French versions, on the other hand, are, with one notable exception, very bad, and Andersen was never satisfied with his French translators. There is also an extremely spirited version of the Tales, where one would have least expected it—in Spain—apparently from the German, and all the Hungarian and Slavonic translations that I know have considerable merit. But in no country is Andersen so well known and so highly appreciated as in England, though here, unfortunately, he has not been very happy in his translators. Omitting school editions and minor selections, there are, roughly speaking, twelve English versions, and of these the earliest is still, on the whole and as far as it goes, the best. I allude of course to the ten tales translated by Mrs. Howitt (*Wonderful Tales*, 1846). Mrs. Howitt knew German and even Swedish much better than she knew Danish, and very often she commits ludicrous blunders which would be the ruin of the average translator nowadays, but nobody ever caught the spirit of Andersen as she has done, and she is loyally literal or fearlessly free according as the occasion demands it. Another excellent selection (it consists of but eight of the best stories) is the gorgeously got-up version by Ward and Plessner (Sampson Low, 1872). Their knowledge of Danish, though not always above reproach, is more thorough than Mrs. Howitt's, but they might take a lesson from her in style. By far the ablest of the larger collections is Madame de Chatelaine's translation (Routledge, 1852; Arnold, 1893, the latter edition illustrated). This lady, who had considerable experience as a translator, is scrupulously exact and painstaking ; her English, too, is pure and simple, and her knowledge of Danish much more intimate than that of any other of Andersen's English translators except, perhaps, Dr. Dulcken. All the remaining English versions of Andersen are distinctly inferior to the first three. Least irritating are the numerous and well-known versions of Dr. Dulcken, to whom the British public owes its first *complete* Andersen. Dr. Dulcken evidently knows Danish very well, but his slavish literalness constantly reminds us of the fact that we *are* reading a translation. His English also leaves very much to be desired. Still less can I recommend the English of Mr. Siever's version (Sampson Low, 1887). Even when accurate (and he is generally accurate) he repeatedly vulgarises his original, and not infrequently both garbles the more difficult and debases the more beautiful passages. I am also inclined to think, from internal evidence, that he owes something to Rydberg's Swedish version. Of Mrs. Paull's version (Warne, 1882), I can only say that it is feebly accurate and hopelessly slipshod. The *naïve* humour of Andersen, his peculiarly strong point, is frequently missed altogether ; but the translator compensates us somewhat by an unconscious humour of her own, especially remarkable in her notes, which reveal a

2 F

perfect genius for blundering. The numerous anonymous
versions published by Messrs. Ward, Lock & Co. are fairly
correct, but their English, generally speaking, is wooden and
wayward. Nevertheless they are preferable to the translations (1846, 1852, Bohn) for which Miss Peachey is
responsible. Other translators may misunderstand, and
therefore misinterpret, their Andersen. Miss Peachey pre-
sumes to embellish and even bowdlerise him. In *The Tinder
Box*, the dog that had the gold is expanded into " the monstrous
guardian of the golden treasure." The soldier, who, by the
way, puts up not at an inn but at a *hotel*, is so modest that he
" kneels down and kisses the Princess's *hand* "—quite a new
departure. We all remember that the Queen in the same
story is described as a wise woman who " could do something
more than ride in a coach." Miss Peachey is careful to add,
" and look very grand and condescending." Four adjectives
suffice Andersen for describing the little match-girl's grandmother : Miss Peachey requires three sentences. Mr.
Wehnert, however (Bell, 1869), is still more presumptuous
for his fondness for big words, goes hand in hand with a perfect mania for moralising. Andersen himself would scarcely
recognise *The Wild Swans*, when it emerges from beneath
Mr. Wehnert's deforming pen. The heroine, poor Eliza, to
take but a few instances, leans against the stump of a tree,
" *which in all probability had been destroyed by lightning.*"
When she plaits her hair it is " *simply but prettily.*" When
her elder brother tells her they must all fly away on the
morrow, " the other ten confirmed these words *with evident
emotion,*" so Eliza puts her trust not in " God," but in " *the
ruler of the destinies of man,*" all the italicised words being
gratuitous amplifications of the translator. But the *ne plus
ultra* of pretentious pedantry is reached by Mr. Gardiner
(Heywood, 1889), who takes unheard-of liberties with his

text; devotes a note of ten lines to endeavour to prove that the old Court lady in *The Tinder Box* wore goloshes and substitutes the name Ludvig for that of Hjalmar in *Ole Luköie*, as conveying "the general idea of the orginal, and also because a foreign name better suits the spirit of the story." Andersen's latest English translator is Mr. Oscar Sommer, who has given us a version of not quite two-thirds of the immortal *Eventyr*, under the title of *Stories and Fairy Tales*, by H. C. Andersen (Allen, 1893). As compared with the general run of Andersen's English translators, Mr. Sommer may be said to have done his work fairly well. He is not quite so accurate as Dr. Dulcken, and nothing like so convincing as Mrs. Howitt, Miss Plessner, and Madame de Chatelaine; but he avoids the pitfalls into which such translators as Mr. Wehnert and Mrs. Paull invariably fall, and never takes the liberties with his text which disfigure the pages of Miss Peachey and Mr. Gardiner. Where Mr. Sommer seems to me to fail is in the apprehension of those delicate and subtle *minutiæ*, those exquisite little touches of humour or fancy which are of the very essence of Andersen's unique art and the secret of his peculiar charm. For such *minutiæ* Mr. Sommer only has half an eye, and even when he sees and grasps them, it is, generally speaking, only to crush them out of recognition in the handling. I will take a single instance of what I mean from one of the simplest of Andersen's stories, *The Little Match Girl*, where it might be supposed it would be almost impossible to go wrong. It will be remembered that the poor little heroine's misfortunes began with the losing of her shoes, and Andersen, in his inimitable way, has tried to bring home to the mind of a child how very vast those ancient hereditary slippers really were. Now I will give in parallel columns .Mr. Siever's and Mr. Oscar Sommer's versions of the incident :

*Mr. Siever's Version.*

" In the cold and darkness a poor little girl was wandering in the streets with bare head and feet. She had had slippers when she left home, but what good were they ? They were very large—her mother *had worn them last*, so big they were—and the little girl had lost them as she hurried across the street to escape two rapidly driven vans. One of the slippers was not to be found, and the other a boy ran away with saying he would *use it for a cradle* when he got children [of his own]."

*Mr. Sommer's Version.*

" In the cold and darkness a poor little girl with bare head and naked feet went along the streets. When she left home it is true she had had slippers on, but what was the use of that ? They were very large slippers; her mother had worn them till then, so big were they. So the little girl lost them as she sped across the street to get out of the way of the carts driving furiously along. One slipper was not to be found again, and a boy had caught up the other and run away with them."

Now I don't mean to say that Mr. Siever's version is perfect, but anyhow he is faithful and intelligent, and has grasped the force and point of the words I have italicised, which are vital to the meaning of the whole paragraph. What a vista of endless proprietorship the expression " *had worn them last* " opens out to us ! Mr. Sommer's " had worn them *till then*," is not merely inadequate, it is incorrect. The little match girl's mother had *not* worn the slippers *till then*, she was only their last proprietress. The humorous little final touch as to the fitness of the enormous odd shoe to form a cradle for some future generation, Mr. Sommer omits altogether. Such an obliterative method of interpretation can scarcely commend itself to reverent lovers of " the good old poet."

# INDEX

## A

ABDUL MEDJID, *Sultan of Turkey*, 220.

ADLER, *Privy-councillor*, 238.

AINSWORTH (William Francis), impressions of Andersen, 222-224.

ALBERT EDWARD, *Prince of Wales*, 267.

ALEXANDRA, *Princess of Wales*, 426.

ANDERSEN, *Madame, the Actress*, 42.

ANDERSEN, afterwards JORGENSEN (Anna Maria), character, 4-5 ; death, 113.

ANDERSEN (Hans) *the Elder*, character, 5-6 ; death, 14.

ANDERSEN (Hans Christian), birth, 3 ; infancy, 4-12 ; early schooling, 13-14, 18-19 ; confirmation, 19 ; early trials and adventures at Copenhagen, 21-47 ; at Slagelse, 48-67 ; at the Collins' house, 69-70 ; first work *Fodrejse fra Holmens Canal*, 1829, 72-3 ; first visit to Jutland, 1830, 76-77 ; *Phantasier og Skizzer*, 1831, 81-83 ; first continental tour, 1831, 84-90 ; *Skyggebilder*, 1831, 84-89 ; earliest dramas, 91-94 ; *Digte*, 1831-3, 95 ; first visit to Paris, 1833, 102-106 ; *Agnete og den Havmand*, 1833, 107-109, 114-116 ; in Italy, 1834, 110-112, 118-123 ; in Bohemia, 123-4 ; *Improvisatoren*, 129-133 ; first *Fairy Tales*, 1835-37, 138-145 ; at Lykkesholm in Funen, 147-152 ; *O.T.* 152-4 ; first visit to Sweden, 156-9 ; *Kun en Spillemand*, 159-165 ; first pension, 172 ; more *Fairy Tales*, 178-9 ; dramas, 180-182 ; *Mulatten*, 1838-9, 182-195 ; *Maurerpigen*, 199-206 ; in Italy, 1840-41, 209-215 ; at Athens, 1841, 217-18 ; at Constantinople, 219-221 ; on the Danube, 222-6 ; *En Digters Bazar*, 1842, 227-8 ; *Fairy Tales*, second series, 1838-42, 230-31 ; third series, 1845, 231-36 ; *Billedbog uden Billeder*, 1840, 234 ; dramas, 1843-5, 236-43 ; *Herr Rasmussen*, 1846, 242-3 ; second visit to Paris,

## C

## V

VIEWEG, 235.
VIGNY (Alfred de), A.'s account of in 1843, 245-6.

## W

WEBER, 261.
WEIMAR, *Grand Duke of*, 249 ; intimacy with A., 254, 256, 266, 300.
WEYSE, *Prof.*, kindness to A., 28-29.
WILLESEN, *General*, 302.
WINTHER (Christian), 227.
WRIGHT (Henry Clarke), 274.
WULFF, *Admiral*, description of young A., 38-9, 45
WULFF (Henrietta), 71, 192, 290 ; dreadful fate, 360-61.

## Z

ZIERSDORFF, 166.

*Printed by* BALLANTYNE, HANSON & Co.
*London and Edinburgh.*

www.ingramcontent.com/pod-product-compliance
Lightning Source LLC
Chambersburg PA
CBHW052345110726
47901CB00005B/1361